Two Baker's Dozen

BY

Jay Dubya

Two Baker's Dozen

By

Jay Dubya

Published by
Jay Dubya
Hammonton, NJ 08037
2065_3

ISBN 978-1-58909-406-2

Printed in the United States of America

Other Books by Jay Dubya

Adult Fiction

Black Leather and Blue Denim, A '50s Novel
The Great Teen Fruit War, A 1960' Novel
Frat' Brats, A '60s Novel
Ron Coyote, Man of La Mangia
So Ya' Wanna' Be A Teacher!
Pieces of Eight
Pieces of Eight, Part II
Pieces of Eight, Part III
Pieces of Eight, Part IV
The Wholly Book of Genesis
The Wholly Book of Exodus
The Wholly Book of Doo-Doo-Rot-on-Me
Thirteen Sick Tasteless Classics
Thirteen Sick Tasteless Classics, Part II
Thirteen Sick Tasteless Classics, Part III
Thirteen Sick Tasteless Classics, Part IV
Thirteen Sick Tasteless Classics, Part V
Nine New Novellas
Nine New Novellas, Part II
Nine New Novellas, Part III
Nine New Novellas, Part IV
Mauled Maimed Mangled Mutilated Mythology
Modern Mythology
Fractured Frazzled Folk Fables and Fairy Farces
FFFF & FF, Part II
One Baker's Dozen
Random Articles and Manuscripts
Snake Eyes and Boxcars
Snake Eyes and Boxcars, Part II
Shakespeare: Slammed, Smeared, Savaged and Slaughtered
Shakespeare: S, S, S and S, Part II
O. Henry: Obscenely and Outrageously Obliterated
Twain: Tattered, Trounced, Tortured and Traumatized
London: Lashed, Lacerated, Lampooned and Lambasted
Poe: Pelted, Pounded, Pummeled and Pulverized
Time Travel Tales
UFO: Utterly Fantastic Occurrence
Suite 16
Snake Eyes and Boxcars

Snake Eyes and Boxcars, Part II
Prime-Time Crime Time
The FBI Inspector
The Psychic Dimension
The Psychic Dimension, Part II
First Person Stories
The Arcane Arcade
13 Tantalizing Tales
PLOTS
PLOTS, Part II
THEMES
Hawthorne: Hazed Hooked Hammered & Hijacked
Hathorne Hacked, Shakespeare Sacked, & Thurber Thwacked
Homer's Ill Iliad
Homer's Odd Sea Odyssey
Homer's Ill Iliad & Odd Sea Odyssey
The Timeless Time Machine
War of the Worlds
The Invisible Man
Parody Paradise
Parody Paradise, Part II
Parody Paradise, Part III
Parody Paradise, Part IV
A Christmas Carol
Bee 17, Short Stories
Bee 17, #2, Short Stories
Bee 17, Part III, Short Stories
Bee 17, Part IV, Short Stories
Bee 17, Part V, Short Stories
Bee 17, Part VI, Short Stories

Young Adult Fantasy Novels

Pot of Gold
Enchanta
Space Bugs, Earth Invasion
The Eighteen Story Gingerbread House

Contents

Introduction

Two Baker's Dozen is a collection of twenty-six short stories and is author Jay Dubya's ninth story collection written in the spirit of *Pieces of Eight, Pieces of Eight, Part II, Pieces of Eight, Part III, Pieces of Eight, Part IV, Nine New Novellas, Nine New Novellas, Part II, Nine New Novellas, Part III and Nine New Novellas, Part IV.*

Two Baker's Dozen contains original works of science fiction, paranormal and mystery tales. Many of the stories feature suspense and surprise-endings, writing techniques that the author enjoys utilizing.

“Story Behind the Headlines”

The relationship between big city police departments and the press is often both adversarial and contentious. It is with good reason and justification that many policemen possess a distinct animosity for the mass media. News commentators, and on-the-scene reporters, often interfere with crime-scene police activities and complicate arrests and indictments with *their* apparent ubiquitous presence. This narration verifies the disdain that many on-the-beat cops have for the ravenous media, particularly tenacious and interfering newspaper reporters. Relentless journalists have been known to jeopardize investigations, just so that the scribes could develop a good “hook” to introduce their sensationalized front-page columns.

Detectives Mark Harmon and Dave Damon were sitting behind their cluttered desks in their third-floor office at the famously designed “Round House” police headquarters. Harmon was reading aloud an article from the *Philadelphia Inquirer's* “Metro Section” headlined “Cab Driver Killed on Job”, while Damon was preoccupied staring-out the grimy window and watching the traffic flowing between Pennsylvania and New Jersey on the very busy, seven-lane *Ben Franklin Bridge*.

“The carnivorous newspaper writers ought to leave investigation work up to the police!” Mark Harmon criticized. “They're falsely reporting here on Metro page one that cab driver Alfonso Giorno had been randomly killed on the job near his Kensington apartment. The article maintains that an armed fellow named Ronald Hutchinson deliberately murdered the cabby in cold blood, by emptying six bullets from a .38 into the cabby's head and chest.”

“What was the motive?” Dave Damon asked as the have-seen-it-all companion apathetically observed the *Lindenwold High Speed Line* train crossing the *Ben Franklin* from ‘Philly, heading toward Camden. “Was the cabby robbed? If so, how much dough was stolen? Or did this suspect, Ronald Hutchinson, have a personal grudge to settle with Alfonso Giorno?”

“Violent crimes like this one tend to be more personal than random ones between the perpetrator and the victim,” Mark Harmon elaborated from twenty-four years of on-the-job experience. “As you know, Dave, I had been assigned to *this* particular case. The *Inquirer's* early morning edition has three separate stories occurring on two distinct days, appearing on three separate pages, describing the facts. But their devil-may-care amateur reporters didn't have the wherewithal to lace the three odd accounts together.”

Mark Harmon believed that the police should write the news stories *after* the trial, instead of having the clueless press incompetents screw-up everything, while precious evidence is being gathered and evaluated *before* the trial.

"Now that you've gotten my attention," Detective David Damon answered, "how about filling me in on all the essential details. I have deep aspirations of becoming a journalist and an accomplished author after I retire from police work, during my much-anticipated 'Golden Years'. Maybe then, Mark, I'll become rich and famous, and finally earn the big bucks that I now deserve. Walk me through the specifics of your case."

Mark Harmon ignored his cynical colleague's prattle and focused on his already-stated principal concern. The dedicated investigator thumbed through the bulky newspaper to a small article appearing above a clothing store advertisement. Harmon then orally read, interpreted, and discussed the information provided in the news report.

"Dave, it explicitly states here on page thirty-eight that a young woman named Lisa Jacobs had her car stolen inside a high-rise parking garage near Eighth and Walnut. The article also indicates that Miss Jacobs was a nursing student at *Thomas Jefferson University Hospital,* and that the young woman worked as a waitress at Portofino's Restaurant on Walnut near Broad."

"Ah yes," Dave Damon's eyebrows raised as the cop recognized and acknowledged a familiar name. "Portofino's has great Italian food. My wife and I eat there all the time. 1227 Walnut is the exact location, I believe. The place has really terrific cuisine. I especially like the authentic white marble bar near the entrance. It gives the place a special ambiance!"

"As usual, you're distracting me off subject," Detective Harmon mildly rebuked. "Thanks to the *Declaration of Independence* and the *U.S. Constitution* drafted just several blocks down the street, we have in this crazy country Freedom of the Press, but as we were discussing earlier," the argumentative-but-efficient detective affirmed, "cops ought to be writing the newspaper columns involving crime, and not rank amateur reporters that don't have the proper education, the necessary investigative skills, or the basic ambition to get the stories straight."

"Okay then, Sherlock Holmes," the somewhat amused Detective Damon countered "Review for me what happened to Miss Lisa Jacobs on illustrious page number thirty-eight. And please make your rendition short and sweet. I have an appointment to take my wife clothes shopping at the *King of Prussia Mall* in just three short hours."

Mark Harmon cleared his throat and initiated divulging the "isolated" page thirty-eight story, explaining how Lisa Jacobs had been accosted and held at gunpoint by (according to the press release) an "in-need-of-a-fix" drug addict. After attempting to rob the frightened young woman, the suspect grabbed her car keys from her pocketbook; hopped into the young lady's pale green *Nissan Sentra;* started the engine, and then sped-out of the high-rise parking facility. Miss Jacobs' fiancé, who was scheduled to meet her at the parking garage, saw the familiar green auto' speed-out of the building, and foolishly chased after it on foot.

"Of course, Mark, I presume that the *Inquirer* reporter failed to give the name of Lisa Jacobs' fiancé," Dave Damon accurately interrupted. "I believe I read that page thirty-eight article during lunch, and clumsily spilled some freshly-brewed coffee on my edition. The young woman's fiance' was described as a big fellow that was infuriated by the auto' theft. It's too bad the boyfriend didn't catch that vile thief, and then we would've had another easy murder case to investigate."

"Stop being so damned facetious!" Detective Mark Harmon admonished his comrade. "It's no wonder that newspaper stories get fragmented when reporters interview cops like you. And Dave, don't be surprised that you happen to be closer to the pathetic truth than you might think!"

"Okay, Mark. Thanks for the backhanded compliment! I promise to be polite and courteous during the rest of your profound dissertation," Dave Damon pledged. "When your face turns as red as a beet like it is right now, I fully realize that it's time to drop the frivolity and respectfully listen to your rhetoric. Tell me more about this remarkable crime case."

Harmon explained to his impatient partner that while Lisa Jacobs' muscular fiance' was preoccupied pursuing the stolen *Sentra* on foot, the victim gathered her composure; asked the startled garage cashier which way her *Sentra* had turned; exited the parking garage, and anxiously flagged-down a taxi heading westbound on Walnut. A high-speed chase then ensued, all the way from Eighth and Walnut, across Broad, to Eighteenth Street, the location of ritzy *Rittenhouse Square.*

"They flew right by Portofino's Restaurant at 1227 Walnut without even stopping for pasta and some fine vino," Detective Dave Damon sarcastically jested. "I'm mighty sorry, Mark, but I just couldn't resist the temptation of injecting that fabulous footnote into our pathetic conversation. Unfortunately, for me, your drab story lacks suspense and drama!"

"You're just lucky you caught me in a good mood this afternoon!" Mark Harmon admitted with a degree of indignation. "The high-speed-chase eventually ended near *Rittenhouse Square,* when the stolen *Sentra* smashed into a parked utility truck. The page-thirty-eight story ends with the accident, and the entire sequence of events is simply reported as an attempted robbery/pilfered car type theme. As you can plainly determine, Dave, so much for the *Inquirer's* inefficient staff for failing to stitch two seemingly unrelated items together! Do you follow my trend of thought here?"

"Well, what about the alluded-to third story?" Dave Damon demanded knowing. "Now that you've captured my curiosity, exactly where does that interesting third factor come into play? On page seventy-two?"

"On page forty-seven," Mark Harmon corrected in an aggravated tone of voice. "The article linking the two seemingly isolated stories definitely appears on page forty-seven. Now, if it were up to either you or me," the loquacious speaker authoritatively continued, "then naturally…"

"Then naturally the Lisa Jacobs adventures would've been organized into one firm cohesive story, instead of into three seemingly unrelated incidents haphazardly reported by journalistic imbeciles," Damon concluded and recklessly verbalized. "Certainly Mark. If allowed by fate to explore another profession, we would've brought *justice* and thoroughness to the art and science of medieval newspaper journalism!"

"I don't know if you're being nastily sincere or being obnoxiously deceitful!" Detective Harmon opined. "There's no doubt in my mind that you've been involved in the drudgery of police work at least five-years beyond your tolerance level! I believe it's time for you to take a Sabbatical!"

"Was the nefarious assailant/carjacker finally apprehended?" Dave Damon apologetically asked. "I believe I had glanced at a confidential report concerning the incident that had somehow accidentally crossed my desk."

"Yeah, Dave. The parked utility truck was stopped and its driver was up in a cherry picker, repairing a faulty traffic signal. The felon left the incapacitated *Sentra* and then sprinted diagonally through *Rittenhouse Square,* but thank goodness to our well-trained department's quick response, the repugnant thug was collared two blocks away."

The now-captive listener concurred that two of the three stories were related and expressed interest in how the third crime was connected with the two other newspaper incidents. Inspector David Damon discreetly inquired about the third and most serious part of his friend's investigation. The man was intrigued to know "the missing link" connection.

"Well, Dave," the senior detective proceeded with his strange presentation. "I'll tell you my vital source of information at the conclusion of my story. I learned from an anonymous waiter at Portofino's that Alfonso Giorno, the cooperative cab driver, had accepted Lisa's grateful invitation to take her out to dinner. The young lady wanted to express her thanks for the cabby's help in having the police apprehend the culprit that had stolen her car. Now you and I had casually discussed Portofino's Restaurant in our recent conversation, and coincidentally, that's exactly where Lisa Jacobs and Alfonso Giorno had their supper that evening," Harmon informed Damon. "After dinner, the pair exited the premises. and in an alley near the restaurant, Alfonso Giorno made advances towards Lisa, who immediately refused his amorous overtures. According to a shocked eyewitness, a terrible quarrel ensued, and Lisa fumbled in her pocketbook for her pepper spray. But instead, removed a steak knife that the wary girl always kept for protection purposes. During the wild scramble, Alfonso Giorno disarmed the knife from Lisa's grasp...."

"And she was stabbed in the chest, abdomen, and arm in the process," finished Dave Damon. "I recollect reading about the attack this morning on page fifty-eight of the *Inquirer,* but no names were given. But as *you* have related, this third incident is really an extension of the second episode. I speculate that Lisa had told her parents about Alfonso Giorno at the hospital before the victim lapsed into unconsciousness. The cabby surely had a strange way of expressing his gratitude for a free dinner! Whatever happened to good old-fashioned values, and to the existence of courtesy?"

"Precisely, Dear Watson!" agreed Detective Mark Harmon. "But the press never got the scattered pieces of the entire story systematically arranged into a lucid-looking jigsaw puzzle. Now, here's where Lisa's fiancé, the very jealous and possessive Ron Hutchinson, again comes into the picture."

Detective Harmon revealed to Damon that after Ronald Hutchinson found-out about Lisa Jacobs being assaulted and hospitalized at *Thomas Jefferson Hospital,* Lisa's favorite man went absolutely berserk. After talking with Lisa's father, Mr. Jack Jacobs, on *their* cell phones, and then conferring with the chief investigating

Detective, it was learned that Ron Hutchinson next researched Alfonso Giorno's address from a city telephone book. The angry brute then drove his vehicle over to Giorno's apartment in the Kensington section, and soon methodically proceeded to administer a brutal beating, and next emptied the contents of a .38 caliber into the flirt's head and chest. The coroner's men pronounced Giorno 'dead on the scene'. Quite a spectacular ending, huh Dave?"

"Well, Mark," Dave Damon conjectured and stated to his astute associate in crime prevention and case solution. "Where did you arrest Hutchinson? To tell you the truth, I too would've probably gotten on the wrong side of crazy if a similar thing had happened to my wife or to my daughter. It's hard to be objective and rational when someone close to you is nearly killed!"

"That discovery was quite easy, Dave," the veteran detective revealed. "Lisa momentarily regained consciousness over at *Jefferson Intensive Care Unit,* and she was able to recall and identify Hutchinson's street and house number over in Bristol. I contacted the Bristol Police, and we jointly raided the home and made the arrest. The rest is all criminal history! But the naïve newspapers don't have the ability to assemble three separate incidents into one in-progress series of events," the speaker reminded his audience of one. "The high-rise garage robbery; the stolen *Sentra;* the high-speed chase down Walnut Street; the *Sentra's* collision with the parked utility company truck; the desperate on-foot pursuit through *Rittenhouse Square*; the violent altercation in the alley near Portofino's, and the consequential murder of Alfonso Giorno were all relevant extensions of the vile criminal activity that had victimized Lisa Jacobs inside the high-rise parking garage. The original suspect that had stolen the *Sentra* is one Matthew Wilson, but ironically, his name's not cited anywhere in either the *Inquirer* or in the *Philadelphia Daily News*. Wilson had been released on bail for the auto' theft, but the crook has a record of being a common thief/drug addict, with a chronic history of felonies."

"If those damned reporters had as much on-the-ball as *we* do," Dave Damon boasted, "then the public would be much better informed, and wouldn't have to watch TV *Action News* or *Eyewitness News.* Talk about lazy journalists' bein' incompetent! The press inaccurately reported that Alphonso Giorno was murdered on the job near his Kensington Apartment, when he actually was killed at his Kensington Apartment, and the newspaper article made it sound like all three incidents had occurred on the same day. Say Mark, there's one aspect of this whole scenario that's rather troubling me!"

"What's that, Dave?" Detective Harmon nonchalantly questioned. "What minor detail evaded *our* collective memory? As you know, I pride myself on being precise and thorough!"

"How did Ron Hutchinson ever find-out about Alfonso Giorno, if Lisa Jacobs was unconscious most of the time in the *Jefferson Hospital* Emergency Ward? Was the guy psychic, or what?"

"Well Dave, confidentially, between you and me," Detective Harmon disclosed, "Lisa's father, Mr. Jack Jacobs, never learned of Ron Hutchinson's involvement regarding the cab driver's murder! I had inadvertently spilled the beans and told Hutchinson Giorno's name and address two days ago. I had no idea that the former college football linebacker would take the law into his own hands and practice cold-blooded murder!"

"It was a crime of passion, jealousy, and revenge! Now Mark, I promise not to tell anyone of your unprofessional indiscretion in sharing confidential information with the alleged murderer!" Dave Damon confided. "I'm certain that the Commissioner has more challenging obstacles and problems to deal with, other than suffering through a painful internal investigation! And thank goodness that the press is too encumbered and too lazy to sort and figure-out all of the pertinent facts. Just think of all the expensive bureaucratic red tape you had eliminated. Mark, I gotta' confess with admiration and envy, that you're a true credit to the crime-solving business, and I'll never reveal your little secret!"

"And the lame-brain media buffs actually think that all three newspaper stories that the reporters had written are unrelated," Mark Harmon assessed and declared. "No wonder why the world seems so confusing to the average citizen, who watches the news on TV, or who innocently reads isolated fragments of minutia in the daily tabloids!"

"Irrigation Irritation"

Robert and Rita Randazzo had experienced a pleasant weeklong *Pocono Mountains* vacation at Fernwood Resort in Bushkill. In addition to playing golf and swimming, the couple also relished visiting the picturesque *Delaware Water Gap* situated just below East Stroudsburg, rented and paddled a canoe on the tranquil *Delaware* up near Milford, felt adventurous and tried white water rafting on a mountain river and attended various popular entertainment venues at other area resorts at Mt. Pocono, Analomink and near Swiftwater. The three-hour ride back to Hammonton, New Jersey was also especially carefree and enjoyable. Everything including the normally abominable traffic congestion on *Route 206* was (in Bob's judgment) "copasetic."

"That was a great escape from reality," the husband commented to his wife from behind the wheel of his *Mercury Mountaineer* as the tan *SUV* sped south by Atsion Lake at noon on Friday, August 5, 2005. "No flat tires, no complications and thanks to your sister staying at her place at the Jersey Shore," the Ford/Lincoln/Mercury new car salesman evaluated, "our two teenagers were being expertly supervised while hittin' the surf and walkin' the Wildwood Boardwalk."

"Don't jinx us before we get safely home," Rita Randazzo cynically answered while reflecting her typical Sicilian demeanor. "I'm superstitious about certain things and I don't want you causin' a reverse black cat. When events are goin' smoothly and seem too good to be true," the leery wife related, "just pretend letting matters be and start thinking about something else. But Bob, the *Poconos* were terrific and exciting but frankly it's great being back on flat South Jersey land again."

Upon reaching the familiar horseshoe-shaped driveway of 569 North White Horse Pike, Bob stopped and removed the week's mail from his highway box. He then re-entered the *SUV*, parked in front of his well-kept gray two-story colonial house and next brought the travelers' four pieces of luggage inside. After depositing two bags of dirty clothes in the laundry room the husband cooperatively carried the other two suitcases upstairs to the master bedroom. Returning downstairs to the kitchen table the man-of-the-house sifted through the accumulated mail, casually sorting junk solicitations from the more relevant bills and correspondence. Soon, something important in the mail grabbed his attention, and Robert Randazzo anxiously opened the missive.

"Honey, here's a letter from your old high school boyfriend Brian Raso, Esquire," Bob yelled from the kitchen in the direction of the laundry room. "I haven't seen him since your last class reunion five years ago. Just think. I always beat the wimp up my junior year and now he's a prominent judge over in Mays Landing also practicin' law here in Hammonton!"

"What does Brian want?" Rita hollered back from two rooms away. "Is he tryin' to sell us a hundred-dollar ticket to the Lions Club Gold Raffle? If so, let's just buy the ticket for a hundred bucks. If we go to the dinner and drawing it'll cost us a hundred and seventy smackeroos!"

"Holy mackerel!" Bob exclaimed in a shocked and astonished tone of voice. "We're bein' sued and your old beau is representin' the plaintiffs. At least that's what's described in the first paragraph of this legal-lookin' document!"

"What's this postal nonsense all about?" a puzzled-looking Rita Randazzo answered as she quickly exited the laundry room and approached the kitchen in a strident gait. "This rude interruption sounds absolutely absurd! Who would possibly be suin' us and for what reason?"

The husband checked the calendar hanging on the kitchen door leading to the cellar. "Today is Friday, August 5th," the aggravated spouse confirmed to his equally upset marital partner. "It states in this lousy letter that at six p.m. on Wednesday, July 28th a certain couple named Philip and Elsie Mangano from Berlin were drivin' by our place when the irrigation sprinklers were runnin'. Some water from one of the three front-line sprinkler heads splashed onto the windshield of their car, frightened the driver, who incidentally was Elsie Mangano, and then their auto' swerved off the highway and hit a tree. The Manganos' sustained lacerations, bruises and other injuries in the mishap and were taken by the Hammonton Rescue Squad to Kessler Memorial Hospital."

The husband further explained that Mrs. Mangano had several deep cuts on her face that might require plastic surgery and that her husband had sustained a broken wrist. "The 2001 Ford Focus, which by the way, I did not sell to them, required two-thousand-dollars to repair, and the letter also states that we're liable for that added compensation, also."

The newly arrived vacationers were not-too-thrilled with the disappointing newfound information. Rita Randazzo soon felt nauseous in her stomach. "How long has it been since those sprinklers had been installed?" the still-in-surprise wife asked.

"If you recall, your cousin Nino acquired a trench diggin' machine, and next, he helped me put in the plastic pipes, risers, and sprinkler heads before I finally got around to seeding the lawn," Bob Randazzo remembered and reluctantly reported. "That was two years after we moved into this home, which was new in 1970, so it had to have been in the summer of '72. Yes, it was a year before Steve was born."

"That front line has always been a problem," the wife admitted, "and sometimes the water does squirt out onto the highway. I've warned you to get the nuisance fixed!"

"Yes," Bob guiltily acknowledged in a disgusted tone of voice. "When the wind's blowin' north to south the water carries about ten feet farther than usual and it does land in the right-hand-lane goin' west towards Philadelphia. But that only happens occasionally, maybe three times a summer. If I'm home, I don't run the front line on a windy day. But since I had the irrigation system set on 'Automatic' during our *Poconos* hiatus," the husband mentioned with regret, "then it could be true that *we're* responsible for causin' the accident."

"Our society is becomin' so litigious!" Rita instinctively complained. "Exactly how much are these money-hungry people the Manganos suing us for?"

"For $250,000.00 if your old beau Brian Raso can prove negligence on our part," Robert Francis Randazzo revealed while again examining the legal dispatch. "But the hospital expenses and the damage to the 2001 Ford Focus come to a mere three thousand bucks, which I think we'll certainly be obligated to pay. And that's not counting court expenses too."

"Will our homeowner's insurance policy cover the $250,000.00 negligence claim if the judge is crazy enough to award that amount?" the disbelieving wife inquired. "Is there no more sanity in this chaotic world? I hope that Brian doesn't carry a grudge against you after all these years!"

"I don't know that answer!" Bob replied and then hesitated. "Maybe. I'll have to get on the phone with our insurance agent and ask him that. And then after I speak with Mike Garrison I'll give my old high school buddy Nelson Donio a call. He's reputed to be the best defense lawyer in town. This ugly misadventure looks as if it's goin' to cost us more than a pretty penny!"

"I have a serious question to ask," the wife declared. "Why couldn't you have gotten a professional sprinkler installer to put in our system?" the wife criticized and indicted.

"Honey, at the time we were strugglin' makin' ends meet when we first got hitched," the husband snapped back in a defensive baritone. "You were talkin' to Nino at a family get-together and he volunteered to help us out. And now thirty-three years later we're gonna' pay the piper big time! I hope we don't have to declare bankruptcy after the smoke clears! This sudden legal challenge might mean financial ruin for us!"

"You'd better get on the horn and set-up an appointment with Nelson Donio right away," Rita emotionally commanded. "I hope *he* doesn't still hold any old high school grievances against you *too*!" "Not a chance!" Bob said in an attempt to put a positive spin on the bad-topic-conversation. "You just gotta' hope that if Nelson can't perform a minor miracle in this extraordinary case then at least he could partially rescue us by pullin' a legal rabbit out of his hat, perhaps on the basis of a procedural technicality, or something imaginative like that. Rita," the husband expressed in a more civil tone of voice, "and maybe there is such a thing as creative justice! Please hand me the yellow phone book in the top drawer. This unexpected dilemma that's all-too-quickly surfaced from nowhere requires instant attention."

* * * * * * * * * * * * *

Nelson Donio, Esquire was sage in regard to cases similar to the one perplexing Bob and Rita Randazzo and at their first consultation the veteran attorney convinced the couple that the best tact would be to delay the case for six months to frustrate the plaintiffs and to perform comprehensive background checks on the lawsuit's propagators. The Randazzos wholeheartedly endorsed the reputable lawyer's advice and anxiously gave him a retainer of one thousand dollars.

"I'll need some additional money allowance!" Nelson Donio stated in a mailed written addendum to his retainer fee. "I'll have to hire a private investigator to dig-up some pertinent information on the Manganos. The method by the way is common practice. This infighting can get a little dirty and messy at times and if I need to use past practices that the plaintiffs may have committed, I want to be on solid ground. So, Bob and Rita," the lawyer conveyed to his new clients a week later in his richly furnished Bellevue Avenue office, "Here's the present situation, folks. I'll need another fifteen-hundred dollars to initiate an investigation that needs to be done. We're hiring two gumshoes that I've had past associations with to gather evidence.

He and his partner are very good and I have a hunch that this *P.I.* enterprise will yield positive results. Sometimes you have to go the extra mile to outwit your opponents in the Legal War battles, particularly this bizarre one that you've been inadvertently thrust into."

The Autumn months passed by very slowly for Robert and Rita Randazzo as they worried about the outcome of their "unfortunate sprinkler predicament." Soon *Thanksgiving* and the *Christmas* holidays had passed and on Friday, December 26th the husband received a call from Attorney Donio.

"Bob, the case has been scheduled for Thursday, January 6 at 10 a.m. in the court chambers in the Hammonton Municipal City Hall. I know that doesn't quite sound like a 'Happy New Year' statement but that's when the judge is available and he's tired of us postponing the trial. But Bob, there's one good aspect to this announcement. The case will be held in private session without any local reporters there to pepper us with annoying questions after the trial."

"Can you tell me anything about what your private investigator friend has discovered?" Bob curiously inquired. "After all Nelson, I am your client and I'm paying the freight here."

"Believe me Bob, I take my profession seriously and the revelation of that information, at least in my mind, constitutes a violation of professional ethics between the private investigator and me. His research is still ongoing. You'll learn what details have been excavated either during or after the court proceedings," the attorney pledged. "And in addition Bob I'll try to see to it that you won't have to testify because you weren't at home during the time of the accident when the automatic sprinklers had been activated."

"Thanks Nelson! Rita and I will see you at Town Hall on the morning of January 6th," Bob indicated. "I'll jot that date down on the cellar door calendar and also in my personal memo' book. If Rita and I have to cough up a quarter of a million dollars we don't have, then we'll have to secretly leave town in the middle of the night and move to Afghanistan or some other remote country like that and start our lives all over again! Nelson, we just can't afford to pay any excessive settlement!" Click.

At precisely 10 a.m. on the morning of January 6, 2006, Bob and Rita Randazzo (represented by Attorney Nelson Donio) appeared in Town Hall Municipal Court before the Honorable Judge Vincent C. Curcio in the predominantly Italian community of Hammonton, N.J. The Randazzos waived their right to testify, and Nelson Donio read an opening statement where his clients accepted full responsibility for the "front irrigation sprinkler line shooting water out onto *Route 30*, the White Horse Pike." The Manganos sat behind a desk on the opposite side of the courtroom having smug and confident expressions on their faces.

Judge Curcio then heard testimony from Philip and Elsie Mangano', whose statements and answers supported each other's account of what had transpired at 6 p.m. on Wednesday July 28th, 2005. The Randazzos were quite dismayed about the flow of events and they felt that Attorney Donio was veritably conceding the case and that they (the defendants) should speak-up and defiantly challenge their lack of an organized defense. After the Judge patiently listened to the plaintiff's version of what had occurred Nelson Donio courteously asked the Solon seated at the bench if he and Brian Raso could temporarily adjourn from the formal proceedings and have a "necessary threesome sidebar conference" in the Judge's chambers.

A full hour elapsed with only the Manganos, the Randazzos, the court stenographer and a conscientious bailiff occupying the silent courtroom while the private conference (that the all-too-shrewd Attorney Nelson Donio had requested) was in progress. Then the legal experts all re-entered the courtroom and the dignified proceeding continued with Judge Curcio rendering his verdict from his black leather swivel chair. All scrutiny from the four principals involved in the dispute respectfully focused on the judicious man wearing the black robe.

"Mr. Robert Randazzo, this court warrants that you get your sprinkler system adjusted and immediately move your front line back ten feet so that your irrigation does not drift out onto *Route 30* on certain windy days," Judge Curcio austerely mandated. "I don't want to see any recurrence of the unfortunate events of July 28 or else the consequences will be severe next time."

Philip and Elsie Mangano momentarily stared at each other with very evident smirks on their countenances. The plaintiffs both believed that their negligence case had been bolstered by the Judge's attitude and that civil damages would definitely soon be awarded. Then Judge Vincent C. Curcio continued disclosing his decision.

"And Mr. And Mrs. Randazzo," the prudent enforcer of justice explained from his elevated courtroom position, "I hereby rule that it is not necessary to compensate the plaintiffs, otherwise known as Mr. and Mrs. Philip Mangano, for either hospital debts or for damage to their automobile. Furthermore, Mr. And Mrs. Mangano," Judge Curcio forcefully declared, "by virtue of additional evidence presented by the defendants' attorney, I am hereby ordering the two of you to appear in this court four Thursdays from now to answer to certain charges that your reputable lawyer Mr. Brian Raso shall discuss with you. Secondary facts have entered into this case that demonstrate that fraud might be involved," the Judge divulged to the suddenly appalled plaintiffs. "My clerk will be sending you a letter via certified mail outlining the specific violations to which you will have to answer. This court now stands adjourned!" Judge Curcio determined as he smacked his gavel on his mahogany desk's wooden panel.

Mr. And Mrs. Philip Mangano appeared quite perturbed and distraught at the case's outcome and vehemently protested to no avail to their embarrassed attorney Brian Raso, who seemed to want no part of their acrimonious insinuations.

An hour and a half later, Bob and Rita Randazzo met with Nelson Donio in the lawyer's plush downtown Bellevue Avenue office. The attorney thoroughly disclosed what pertinent information had been reviewed and analyzed in Judge Curcio's chambers and explained why Brian Raso, Esquire had acceded to the final verdict without providing aggressive legal arguments (or challenges) for his vitriolic Berlin, New Jersey clients.

"Bob and Rita," Nelson Donio prefaced with a broad smile, "much to my satisfaction the investment in my private investigator friends indeed paid off handsome dividends in your favor. First of all we caught the Manganos in the middle of a blatant lie."

"This is all rather confusing, so could you please go back to square one?" Bob Randazzo insisted. "We had no inkling that the Manganos were lying about the accident? I mean to say, they did sustain physical injuries, didn't they?"

"Well, Bob, in the beginning, neither did I question their integrity!" the very efficient attorney admitted. "You see folks, the Randazzos had passed your place a first time going west toward Philadelphia and perceptively observed that the irrigation was squirting out onto the *Pike*. They drove a quarter mile past your home and turned around at the Silver Fox Tavern onto *Route 30* and then headed back east. Next they turned around at Ideal Clothes Manufacturing Company and by that time the troublemakers had fabricated a story that each agreed corroborating to the police. It pays to have observant honest citizens in your neighborhood."

"But how do those particular occurrences prove that a lie existed?" Rita Randazzo piped-in. "I just don't understand how these things are even vaguely connected. There's a missing link here somewhere."

"You'll see in a minute," Nelson Donio assured his grateful-but-confused clients. "The owner of the Silver Fox was just finishing-up mowing his lawn when he noticed the Manganos' red Ford Focus turning around in the establishment's driveway. Then the tavern owner stepped inside his place of business and five minutes later heard on his police radio scanner that a car had hit a tree near your residence. The tavern proprietor rushed to the accident scene and noticed that the dented vehicle was the same one that had just turned around in his driveway. Since nobody was seriously maimed or killed in the accident," Attorney Donio uttered and then paused, "the Silver Fox owner did not issue a statement to the Hammonton Police because he didn't desire getting immersed in having to make a court appearance to testify about making what he considered a minor observation."

"I see!" Philip Mangano interrupted. "The Silver Fox Tavern owner's statement as told to you and to your private investigator proved that the Manganos had turned around in the restaurant's driveway just prior to hitting the tree so that they could again pass by our property and then deliberately collide into the sturdy oak, blaming the incident on my errant front sprinklers."

"Now you're cooking with gas!" the lawyer enthusiastically praised. "And when the Manganos had turned around at Ideal Manufacturing they were spotted by the caretaker of Oak Grove Cemetery situated just across the street. The caretaker four minutes later also heard the ambulance call over his police monitor he keeps in his storage garage. And next we got the police dispatcher's transcript records to identify the exact time of the call, 6:03 p.m. It's a good thing that the people in and around Hammonton are both nosy and concerned and keep their police monitors active most all of the time."

"Naturally, Nelson, your private investigator interviewed both the tavern owner and the cemetery caretaker," Rita Randazzo concluded and verified.

The attorney heartily laughed and then communicated other interesting facts that had eventually persuaded Judge Curcio to dismiss the Manganos' negligence claim and that ultimately dissuaded Brian Raso from actively representing his disenchanted clients. Evidence presented inside the judge's conference chambers exposed that Philip and Elsie Mangano had previously demonstrated a long history of filing frivolous lawsuits. Mrs. Mangano had once fallen down outside the Berlin ShopRite Supermarket and collected ten thousand dollars for her premeditated tumble that incidentally happened with only her husband as a witness. Then on two separate occasions the devious Manganos were involved in "similar suspicious-in-nature" Berlin, New Jersey area auto accidents.

"The Manganos would look in the rearview mirror for a fast traveling car in the passing lane, while approaching a traffic light that was turning yellow," Attorney Donio eloquently divulged. "At the last minute the Manganos would switch lanes and then be rear-ended when the speeding vehicle in the passing lane jammed on its brakes to avoid a violent impact. Berlin Police records describe in detail this scam happening twice with the Manganos collecting medical expenses, car repairs and then aggressively suing the other driver for carelessly operating a motor vehicle. The auto' insurance companies suspected fraud and alertly filed counter-claims that are still in litigation."

"I had no idea that we were being sued by such deceitful nefarious people!" Rita Randazzo gasped while shaking her head in disgust. "Who would ever think that anyone could be so furtively greedy and so untrustworthy?"

"Anyway, the Manganos have already been convicted for claiming to have their previous car stolen in April of 2000," Nelson Donio informed his thoroughly delighted clients, "and Pennsylvania court records indicate they had sold that particular vehicle to a notorious chop shop in Philadelphia and then collected insurance money too. That was another example of the pair conspiring to cheat an insurance company out of money while also getting paid by the chop shop dealer, who claimed to operate a legitimate auto' repair business. And thank goodness the South Philly' chop shop was recently raided and the Manganos' records were found kept in computer files that had been confiscated. And finally, according to Camden County police records, Philip Mangano had broken his right wrist in a Berlin barroom fight on Monday evening, July 26th."

"We're sure glad we hired you Nelson to take our case," Bob Randazzo praised. "Ironically it only goes to prove the maxim 'Honesty is really the best policy'."

"Maybe yes and maybe no!" Attorney Nelson Donio cryptically answered tongue-in-cheek. "It also pays to have the Honorable Judge as my loyal third cousin. Nepotism is quite common in small towns, you know! That's not to definitely say that bein' a blood relative of the Judge affected the disposition of your case. And besides that' distinct relationship Bob, you stand to directly profit from this deal and then have enough cash left over to pay for your new irrigation system and to travel to Hawaii, too!"

"It sounds like you're talkin' in riddles!" Bob Randazzo exclaimed. "What on Earth are you referrin' to?"

"Well Bob, you're a new car salesman over at the *Route 30* Ford/Lincoln/Mercury distributorship, aren't you?"

"Why yes Nelson!" the rather bewildered new car salesman responded. "Yes, I am!"

"Bob, I was talkin' to cousin Vince Curcio over the telephone just before you two Hammontonians arrived at my office for your briefing conference. And it coincidentally appears that the Judge and I are both in the market for two brand new Lincolns. Congratulations Bob! You've just merited commissions that'll more than pay for your irrigation alterations, your grand Hawaiian vacation and for your wise hiring of my sagacious Berlin private investigator friends to boot!"

“Illumination”

Henry Hugh Hendrix was an unhappy burned-out Hammonton High School English teacher whose only true classroom love was textbook literature. The thirty-four year New Jersey teaching veteran immensely enjoyed teaching the acclaimed works of Edgar Allan Poe, Mark Twain, Jack London, O. Henry, Washington Irving, Saki, H.G. Wells, Charles Dickens, Sir Arthur Conan Doyle and John Steinbeck to mostly apathetic hormone-driven juniors and seniors. The instructor was dissatisfied with his daily academic existence and Henry often found sanctuary in his ongoing dream of becoming a bona fide famous twenty-first century author.

‘Soon, I’ll be retiring from this misery and will be earnestly collecting my mediocre hard-earned pension,’ the fifty-seven-year-old pedagogue considered before his obnoxious eighth period General English class entered his Room 214 sanctuary. ‘Then, I’ll be able to publish several of the twenty controversial manuscripts I’ve meticulously and secretly written over the past three decades. I didn’t want to jeopardize my pension or my teaching career by publishing something risqué and adult-oriented that’s out of the mainstream,’ the aspiring author contemplated. ‘On July 1, I’ll officially have the *First Amendment* rights and freedoms guaranteed to Americans in the *U.S. Constitution.* Now I know how Martin Luther King felt when he proudly proclaimed ‘Free at Last’!’

Henry Hugh Hendrix was not a religious-oriented man in the traditional sense but he frequently professed being “spiritually inclined” when conversing with various relatives and acquaintances. The English instructor seldom accompanied his wife Marie to St. Joseph Catholic Church, preferring to believe that God was a force that deliberately disguised Himself as Evolution. In Hendrix’s personal interpretation of the Almighty, the Life Force specifically governed by Evolution had indiscriminately perpetuated both biochemistry and the prospect of intellectual genius throughout the Universe. And so the prospective author believed in God as a ubiquitous Spiritual Energy and not as a Divine Someone (intent on creating the world) as portrayed in *Genesis* or (benevolently giving Moses two stone tablets atop *Mt. Sinai*) as described in *Exodus*. Mrs. Marie Hendrix was not enamored with either her husband’s self-tailored philosophy or with his apparent eschewing of conservative Catholic Church doctrines.

The second week after officially declaring his retirement (in fact on July 4th, *Independence Day),* Henry sat behind his familiar desk and blankly stared at his flat-panel computer screen. 'This collection of short stories is not nearly as good as I had thought it was twenty-seven years ago. I remember writing the tales shortly after I achieved tenure at the high school,' the retiree recollected. 'Now I realize that this work is at best average quality, actually inferior to the caliber of literature developed by the masters I used to teach to my bored English classes. Time has certainly put a damper on my formerly rampant enthusiasm!'

The determined writer always believed that he worked best at his craft between the hours of five and eight a.m. 'That's when my mind is freshest and when I can think lucidly,' Henry stubbornly evaluated his predicament. 'But first I'll superstitiously engage in performing a small ritual that I hope will bless my endeavors. Perhaps what I have in mind will inspire me to organize my short stories into a legitimate science-fiction/paranormal collection worthy of praise from critics and pundits alike. This little ceremony I'm about to enact ought to confer on my stories a degree of dignity. Well, here it goes!'

In the corner of his computer room (which was actually his eldest son's former bedroom), Henry reverently approached a six-foot-high brass lamp stand. Although not a deeply religious man (in the conventional sense) the writer respectfully bowed his head and prayed, 'Oh lamp of light and beacon of intellectual illumination, please grant me the talent to rewrite my first literary work into a praiseworthy book. Allow me to transcend my limitations, this I pray, oh Lamp of Wisdom!'

After raising and again bowing his head in veneration, the on-a-mission author turned, stepped forward, sat down at his mahogany desk and soon began conscientiously editing and amending his 'lackluster manuscript.' And then predictably each morning without deviation at five a.m. Henry Hugh Hendrix loyally pursued his lofty goal, and after three consecutive months of assiduous daily labor the 're-creator' finally finished his masterpiece. The word composer was quite exuberant about the product of his toil.

'I'll self-publish my short fiction in Adobe Reader, in Microsoft Reader and in Mobipocket encryption formats,' the ambitious fellow imagined, 'and with the growing popularity of Print-on-Demand technology I'll also be able to produce the book in paperback and in hardcover formats. It'll be like five different books all consolidated into one, and the entire enterprise with cover artwork and *Internet* display all-included will cost me less than two-thousand-five-hundred dollars. I'll not be discouraged or dissuaded from accomplishing my objective!' Henry vowed to his conscience. 'And I'll doggedly keep generating manuscripts until I finally become rich and popular. And my personal success secret will be that wonderful six-foot-high halogen lamp situated in the corner of Joey's former bedroom,' Henry sentimentally mused. 'Now it happens to be time to start reviewing and rewriting my second excellent story collection. Thank you Magnificent Lamp of Wisdom! Thank you for showing me the light!'

After subsidizing his first independent publishing venture, Henry Hugh Hendrix commenced piecing together his second literary initiative, a compilation of eight imaginative novellas. Remarkably, the powerful corner brass halogen lamp provided the author with a unique and distinctive writing style as he marvelously incorporated the talents of his favorite contributors to literature into a phenomenally compelling new writing voice. By virtue of his admirable diligence, Henry's stories now had fabulous organization, coherency, consistency, rhythmic flow, terrific transitions between narrative and dialogue elements and also 'smooth seamless bridges' appearing between paragraphs. His exceptional work was actually peerless, virtually flawless and the envy of other authors that begrudgingly would soon be reading it.

'Oh, Lamp of Light and of Intellectual Illumination, please grant me the talent to finish the last story of my new novellas collection,' the man sincerely prayed with his chin lowered to his chest in genuine submission. 'Gee, this fantastic vertical lamp is just as indispensable to me as Aladdin's magical lamp was to him. Of course Aladdin was only a fictional character so my analogy is really a bogus one. I wonder if Shakespeare, Faust and Cervantes had magic candles, mystical plumed pens or other supernatural physical aids that allowed them to achieve literary greatness?' Henry considered. 'Why must I speculate about remote trivialities when I could be dedicating my soul to developing my next masterpiece?'

Soon, Henry completed his second creative compilation and had the exceedingly imaginative work produced and available on the *Internet* in Adobe Reader, in Microsoft Reader, in Mobipocket Reader, in paperback and in handsome Print-on-Demand hardcover versions. And amazingly the ambitious author's books began selling nationally and internationally with hungry-minded readers giving the new self-published author instant credibility and recognition. Henry was regarded as quite an aberration because his work transcended the pulp fiction being published by giant New York publishing houses and Hendrix retained all of the rights (movie, TV, radio, book clubs, subsidiary) to his fascinating stories. Despite his remarkable public acceptance, the 'all-too-arrogant publishing and book review establishments' basically had shunned the author's two spectacular triumphs.

In spite of being ignored (and denied honor) by the traditional and entrenched literary industry, the following year Henry had two more novellas collections titled *The Clean Dozen* and *The Clean Dozen, Part II* on the *Internet* marketplace and the brilliant entrepreneur believed that the time was ripe to fine-tune his first five-hundred-page novel into a sensational meritorious venue. But regarding the marvelous lamp the very superstitious author still kept his extraordinary 'illumination secret' all-to-himself.

'Not even Marie knows how I've been receiving direct assistance from 'The Lamp of Wisdom'. I must exercise humility and not show any hint or trace of pride or hubris,' Henry worried fearing the consequences of 'Divine Justice'. 'I have no desire to jinx my meteoric rise to fame. Even though my books are only sold by large *Internet* distributors and by mass market online bookstores my works are not available in libraries, are not sold in regular bookstores and are not reviewed by established newspapers like the *New York Times*. My sincere desire is to become the first self-published author to challenge and to defeat the powerful New York publishing syndicate and so far thanks to my faith in 'The Lamp of Wisdom' my efforts are astounding the powers-that-be in the industry. Now I must get down to important business again!'

Just before Henry was to begin editing his 'breakthrough novel', the halogen bulb suddenly burned-out inside his 'mystical lamp.' Overcoming the onslaught of a panic attack, the perplexed fellow apprehensively drove the twelve-mile-distance from Hammonton to Berlin, New Jersey and bought a three-hundred-watt replacement bulb at a busy *Home Depot*. Upon returning home to his Oak Road residence the anxious author immediately inserted the new bulb into the top of the mysterious lamp. The writer was ecstatic to soon observe that the lamp again glowed brightly and that the 'sacred object' still afforded him the confidence and the acumen to generate quality literature. Soon the relieved-but-serious author was knocking off three stellar chapters a day.

'At this astonishing rate, I'll finish rewriting this action/adventure novel in less than a month,' Henry conservatively estimated. 'I'm absolutely thrilled that the second bulb is just as effective as was the first one. Even Marie hasn't detected any dramatic change in my mood or in my attitude. I'll try to maintain a normal healthy marital relationship while dealing with the enormous pressures involved with producing a class novel. My wife can't imagine how tedious and nerve-racking writing and editing a novel can be, even with the assistance of a rather exceptional Lamp of Wisdom!'

Several days later, Marie insisted that the couple drive up the *New Jersey Turnpike* and the *Garden State Parkway* to Saddle Brook in Bergen County to visit and stay overnight at their son Stephen's Coger Street home. 'Steve and Michelle are christening their second daughter Lindsey Anne tomorrow, so it's our responsibility Henry to attend the *Baptism* ceremony and the restaurant reception afterwards. I know that you don't want to leave your novel," Marie reminded her obviously disgruntled husband, "but sometimes family commitments take priority over personal interests. I promise that you'll be able to return to your coveted *Dell Computer* Monday morning."

"You gotta' understand Marie that when an author is involved in a story that virtually everything else is perceived as being clutter. I know it sounds selfish but everything else is picayune and must be relegated and must therefore take a back seat to the pursuit of literary perfection," the husband insisted. "Even a granddaughter's *Baptism* comes along as a vexing inconvenience!"

After the Saddle Brook Baptism festivities had ended, Henry Hugh Hendrix was completely devastated upon returning to Hammonton late Sunday night. Vandals had broken into the couple's two-story colonial home and had ransacked the living room and the upstairs bedrooms. The treasured standing 'Lamp of Wisdom' had been savagely smashed against a bedroom wall and was all twisted and bent out of shape. The electrical appliance no longer worked and evidently was beyond reconstruction or repair. Henry's emotional state of mind was now borderline insanity and his fragile spirit was inconsolable.

"Gotta' be delinquent high school kids needing money for drugs and alcohol," Henry surmised and shared. "I just hope it wasn't some former students I had flunked on a rampage seeking their own personal vendetta!"

"Henry, after we notified the police about the destruction you seemed more distraught about your lamp being abused than about your computer being stolen," Marie Hendrix noticed and inquired. "What's so special about that cheap brass lamp? You can tell me the truth now!"

"All twenty of my manuscripts I've copied on floppy and large memory compact disks that I've hidden in the upstairs cedar closet so my life's work is safe since all of the books remain intact on backup files," the husband explained in a very melancholy and disgusted tone of voice. "But Marie, I gotta' confess that the standing brass halogen lamp was quite lucky for me. I believe it gave me the strength and the aptitude to write my fiction but now that it's been so severely damaged," the husband lamented, "I think that I'll no longer be able to write sophisticated and innovative stories without it. My second career's been maliciously ruined! All future endeavors are hereby doomed to being commonplace material! Now that the cat's out of the bag I might as well be honest with you! Without my lucky magic lamp Marie I'm on the same condemned shelf with all other fledgling writers! I'm just another crab in the bushel squirming hopelessly around seeking guidance and inspiration! Just another trapped crab in a damned bushel, mind you!"

"Don't' be ridiculous, Henry!" Marie undiplomatically chided. "Sometimes you're your own worst enemy! You're under duress from the vandalism and you don't sound sober even though you haven't been drinking! How could you possibly believe that your fate is dependent on an inexpensive brass-gilded lamp?"

"That's easy for you to say because I'm the one that's lost his outstanding writing skill and his formerly unparalleled storytelling ability!" the still-disturbed spouse vehemently answered. "I want you to know that I need that brass lamp stand intact as much as I need oxygen in my lungs and food in my stomach! It's a necessity I can't live and function without! I do believe that the brass lamp was a medium that allowed my mind to synchronize and communicate with a Greater Intelligence!"

"That's really ludicrous for you to even suggest such preposterous comparisons!" Marie rebuked her usually tranquil mate. "To tell you the truth I think you need asylum from yourself! I should be recording this conversation on tape!"

"What is that unwarranted insult supposed to mean?" Henry nastily asked. "Now I'll never win a *Nobel Prize for Literature* without special guidance from the *Lamp of Wisdom*!"

The wife then broke-out into a hysterical laugh that further infuriated her thoroughly upset husband even more. Contrary to his normal docile demeanor Henry Hugh Hendrix's temper was about to explode. The man could not fathom the basis for his wife's inexplicable state of levity.

"Look Marie, first our house is violated by being vandalized and robbed by area hooligans, and then my cherished good-luck-charm halogen brass lamp is destroyed by maniacal barbarians," Henry loudly rankled. "

"You ought to appreciate that no one was injured or killed!" Marie replied while still laughing. "And I do think you're being rather presumptuous in your biased conclusion about the age bracket of the insidious vandals. The wonderful world has not ended," the wife melodramatically emphasized, "and you now have four beautiful Baptized grandchildren and I must wholly stress the fact that property can easily be replaced thanks to our homeowners' insurance policy. And in regard to the brass lamp…."

"Don't tell me that you believe it can be replaced by a *Wal-Mart* special!" Henry bitterly yelled in defense of his frail ego. "In that case I'll never be able to jot-down a decent grammatically correct sentence again! *Wal-Mart* can't cut the mustard when it comes to finding a new omniscient *Lamp of Wisdom*! Don't you see that my confidence too has been plundered and has been reduced to rubble?" the distraught husband angrily argued. "Where's your sensitivity to my current plight? Learn to support your husband! You've lost your trademark! Your strong suit in our marriage Marie has always been sensitivity!"

"Henry, you aren't too observant when it comes to noticin' common everyday things! Haven't you ever realized that your oldest son Joseph now has a duplicate brass lamp stand in his new residence's spare bedroom?" the wife asked her irate spouse. "He insisted on having it as a memento from his coming-of-age high school days so while you were away in January gambling in Atlantic City with your retired friends at Harrah's Casino, I had delivered your original lamp to his apartment. Then I drove over to *Wal-Mart* and purchased an identical model brass lamp and took it home. I must admit that it was really pretty easy to assemble! All I needed was a regular screwdriver and a pair of pliers."

"You mean to say that I wrote the first two short story/novellas collections with the lamp that is presently in Joe's condo' over on Egg Harbor Road and that I wrote the novel with the aid of a *Wal-Mart* special that you had assembled without my knowledge?" the husband incredulously asked. "This is all rather unbelievable!" Henry anxiously exclaimed as he gingerly plopped down into his favorite black leather reclining chair. Sweat beads were rapidly accumulating on his forehead.

"I think Henry you've attached too much power to the first brass lamp stand, which if you remember had been purchased at *Home Depot* over in Berlin," Marie Hendrix recalled and stated. "And then your action/adventure novel was written with the supreme guidance of the second identical brass halogen lamp, which I incidentally had bought at the Hammonton *Wal-Mart*. I hate to inform you," the wife wryly announced tongue-in-cheek, "but those two cheap brass lamps were no more magical than any fork, knife or spoon in our kitchen flatware drawer!"

"What!" Henry hollered in absolute amazement. "Do you mean to say that all the while…."

"Exactly!" Marie reflexively confirmed. "The lamp was just a crutch that you superstitiously attributed your literary dynamics to. All the while the illumination for your superb stories came from within your own mind and not from any cheap *Home Depot* or *Wal-Mart* brass halogen lamps! Now that you're aware of all the facts, buy a new computer and sit down and write your glorious novel using whatever light you like," the wife suggested. "And now in conclusion my beloved Shakespeare, I must reiterate that your true illumination came from the depths of your immortal soul and not from a pair of cheap merchandise box-store bargain-basement brass halogen lights!"

"Double Play"

Michael and James Metz were sixty-two-year-old identical twins whose deep friendship had originated prior to kindergarten. The brothers even played on the same Levittown, Pennsylvania Meenan Oil *Little League* team in 1954-'55, dated, married and later divorced twins Barbara and Carol Zella and persevered and triumphed by becoming successful business partners, owning a small chain of six novelty gift shops in various Philadelphia suburban malls. Despite several difficult financial setbacks, the pair enjoyed engaging in their daily pursuit of "the American Dream."

The Metz twins were avid *Phillies* baseball fans and being loyal season-ticket-holders, they faithfully attended (from 1970 up to 2005) the Philadelphia club's home games at *Veterans Stadium* and then in later summers at *Citizens Bank Park.* In early October of 2005 the pair decided to escape the burdensome pressure of running their retail stores and drive cross-country before winter weather pestered and tormented the continental United States. Mike and Jim Metz had arranged to stay at the splendid Doral Country Club in Palm Springs, California for a week of golf, spend a second week of relaxation at the Sea Lodge Shores Resort overlooking the *Pacific* in La Jolla and then motor back to the East Coast before the deciduous trees completely lost their autumnal splendor.

"It's been great getting away from the nagging problems of American capitalism," Mike remarked as he sipped a mouthful of rum and *Coke* inside the Chart House Bar and Grille on La Jolla's ritzy Prospect Street. "We're blessed havin' competent management and efficient help lookin' over our thriving enterprises. And things are goin' like clockwork at all six of our retail outlets despite our absence. It's as if we've created something tangible that can now operate all by itself' without us! We'll have to return home and reestablish our authority over our loyal subordinates!"

Jim Metz was a little more nostalgic of the past than was his profit-driven competition-oriented twin. "Mike, I still remember when we played *Little League* back in 1955!" the less aggressive brother stated with reverence. "Meenan Oil was involved in a crucial game against Bristol Trust. We were tied in the top of the seventh inning with that big awesome kid Dick Brown on the mound hurlin' for our opponents."

"Yeah, I now remember the exact circumstances!" Mike Metz interrupted and commiserated. "There was only one out! I had laced a single to left field and was occupyin' first base. Then you had to smack a hard one hopper to shortstop and Bristol Trust skillfully executin' a really clean double play that erased our budding rally. Ya' really let Meenan Oil and Coach Siegel down!" Mike chided his twin. "And then, to aggravate us some more that dreaded thick-necked athlete Dick Brown hit a game-winning homer in the bottom of the seventh! I'll tell ya' Jim that was a heart-breakin' loss that remains with me to this very day! It was a rather traumatic experience for a couple of hopeful twelve-year-old kids like us."

"Yeah, but that hurtful loss built character!" Jim Metz reminded his self-centered sibling. "Dick Brown then played with us on the Levittown National League All-Star Team and *we* cooperated and became decent friends workin' toward common goals. The Goliath was no longer our dreaded adversary playin' for Bristol Trust. Mike, do ya' remember when we defeated the American League All-Stars in that close contest! That memorable game was suspenseful and pretty excitin' for players and fans alike! I'll take it to my damned grave!"

"And then, after bein' victorious over our American League rivals Levittown National played Morrisville," Mike Metz recollected and vociferated. "They had two six-foot-tall kids that dwarfed everyone on our squad with the exception of maybe Dick Brown. And Morrisville broke the game wide open in the top of the fifth when Dick Hart hit a mile-high triple to centerfield."

"That's right!" Jim recalled and verified. "The ball broke the webbing in Jerry Friedrich's glove and the bases were cleared. And then Morrisville continued on in the tournament and wound-up capturin' the *Little League World Series* in Williamsport. We listened to each and every one of their games on dad's portable radio! What a thrill that was! And to think that...."

"That *we* could've been the World Champions, if Jerry Friedrich had taken better care of his withered leather glove!" Michael Metz declared before ordering another round of drinks. "Jim, we could've gone to Williamsport and gotten attention in all the big city papers. But who can predict the whims of fate?" the more extroverted brother rhetorically asked. "All I can tell ya' Jim is that goin' up against Morrisville in the summer of '55 was a once-in-a lifetime opportunity that was destined to go against us!"

The pair left the bar area and then enjoyed delicious Chart House sirloin steaks and after paying the bill and leaving a generous tip to the attractive blonde waitress the two exited the premises and next casually strolled along La Jolla's retail store promenade. The impressed vacationers marveled at some lazy *Pacific Ocean* seals resting comfortably on massive rocks just off the shoreline and soon the duo sauntered back to their superior Sea Lodge accommodations. *Sea World* and the renowned *San Diego Zoo* and *Balboa Park* would consume the following two days' La Jolla and vicinity stay and then the itinerant Metz twins would be heading back to the East Coast with the initial-leg stopovers being a two day hiatus at Las Vegas's New York, New York followed by scheduled day visitations to Salt Lake City and then Denver. Everything on their structured agenda was going smoothly without a hitch.

After leaving the scenic *Rocky Mountains* and the "Mile-High City" behind, Michael asserted his dominance and again took command of the wheel and in several hours the more gregarious brother was driving his coveted black *Lexus* eastward on *Interstate 70.* While en route to their next scheduled destination the pair shared some fond memories that soon shifted from magnificent La Jolla (along with its swanky retail emporiums) and also Las Vegas gambling palaces to their childhoods growing-up in middle-class Levittown, Pennsylvania. As usual Michael Metz controlled the flow of the conversation.

"Jim, I wouldn't mind livin' on the West Coast where it's tolerable spring-like weather all-year-long," Mike commented to his less garrulous passenger. "Maybe we can sell our stores and duplicate our prosperity by becomin' the founders of a chain of California novelty outlets. We could even set-up a couple of shops in Vegas just off the Strip."

"You're too entrepreneurial for me! You're always motivated to start something new," Jim politely praised and responded, "but on the other hand I'm totally satisfied with what compensation I have and with where I'm at in life. I feel quite comfortable with our current security situation and our level of prosperity. Say Mike, where do we have reservations tonight? I don't want to sleep out on some park bench or inside a smelly garbage dumpster!"

"We'll be stayin' at a newly renovated *Ramada Inn* just west of Topeka," the more talkative brother amiably answered. "I looked at one of the glove compartment's maps this morning, and I believe we're now between the towns of Ellis and Hays. There sure aren't a lot of trees in this part of the country. Compared to Colorado Jim, Kansas is like flat prairie land and its dotted with wheat fields in the western part and occasional cornfields towards the east," the driver academically informed. "I can't wait until we reach Kansas City, and then drive northeast over toward Pittsburgh. You're quite right, Jim, in your sage conclusion. Philadelphia, *TastyKakes*, cheese steaks, and soft pretzels never seemed so wonderful to the imagination. On second thought we oughta' stay put on the East Coast regardless of what powerful temptations allure my wanderlustin' spirit!"

"Say, Mike. Watch your speed. You're goin' eighty-five, just about as fast as Dick Brown's Little League fast ball. It's amazin' how people come in and out of your life and then vanish into infinity," the *Lexus's* passenger aptly philosophically observed and related. "I wonder what Dick Brown, Jerry Friedrich and Dick Hart are doin' right now."

"Dick Hart, I know, played pro' football for the *Eagles* back in the '70s, and as far as Dick Brown and Jerry Friedrich are concerned," the driver paused and exhaled, "they could be married to the former Barbara and Carol Zella. So much for Italian beauties doubling as ex-wives and for old friends!" Mike added with a trace of regret. "I just wish I could be more sentimental than I am, but as my favorite cartoon character Popeye used to say to Olive Oyl, 'I am what I am, and that's all that I am'!"

"Maybe we could've had distinguished baseball careers playin' *Major League* ball for the *Minnesota Twins!"* Jim innocently joked. "That sort of coincidental fate would've seemed quite appropriate! In a way it might've been a blessing in disguise losin' that big game to Morrisville! Just think about it Mike! If the all-important Morrisville game outcome had happened in reverse," the normally laconic rider speculated and stated, "we might not have ever become the retail store tycoons we are right now!"

The pair engaged in their impromptu exchange of banter for several more miles, until Jim's keen perception spotted a dark funnel cloud forming off in the distance to their right. He immediately brought the meteorological phenomenon to his brother's attention. "Mike, there's a mean-spirited cyclone coming this way! It looks just like the one that swept Dorothy and Toto's house all the way to Oz. And wouldn't you just know it. Ironically, Dorothy's last name was Gale?"

"I think they call those wild twisters' tornadoes out here in this part of the country," Mike uneasily elaborated. "It's funny that you mentioned Oz. I was readin' in a newspaper several months ago where the author of *The Wizard of Oz* got the idea for his magical kingdom from lookin' at a file cabinet. The top drawer read 'A-To-N' and the bottom tray read 'O-To-Z.' That's how L. Frank Baum invented the name Oz, and that story's as true as Gospel. But you're geographically correct Jim," the driver commended the more anxious rider. "Tornadoes like the one that transported Dorothy and Toto to Oz are

are common in this flatland region between the *Appalachian* and *Rocky Mountains.* Hot and cold pressure systems are always fighting each other and that's what causes all the atmospheric turbulence in this part of the country. But Jim," the driver remarked as he glanced at the darkened sky to their right, "don't ask me how the brainless Scarecrow, the squeaky Tin Man and the cowardly Lion were invented. That's all open to speculation! What's the status of that over-aggressive tornado?"

"Er Mike, the cloud is only about half a mile away, and there's a distinct chill in the air!" James Metz uttered in a rather alarmed exclamation. "Forget about drivin' to Hays right now! Why don't ya' just pull over under that sturdy overpass up ahead and let the tornado determine its own path? If we're lucky, it'll veer north, or sweep right on by, and then we could continue our merry ramble through Kansas! What's your opinion?"

"Should we stay in our car, or latch onto the bridge guardrail?" the suddenly nervous driver asked. "I'm not that much of an authority on swirling air masses! All I know is that we're caught in the middle of some extraordinary weather war goin' on close by!"

"I believe we oughta' leave the car and grip the guardrail!" Jim strongly recommended. "I saw on TV where a wicked cyclone could pick-up an automobile with passengers in it, and convey the object clear into another county! I think our chances are much better if we quickly leave the vehicle, clamber up the concrete embankment and clutch onto the metal supports!" the now-very-concerned passenger advised. "I don't want to be a mere obituary statistic prematurely appearnin' in the local newspapers!"

Michael Metz pulled his black *Lexus* under the overpass without even realizing that all other cars, trucks, buses and *SUVs* had already abandoned *Interstate 70*. The brothers hastily evacuated their auto' and then swiftly scaled the concrete incline under the abutment as the first evidence of the raging twister began flapping around *their* outer garments.

"Hold on tight!" Mike instructed while feigning courage. "These intense Kansas tornadoes only last a minute or two! This is a very good method of losin' your dandruff!"

"I'm glad we only get an occasional hurricane or flood back home in the East!" Jim hollered above the ascending roar and accompanying wind eddy. "This confrontation really makes me respect nature's fury! What tremendous wind velocity! I feel like my legs are gonna' be blown out from under me, and that this metal bridge support will soon be our clothesline!"

After ninety-seconds of violent whirling, the cyclone's potent wrath gradually subsided and the men felt exhausted from enduring their excessive struggle. Both beleaguered brothers momentarily collapsed to the cement incline to rest their fatigued bodies along with their aching arm and leg muscles. Several moments of deep breathing allowed for sufficient oxygen to replenish their lungs and then finally the physically challenged pair had the wherewithal to resume intelligent dialogue.

"Thank goodness my *Lexus* wasn't damaged!" Mike Metz noticed and disclosed to his exhausted companion. "The next time I see the *Wizard of Oz* on cable TV I'm gonna' frantically change the channel. Jim, we almost wound-up in Oz I tell ya', we almost had a one-way excursion to visit the Emerald City! That's the first and last tornado I ever want to experience! We could've been killed!"

"Let's evacuate this place and get on our way to Topeka!" Jim advised. "It's just like we miraculously escaped some sort of suspended animation! Maybe there'll be radio and TV reports about this tornado and we can learn of any casualties or property destruction. All I can say is that I share your sentiment and never want to be in another cyclone again! This type of encounter we just escaped would make a drunken man sober again in a hurry!"

The pair re-entered their black *Lexus* and Mike turned the ignition key and fired up the engine. Soon the twins were again heading east on empty *I-70* and no traffic for miles in either direction was detectable. Mike hit the radio button and scanned for a local station but had little success in his exploratory enterprise. All FM and AM frequencies had simultaneously become silent.

"That's mighty strange!" the driver muttered to his still-in-shock now-neurotic passenger. "The storm must've affected the radio transmissions! I can't seem to get any reception or signal from anywhere!"

"The sign up ahead doesn't read Hays!" Jim apprehensively indicated. "It says Peaceful Valley, but Peaceful Valley isn't on your Triple-A map or on your car's automatic map finder. Honestly Mike, this trip and that twister are really givin' me the grand creeps. Pull off the ramp and we'll locate a diner or a gas station. Then maybe we can discover some details about our most recent misadventure with Mother Nature!"

Mike Metz reluctantly-but-obediently exited *I-70*, which still was devoid of human activity. Several miles down a winding, two-lane country road, a green sign with white lettering read: "Welcome To Peaceful Valley!"

"Sounds almost like a morbid greeting to a cemetery!" Mike interpreted to his identical twin. "Looks like some kind of baseball game is in progress up ahead. Let's stop and see if we could buy a couple of hot dogs and two refreshin' soft drinks! Say Jim, the blasted concession stand is closed with the counter padlocked and their aren't any fans sittin' in the stands! What kind of peculiar illusion is goin' on here? I've heard of fantasy baseball but this eerie event is absolutely ridiculous! Even the two bathrooms are locked! Talk about the damned *Twilight Zone!"*

The men climbed the green wooden steps into the empty bleachers and ascended four rows to bench seats elevated directly above the home team's dugout. Mike and Jim were equally stunned upon realizing that the two Little League teams (having the Peaceful Valley contest before their very eyes) were Meenan Oil (at bat) and Bristol Trust stationed out on the field and also in the visiting team dugout on the opposite side of the well-manicured perfect-looking baseball diamond.

"This is beyond a shadow of a doubt absolutely incredible!" Mike whispered to his partner in an intimidated and frightened tone of voice. "That's Dick Brown, standing on the mound, a twelve-year-old Dick Brown! And the centerfield scoreboard says the top of the seventh inning with the damned score tied three to three. Is this the ultimate nightmare or what Jim? Hey, there's Coach Siegel nervously sittin' at the end of the bench!"

Jim Metz not only noticed the presence of Meenan Oil Coach Bill Siegel at the end of the dugout bench, but the bewildered spectator also observed that he and Mike were again acne-faced twelve-year-olds wearing their #5 and #7 black and gray Meenan Oil uniforms. Somehow he and his equally astonished brother had been conducted from the stands as adults and were now also twelve-year-old kids sitting in the home team' dugout and impatiently waiting their turns at bat. Coach Siegel motioned for Mike to get into the on-deck circle and the stunned young man obediently complied. Moments later, the boys incredulously peered at each other as their childhood friend Mike Hunter popped up to the second baseman just as he had done on June 18, 1955. But both Mike and Jim rationally knew that today's date was Wednesday, October 19, 2005. Their hearts were now wildly palpitating inside their chests.

Just as had transpired back in 1955, Michael Metz swung at the second pitch and smashed a solid line-drive single to left field. Jim then assumed his left-handed batting stance in the batter's box and stared-out at the formerly formidable Dick Brown stoically standing on the pitcher's mound. 'I'll swing at the third pitch and not the second as I had done back in 1955,' Jim mumbled to himself and promised his conscience. 'According to sports' folklore Abner Doubleday was the legendary inventor of the game of baseball but ever since 1955 Mike and the other guys have mockingly called me Abner Doubleplay. Now's my chance to redeem myself with a clutch hit or maybe even a dramatic home run!'

Everything was still and quiet on and around the phantom baseball yard, and all the players and coaches both on the field and in the dugouts remained mum. Mr. Irvin, the reticent third base coach gave Jim the same signal as had been communicated a half-century before, the sign tacitly instructing the batter to take the first pitch, which just like in 1955 was a Dick Brown blazing fastball for a strike.

Jim Metz instinctively glimpsed-up at the centerfield scoreboard and recognized that the score was deadlocked at 3 to 3 just as it had been in 1955. 'The next pitch is goin' to be a curveball slightly out of the strike zone!' Jim accurately remembered and considered. 'I'll take it and even-out the count at one ball and one strike. I'll be damned if I'm again gonna' hit a grounder to shortstop for an easy double play! This time I'm goin' to avoid disgrace and achieve something a little more sensational and honorable!' the batter promised himself as he peered out at the stationary but mentally focused Bristol Trust players ready for action on the crazily weird and very uncanny fantasy baseball field.

Dick Brown stared-down at his catcher's glove target with an extreme frown on his chubby face, and soon the hurler snarled at the determined young man standing with trembling legs at the plate. Jim noticed his adult counterpart sitting in the stands and then firmly gripped (choking-up) on his bat as tension mounted in every limb and fiber of his twelve-year-old body. The twin keenly desired to alter the past embarrassment with one steady swat of his bat.

Just as Dick Brown initiated his all-too-familiar windup, a gust of wind spiraled the loose dirt on the field around, making the odd baseball diamond scene into a veritable dust bowl. Then a massive tornado spontaneously enveloped the entire miniature baseball stadium. Everyone and everything had been violently sucked-up into the gigantic vacuum that resulted. Mike and Jim succumbed to reality and now finally understood too late that they were merely actors serving as props' in a terrible natural disaster being staged. Then, to *their* nebulous perception, the whole *Little League Park* scenario went black and lifeless.

* * * * * * * * * * * * *

A front-page article was featured in the next day's edition of the *Hays Daily News*. Local residents were shocked reading the particulars of the gruesome story, which also appeared in the *Wichita Eagle* two days later.

"Tornado Kills Two Pennsylvania Men"

> Yesterday, an unexpected funnel cloud descended onto *Interstate 70* and took the lives of two Pennsylvania men that local police assume are brothers from credentials found inside the dead men's wallets. State Police and Hays Law Enforcement Officers are still investigating the details of the horrible mishap.
>
> Apparently, the men were traveling eastbound on the *Interstate* several miles past Ellis when they were surprised by the appearance of the oncoming twister. They left their *Lexus* and sought temporary shelter and safety underneath an overpass as the weather pattern swooped down from the sky. Unfortunately the twister picked up the black *Lexus* and crashed the vehicle onto the bridge's support structure, instantly crushing and tragically killing the two victims.
>
> More pertinent information about the *twins' killing* should be available from authorities by press-time tomorrow following necessary notification of the victims' next-of-kin.

"Calendar Man"

Wilson Parkhurst grew-up as a shy bashful kid on his family's Central Avenue estate pleasantly situated on tranquil Hammonton Lake. Wilson attended the South Jersey somnolent community's high school, graduated from *Glassboro State Teachers' College* with a Mathematics Degree in 1965, and then phlegmatically worked on his father's five-hundred-acre fruit and vegetable farm as the company's office manager. When half of Hammonton agriculture went flat in the early '80s with the area peach crop losing favor to California and Georgia fancy fruit, the Parkhurst family abandoned orchard farming, rented their acres to various other "industrious but impractical stewards of the land," purchased a profitable construction company eight miles west on *Route 30* in Atco, and the extraordinarily withdrawn Wilson Parkhurst was again actively involved in keeping the books of a prosperous thriving enterprise.

Wilson Parkhurst handled all of the company's contract bids, machinery acquisitions, and payroll. The meek man didn't like mingling with others or kibitzing at the firm's holiday socials, especially the annual *Christmas Party* and the traditional *Labor Day* picnic. The introvert liked analyzing human behavior from a distance, preferred interacting with others on strictly an impersonal business basis and the low-level executive generally frowned on overtly giving and receiving affection. Thus Wilson created his own little fantasy world to compensate for *his* real-world apathy and he only felt comfortable when entranced in his own secret comfort zone, with Parkhurst deliberately insulating himself from commonplace gossip, drivel and prattle. That particular withdrawal practice was not to say that the accountant's acquaintances didn't gossip, drivel and prattle about him and his self-mandated isolation.

In 1990, Wilson Parkhurst's wife Jenny filed for divorce citing "irreconcilable differences" as the principal reason for initiating the permanent separation. According to the divorce court judge's order Wilson had to pay a monthly stipend of three thousand dollars for child support and alimony, and the staggering amount effectively crippled the shy fellow's finances. Although Parkhurst was a member of a prominent Hammonton family he only commanded a ten percent share of the family businesses and a fifteen-hundred-dollar weekly salary. His stubborn father was parsimonious and also favored the accountant's three older brothers over "the lackadaisical dreamer." Thus the former Jenny Dickinson became disenchanted with her unmotivated husband's past, present and future in regard to his share of the company's assets, and the all-too-greedy woman sought the emotional security that was absent in their "strained relationship" a year later in a second marriage to a successful stock broker.

On the Saturday morning of July 9, 2005, Wilson Parkhurst woke up early and pondered, 'I have weekends off so today I'll get caught-up on some personal responsibilities and interests. Perhaps a little diversion will allow me to escape my noticeable lethargy that dad and my brothers are always criticizing. Maybe Jenny was right after all. I never learned how to open-up and share my personality and inner feelings with others and meanwhile enjoy their company! Today I'll set out to change some of my negative habits.'

The quiet man arose from bed, showered, shaved, and then glanced at the daily date hanging on his bedroom closet's door calendar. Wilson gently ripped off Friday July 8th but accidentally tore two dates off the suspended data document. The new date remarkably read Sunday July 10th when it should have been Saturday, July 9th. Inspecting the remainder of the "oddball calendar", Wilson Parkhurst recognized that every additional date for the remainder of the 2005' year was Sunday, July 10th as if time had stood still and as if the eccentric Parkhurst had been wickedly trapped in an inescapable 'suspended animation time situation!'

'This is awfully strange!' the born-again-bachelor contemplated and evaluated. 'It must be a misprint! Some careless incompetent employee at the date/calendar firm was probably distracted by a pretty girl and momentarily lost his concentration,' Wilson speculated as he shook his head in consternation. 'We've got similar men working at construction sites and smashing their heavy equipment into walls or into other vehicles whenever a good-looking woman wearing a tight sweater or a sexy bikini appears somewhere around the work scene!'

After meticulously making his bed, Wilson Parkhurst thought about how he would selfishly spend his day. First, he drove his white Ford Fairlane to the nearest *WaWa* convenience store at the corner of *Route 30* and Fairview Avenue, purchased three glazed doughnuts and a cup of freshly prepared coffee and observed the other more sociable early morning shoppers picking-up snacks and junk food to further contaminate their digestive systems and to involuntarily increase the girth of their paunches. In a short seven minutes the three glazed doughnuts and accompanying twelve-ounces of coffee had been consumed and feeling uncomfortable and "out of place" the generally self-isolated, private fellow abandoned the popular establishment to pursue other duties, responsibilities and pleasures.

'It's a little after 9 a.m.,' Parkhurst realized after re-entering his modest white Ford Fairlane. 'I need a haircut, so I'll zip over to Salon FX in the Village Mall. No wonder why kids today can't spell correctly. Salon FX is code language for Salon Effects, just like that rock group INXS stands for *in excess*. The whole vernacular and its grammar are being convoluted and corrupted with companies like *Cingular* and *Conectiv* further complicating matters and thoroughly confusing the minds of already disoriented teenagers!' the critic cynically assessed. 'It's not only our American schools that are dumbing-down the gullible minds of acne-faced kids! Let's have less of all these pathetic anagrams, or whatever they're called! When I was a kid, every word spoken or read was sacred and had special meaning! There's no longer any rigid border between right and wrong and between sanity and insanity!'

Parkhurst always deliberately avoided the Hair Cuttery on Third Street or the Hair Hut on Egg Harbor Road because Jenny and her sisters frequented those business establishments, and a confrontation with his former spouse or any probing discussion about *their* college-age children Bill and Jackie was exactly what the keep-to-himself accountant shunned and dreaded. So to evade any undesirable encounter or incidental meeting Parkhurst preferred patronizing Salon Effects early on weekend mornings when most women were still putting on their makeup getting ready to venture out to their preferred hair-dressers. That particular morning, Annette was available for the next customer and so Wilson jotted his name on the third line from the top on the receptionist's counter notebook list and requested the stylist whom he noticed was free.

"Hello, Wilson!" the attractive frosted-haired brunette greeted. "What'll it be, a summer cut?"

"Yes, and you can shave off the sideburns too!" Parkhurst emphatically instructed. "Just leave a little showing above my ears. I mean Annette, it seems like I was just here yesterday. Gosh, my hair is growin' faster than the weeds in my garden. I must be swallowin' too many powerful vitamins or something! Maybe my hair follicles are overactive?"

"I'm sure you're exaggeratin'!" the accommodating hair specialist answered with a forced grin. "I don't remember seein' you in here yesterday, Mr. Parkhurst! And I gotta' tell ya' I was slavin' away inside this place all-day-long, too!"

"Isn't today Saturday, July 9th?" the customer asked with an air of confusion evident in his tone of voice. "For some remote reason I must've thought that yesterday was Saturday, July 9th! I must be havin' one of those senior moments!"

"This is the most humor I believe I've ever seen you exhibit," Annette complimented while un-meritoriously contemplating a huge tip, "and to tell you the truth, Mr. Parkhurst, I think it's good to see you loosen-up a bit, even if you're jokin' about bein' here yesterday!"

'I'd better keep my mouth shut, or else Annette will think I'm ready for a straightjacket,' the man in the chair imagined. 'But it certainly does seem like I was here yesterday, getting my head trimmed. I'll have to be very careful about this crazy July calendar business or else someone in my immediate family will have me permanently committed!' Then the man's mind snapped back to reality. "You can call me Wilson, Annette, but mind you that privilege pertains only for today! I hereby announce that excessive formality is taboo for this morning only!"

"Well Wilson, how's the construction business goin'?" Annette asked to fill a momentary void in the conversation with some impromptu small talk. "I see your family's trucks all over Hammonton, Atco, Egg Harbor, Vineland and even over in Berlin. The public's demand for new roads to access new buildings and homes must be goin' right through the roof!"

"As they say Annette, the grass is always greener," Wilson smartly answered. "That cliché has never been more applicable. When things' look too good to be true, they' generally are too good to be true. Union workers incessantly want higher salaries and benefits, along with better workin' conditions, the cost of materials keeps escalatin' and new expensive equipment must always be purchased once the old bulldozers and front-end-loaders are fully depreciated on the tax statements. And interest rates are now rising on borrowed money and health insurance expenses have no ceiling," the newly transformed man in the chair pontificated. "Just learn to be glad and happy Annette that you're makin' a decent livin' cuttin' hair without all the colossal headaches and problems associated with ownin' your own business. I assure you that financial independence has a dear price, actually a very high dear price one must pay! Confidentially, if I had a second opportunity to turn back the clock and do it all over again, I'd enter the seminary!"

Annette indulgently laughed at Wilson's inordinate wit as she brushed off the silver and brown hair cuttings off the black cloth' cape draped-around Parkhurst's narrow shoulders. The affable attendant wrote out the customary check and Wilson thanked the courteous woman for her skilled services. He then awkwardly ambled over to the cashier, removed his wallet from his back pants' pocket and handed the Asian woman a twenty-dollar bill. "Please give Annette a five-dollar tip," the satisfied customer affably requested. "She really performed a great miracle this mornin' with my unmanageable wiry wig!"

Upon feeling good because he coincidentally looked good, Wilson again entered his white Ford Fairlane, eased out of the Village Mall's asphalt parking lot and steered east on *Route 30* in the direction of Atlantic City. 'Harrah's Casino is only thirty miles from here, or maybe instead I'll try a little gambling over at the *Showboat* on the boardwalk. It's just three miles farther down the road. I remember taking this highway back in the late '50s and early '60s' when I was dating Jenny,' the driver lamented as he sped through a yellow light in downtown Egg Harbor City. 'But back then, we' called this deathtrap highway the White Horse Pike. We still do, but most folks refer to it as *Route 30* nowadays.'

On his drive east, Wilson reminisced about the good old days in the late '50s and the early '60s, about the glorious Atlantic City Boardwalk, the fabled Steel Pier attractions featuring the High Diving Horse and the submarine-like Diving Bell, and the fabulous Million Dollar Pier with its many amusement rides and its "World Famous Flea Circus." The innocence of the 1950s was what Wilson Parkhurst's lonely heart yearned for.

'There were at least a dozen movie theaters on the boardwalk and on Atlantic Avenue that were jam-packed every Friday and Saturday night, but all of that local nostalgic stuff has changed with the advent of casino gambling, color TVs, VCRs and DVDs,' the driver regretted. 'If only I could time travel back to the '50s and live my young-adult life over again. I suppose that dream's just a lot of naïve wishful thinking! I suppose I've made my bed and now must learn to sleep in it too even though lately it's had a lousy mattress and broken box springs.'

After parking his Fairlane in the Showboat's high-rise-garage, the somewhat depressed visitor entered the swanky casino that was glittering with flashing lights and alluring flickering neon. 'Jenny had originally miscalculated my status and role in the farming enterprises and later overestimated my percentage of the family construction company,' Parkhurst thought as he gritted his teeth and then smirked as he responded to temptation and put a fifty-dollar bill into a dollar slot machine. 'These machines require a dollar to play, but they really make you feel compelled to feed three dollars at a time into them in order to qualify for the seldom-seen big-jackpot payoff. Oh well, nothing ventured, nothing gained.'

Wilson's luck at his randomly chosen slot machine was rather phenomenal. On his third pull the amateur gambler landed three sevens, which paid a handsome thousand-dollar-prize, and on his "lucky seventh tug" of the one-arm-bandit the fortunate fellow landed three double diamonds, which afforded him an award of two thousand genuine American bucks.

"Your luck is rather incredible!" the slot machine attendant congratulated the now elated two-time winner. "Maybe you ought to parlay your luck on the super progressive machines over there against the wall! Like they say, when you're hot, you're hot! Keep the streak goin'!"

"No thanks!" Wilson sternly replied with noteworthy discretion. "I'm an accountant and good with figures and knowin' the odds I'm aware of precisely how these things work. I don't want to defy the laws of probability! Once a player is ahead like I am right now, the wise action to take is to cash in my winnings and come back in a month or so and try my luck again. That system always seems to be the most beneficial for me."

"You have this place figured-out!" grinned the manager, as he individually deposited twenty additional crisp hundred-dollar bills into Parkhurst's right palm. "But as they say, the swallows always come back to Capistrano and winners always return to see if they can duplicate their feats! Good luck to you sir!"

Wilson smiled and gave the attendant and the manager forty-dollar tips each, and in return, only asked for their blessing, and the two employees instantly obliged. Then the jovial newly changed fellow departed the glitzy tourist trap, stepped into the high-rise parking garage to retrieve his white Ford Fairlane, fired-up the motor and drove out onto Pacific Avenue with a broad grin and a blithe disposition. 'I'm sure happy that I didn't play blackjack, roulette, or craps like I usually do,' the thrilled driver considered while proudly shaking his head. 'For once in my life I made an intelligent lucky choice! I ought to savor this moment for the rest of my monotonous existence on this rather dull and humdrum planet.'

Parkhurst decided to take *Route 322* (Black Horse Pike) out of Atlantic City west to *Route 50* south, so that the winner could stop off and privately celebrate his good fortune at Joanne's Pizza in Mays Landing where not-too-many Hammonton people lunched. After the

Italian food lover had entered the eatery, the only familiar Hammonton face belonged to Michael Donio, a Superior Court judge who presided over criminal cases at the Mays Landing County Seat. The Solon recognized the new arrival, and gave Wilson a tacit wave, and Parkhurst reflexively reciprocated the polite gesture. Then Judge Donio continued his symposium with three important-looking colleagues, all dressed in dark blue suits.

"What will it be for you today, Mr. Parkhurst?" a familiar voice asked. "Haven't seen you here for lunch in a couple of months! Care to scrutinize a menu?"

"Oh, hi Darlene, that's okay, I know exactly what I'd like. I just want a quiet table all to myself, a small personal-sized pizza, extra-thick with just tomato and cheese, and a large *Coke* to wash the delectable meal down!"

"Okay, how about situatin' yourself' at the corner table next to the front window," the short convivial Italian waitress suggested. "That's always been your favorite place ever since you've been comin' here."

"Great!" the regular patron ecstatically replied. "Heard anything worthy of mention about Jason? My former wife has my son brainwashed against me."

"I still date Jason now and then, but our relationship has changed ever since I moved out of Hammonton. Mays Landing' is a much less clannish town and I gotta' admit that I fit in much better here. But Jason still occasionally asks about you, and I tell him you're doin' just fine."

"Well, Darlene, tell my son I said 'hello' and that he could come and visit me if and when he has the time. After all," Wilson qualified with feigned seriousness, "you might someday be my daughter-in-law."

After consuming his extra-thick personal pizza and enjoying his refreshing large *Coke,* Wilson dutifully paid his check, left a handsome ten-dollar tip, nonchalantly waved again to Judge Donio and departed the establishment in an uncharacteristic jubilant mood. His spirit was still buoyant about his recent mini-bonanza at the *Showboat*. 'I think I'll take *Route 50* back to *322* and then head west to *County Road 559*, known to locals as Weymouth Road,' Wilson imagined and then decided. 'I'll stop at Atlantic Blueberry Company and buy a flat of Blue Crop variety. July 9th or July 10th usually marks the midway point in the berry harvest season when the fruit's flavor is at its peak.'

Atlantic Blueberry Company is the largest cultivated blueberry farm in the world growing over fifteen million pounds of the luscious fruit on thirteen hundred acres of pristine white sandy soil. As a youth (after a dispute with his father) Wilson had worked one summer as a skid loader and he recalled meeting Jenny at the blueberry farm where she had been employed for the season as a packer.

'Today, the berries are packed on ten automated assembly lines but in the late '50s over a hundred high school girls were employed at the packinghouse putting cellophane over each pint along with a blue rubber band and then inserting twelve pints into each flat. Times have really changed. Local kids back then earned money for their fall clothes and for college tuition,' Wilson recollected, 'but today it's hard for a young country fella' to meet a pretty girl at a farm packinghouse. But in the '50s, whether it was peaches or blueberries bein' packed and shipped, area teenagers were employed, and that was the tradition in and around Hammonton.'

Normally, prudence and caution were Wilson Parkhurst's watchwords, but after obtaining and paying for his flat of Blue Crop variety the exhilarated man climbed back behind his Ford's steering wheel and after turning his auto' around hit the accelerator hard, peeling out of the farm's front parking area onto Weymouth Road just as he had audaciously done in 1959. While in college the driver had owned a dark green Triumph Spitfire convertible and now on July 9, 2005 he recalled (and re-enacted) sitting behind the wheel and taking Jenny on exciting excursions down winding *County Road 559* with the top down.

'Those were the days!' Wilson mused with a prodigious smile on his countenance as his Ford Fairlane gradually increased its speed up to fifty-five miles an hour. 'I had plenty of spunk, a neat car, and this snake-like road presented itself as a challenge to any sports car enthusiast.' Then the driver reflected some more. 'July 10th, 2005! This might be the day that alters my life forever! I'll just pretend I'm again in my Spitfire zipping around these dangerous curves! I did it in my youth! I'll do it again!'

Wilson zoomed around curve number three at sixty-miles an hour, and then soon was approaching bend number four with the speedometer registering sixty-five when suddenly a behind schedule tractor-trailer refrigeration truck was observed speeding south in the opposite direction on its way to Atlantic Blueberry Company. The monstrous eighteen-wheeler veered into the oncoming lane and Parkhurst desperately turned his steering wheel and frantically swerved away from the enormous moving object. The tractor cab's left front wheel clipped Wilson's back fender, and the Fairlane skidded out-of-control across the two-lane highway, and then sheered a telephone pole in half. The white Ford next spun around and flipped over into a pine tree woods, and after that, the vehicle caromed off of three evergreens before finally coming to a halt upside-down. The automobile was virtually demolished, and its occupant was unconscious, barely breathing and very close to death.

* * * * * * * * * * * * * *

Dr. Philip Evans was professionally speaking with nurses Meg Duncan and Marcia Williams outside Hammonton's Kessler Memorial Hospital's Intensive Care Unit. The subject of their grim discussion was automobile accident victim Wilson Parkhurst and the bottom-line prognosis was not encouraging. All three medical specialists were extremely concerned about the man's prospects for recovery.

"Mr. Parkhurst has been unconscious for three days now ever since his admission," Dr. Evans marveled and related. "It's amazing he survived the ambulance ride here. It's also rather remarkable he's still alive because of the extensive internal bleeding he's sustained and because of the multiple fractures and various injuries he's incurred all over his body. The man has an unrelenting will to live and I must say with the utmost admiration, he absolutely refuses to die."

"Today's Tuesday, July 12th, but Mr. Parkhurst keeps mumbling and insisting that it's still Sunday, July 10th," Nurse Meg Duncan contributed to the topic of conversation. "That terrible series of collisions out on Weymouth Road must have had a traumatic effect on his mind. July 10th must be deeply embedded in our patient's psyche."

"Yes," Nurse Marcia Williams said as she handed Dr. Evans Wilson Parkhurst's medical chart. "He keeps describing a strange calendar with each day being July 10th. That day has become a sort of mantra with him! And the patient has been repeating certain events over and over again, ever since he's arrived at the Emergency Suite," Nurse Williams indicated. "All the staff members on duty now know and have memorized his exact routine in its precise chronological order, including his brief visit to the Fairview Avenue *WaWa*, his haircut, his casino expedition, his pizza stop in Mays, his blueberry flat, yes, everything that happened that day up until….."

"Up until his terrible encounter with the speeding tractor-trailer," Nurse Meg Duncan finished. "It's as if he's pathetically trapped in the same day, and his soul can't escape his badly damaged body. But Mr. Parkhurst keeps mentioning a green Triumph Spitfire, when actually he was driving a white Ford Fairlane, and was actually hit by the oncoming tractor-trailer on Saturday, July 9th. This man has without a doubt…."

"An implacable will to survive!" Dr. Evans theorized and eloquently stated. "Let's hope and pray that Mr. Parkhurst's spirit stays embedded in the past until his body finds sufficient strength to heal and replenish itself. I'm afraid that if our courageous patient's mind prematurely crosses the psychological bridge to the present date," the doctor revealed and then took a deep breath, "his fragile psyche might lose its need to endure, and then our struggling patient might inadvertently give-up the ghost!"

“New Jersey Transit”

Thomas William Mills was examining the front-page headlines of the *Atlantic City Press* and noticed the early morning edition’s date: ‘Monday, August 15, 2005,’ the retired Hammonton Middle School guidance counselor perceived and read to himself. ‘The national and local news stories are so depressing that I’m feeling a tad despondent from all the negativity. Hey, I have a brilliant idea! I’ll simply treat myself to a pleasant afternoon on the Atlantic City Boardwalk. That stroll will bring back many fond memories to reminisce. I’ll even gobble down some saltwater taffy and fresh-baked pizza. Those self-rewarding activities ought to revitalize my spirit and get me out of the doldrums!’

Much to his mental relief, Mills’ bossy wife Anna was staying the full week at an expensive modern-designed rental home at 17th and the Boardwalk in Ocean City, New Jersey. His three sons, their wives, children and several ‘freeloading in-laws’ were also staying in the massive six-bedroom guesthouse. Mills’ wealthy elderly mother-in-law had forked-over ten thousand dollars for the weekly summer residence, but crying grandchildren, plenty of confusion and communal living with seventeen other people were not Thomas Mills’ forte. The quiet fellow preferred seclusion, contemplation, marital intimacy, watching old ‘40s and ‘50s movies on cable television and reading good novels in peace and quiet rather than ‘contributing to excessive domestic noise pollution.’

‘I know what I’ll do!’ the confirmed loner eventually decided. ‘I’ll drive to the Hammonton Station, park my car and catch the New Jersey Transit noon train to Atlantic City. The relaxing ride will be a welcome change, because if I drive to the shore, the traffic will be too hectic and congested. The thirty-mile excursion should only take about forty-five minutes and then I’ll connect with a jitney waiting for pickups at the Atlantic City Terminal and get dropped-off at one of the classy boardwalk casino/hotels,’ Thomas reckoned. ‘I’ll gamble and take my time sacrificing a hundred bucks in air-conditioned comfort for an hour or two and then casually amble the Boardwalk at my leisure and I’ll attempt refreshing my dissipated energy level.’

The seventy-year-old man changed into some comfortable blue denim Bermuda shorts, a colorful Las Vegas tee shirt, and a pair of sturdy baseball umpire black shoes. At 11:35 a.m. Thomas backed his black *Mazda Protégé* out of his garage, lowered the door with his remote control, and drove from his Pine Road ranch home to *Route*

30 and then turned onto Bellevue Avenue. He proceeded through downtown Hammonton to Egg Harbor Road. A left turn was expertly negotiated and soon Thomas William Mills reached Line Street, and after making a ninety-degree right' a half mile down the road he eased his shiny automobile into the Hammonton Station's New Jersey Transit Parking Lot. After carefully locking his car and leaving the four windows partially cracked (to allow compensation for the intense summer heat), the prospective passenger ascended the ramp leading to the train platform and approached a ticket dispenser with sufficient dollars and change to procure a two-way-pass to show the conductor.

'This is awfully strange!' Thomas logically assessed with mild surprise. 'I realize that it's noontime but I'm the only person standing on the platform. Oh well, I see the locomotive's light a mile or so west. I suppose I should feel lucky getting here without any complications and making such an excellent connection without any hassle whatsoever!' Mills assessed while putting a positive spin on his situation. 'Maybe Friday I'll feel relaxed enough to motor on over to 17th and the Boardwalk in Ocean City and show my face to avoid being the subject of family gossip about my extended absence!'

When the New Jersey Transit Local loudly rumbled into the almost deserted station, it soon stopped and like clockwork the automatic electronic doors opened. The sole individual on the platform incredulously looked around and then reluctantly entered the carriage. Tom Mills slowly stepped toward the anterior section and in a bewildered frame of mind plopped himself down in a comfortable cloth-fabric seat. His eyes surveyed the remainder of the car and his mind quickly discerned that no other riders were aboard what he imagined to be "the phantom train." A chill wandered up and down Mills' spine and a primitive atavistic-type feeling spontaneously dominated his being.

'This is totally absurd and completely contrary to reason!' the fellow skeptically rationalized. As Mills' pupils made a swift inspection of the aisle of the car directly ahead the now-neurotic passenger determined that it too was devoid of human occupancy. 'Perhaps there's some feasible explanation for this anomaly!' Thomas considered in an effort to allay his mounting fear. 'I wonder if my nephew David is the engineer today. He works for New Jersey Transit and sometimes rides these rails between Hammonton and the shore. But it can't be David sitting at the controls!' the man acknowledged. 'He's vacationing down in Ocean City socializing with the rest of the family! Does this diabolical eastbound train have any engineer at all? This entire matter is quite abnormal to say the least!'

The train lurched out of the Hammonton Station and sped-off eastward towards the Jersey coast, a mere thirty miles away. The chain of five cars soon entered a section of the New Jersey Pine Barrens and the train's route paralleled familiar *Route 30,* the White Horse Pike, whose traffic and landmarks were visible every now and then outside the left glass panel windows with every momentary flickering break in the evergreen forest. All the while deciduous, cedar and pine trees were whizzing by as the sinister train gradually accelerated along while conducting its daily itinerary.

'Maybe some passengers will get on at Egg Harbor City?' Thomas anxiously worried and wondered. 'Oh well, I'll just have to wait ten more miles of annoying suspense before learning how true my rampant imagination turns out being. Hey! Now that's impossible!' the rider dubiously ascertained as he' glanced to his left and then sighted a unique relevant structure from *his* past. 'Laura's Farm Market located on *Route 30* in the lazy rural rustic village of Elwood had been demolished back in 1980!' Mills recollected. 'How could it still be here?'

Thomas Mills had dated Anna Curreri since high school, and his future wife's mother had owned Laura's Farm Market from the early '50s right up to 1980 when the building had been knocked down by bulldozers. And to add to Mills' present quandary vintage cars of the nostalgic late '60s era (belonging to fruit and produce retail customers) had been parked in front of the authentic-looking farm market. 'I must be hallucinating!' the sole passenger uneasily contemplated. 'All of this difficult introspection is not healthy for my emotional stability! In fact it's very detrimental! I feel weak and confused! Egg Harbor City can't come into view too soon!' Thomas admitted with flagging confidence. 'My mother-in-law abandoned the farm market business over twenty-five years ago and she's now vacationing in Ocean City entertaining the rest of her extended family. I wonder what wicked demon is causing this accursed aberration?'

Thomas William Mills' apprehension ascended to a new height as an eerie voice ominously announced over the train car's speakers: "Now approaching Egg Harbor City Station." The only rider recognized that he was involved in an inexplicable weird situation where his assumed faith and trust in New Jersey public transportation had been mysteriously violated. Yet the affected passenger was so petrified that he dared not get-up from his seat out of fear of some unbeknownst evil supernatural consequence.

When the phantom train's wheels eventually grinded to a halt, Thomas was in for another unanticipated shock. Standing on the Egg Harbor platform were three former acquaintances, Carol Engles, Bob Macrie and Janet Weldon, all chatting amongst themselves seemingly oblivious to and unconcerned about the train's arrival. Their casual clothes were of mid-1960s style and several dozen automobiles of that same era filled the station's parking lot, yet the three friends from Thomas's past were the only humans standing on the Egg Harbor City platform. The awed observer's face turned pallid as his bleary blue eyes continued witnessing the unbelievable spectacle. The formerly predictable world now made no sense whatsoever.

'I had frequently gone out with Carol Engles during our college years back in '64 and '65 when Anna and I had been intermittently on and off in our rocky unsteady relationship,' Mills' recalled, 'and *we* often double-dated with Bob and Janet to the *Route 30* Circus Drive-in across the Pike from the Hammonton Rollway Roller Rink. But both of those places went out of business in the early '70s and oh my God! Carol was killed in an auto' accident in 1985, Bob died of cancer in 1990, Janet moved to California in the fall of 2001 and I haven't heard of or seen her since! This strange illusion is getting more terrifying and macabre by the minute!' And then another peculiar realization occurred to the very perplexed rider. 'This unearthly train is journeying backwards in time! The Laura's Farm Market scene was without a doubt from the late '60s and this current Egg Harbor nightmare is from the mid-'60s! And why aren't the carriage doors opening and why are Carol, Bob and Janet conversing and ignoring both the New Jersey Transit and myself? What am I thinking? Two of them are deceased! I knew I should've driven my *Protégé* to Atlantic City!'

Thomas was in for another shocker when the New Jersey Transit Train departed the Egg Harbor City Station. He nervously glanced down and closely examined his boarding ticket and immediately fathomed in disbelief that the print on the admission pass read "One-Way to Atlantic City." 'I know I had purchased a Two-Way ticket! What gives here?' the addled Mills conjectured with palpable trepidation. 'What abominable thing have I done to deserve this sort of wicked treachery? I honestly feel in my soul that I'm on a One-Way trip to Hell! I have no desire to meet Lucifer in this world, or the next.'

The ill-omened train picked-up speed and followed its tracks meandering through additional dense pineland forests and the locomotive and its cars passed by occasional pristine fresh-water lakes on both sides and whenever Thomas William Mills was able to catch a glimpse of the parallel White Horse Pike he incomprehensibly observed that the vehicles-in-transit were all 1950s design or older and that all the cars on the four-lane highway appeared to be entries being exhibited in a classic antique automobile parade, simultaneously happening in both eastbound and westbound lanes. The emotionally distraught passenger sat still as a statue as his attentive psyche endeavored determining how and why he had become a prisoner being held hostage in such a bizarre in-progress anachronism. 'This mystery train is definitely journeying backwards into time!'

The next doomful stop on the ghastly itinerary was soon announced when the words "Absecon Station" echoed from the intercom speakers off the carriage's gray painted metal walls. When the New Jersey Transit screeched to a stop at the empty Absecon Station Thomas noticed off to the north a traffic accident at a dangerous *Route 30* intersection. 'Holy Toledo!' the intrigued fellow thought as he held his throat and gasped for air. 'That's my green and white '55 Chevy Bel Air! I was sideswiped at that exact corner on August 15, 1956. Jack Melora, Jim Amari and Joe Sindoni were passengers and there they are, all milling-around and inspecting the damage with the investigating Absecon Police Department officer! I feel nauseous in my stomach!' Thomas realized. 'I know what that sour taste in my throat and mouth mean! I've felt it before and don't savor it one iota!'

The next stop on the New Jersey Transit's daily schedule was the concrete Pleasantville Station and it only confirmed Thomas William Mills' suspicion that the dreadful shore-bound train was actually traveling backwards in time. A delinquent Hammonton car gang "The Ramrodders" (to which Mills had been a member) was assembled in the parking lot ready to have a rumble with The Matadors, a mixed Hispanic band of Pleasantville hoodlums that had dared invade Bellevue Avenue and Central Avenue and crash Augie's Hamburger Paradise and the Gem Burger Parlor on August 15, 1955. The Ramrodders sought revenge for the incursion of their town and then traveled to Pleasantville to even the score. The formidable Matadors organized and intercepted the Hammonton kids' on the rampage seeking street justice, and soon a major magnitude brawl ensued with forty-six rowdy teenagers being arrested.

‘My father wasn’t too keen driving over to Pleasantville and bailing me out of my law-breaking predicament,’ Tom sadly recollected. ‘We thought we were big men having the audacity to invade Pleasantville in six carloads and retaliate against the Matadors but we wound-up regretting exercising our need for retribution. Thank goodness the cops arrived en masse and quickly intervened or else serious injuries could’ve been inflicted during the wild escalating melee!’

The ghostly train soon abandoned the Pleasantville Station, and continued onward towards its ultimate destination, the newly constructed Atlantic City Train Terminal that had been specifically built to accommodate the influx of casino gamblers and employees. The now ‘one-stop spectral express traveled through the high-reed meadowlands, and the totally spooked Thomas William Mills could distinctly see that the automobiles on the White Horse Pike, a half mile to his left, were all of early 1950s vintage. As the now-paranoid passenger turned his attention to the right-side windows, Mills was again stunned to *not* see the *Atlantic City Expressway*, which had been built in the early ‘60s. Instead the familiar Black Horse Pike was evident and the vehicles heading from the mainland across the reed lands into Atlantic City were comparable to those traveling on the White Horse Pike but amazingly, the aforementioned *Atlantic City Expressway* was not sandwiched in between the two older thoroughfares. An antiquated early ‘50s billboard situated on *Route 30* was visible advertising the *World-Famous Summer of ‘54 Steel Pier*, and that particular phenomenon also greatly disturbed Thomas William Mills’ already puzzled mind.

‘I’m so upset I’m sweating profusely and hyperventilating!’ Mills thought as his lungs struggled to access and admit more oxygen. ‘I’ll probably die of fright before I ever complete this terrible excursion into the past!’

Suddenly, the sides and roof of the train carriage appeared as a flickering apparition as the locomotive pulled into the vacated Atlantic City Terminal. When the doors opened Thomas William Mills rose from his seat and rushed forward to evacuate his hostage situation but the ill-fated fellow instantly found himself’ incarcerated in a black void that effectively sucked his entire body inside it. And the supernatural vacuum methodically conveyed the victim next to the *Steel Pier* with his position being two hundred feet out into the *Atlantic Ocean*. The beach, pier, and boardwalk were completely empty, and Atlantic City appeared to the drowning man as a creepy, surreal ghost town. A powerful riptide current was slowly dragging the desperate fellow out to sea.

"Oh, no!" Thomas hysterically screamed but to no avail. "The same horrible thing had happened to me in 1954. The lifeguard was on the boardwalk getting lunch and my older cousin Ray Bucci leaped into the ocean and rescued me. But Ray had died of a heart attack in 1981!'

Then, Thomas Mills frenetically churned his arms and finally understood that he was again a frail nineteen-year-old wearing the same bathing suit that he had donned and had nearly drowned in back on August 15, 1954! 'God save me!' the alarmed young man desperately shouted to the empty and apathetic resort city. 'God save me!' the scared-to-death victim deliriously repeated.

"The FITS Project"

Whenever people think of Hawaii, they automatically conjure-up a mental vision of a tropical *Pacific* paradise, possessing lush vegetation, colorful luaus, beautiful native girls in hula skirts, resplendent rugged mountains of natural beauty, and *Pearl Harbor,* along with Waikiki Beach. having picturesque *Diamondhead* in the background. But the State of Hawaii is a geographic collection of many islands, and the entity is not just Honolulu nestled on gorgeous Oahu. Other less popular islands such as Maui, Molokai, Lanai, and the less-tourist-frequented Niihai and Kauai are distantly located in the northwest sector of the exotic Hawaiian chain.

The 'Big Island" specifically known as Hawaii is the largest land-mass of the famous group, and it covers approximately 4,038 square miles. Hawaii is ninety-three miles long, seventy-six miles wide, and is located around sixty-miles southeast of neighboring Maui. The "Big Island" was geologically formed from lava that had spewed from five separate volcanoes. Maunaloa and Maunakea are situated near the center of Hawaii, and the twin peaks represent the island's highest summits, each rising about 14,000 feet above the majestic *Pacific.* Haulalai is found to the west; Kohala to the north, and the most famous volcano, Kilauea, is prominent on the southeastern extension of Mauna Loa.

Volatile Kilauea and then Mauna Loa (in the former *Hawaii Volcanoes National Park*) are the island's only active volcanoes, with the former erupting more often and more spectacularly, and with the latter mountain releasing molten lava with less regularity.

Bountiful vegetation on Hawaii is the result of abundant annual rainfall with approximately a hundred-and-fifty-days featuring brief showers. Throughout its history. the "Big Island" has been imagined as an ideal sightseeing environment with annual temperatures ranging from a very comfortable sixty-two to seventy-eight degrees in January, which is generally Hawaii's coldest "winter month." Many breathtaking scenic cliffs overlook the blue *Pacific,* and fabulous waterfalls exist on several sides of the tropical wonder. And up until the year 2046, the orchid industry flourished in the city of Hilo, and coffee and cattle ranches prospered on the island's west side. All of that human enterprise soon ceased because of certain relevant socio/political circumstances.

In January of 2046, the United States Environmental Commission determined that the Island of Hawaii constituted "a looming environmental hazard to human health and welfare", with violent volcanic activity threatening the population because of excessive carbon monoxide being continuously released into the atmosphere from the island's two major craters, Kilauea and Mauna Loa. With the inhabitants being in "serious physical jeopardy", federal authorities mandated that Hawaii had to be evacuated, and its residents relocated on other "less-dangerous islands".

First, Hilo's population was transplanted to Maui, to Lanai, and to Molokai, where a new dynamic orchid industry would quickly be established. And the remainder of Hawaii's scattered population (particularly the coffee plantation growers and workers, and the cattle ranch owners and employees) were also generously compensated and assisted by the federal government in relocating on other Hawaiian islands, and in the process, escaping "probable impending disaster". This incredible and creative central government ruse allowed for the initiation of project *FITS,* an appropriate secret/confidential file acronym for "Felony Island Transfer Selections".

* * * * * * * * * * * * * *

Air Force Major Jeffrey Peterson and Colonel Daniel Arness were relaxing in their *Edwards Air Force Base* office, discussing their unexpected recent reassignment from *McGuire Air Base* outside Trenton, New Jersey to the legendary California facility, bordering the western perimeter of the *Mojave Desert.* Being eighty-miles northeast of Los Angeles was, in many respects, comparable to being eighty-miles southeast of New York City. The subject of duty transfer in the officer's verbal exchanges soon switched to a more significant July 1, 2047 topic, the threat of nuclear war with China and India. Both service men had strong convictions about the issue.

"China and India have been recklessly and wantonly polluting the air for over a century now," Major Jeffrey Peterson reminded his astute colleague. "And Dan, it looks like conflict with those rogue nations is inevitable. The two hostile countries have been ignoring UN resolutions and U.S. warnings for over two decades now, and it looks like military preparations are heating-up in a dire hurry with each successive diplomatic failure."

"Gotta' agree with you on that count, Major," Colonel Dan Arness concurred. "The problem's been going on ever since the Industrial Revolution. Acid rain has saturated the skies and weather patterns. Air currents are constantly moving from continent to continent in both the Northern and Southern Hemispheres. Now that the U.S. economy almost exclusively consists of services and high technology, the smokestack and manufacturing industries have all migrated to India and to Asian countries. But as you had mentioned, Jeff, China has been a principal violator to atmospheric contamination for many years. But in my humble estimation, the whole difficulty is the simple fact that...."

"That China and India's lack of restrictions on their industrial complexes is harshly contributing to global warming, and pretty soon the polar ice caps and Alaskan glaciers are going to melt. And coastal cities all over the globe are going to be inundated up to their penthouses," Major Peterson asserted and exaggerated. "Dan, the U.K. and Russia are also tired of protesting against the chronic polluters, and the word is out on the military grapevine that war is imminent. If we fail to grab the bull by the horns, and don't stop China and India now..."

"Then, the entire human race is guaranteed to become an endangered species," Colonel Dan Arness suavely finished his immediate superior's thought. "Either way, Major, disastrous global warming, or an almost certain nuclear holocaust, obviously, the Earth is on a rendezvous with Armageddon."

"Let's hope that our diplomats and our ambassadors can show some compromising skills and stave-off senseless worldwide catastrophic devastation," Major Jeffrey Peterson articulated to his loyal subordinate. "Our wives and children should not have to live in a world that's so threatened by human folly, ignorance, and greed. And ya' just gotta' worry right down to your soul, Dan, that we've been reassigned from *McGuire* to *Edwards* to participate in some important secret project. My reputation is that I'm not a gamblin' man, but I'll bet ya' a good steak dinner that our transfer to California is not about China and India. I suspect it involves domestic, and/or international terrorism."

"Major Peterson," Colonel Dan Arness seriously addressed his commanding officer. "You know as well as I do that *McGuire* and *Edwards* would've both been closed a half-century ago if it weren't for the ongoing and very frustrating *War on Terror*. We've been shuttling supplies and prisoners back and forth between Europe and New Jersey for over ten-years now. But I gotta' confess, Major, that it's a little sad leaving the McGuire Twenty-first Air Force Airlift Command behind, and bein' reassigned out to the California desert. And pretty soon our wives and kids are gonna' have to pull-up their roots and be moved, too. That's one very apparent penalty connected with bein' dispensable pawns on the U.S. Military chessboard."

"Yes, Dan. Sheila is bringin' Tommy and Jean out west next week, once *we* get settled in," the Major affirmed. "What about Agnes takin' Jimmy and little Helen out to the West Coast? Your wife must also be peeved, being forced to migrate three-thousand-miles on such short notice to another part of the country. But as the pundits say, both inside and outside the *Pentagon,* 'It comes with the territory'."

"Yes, Major. Agnes is also complainin' and balkin' about being so inconvenienced with such short notice," Colonel Arness verified. "But when ya' work for fickle Uncle Sam, ya' gotta' adapt to his whims. Just look at what happened to the dinosaurs when they couldn't modify their livin', huntin', and eatin' habits. And thanks to the demise of those large beastly reptiles," Dan Arness academically added, "mammals were allowed to ascend among the various phylum, and eventually, dominate the Earth after the giant asteroid had hit off the eastern coast of Mexico millions of years ago. But if mankind doesn't get its act together soon, then....."

"Then, we're all destined to go the way of the dinosaur," Major Peterson aptly articulated. "I despise bein' a minor character in this doomed tragic play, Dan. If that ugly last chapter in human history ever arrives, then three-thousand-years of developin' culture and civilization will go straight down the tubes. You don't know, Colonel, how much I wish and pray that there's a benign God directin' and overseein' all human activities down here on terra firma! I'd hate to leave history to the disposal of chance, coincidence, and human circumstance!"

* * * * * * * * * * * * *

Two weeks later, the transplanted, loquacious officers exchanged and interpreted the morning's *Yahoo Internet Headlines*. Eight Arab terrorists had blown-up the *Universal Artists Movie Studios* in protest of *Hollywood* films perpetuating decadence and immorality that *they* believed contradicted the *Koran*'s teachings. Several Islamic Jihad *Internet* web sites explained the basis for the twelve destructive explosions, that had its toll accounting for the taking of three-dozen, innocent, American lives.

"How did the terrorists get the explosives inside the studios?" Colonel Arness curiously asked his companion seated in front of *his* computer screen. "Weren't there any security guards posted at the gates who could recognize trouble?"

"Yes, there were Dan," Major Peterson acknowledged. "But because the myriad studios in and around *Hollywood* had been compelled by specific court rulings regarding certain controversial cases endorsed by the *ACLU,* the large production facilities were compelled to employ a quota of Muslim minorities, even if the newly hired employees were illegal aliens, which as you know, doesn't matter one iota any more. Bein' politically correct is now more vital in America than bein' alive and breathin'," the Major bluntly editorialized. "The irony of it all, Dan, is that liberal *Hollywood* is bein' attacked by evil terrorists, and that the movie industry has been tacitly, and sometimes openly, promotin' the civil rights of illegal aliens and also those members of Muslim hate cells scattered throughout the United States! *Hollywood,* in effect, his inadvertently authored its' own demolition. I suspect that certain guards hired to watch the gates were actually Arab sympathizers, or part of a malicious Los Angles jihad terror cell."

"But because of the social agenda of the *ACLU* and the fanciful dreams of pinheaded politically-correct liberals occupyin' seats in *Congress,"* Colonel Arness elaborated and opined, "companies are pressured and coerced into bucklin' to their knees to appease trouble-making ultra-liberals. Otherwise, employers that oppose the militant radicals are picketed; their products boycotted; their places of business demonstrated against, and their reputations smeared by bullying multi-culturalists and by vociferous civil rights activists. All of that socialistic burlesque is well disguised, and ironically, happens under the cloak of American democracy. Needless to say, Major, our great capitalistic society is rapidly decayin' and swiftly destroyin' itself from within."

"No wonder why the President is confidentially tellin' his most trusted aides that California is now Mexifornia, rapidly evolvin' into Arabfornia," Major Jeffrey Peterson confided to his close friend. "And to tell ya' the truth on the *QT,* Dan, gossip among the top brass has it that something drastic and extremely vital is in the works to deal with Arab saboteurs havin' wicked aspirations of cripplin' the American economy through random acts of violence and terrorism. When I get wind of exactly what's happenin' in the *White House* from the drawin' board to actual implementation," the Major specified to his chief assistant, "then I'll fill you in on all the essential details. Now Dan, I'm just as curious about the secret operation as you are!"

Colonel Dan Arness pondered his family's safety, the preservation of American values, and the nation's way of life and high standard of living. And next, the Air Force officer contemplated his planet's future, and his sacred call to duty to uphold the *Constitution*, a *Constitution'* that was being manipulated by fast-talking, cowardly lawyers, and by unscrupulous, craven politicians, fraudulently lining their deep pockets with good American money. "Yes Major, I want to be in-the-loop about this new secret Government Project to which you've alluded. I strongly desire to participate with the program in any way that I can," Colonel Arness promised. "I want to help my country, and live to be a benefactor, watching my grandchildren enjoying good old-fashioned, wholesome American values. Jeff, in my heart, I want to protect my family from the satanic dangers that are egregiously convergin' and envelopin' the USA from all possible angles!"

"All I know at present is that the latest secret operation at the highest level has been dubbed Secret Order *FITS,"* the Major divulged to the Colonel. "But that's the extent of what I've heard from several tight-lipped generals that I know over in Denver. When I learn or decipher more from my anonymous sources, I'll clue you in. Dan, I really appreciate your unwavering allegiance to me, and also your very evident dedication to your country!"

* * * * * * * * * * * * * *

On August 15, 2047, Dan Arness was both apprehensive and quite exhilarated about flying his first mission involving high-priority/top secret *Project FITS* as the pilot of a giant *C-230* cargo transport, the largest airplane is the Air Force's recently modernized fleet. On the strategic flight originating from *Edwards Air Base,* the highly-skilled pilot was accompanied by General Andrew Bennett', who had been assigned to brief his fledgling apprentice about the more pertinent aspects of *Project Fits*. The General got-down to brass tacks as the *C-230* approached its *Pacific* destination, after taking-off three-and-a-half-hours earlier from *Edwards*.

"Just continue following Major Peterson and General Earhardt in the lead *C-230,"* General Bennett instructed his enthusiastic protégé. "We'll be over our designated drop point in another fifteen-minutes, or so. I suppose you're wondering what this mission is all about?" the florid-faced mentor rhetorically asked the more reticent pilot. "Well Dan, now that you've been promoted to the rank of Major, you've qualified being an integral part of *Project FITS*. Only selected

Majors and Generals are aware of the specifics of this very strategic national security operation."

"Well, General Bennett, thank you for your kind endorsement and for your confidence in my ability and patriotism," the newly promoted Major Arness politely answered. "I suppose my first question is: 'Are we carryin' the same cargo as the lead *C-230?"* And also, 'Do we have the same set of directives'?"

"Very perceptive questions indeed, Major!" General Bennett complimented his mission partner. "Yes, we sort of have the same instructions and share a common operation. But no, our drop-off materials will be considerably different. But first," the General sternly indicated, "you must learn that the official military code name for the large Island of Hawaii is *Felony Island.* And to add to your empirical knowledge, Major Arness, Project *FITS* stands for 'Project Felony Island Transfer Selections'. The dossier you'll read after the first airlift is of paramount importance, both to you and to the *Air Force Command."*

"Okay, about that," the pilot replied to his knowledgeable source of information. "But what is the first *C-230* haulin' way out here in the middle of the *Pacific?"* I thought that Hawaii has been declared off-limits because of serious carbon dioxide emissions from Mount Kilauea and from its sister volcano Mauna Loa. What's really goin' on here?"

"Ha, ha, ha!" General Bennett indulgently laughed. "That contrived environmental disaster story was just a diversionary canard to get everyone off the big island in fire drill fashion. It was done so that *Project FITS* could be activated, without any interference from the nosy press, or from radical civil liberties' lawyers, and from insane power-hungry activist judges."

"Okay, about that!" Major Arness granted and repeated. "But what are Major Peterson and General Earhardt transporting in the first *C-230.* Excuse my lack of knowledge, General," Dan Arness humbly apologized. "But what is in the lead aircraft? I feel somewhat in the dark here, and my mounting curiosity is overwhelming me!"

"Well, Major, now that you've insisted on learning and knowing full disclosure," General Bennett deliberately paused to build even more suspense, "the first *C-230* is airlifting water; Army food rations, and discarded clothing to be parachuted down onto Hawaii. The enormous isolated island has been clandestinely converted into a permanent detention facility, where hardcore terrorists, prisoners of war, and repeat felons are transferred to, so that the thugs can survive on their own."

General Bennett proceeded to inform his astonished "mission amigo" that *Felony Island* now had over twenty-five thousand convicts and three-thousand "enemy combatants" (better known as "captured jihadist terrorists") living independently (and possibly barbarically) on the island, as "transplanted unsupervised prisoners". The expense' of keeping the rabble incarcerated in federal penitentiaries and in remote detention facilities like *Guantanamo Bay, Cuba* became too cost prohibitive and too much of a burden to the beleaguered American taxpayers. "Consequently, Major, the easiest cost-effective solution was to evacuate the Big Island and then re-position the "scum of the Earth" on various sections of the secluded, natural paradise."

"Notice down there, Major, that two huge parallel fences have been erected several-hundred-feet offshore," the General informed his new-found assistant, who still had his mouth agape. "Around three-hundred-feet separate the two ocean partitions, and thousands of hungry sharks infest that three-hundred-foot division. Should someone from the island manage to successfully scale the first seventy-five-foot-high fence, then ravenous, carnivorous sharks will attack the audacious escapee," General Bennett informed his newly assigned colleague. "Ya' gotta' admit, it's quite an in-genius plan, based on a disingenuous lie about Hawaii being an environmental hazard, isn't it Major? All ships sailing the *Pacific* have been notified to keep at least a twenty-five-mile distance from Hawaii. And the immense island is constantly bein' patrolled from the air, and surveillance teams are continuously on the lookout for errant ocean ships, pleasure yachts, fishing boats, sightseeing vessels, as well as off-limits' small private and commercial airplanes."

"Are there any military guards stationed on the island?" the Major inquired after fully regaining his sensibilities. "Most of the prisoners down there are desperate people that don't respect either life or property."

"No, Major. There's no need for the presence of military correctional officers on *Felony Island,"* General Bennett explained. "It's basically back to Darwinian survival of the smartest and of the fittest, without too much natural selection involved. We humanely provide the scumbag dregs with food, water, and clothing, Major, and it's up to each inhabitant to build his own shelter, to form alliances, and to establish a viable pecking order, so that the criminals can continue existing by some rule of improvised law. Hopefully, somehow Major Arness, the foul occupants will create some semblance of a primitive society, and learn how to organize some kind of rudimentary government structure. Government."

"Now I understand, General. In time, the island' will be doomed to chaos and to anarchy! Ten-to-one, the more demonic Islamic terrorists will eventually dominate and eradicate the more sophisticated and docile American felons, kidnappers, murderers, child molesters, and rapists. But in the end," stressed the alert pilot, "their demise and elimination will be no big loss to the productive, civilized world. Now General, how did the brass and the State Department come-up with this imaginative idea of systematically converting Hawaii Island into a mass prison, where all the convicts are entirely on their own?" the still-astounded pilot queried.

"The inspiration came to the President when he was watching on TV an old Burt Lancaster movie titled *The Birdman of Alcatraz,"* General Bennett confidentially explained. "As you know, Major, *Alcatraz* was a terrific prison intelligently constructed out in *San Francisco Bay.* The facility discouraged its dangerous inmates from attempting to break-out and flee. Then, the crooks would have to risk almost certain drowning after swimming off 'the Rock'. And so, Dan, as you can plainly understand, Hawaii is just like a gigantic *Alcatraz* that can easily contain and accommodate a huge prison population."

"Well, General," Major Arness stammered as his colossal *C-230* approached the center of the island paradise, teeming with felons and committed jihadists. "What's in *our* cargo hold if I might ask?"

"It's definitely a lot easier to show you than to adequately describe it with words," the General announced and then chuckled. Three-Star General Andrew Bennett pushed a button on *his* side of the plane's instrument panel, and an overhead portal opened, revealing a previously concealed colossal television screen. The expression on Major Arness's face suggested that he had been momentarily shocked beyond belief.

"But won't these felons' families learn that they aren't bein' kept in regular prisons, and then report the whole matter to the press?" the veteran pilot asked. "How can we successfully smuggle *them* onto *Felony Island* without detection?"

"The punks and thugs sittin' in the compartment behind us have recently been captured by military and civilian authorities, but the *FBI* and the *CIA* publicly claim that they're still at large on the lam, runnin' away from justice," the high-ranking co-pilot disclosed. "Ya' gotta' admit, Dan, that the President's *Felony Island* experiment is a practical solution to our overcrowded prisons. Those desperate degenerates restlessly sittin' behind us are still reputed to be wicked fugitives and renegades."

"This is almost too much to comprehend!" Major Arness marveled and shared. "I never imagined that the government was up to this kind of stealthy answer to rampant crime and terrorism!"

"Please observe, Major, your precious cargo is just waking-up after being administered a controlled dose of sprayed nerve gas," General Bennett communicated. "Notice also that exactly two hundred felons and criminals are wearing parachutes. Let's just presume that they're listening to the taped instructions bein' broadcast over the intercom on how to pull their ripcords!"

"But General, I'm sure that these two-hundred parachutists aren't going to jump out of this *C-230* voluntarily! They've had no formal training, whatsoever!"

"Nobody wants to die, not even the bottom basement dirt bags of society!" the General tersely answered. "When I push this button in front of me, a nifty back compartment trap door will open in this modified airplane, and then a tremendous hydraulic piston will push the hold compartment metal wall forward, and thus dump all two-hundred carefully selected candidates fifteen-thousand-feet down to *Felony Island.*"

"This is totally bizarre and amazing!" Major Dan Arness commended before clearing his throat. "But tell me, General, why are a dozen of those prisoners with parachutes, against *their* will, wearin' dark blue business suits?"

The General hardily laughed before responding to the pilot's interrogative. "Major Arness, you ask the damnest comprehensive questions! Those dozen idealistic idiots represent the biggest threat to freedom on the entire planet! Those blue-suited buffoons are *ACLU* attorneys and civil rights lawyers!"

"But won't their families become suspicious of their absence? They aren't fugitives or renegades runnin' away from justice? How could you, the *Pentagon,* and the President classify them as criminals?" the inquisitive Major asked.

"Whoa there, cowboy; one pertinent question at a time! The corralled attorneys will simply be labeled and identified as 'Missing Persons'. Lawyers in general, and *ACLU* creeps in particular, Dan, are the worst and lowest elements of our great American society," the General reasoned and firmly uttered. "They're basically legal criminals that bilk our treasury and our citizens of billions of dollars annually, and the disgustin' parasites are ten-times more detrimental to civilization than any equal number of vile felons, real criminals, or radical Islamic jihadists! Now, Major Arness, let's get busy pursuing this phase of *Project FITS* in order to ensure the necessary continuation of the *United States of America!"* And let's diligently and patriotically do our duty for the land of the free, and for the home of the brave!"

* * * * * * * * * * * * * *

Just before the release button was to be pushed on the second C-230's instrument panel, an immense UFO appeared and hovered above the designated transport jet. Then, a powerful tractor beam gently pulled the state-of-the-art Air Force jumbo jet into the mammoth saucer's entrance platform.

"This is a cheap way of obtaining prisoner and slaves to perform basic labor on our home planet, Carthos," Commander Greck said to his co-pilot, Captain Sant. "It pays to electronically monitor military transmissions between Earth aircraft and their Air Force bases."

"Yes, Commander," Captain Sant readily agreed. "And we even got a pilot and a co-pilot while conducting this minimal-risk mission. "I'll bet the two won't miss their wives and families one iota, once the officers acclimate to the high standard of ultra-modern living across the Milky Way on good old planet Carthos! Indeed, Commander Greck, their capture *fits* our agenda perfectly.

"Life on the Blueberry Farm"

Being a New Jersey public school teacher for thirty-four years meant that I had to find summer employment to supplement my mediocre yearly income. Since schoolteachers are "contracted" employees they're not eligible to collect unemployment benefits during their ten-week unpaid summer vacations. And in fact teachers don't receive paid vacations or paid holidays at all since they're contracted to work a hundred and eighty school days! My job predicament allowed me to find and explore many different alternative occupations during the summertime that I wouldn't have ordinarily dabbled-in if I had been employed in a profession that demanded a twelve-month-commitment and a corresponding twelve-month-remuneration.

In the summers of 1965 through 1967 I worked on my father-in-law's four-hundred-acre fruit and vegetable farm on the White Horse Pike (*Route 30*) in Elm just outside Hammonton, New Jersey. I drove a forklift, loaded tractor-trailers, drove a bus, spent many hours in the packinghouse's cold storage, and generally helped manage the growing, harvesting and shipment of peaches, nectarines, apples, sugar plums, zucchini squash, corn, peppers and tomatoes, for those were the principal crops raised on White Horse Farm. My father-in-law was a tough Sicilian taskmaster and we often didn't see eye-to-eye in regard to personnel management and our colliding philosophies pertaining to regular day-to-day operations were often at different ends of the thought spectrum.

From 1968 to 1981 I co-owned and operated Dealers Choice, an amusement arcade doing summer business under the Atlantic Hotel at 410 South Boardwalk in Ocean City, Maryland. People (mostly tourists with money to burn) would come into the establishment and play poker machines that were activated upon the dropping of dimes into slots, and if the players obtained hands of "Jacks or Better" the customers received coupons of different values depending on whether the hand was a pair, two pair, three of a kind, a straight, a flush, a full house, four of a kind or a fabulous straight flush. If a rare Royal Flush occurred the player was entitled to "Choice of the House," which constituted the top-value-prizes ranging from a giant stuffed animal to a blender, a roaster oven, a desk radio or an electric frying skillet. The boardwalk arcade also featured "money pushing games" like Flip-A-Winna', Splash Down and Pot of Gold where the player would insert a dime, or a quarter, and moving arms would push the inserted coin against a big pile of similar coins. The object of the "Money Pushing

Games" was to force coins to accumulate and then fall down a chute. Let's say if seven coins plummeted down the appropriate opening seven tokens would be won and would be ejected into the winning tray situated below where the player was standing. Each token was equal in value to a ten-cent coupon won on the poker machines thus making the coupons and the tokens wholly compatible in terms of monetary exchange.

From 1972 to 1981, I also co-owned the New Horizon Gift Shop on the boardwalk in Rehoboth Beach, Delaware where the enterprise specialized in applying decals to tee shirts using special heat transfer machines. And for four summers I was also a partner in an arcade business called Wheel and Deal on the Atlantic City Boardwalk near Missouri Avenue that was similar to the Ocean City, Maryland operation. Wheel and Deal lasted until legalized gambling was passed to salvage the famous but declining New Jersey resort. My two partners and I lost our lease as competition for boardwalk space heated-up and when prospective casinos began buying-up strategic real estate all over the *Queen of Resorts*. So, from 1977 to 1981 I was frantically hopping back and forth like a neurotic jackrabbit from New Jersey to Delaware to Maryland riding the *Cape May-Lewes Ferry* delivering and shuttling around merchandise for the three independent summer operations.

In the sweltering summers of 1982 and '83, I returned to White Horse Farm to give the place (and my obstinate Sicilian father-in-law) a second chance but the aging man stubbornly refused to relinquish any authority so I again bolted from that Hammonton, New Jersey business and began managing an almost defunct farm market a mile west down *Route 30*. Much to my father-in-law's chagrin in three short summers Pastore Orchards Farm Market had been miraculously transformed into the busiest and best retail produce outlet on the busy highway.

From 1987 to 2004 I diligently worked the hot summers as a field manager for Atlantic Blueberry Company, the largest cultivated blueberry farm in the world. The farm owned by the Galletta Brothers and Sons actually consisted of two pretty massive plantations. The main farm called the Weymouth Division was located just southeast of Hammonton and was comprised of eight hundred and fifty acres growing the luscious blue fruit and eight miles away on *Route 322* (the Black Horse Pike) the Mays Landing Division of Atlantic Blueberry sported five-hundred and fifty acres. All the berries harvested on the smaller New Jersey farm were transported by large company trucks from the 600 acre Mays Landing plantation to the Weymouth Farm, to be packed and then shipped via tractor-trailers all over continental

United States and Canada. Atlantic Blueberry was a massive operation growing anywhere from twelve to fifteen million pounds of the blue fruit (depending on seasonal crop volume) in what constituted an eight-week harvest season. The biggest problem with blueberries is that the crop is very labor intensive. A hundred men could operate a fourteen-hundred-acre peach farm but a fourteen-hundred-acre blueberry operation required anywhere from fifteen hundred to two thousand pickers a day during the height of the season. It was impossible for the owners of Atlantic Blueberry Company to house that many workers on their two properties.

The Weymouth Road camp accommodated three hundred Mexicans, a hundred of whom worked in the packinghouse and in the bulk house next door while the remaining two hundred men picked with the "Home Gang," which was supervised by brothers Mike and George Estrada, Puerto Ricans that had started as pickers back in the '60s and who had eventually been promoted to lower management positions. Mike and George each have small houses situated on Farm #1 and they and their families live rent-free as permanent year-round employees. And the smaller Mays Landing camp houses approximately two hundred and fifty men, all of whom' pick berries on that very scenic plantation. Juan Lopez (Lopey) and Ephraim Torres, long-time Puerto Rican employees, had the chore of overseeing the "Home Crew" and the prodigious harvests at the Mays Landing Division.

Because the combined farms only housed four hundred and fifty pickers in their respective camps Atlantic Blueberry had to contract with "Day Haul" crewleaders that could provide additional farm labor. Modesto Flores (a mild-mannered long-time Puerto Rican employee) and I managed the "Day Haul" pickers at Plantation #1 and I was the Weymouth Road farm's liaison to the "outside crewleaders" and in the process had authority over their respective gangs.

In the mid-1980s the outside gangs were mostly Oriental with pickers (commuting from Philadelphia in vans and Farm Labor Transport buses) of Laotian, Cambodian and Vietnamese origins all possessing "green cards" showing that they were "legal resident aliens." The Oriental crewleaders had hard-to-remember names like Bunyan Yang, Lu Vang, Vang Kusanni, Inxay Pathatogong, Chia Lin, Muoa Lo, Khammy Pathong and Yang Lo. One black gang working at the Mays Landing Farm still remained from the 1950s and it was commandeered by a woman crewleader, Frances Dantzler, also known as "Miss Frances" by her fifty-member squad of obedient, Bible-toting underlings.

But in the mid-1970s, area Puerto Ricans that had started-out working on the local South Jersey peach and blueberry farms had found employment and more lucrative paying occupations in other industries, and *that* job migration left a giant agricultural workforce vacuum that needed to be filled.

Soon, an abundance of Mexican crewleaders and their followers began appearing in the early 1990s and these new groups rapidly replaced the Oriental gangs that had previously fulfilled the farms' labor needs. The Laotians, the Cambodians and the Vietnamese pickers had been sponsored by their crewleaders, who in effect practiced a modern type of indenture system. The employees loyally toiled for their crewleaders for seven or so years and then migrated to and assimilated into performing various factory jobs, construction work, laboring in fish canneries, engaging in lawn care services and toiling in tree and plant nurseries. Most of the Oriental blueberry pickers had traveled early each morning in "Farm Labor Transport" buses and in vans thirty-miles from Philadelphia to begin work on the New Jersey blueberry farms at 6 a.m.

The Mexican crewleaders that replaced the Orientals in the 1990s had names like Hermann Castro, Juan Bravo, Mario Valesquez, Francisco Fuentes, Tomas Agguire, Margarito Gonzalez, Marco Rodriquez, Carlos Lopez, Olegario Garcia and Marco Sanchez. Most of the Mexican pickers now come to Atlantic Blueberry on yellow school buses hired by the company to transport them up to the Weymouth and Mays Landing farms from Bridgeton and Vineland, New Jersey, communities where most of the Mexican pickers temporarily reside during the summer harvest season. This is a win-win situation for all parties involved. The farm benefits because the workers now arrive safely to work on state inspected school buses that have the proper insurance coverage. The school bus company benefits because their drivers now have summer employment and the bus owners can generate additional revenue when area schools are not in session. The "outside Day Haul" crewleaders like the new school bus transportation method because they save the expense of having their own "Farm Labor Transport" buses that in the past had required costly gas, maintenance and high insurance and inspection expenses.

My responsibilities at Atlantic Blueberry were manifold and the farm owners had amusingly dubbed me "the Director of Documentation." Each "Day Haul" picker had to fill-out a federal I-9

Form (Immigration Paper) proving that he or she was legally eligible to work in the United States. Many of the older Orientals and Mexicans were illiterate and could not read or write, so the crewleaders would fill-out the I-9 for them and I would check the forms to make sure that the information was correct before approving and collecting them. For example, a social security number on the I-9 would have to have nine numbers and an alien green card cited as an official credential contained either eight or nine digits. For pickers that were U.S. citizens, a bona fide state driver's license and a valid school I.D. or a recently updated voter registration card or a government-issued welfare card had to also be presented for me to check.

The federal I-9 forms were a real challenge to keep track of because pickers would often get on different yellow school buses and travel to different South Jersey farms and work for other crewleaders from day to day so the daily work force was continually changing. The Weymouth Farm would have anywhere between five hundred and a thousand "Day Haul" pickers show-up at the south-end dirt parking lot every morning and the Mays Landing Farm would have anywhere between three and eight hundred prospective day workers waiting in line at the front gate to hook-up with a crewleader and then be admitted onto the property at 6 a.m. A crewleader would usually have anywhere from fifty to one-hundred-and-fifty workers that he or she would bring (or have transported) every morning to Atlantic Blueberry.

Another farm duty I had besides keeping track of the ever-challenging I-9 forms was monitoring and collecting daily pay slips. Every "Day Haul" picker was paid cash by his boss (the subcontracted crewleader) in the farm's parking lot after the workday had been completed. At the end of each afternoon every crewleader had to fill-out a pay slip contract (on color-coded triplicate forms) for each worker with the worker's name, social security number, home address, date, hours worked, time in and time out, units picked and total daily wage jotted-down. The white copy went to the field worker', the yellow copy to the farm's main office and the pink copy was kept by the crewleader. The following morning or afternoon I would drive my pickup truck to the crewleaders' fields (Atlantic Blueberry Company had over a hundred and twenty separate fields) and check each worker's yellow form to ascertain that everyone had made more than minimum wage the day before. Then, I would drop off the crewleaders' yellow copies to the farm's main office on Weymouth Road, *County Route 559* for Farm #1, or to the May Landing Division Farm Office on Route 322.

Checking each Day Haul worker's yellow pay slip was necessary, because the pickers were all paid by piecework or "units picked" and not by hourly minimum wage (the "home gang pickers" that lived in the camps on the two farms were paid weekly by Atlantic Blueberry checks). The piecework system was good for all parties concerned because it provided incentive for the Day Haul workers to fill flats fast since they were not paid by the hour and thus they could make much more than minimum wage if they hustled (around forty-two dollars for an eight hour work day would have been the minimum wage daily salary). Most pickers earned between fifty and a hundred dollars a day on piecework being able to fill thirty-three trays to make a hundred dollars. Some conscientious swift-handed pickers earned over a hundred and thirty dollars a day.

Each picker was distributed a plastic picking basket attached to a cord, which the field worker was required to wear around his or her waist. Usually, two full picking baskets would constitute a "full red picking tray," which was equivalent to a "flat" of twelve pints when brought to the packing house by one of the crewleader's drivers. When two red picking trays were completed the picker would carry the "two flats" to the crewleader's company owned field truck and then the worker was given a ticket for each flat by the driver. Each "movie ticket" (with the crewleader's color code and name printed on it) represented one flat' picked and the worker was later paid three dollars and twenty-five cents for each tray filled. The farm would pay the crewleaders three seventy-five for each tray picked so each "gang master" made on-the-average fifty cents a tray, with some of the bigger crews during the height of the season picking over two thousand flats a day for their ambitious bosses.

The crewleaders were also accountable for maintaining quality control in their assigned fields. The blueberries on their trucks destined for the packinghouse had to be hard and not green. Each flat when brought to the field truck had to be inspected by the driver and/or by his loader to make sure it was acceptable to take to the packinghouse. After that quality standard had been met a picking ticket for each red tray was then handed to the worker, who would redeem his or her total tickets at the end of the day for cash in the dirt parking lot, the earned money (according to New Jersey Labor Law) being strictly disseminated by the employee's crewleader.

The farm provided each "outside Day Haul crewleader" with two box trucks. The crewleaders' drivers would circle their fields until four skids of forty-nine trays on each had been loaded onto one of the two assigned farm trucks. Then the berries were carefully driven to the packinghouse where each skid would be picked-up by forklift operators and separately put on a scale for weighing. If the weight did not conform to a specified standard, then the crewleader would be "docked" (deducted) trays from his percentage of making fifty cents a tray, so the workers were constantly reminded to pick hard berries and to sufficiently fill their red trays, so that their bosses made a decent profit.

At the packinghouse, each skid was labeled with the crewleader's name, Field Number and Blueberry Variety and then the berries were transported and temporarily held in the farm's cold storage, which for blueberries had to be maintained at forty-two degrees (conversely a peach farm's cold storage would be set for thirty-two degrees). When the packinghouse production crew was ready to pack the berries from the cold storage, a forklift driver would transport the skid of forty-nine red trays (neatly stacked seven flat by seven high) to one of ten conveyor belts on production lines. Next each red tray was carefully dumped onto a slow-moving belt.

Four sorters on each working line would take out the soft berries and the green ones to again ensure quality control. A weighing device would then insert the exact number of berries to make a standard satisfactory weight for each filled plastic pint. Another machine would then automatically close each lid on each plastic pint. Next the pints were trafficked to one of ten rotary tables at the end of each packing line and finally the finished product was hand inserted into a handsome company shipping flat neatly containing twelve pints each. The flats were then neatly stacked on skids and immediately loaded onto tractor-trailer refrigeration trucks to be shipped and transported all over continental United States and to destinations in Canada.

When the berries arrive from the field to the packinghouse's unloading dock, and accepted in terms of weight for each skid, the packinghouse manager gives the crewleader's driver a yellow receipt for four skids (usually 196 red tray flats). Late in the afternoon the crewleader takes all of his "yellow slips" to the farm's main office and a secretary adds up all the receipts and then issues a farm check to the crewleader. The field boss then goes to either the Hammonton or Mays Landing bank and cashes the farm check, getting the cash to pay his or her people paper money at the end of the day in the farm parking lot. Of course the following morning or afternoon I would visit each crewleader in his assigned field and check and collect the yellow copies of the pickers' previous workday contracts.

Another duty I had as a field manager was filling-out and checking working papers for children between the ages of twelve and sixteen that had shown-up on the farms each morning as part of a crew. These kids were sorted-out each morning and not allowed to pick until proof of proper work-eligible documentation had been obtained. Even if Asian kids had Pennsylvania working papers or if Mexican children had working papers from another state, those substantiating documents were not valid in New Jersey. I had to make sure that each new arrival had an authentic birth certificate or alien card along with a social security card and an available parent to sign the working papers. Then I would transport the kids to either Hammonton High School for the Weymouth Farm or to Oakcrest High School for the Mays Landing Farm to get their credentials officially certified. Since the schools' main offices weren't open on weekends kids that came with working papers completed and registered with the farm on Saturday or Sunday could not go into the fields to pick. And kids under the age of twelve were ineligible to perform labor for wages and were not allowed to work at all and had to remain in the parking lot until quitting time.

I also drove a bus for the Weymouth Farm. Modesto Flores and his son Willie (the farm's parking lot guard) would have each crewleader line his or her people up in single file at 6 a.m. each morning and four buses would transfer each "gang" to their designated picking fields. First the "Home Gang" had to be transported from the camp to their field and I would assist Mike Estrada driving his bus accompanied by my bus, good old faithful "Number 74." After the two-hundred home crew pickers were efficiently deployed to their assigned field I then drove white Bus Number 74 to the dirt parking lot where I joined the other three buses in transporting the eight hundred or so "Day Haul" pickers to their respective fields. A crew could not go into a field without its crewleader present or a state registered crewleader's agent wearing an appropriate state-issued badge. Usually, I would make six or seven bus excursions each morning.

The crewleader would assign two pickers to each row in a particular field. The two workers would stand on either side of the row and together pick each bush thoroughly. When a crew had finished picking a field I ("Unit 13") would be called on my radio and I would quickly transport the workers from (let's say) Field #14 to Field #48, which might be over a mile away. Then at the end of the work day, I would again drive white Bus Number 74 around the distant fields and pick-up tired workers at various waiting stations near irrigation pumps on the main gravel roads and courteously return them to the parking lot where they would eventually be paid by their bosses.

Usually, each field was picked three times by hand at eight-day intervals. These are the berries that are sorted and packed in the packinghouse and then sold to the "fresh market" grocery and chain stores. After the third handpicking by the crews, large farm machines are deployed to do the fourth picking. The machine-picked berries are generally smaller and of lesser quality and they are taken to the farm's bulk house where the fruit is graded by hand sorters and then frozen and packed in either ten or twenty-pound boxes (for the better grade) or in fifty gallon steel drums for the lesser grade "fourth picking fruit." The frozen machine-picked blueberries are ordinarily sold to large food processors and subsequently used for mass-produced pies, muffins and jams.

My final responsibility (as the Atlantic Blueberry Company field manager in charge of crewleaders) was to represent them if they received citations for alleged violations from Inspectors from the New Jersey Department of Labor. Citations received might involve an under-aged child working in the field, a child found in the fields between the ages of twelve and sixteen without working papers, a pay slip discovered with a stated salary that did not conform with minimum wage laws, or a crewleader without a badged agent in his field or inadequate insurance on a privately owned van taking workers to the farm. Usually the *New Jersey state inspectors* would visit each farm three times a summer and twice each summer they would stop the yellow school buses carrying workers to or from the farms at certain checkpoints on the area highways to look for violations. *The federal labor inspectors* would check the workers' I-9 Forms along with other requirements (including field portable toilets) and would visit the two farms once each summer.

A crewleader's day might have some significant downsides too. On rainy days the people could not work in the fields and all must go home disappointed without earning any pay. Sometimes it rains at noon and the workers only make a half-day's wages. But some gang bosses manage to compensate for their rainy day losses by running food businesses that sell meals to their workers from their own food trucks constantly roaming around out in the fields.

The Weymouth Road Farm's parking lot at the end of the day seemed like a combination of a carnival food bizarre and an amateur sporting event in progress. Tomas Agguire's wife and brother and Francisco Fuentes' wife would sell tacos and burritos from their enclosed food trucks, Ricky's Tacos and Franco's Tacos respectively. Other relatives of crewleader's would set-up shop and vend food, chicken, cold soda, snacks and clothes from various homemade stalls or improvised benches and tables set-up along the dirt parking lot's perimeter.

In the meantime, children would play impromptu games of touch football and soccer in the center of the huge dirt parking lot until the crewleaders finally arrived with their cash payrolls. Then everyone would quit their preoccupations and get in line to receive their daily wages. In 2004 (my last year at Atlantic Blueberry) the Weymouth Farm had an empty field next to the parking lot seeded and management installed soccer nets to allow for crews to compete against each other in friendly competition. And a baseball field still existed on the Weymouth plantation where Puerto Ricans from visiting Farm #2 would play softball (and sometimes hardball) against its rival Farm #1 home field opponents.

I had witnessed and experienced some rather amusing and crazy things during my eighteen-year-tenure at Atlantic Blueberry Company. One July morning in the mid-1970s a black man and woman pulled up to Field 29 on Weymouth Road where a Mexican crew was picking. The gentleman asked me if any black crews were on the farm.

"No!" I politely answered. "The only black crew belongs to Frances Dantzler over at the May Landing Division. Her pickers call her Miss Frances."

"What's your name?" the man requested.

"John!" I stated. "I'm the field manager in charge of crewleaders here!" I proudly added.

"Well John, could you give me directions to the other farm you mentioned?" the concerned fellow asked. "This woman wants to work."

I provided accurate directions to the Black Horse Pike Farm and later that afternoon when I arrived there to pick-up the yellow pay slips Miss Frances, a *Bible* toting chapter and verse quoter and a notorious stern disciplinarian accosted me at the guard's gate, which was situated between the dirt parking lot and the sprawling plantation.

"John, what's the big idea of you sending that woman over here to my field this mornin'?" Miss Frances demanded.

"The man she was with asked me if I knew of any black crews working and yours was the only one," I innocently and defensively replied, "so naturally I explained to the guy how to get to the Mays Landing Farm."

"Well John, for your information that black man was a lousy pimp and the lady that wanted work was a prostitute!" Miss Frances chastised. "The next time someone wants to work for me please call Lopez on the radio so that I can meet that person at the parking lot gate. I'm a faithful churchwoman John! I'm sure you know that! I don't tolerate no guff, drinking, drugs or sex in my field from anyone! Ya' hear what I'm sayin'!"

"Yes, Miss Frances!" I answered with embarrassment and regret showing all over my crimson face.

Once I was driving a Federal Inspector around the enormous Weymouth Farm to show him that portable bathrooms had been specifically placed next to all fields being picked that day. No sooner did I finish boasting to the examiner how organized and efficient the farm was, that is, having six portable toilets on six different wagons that Modesto Flores would frequently move around the mammoth plantation to accommodate the workers in new fields being picked. Soon the Federal Inspector and I observed something that rendered itself as being rather humiliating to me. An old Mexican was washing his arms and face splashing murky water onto himself from an irrigation canal while a companion was urinating into the same canal only three feet from the first farm laborer.

"That's a serious violation!" the Inspector yelled as he began intensively jotting-down myriad notes, thoroughly describing the reprehensible incident.

"But both men are only ten feet away from the portable toilets!" I angrily hollered back in defense of Atlantic Blueberry's integrity. "It's not *our* fault if these uneducated workers don't have or use common sense!"

"Regardless, John!" the angry Inspector maintained in an austere tone of voice. "All your workers must be advised of the law and how it applies to them. That's why *we* require sanitary facilities with sinks and toilets stationed in the fields. And no worker can be more than a quarter of a mile away from the portable facilities or it's a serious violation!"

"Those two men were only ten feet away from the portable bathroom!" I vigorously argued. "How can the farm be responsible for individual irresponsible behavior?"

"That's for you, Modesto and the Galletta family to figure out!" the incensed Inspector shot back. "I won't give the farm a citation this time but I assure you next time I will! A warning letter will definitely be issued!"

Another time I got into a heated argument with a young New Jersey State Inspector in a field at the Mays Landing Farm. The over-aggressive labor law examiner had found fault with a Cambodian kid's working papers and brought the matter to my attention.

"The school principal did not sign on the line at the bottom!" the overly conscientious inspector insisted. "The kid has an invalid working paper."

"Look!" I snapped back demonstrating a degree of hostility. "There are two kinds of working papers. The first kind is for kids from ages twelve to sixteen that pick berries out in the field. The second kind like the one you have in your hand is for kids sixteen to eighteen that work near machinery, like any kid working up in the packing house. Obviously, the school made a mistake by issuing the wrong working paper to this boy. He needed to be given the field working paper that does not require the principal's signature and not the packinghouse working paper that does."

The young state inspector became quite perturbed that I knew something about his job that he didn't. He pointed to his New Jersey Department of Labor badge hanging around his neck, which looked exactly like a regular policeman's shield. "I'm the authority out in this field!" he boisterously and sanctimoniously hollered in my face. "And I know exactly what I'm doing!"

'This guy is trying to *badger* me!' I sarcastically concluded. As the callow inspector was busily writing out the (crewleader's) citation (for having a kid with an incomplete working paper) a nasty fistfight broke out around fifty feet away. Two Cambodian roughnecks began brawling and then wildly thrashing-around in the bushes.

"Aren't you going to break up the fight?" I yelled at the already rattled inspector. "Now's the time to use your badge and exercise your authority!"

"That's your job and not mine!" the perplexed fellow volleyed back. "You're supposed to be the field boss here!"

I shook my head in disgust and called over the radio for emergency backup. Lopez showed up with six burly Puerto Rican associates and thanks to farm security, order finally was restored and civil behavior prevailed. Many of the migrants carried knives in sheaths, so I was always wary of avoiding arguments with the various field pickers.

On another very interesting occasion, I was driving past "the Aqueduct" (also called "the Artesian Well") that fed water into the Weymouth Farm's main "grand canal." Laotian young men had killed a twenty-foot-long black snake and were standing on opposite sides of a smaller irrigation ditch using the dead serpent as a rope in a weird game of tug-of-war. Suddenly four vernal Laotians on the losing side of the deceased snake lost their equilibrium and then plunged into the shallow-water irrigation ditch below.

Another time I had come across a group of Cambodians that were roasting a small animal on a makeshift rotisserie. Out of sheer curiosity I decided to stop my truck and chat with them for a moment.

"What's that you're cooking?" I casually asked. "Looks pretty delicious!"

"Raccoon!" a young fellow answered. "Want some?"

"Not really!" I laughed in total disbelief as I suddenly lost my appetite. "Where did you get it?"

"Up on the highway!" a second kid replied while pointing out to Weymouth Road. "Probably run over by a truck!"

"That animal might have rabies," I warned. "Be careful! You are what you eat! Rabies is dangerous!"

"What's that?" the first Cambodian kid asked.

"It's a bad disease!" I cautioned. "Make sure you roast that animal really good before you decide to eat it!"

Then one day in July of 2000 I received a call on my radio from Modesto Flores to drive out to Field 39 (Blue Crop variety) and transport a Cambodian to the dirt parking lot.

"Is he sick?" I inquired over the radio.

"No," Modesto answered. "Willie just called me over the radio and said that the guy ya' gotta' take to the gate is the owner of a car that just turned over in the parking lot."

"How did it turn over?" I inquired.

"According to Willie the driver had borrowed the car from the guy you're taking from Field 39," Modesto explained. "The guy was drunk and my son Willie wouldn't let him drive the car into the fields, which isn't allowed anyway! And then to harass Willie, the crazy guy started drivin' the car in circles real fast and then hit some soft sand and turned over! Serves him right!"

"Does the guy I'm gonna' take to the parking lot know any English?" I asked.

"No!" Modesto yelled into his receiver. And don't try tellin' him anything, either. We're gonna' kick them both off the farm as soon as I get down to the parking lot myself!"

I picked-up the puzzled owner of the aforementioned car, along with a friend, and taxied them one mile down main elevated gravel roads to the dirt parking lot. During the lengthy ride the two Cambodians were conversing with each other in their native tongue and I could tell by their expressions and by their gestures that they were wondering what the present in-progress excursion was all about. A funny thing happened on the way to the parking lot (sic, forum). When we finally reached our destination the owner of the white *Toyota* automobile noticed his vehicle resting upside down in the white sand and much to my astonishment the owner loudly yelled at the top of his lungs, "What the hell! Oh shit!" 'At least he knows five words of English!' I thought with a broad smile decorating my facial features.

When I first began working at Atlantic Blueberry in 1986, I was basically unfamiliar with the various fields and their immediate environments. High reeds, weeds and grass grew between certain fields and several times I assumed that roads continued from one field to another and then suddenly (on at least six occasions) I found my pickup plunging into small canals or into irrigation ditches. Then I would call Modesto on Farm #1 or Lopez (Lopey) on Farm #2 over the radio to come by and drag me out of my entrapment using sturdy chains as towlines attached to their trucks.

But one time in the early eighties, I had a really close call. I confidently and nonchalantly drove my empty bus #74 up Puerto Rican Avenue (local farm reference) on Farm #1 to "the Columbian Highway" (another local farm jargon term) that wended through a woods.' The dirt and gravel trail led to seven distant and remote blueberry fields (located above Creek Road) that bordered on the *Atlantic City Expressway*. I had been directed to help Mike Estrada deliver the "Home Gang" to Field Number 14 (The Funny Field). Two buses doing the job could make the transportation of two hundred men a lot easier with fewer trips back and forth for the Home Gang foreman.

At the end of "the Columbian Highway" was a wicked right- angle curve that only a very skilled bus driver could negotiate. I cautiously and slowly approached "Deadman's Curve" in my white #74 bus and after getting halfway around I feared that I had not sufficiently cut the angle. I panicked and then gingerly backed-up, not realizing that my right front wheel was passing over soft sand. Naturally, I really hit the panic button.

The bus began sliding to the right and I feared that my vehicle was going to topple over into a large canal. Luckily the bus stopped its slide down the rugged treacherous slope but then the front door couldn't be opened because it had become embedded in sand. Furthermore the bus's hood and engine had tilted sideways and motor oil had leaked-out and gotten onto the hot engine causing fire and smoke to escape. "I'm trapped inside!" I distressfully yelled to Mike and George Estrada over the radio.

I attempted squeezing out one of the side windows of the old refurbished school bus but my body was too big and bulky. I tried escaping out the back door but it was rusty and would not open. Meanwhile smoke billowed and fire raged out from the bus's very hot motor. Then I remembered that there was an axe under the driver's seat and I was about to smash my way out of the back door when an alert Mexican managed to open the hood and throw handfuls of sand inside, thus effectively smothering the engine fire. A farm front-end-loader was summoned and it dragged the bus out of its precarious entrapment. Once back on level ground I finally was able to open the door and personally thank my rescuers. 'Thank heaven that the empty bus wasn't jammed with fifty screaming, hysterical Mexicans!' I solemnly thought.

In the summer of '99, a tremendous-sized septic truck came rumbling onto Farm #1 to empty and service the several dozen portable toilets strategically stationed between various fields being picked. Apparently the in-a-hurry driver was behind schedule and he was speeding (in the monster vehicle) down the parking lot entrance road, which was elevated eight feet or so above parallel canals that existed alongside the hard gravel thoroughfare. All of a sudden, the immense truck's right front wheel hit a soft spot and before the speeding driver could steer the out-of-control "Honey Wagon" in the opposite direction the vehicle's great weight made it skid and then wildly flip sideways down into the right-side canal. I was the first responder on the scene and I stopped my vehicle on the gravel road, fearing that the septic truck driver had been killed, seriously injured or perhaps was unconscious.

"Hey, are you okay?" I yelled down into the canal. "Please answer me!" No response was forthcoming so I figured I should radio for help. After a third holler I noticed a hand and then a body slowing emerging from the driver's side of the cab, which was partially submerged in water (so to my imagination the fellow appeared to be exiting from a submarine hatch). The disoriented-but-unscathed driver climbed sideways out of the vehicle's open window. And a half-hour later, two large farm bulldozer operators collaborated to extricate the massive septic truck from the brackish-water canal. Luckily (for the truck's navigator on that particular morning) the ditch was not filled to its seven-foot-deep capacity.

On the Fourth of July in 2002, Modesto Flores summoned me over the radio to come to Field Number 23 (Duke Variety) in a hurry and to bring several large sheets of cardboard and a blanket from the office in a hurry. I immediately sped my truck towards the packinghouse.

"What's wrong?" I nervously asked into my radio. "What's going on Mo?"

"A Mexican lady is having a baby and you and me are gonna' be the doctors until an ambulance arrives!" Modesto screamed in a panic-oriented voice.

I rushed to the office, obtained the requested blanket, threw two sheets of cardboard onto the back of my company truck and frenetically raced out to Field Number 23. Dr. Modesto was in the process of delivering the baby and its head was already sticking-out of the woman's womb. I laid the cardboard down and handed Modesto the blue blanket.

"Quick, John!" Modesto ordered as I gazed in amazement at the spectacle before me. "Go out on Weymouth Road in front of the packinghouse and wave down the ambulance that's been called. Have them follow you to this field!"

I did as instructed, and when the Hamilton Township emergency paramedics arrived, I dutifully led them to the scene of confusion. When the rescue squad unit's vehicle came to a halt, I noticed that the baby had already been delivered by Dr. Modesto' and that the infant was being cuddled in its mother's arms with the umbilical cord still attached. The woman and her newborn were immediately conducted to a nearby hospital to receive professional care.

'Thank God there weren't any complications!' I thought. "Modesto, you've performed a minor miracle!"

* * * * * * * * * * * * *

My daily routines with Atlantic Blueberry Company were conducted from mid-June to August 1, the length of the main blueberry harvest. The company raised over twenty varieties of berries with Dukes, Bluetteas and Blue Crop being the most popular and abundant varieties. Many of the farm's varieties were developed on Farm #1 under the supervision of the Agricultural Department of

Rutgers University, New Brunswick. In fact, the Duke variety name originated from Arthur "Duke" Galletta," one of Atlantic Blueberry's founders. The large sweet Dukes had replaced the early-season Weymouth and Collins varieties that were popular and prevalent in the 1950s, '60s and early '70s. The last variety of the season was the Elliotts, a tart berry used mostly for making pies and jellies. The Elliotts were handpicked a second time around August 10th and then machine-picked a third and a final fourth time thereafter.

My workday started at around 5:30 a.m. and lasted until 5:30 p.m. seven days a week for eight action-packed consecutive weeks. I only had off when it rained since the pickers couldn't work in the fields, which in total amounted to around six days each summer. And I drove my white company truck between the two farms and through dirt fields with dusty roads putting on an average of eighty miles on the odometer each and every day.

The crews of various nationalities had to be kept in separate fields far apart from each other in order to avoid conflicts. The Laotians didn't mix too well with the Vietnamese, who also had problems with the Cambodians. And the Mexicans didn't get along too well with the volatile Guatemalans, and several times while driving around "troubleshooting" I had to send out a "Mayday" for help to break-up altercations that would instantly flare-up. In a matter of five minutes, twenty farm trucks would converge on the scene of alarm to calm matters down.

Two crewleaders that hated each other were Laotians Inxay Pathatogong and Khammy Pathong, who both claimed to speak ten languages including Chinese, English and Cambodian. Inxay (pronounced "In-sigh") claimed to be a tank gunner in Laos during the time of the *Vietnam War* and Khammy (pronounced Ka-my) claimed that Inxay was nothing more than a flunky foot soldier and jeep driver working for him when Pathong was a respectable prestigious Captain in the Laotian Army. I tended to believe Khammy's version of their Southeast Asian relationship because I knew that Inxay had started-out at Atlantic Blueberry as a field driver and loader for Khammy and then after gaining experience the maverick demonstrated his propensity for free enterprise and started his own crew and became a "gang leader" on his own initiative. That background (for all intent and purpose) explains the tremendous rift and fundamental animosity existing between the two strong-minded individuals, who absolutely loather one another. Actually, I feared both Laotians, knowing full well their volatile temperaments.

Both Khammy and Inxay always wore paramilitary clothing and heavy combat boots and had gold-framed front teeth showing in their mouths. The two carried knives concealed inside sheaths that dangled from their waist belts. And with the strange farm environments having plenty of canals, ditches, high reeds, thousands of blueberry bushes and accompanying military jets flying overhead from the nearby Pomona National Guard Air Base (located right next to *Atlantic City Airport*) practicing flight maneuvers above and around Atlantic Blueberry (with all of the Oriental and Mexican pickers peering-up at the A-10 Warthog jets), the immense place actually at times seemed like a foreign country to me.

The Galletta family made sure that they assigned Inxay to Farm #1 and Khammy to the *Route 322* Mays Landing Division to keep the two dedicated enemies eight miles apart from one another. Inxay would often hop up on the back of a pickup truck in Farm #1's dirt parking lot and violently yell out instructions to his scared workers in his native language as if he were Pol Pot or a formidable Asian military general laying-out battle plans to *his* hundred intimidated troops grouped below and around him. But Khammy once told me that *he* had worked closely with the *CIA* in Laos during the *Vietnam War* and that Inxay had never had the opportunity or the courage to shoot or kill anyone.

"Did you ever kill anyone?" I respectfully and warily asked Khammy.

"Yes John, I kill many, many people in Laos!" Khammy tersely answered.

"Did you shoot them with a rifle or pistol?" I sincerely inquired.

"No!" Khammy curtly replied. "I kill at least a hundred people with my knife!" the maniac indicated as he removed his sharp weapon from his belt sheath and boldly exhibited it to me. "I cut their throat like this!" the fanatic exclaimed as he gestured menacingly while wielding his knife.

"Okay, Khammy, I really believe you!" I remarked with great apprehension and feigned admiration. "Now you're peacefully living in the United States of America so please put your knife away."

Khammy had at least twenty-five red-bandanna Bloods working in his crew, which consisted mostly of a South Philly' Oriental street gang whose tattooed members looked both fearsome and gruesome. One day at around 5 p.m. a New Jersey State Trooper followed a gang member off of *Route 322* into Farm #2's parking lot with his patrol car's overhead red lights flashing. No sooner did the trooper come to a halt when twenty or so Blood' Cambodians surrounded his patrol car, and the thugs began throwing cherry bombs and firecrackers onto and underneath the cop's car. The young trooper panicked and called for backup and in a matter of three minutes at least twenty State Trooper and Hamilton Township Police cars converged on the parking lot and the responding officers managed to successfully quell the disturbance.

One day, vindictive Khammy surprisingly showed up on Farm #1 and drove out to Inxay's field, took out a rifle and hostilely began shooting at his prime foe. Inxay instinctively fled for cover inside a field of tall blueberry bushes. The State Labor Inspectors had heard about the bizarre incident and issued five citations to Khammy citing the rifle confrontation along with other more minor outstanding labor-related violations the wily Laotian crewleader had committed and accumulated.

"Look, Frank," I told the Chief Inspector before Khammy's hearing inside *his* partitioned office in the State of New Jersey's Hammonton Labor Building. "This crazy guy Khammy is not wrapped too tight. Don't trigger him off or else he might have a flashback to Laos during the *Vietnam War* and then become volatile and uncontrollable! In fact," I elaborated, "Khammy confided to me that he had personally slit at least a hundred people's throats back in Laos and had mercilessly killed them without showing any conscience or remorse!"

"Look, John," the Chief Inspector calmly answered, "he's in the United States now and the rule of law prevails here. And besides," the Chief Inspector bragged, "I myself was in the *U.S. Army* and I know how to defend myself if it becomes necessary!"

The scheduled hearing commenced in a placid manner for the first ten minutes but when Khammy learned that the State of New Jersey was going to fine him five hundred dollars and revoke his Crewleader's license, the dysfunctional Laotian felt threatened and was provoked to take action. Khammy stood-up and much to the Chief Inspector's astonishment and consternation removed his sharp knife from his belt sheath and then almost instantaneously lunged at the Chief Inspector, who spontaneously fled the room as if he were a rattled rabbit (while I stupidly and foolishly wrapped my arms around Khammy's shoulders to prevent him from pursuing after his newly-declared adversary).

But in the final analysis, I must confess that Khammy maintained excellent discipline over his crew of Bloods, who all feared him worse than they feared either a hundred' Los Angeles or South Philly' blue bandanna Crips. His pickers always sent quality berries to the loading dock, and the intimidating Laotian's pay slips were always done correctly with hardly ever an error to be found. Khammy was organized and meticulous and I must confess that he conducted his field operations as if his assigned turf was a sophisticated military staging area, but the State of New Jersey and its Labor Department Inspectors viewed the dangerous and unpredictable cold-eyed surreptitious Pathong as if he were an *FBI* "Most Wanted Criminal."

In the winter of 2001, Khammy and three henchmen slipped into a Philadelphia factory where Inxay was managing a work crew and the culprit maliciously jumped his avowed rival, wantonly beating Pathatogong up badly. Police warrants were issued for Khammy's arrest and the last I have heard of him the itinerant maverick is reported to be a fugitive from justice hiding-out in either Alabama or Mississippi operating a fish store. The following summer Inxay (with his characteristic mercurial temper) had a disagreement with one of the owners of Atlantic Blueberry Company and the temperamental crewleader was promptly dismissed from the farm. Rumor has it that the Laotian now is the proprietor of an Oriental food store in West Philadelphia and his somewhat reputable new business caters to former Laotian, Thai, Vietnamese and Cambodian Jersey blueberry pickers. I presume (with a degree of certainty) that Khammy Pathong is not one of Inxay Pathatogong's current steady customers.

"The Stealth Auto' Device"

On a scorching-hot August Thursday afternoon, Jack Scanlon had just finished mowing his one-acre lawn and thankfully retired his *John Deere* mower to his backyard utility building nestled in between twin tall white pines. 'I've got my monthly chiropractic appointment in Atco in another two hours,' the Hammonton, New Jersey resident remembered. 'And Carol's taken the three kids down to Wildwood for the day in my *Maxima* so I'm stuck with her mint green *Altima.* It's okay, but the merlot *Maxima* has the big powerful engine and the black leather seats and I'm the one who's makin' the payments on it. My wife confiscates the only thing I really cherish besides the kids and her and thinks nothin' of it. Everything's community property to her and I should not have acquiesced to her unreasonable demand! My *Maxima* is my *Maxima* and there should be no compromising about that!'

The 375 Valley Avenue resident marched through the back porch of his attractive yellow brick rancher and next ambled through the dining room over to the kitchen sink to wash the sweat and grime off his hands, arms and face. 'I think I'll now savor a cold bottle of *Coor's Light*, take a relaxing cold shower to cool off and then get dressed to see Dr. John and Dr. Joe over in Atco. My chronic back problem is still giving me a little agony and I think I'm developin' tendonitis by the tenderness I feel in my right shoulder,' the amateur lawn doctor realized and hypothesized. 'Too bad I can't trade this used decrepit old man's body in for a new one just like I habitually do every four years with my *Nissan Maximas*!'

After enjoying his refreshing cold shower Jack changed into comfortable blue denim shorts, a flamboyant-looking Graceland tee shirt and a pair of *Adidas* jogging sneakers. Then Scanlon exited the home, locked the side door, entered his wife's mint green *Altima,* fired-up the engine and after departing his concrete driveway headed west towards Bellevue Avenue, Hammonton's main thoroughfare. At the busy intersection of *Route 30* and *Route 206* the impatient "Alpha-personality" waited for the traffic signal to turn green. Jack pressed his stereo radio button and listened to Fats Domino singing his '50s rendition of "Ain't That A Shame" on *WOGL*-98.1 FM, Philadelphia's premier oldies station. 'Ain't that a shame I'm just a middle-class carpenter and not a dynamic multi-millionaire,' Scanlon regretted. 'Oh well, at least I don't have cancer or chronic heart disease. Things could always be worse for me on this indifferent and apathetic planet!

I'll cruise west and reminisce the good old days. I'm sure glad they're playin' the more memorable Fats Domino version of 'Ain't That A Shame', and not that corny Pat Boone cover version.'

After turning left onto four-lane *Route 30* the seven-mile-drive west from Hammonton to Atco was proceeding smoothly and the *Altima's* air-conditioner was working to perfection while effectively negating the unbearable outside ninety-five-degree heat. The driver soon passed from Atlantic into Camden County, traveled through the rural community of Elm and then the mint green automobile ascended the Ancora Railroad Bridge situated in Winslow Township. Still heading west on *Route 30* the man driving the *Altima* slowed down through the Borough of Chesilhurst, notorious for its two police cars issuing traffic tickets around-the-clock to anyone going fifty-five miles an hour or over in the fifty mile an hour zone. Just past Graziano's Italian Restaurant Jack Scanlon entered Waterford Township. A white *Volkswagen* was hogging the left-hand passing lane just behind Jack and a senior citizen in an old dilapidated automobile was going forty-five directly in front of him. The paranoid fellow didn't want to be "hemmed-in" for the next three miles.

'I'll pass this old geezer and then slow down to the speed limit,' Jack Scanlon planned and decided. 'Just as I thought! That *VW* has a Pennsylvania tag because it has no front license plate. In Pennsy' there's no law for drivers to keep to the right after passing like there is here in Jersey! Why don't those self-centered Philly' drivers learn some basic highway courtesy and stop always going so slow in the passing lane?'

Jack deftly cut in front of the white *Volkswagen*, stepped on the accelerator and easily passed the old motorist in the 1975 green *Pontiac* station wagon. Then Scanlon politely put on his right turn signal and skillfully steered his wife's *Altima* back into the right-hand lane. 'This car doesn't have half the pick-up as my *Maxima* does although I do like its overall design! No wonder why Carol's absolutely enthralled with constantly experimenting with my fantastic set of wheels!'

No sooner had Jack passed Atco Lake on his left that his eyes perceived in the rearview mirror red flashing lights rapidly approaching. A Waterford Township Police *Jeep* quickly pulled directly behind the mint green *Altima*, signaling for Scanlon to stop. Jack disgustedly turned into Shannon Caterers' asphalt parking lot. 'Just what I need!' Jack angrily thought while evaluating his circumstance. 'Another pathetic traffic ticket! One more after this summons and my license will be suspended. I got my last citation just four months ago in Chesilhurst!'

A young, strong-looking patrolman in a black uniform exited his *Jeep* and stridently approached the disgruntled driver's vehicle. The metal nameplate fastened directly above the Waterford Township cop's badge read: "Officer Frank Azzara."

"Sir, could I see your license and registration?" Officer Azzara sternly requested. "You were caught on radar goin' sixty-five in a fifty mile an hour zone!"

"I only sped-up to pass an old gentleman in a green station wagon goin' forty-five because a white *Volkswagen* with Pennsylvania tags was hogging the passing lane!" Jack futilely protested. "Where were you hiding Officer? There aren't too many ground-level billboards on the White Horse Pike anymore!"

"Next to the Maplewood IV Restaurant!" the Officer laconically admitted. "Now Sir, may I see your credentials?"

Jack flashed Officer Frank Azzara his red, white and blue "Community Supporter Card" that indicated that the public-minded citizen generously supported and contributed to local police departments.

"I'm very sorry, Sir," Officer Azzara responded to the tacit communication involving the new information. "But that card is only good for Winslow Township, Elm and Ancora. You're in Waterford Township now! Incidentally, I saw the decal pasted on your left rear window and already knew you had that card in your possession. Too bad you don't have a Waterford Township Community Supporter card in your wallet!" the cop stated and emphasized. "Then the Chief would understand why you haven't been issued a summons, but the police dispatcher has already logged your license number and recorded your violation into the computer system!"

"This is my wife's car and not mine!" Jack informed the disinterested policeman. "I'm not-too-familiar with the *Altima's* speedometer. Its markings are every twenty-miles an hour and not every ten' like the one on my *Maxima*!"

"Regardless Mr. Scanlon," the patrolman suavely answered showing good training and discipline. "You were still speedin' fifteen miles over the limit when my infallible radar picked you up. Where ya' heading?"

"To Atco Chiropractic Center for my monthly crunch!" Jack communicated. "But right now I'm thinkin' about goin' to another clinic in Hammonton. At least I know most of the cops on my town's police force!"

"I went to St. Joe's in Hammonton!" Officer Azzara related. "Played football at that high school. Our team won the state championship."

"Then, you must've played for coach Paul Sacco!" Jack name-dropped hoping to help himself' escape like Houdini out of his current motor vehicle dilemma. "You must know Bill Castone too. I think he's the vice-principal over at St. Joe's."

"Yeah!" Officer Azzara acknowledged with a noticeable frown on his face. "That guy suspended me for a minor violation and I missed an important *Cape-Atlantic League* championship game against Hammonton High. I'm not too keen on the mention of his name! Now Mr. Scanlon," the officer said getting back onto the task at hand, "please be more aware of your speed when traveling through Waterford Township. Here's you traffic citation. It'll cost you a hundred dollars and four points towards losing your license. Be careful! The dispatcher has already told me you've amassed four points on your record. One more ticket in the next six months and your driving privileges will be revoked and you'll be required to attend driver counseling classes!"

"Thank you, Officer," Jack apologetically answered. "I'll try and be more careful the next time I pass through your territory. But to me that Pennsylvania *Volkswagen* violatin' the law hogging the passing lane was the real reason I had to speed-up and move past the old fellow in the green station wagon. As you know, I slowed down thereafter and honored the speed limit until you pulled me over! I'm a pretty obedient guy behind the wheel."

"Yes, Sir! I believe you!" Officer Azzara amiably agreed. "Sometimes though we all need a reality check. But the Chief is getting on all our cases because there's been a rash of fatal accidents all over South Jersey in the last month," the cop shared. "One fatality happened in Vineland, another in Egg Harbor Township, a third in Galloway and a fourth just down the road in Winslow Township. I suppose that today was *your* turn to face the music! Please be more alert behind the wheel. Good day Mr. Scanlon!"

After visiting Dr. John and Dr. Joe at Atco Chiropractic Center, and complaining to the two therapists about the overly vigilant Waterford Township Police, Jack Scanlon stopped on his return trip at the Waterford Township *WaWa* convenience store to pick up a newspaper and a pack of delicious *TastyKake Butterscotch Krimpets*. The *Camden Courier Post* headlines read: "Man Killed in Berlin Township Auto Accident!" 'I can see why the local cops are so jumpy about the recent epidemic of auto fatalities. Maybe I should resist temptation and exercise more discretion when it comes to my propensity for speeding. Maybe I'm a candidate for the practice of road rage?' Jack assessed and speculated. 'Thank the Lord I wasn't in the *Maxima* and passin' the station wagon doin' ninety-five! God, I'd love to bury that speedometer!'

Upon reaching his Valley Avenue home, Jack paraded directly to the refrigerator to acquire a cold can of *Pepsi Cola* to wash down his high-calorie butterscotch krimpets. Soon the telephone rang and Scanlon immediately recognized his neighbor Jim Thompson's familiar number on the caller ID.

"Hi, Jim," Jack greeted in a rather melancholy tone of voice. "Guess what! I just got a speeding ticket on the Pike over in Waterford Township."

"That's too bad!" Jim Thompson sympathized and declared. "I was just readin' in the *Atlantic City Press* where there's been a string of terrible auto' accidents and the cops all over South Jersey are crackin' down heavy. Didn't ya' get a ticket in Chesilhurst just a couple of months ago?"

"Yeah," Jack mentioned after gulping down a mouthful of cold *Pepsi.* "I'm thinkin' about getting one of those elite radar detectors to put on my sun visor. That device oughta' protect me from the aggravation of police radar. I can't afford to get another speedin' citation Jim."

"I see those radar mechanisms advertised all the time in the back of magazines in those small coupon ads," Thompson recollected and suggested. "Or Jack, ya' might want to try the *Internet*. Sometimes you can find a special or one on sale at a bargain price on either *Google* or on *Yahoo*."

"Thanks for your keen advice, Jim!" Jack Scanlon appreciated and replied. "I'll investigate thoroughly into the matter as soon as I get off the phone. I need to know about cops lurkin' in the vicinity before the varmints find out about me. It's now boiled-down to a silly cat and mouse game and to use a relevant cartoon analogy I've got to play the role of Jerry lookin' out for that wise guy predator cat Tom!"

"Okay, Jack, good luck on your' research!" Scanlon's good neighbor wished and verbalized. "Let me know how ya' make out! Talk to ya' soon! So long!" Click.

Jack assiduously researched his desired product on the *Internet* and ultimately discovered a most intriguing item. 'It says here that for a mere $99.00 I can purchase a sophisticated police radar detector with a range of a mile and for another hundred and fifty bucks, I can obtain a stealth device that can make my car virtually invisible to police detection. According to this *Internet* description the stealth eraser device attaches to and then plugs right into the radar detector and the whole system operates' directly from my cigarette lighter located under my *Maxima's* dashboard. That's it, the ideal solution!' Scanlon decisively determined. 'Carol's gonna' be relegated to driving the kids around and going to the shopping malls in the green *Altima* and the radar detector and the accompanying stealth device are definitely gonna' be installed as soon as possible inside my merlot *Maxima!"*

The *Internet* credit card transaction was easily completed and three weeks later the indispensable radar detector with its accompanying stealth evasion device arrived at 375 Valley Avenue via dependable *UPS* delivery. Jack explicitly followed the easy-to-install directions and for the next seven days the radar device worked faithfully without deviation on *Route 30, Route 206, Route 322, Route 54,* Route *40,* and equally as well on mass transit high volume thoroughfares such as the *Atlantic City Expressway, the New Jersey Turnpike,* and the *Garden State Parkway.*

'This radar detector works marvelously, no doubt about it,' Scanlon gleefully interpreted. 'In the final analysis I didn't even have to buy the accessory stealth police, evasion device. But I guess that P.T. Barnum was right when he reputedly said 'There's a sucker born every minute!' I'll have to call Jim Thompson up and tell my neighbor to just order the radar detector and to forget about the crummy expensive and unnecessary stealth-cloaking device. That crazy thing sounds like something science fiction directly out of *Star Trek* but now I'm stuck with it anyway!'

At precisely 3 p.m. on the first Thursday in September, Jack Scanlon clambered into his merlot *Nissan Maxima* to loyally honor his monthly appointment at the Atco Chiropractic Center. 'I'll have to tell Dr. John and Dr. Joe about this nagging pain in my right shoulder. They'll probably say that I'll have to get a medical doctor's prescription in order to qualify for some electric stimulus therapy requiring the appropriate medication applied,' Jack assumed. 'I think the tendonitis is traveling down my right arm and is also now showing-up as a case of tennis elbow!'

After passing over the newly renovated Ancora Railroad Bridge, and going the speed limit west through Chesilhurst Borough Jack got caught in a yellow light at Graziano's Restaurant, and deliberately accelerated through the caution signal. The nervous driver glanced into his rearview mirror and observed a Waterford Township Police

Department Jeep entering the *White Horse Pike* from the west side of the popular local spaghetti house, and the vehicle heretofore had been obscure to westbound traffic.

'That's mighty strange! My radar detector didn't set off!' Jack instinctively worried. 'And now that cop in the Police Jeep is on the prowl following me. I'll bet he's about to flip the switch and activate his overhead lights!' the upset driver feared. 'There's only one viable alternative here and that's to hit sixty-five and put the guaranteed stealth police car evader into action!'

Jack accelerated his awesome *Maxima* and the speedometer soon registered '70' as the foreign luxury sports sedan sped by Shannon Caterers and then streaked through another yellow light at Bartram Avenue, passing like a bolt of lightning by the driver's original intended destination of Atco Chiropractic Center. Scanlan again glanced into his rearview mirror and noticed that the Waterford Township Police Jeep had its overhead flashing red lights turned on and was gradually closing the gap between the two vehicles. 'I'll slow down and gently glide into the right-hand lane,' Jack thought. 'If the stealth device is working as advertised the tricked fuzz will zip right by me in hot pursuit of a vague hallucination!'

Just then, a huge dump truck eased out of Ivystone Estates on the left and the unaware driver inadvertently plowed into the speeding merlot *Maxima*, sending Jack and his splendid automobile spinning and then flipping into a right-hand-side highway telephone pole. The patrolman inside the Waterford Township Police Jeep perceptively observed the gigantic dump truck stopped stationary in the center of *Route 30*, noticed the red *Maxima* upside down against a sheered-off telephone pole and then halted his vehicle to begin conducting an intensive investigation.

Here is Officer Frank Azzara's report as released to all area newspapers:

> I was on traffic patrol when I pulled out of the parking lot of Graziano's Italian Restaurant at approximately 3:15 p.m. on Thursday, September 1. 2005. I was casually trailing a merlot-colored *Nissan Maxima* that appeared to be going slightly over the fifty mile-an-hour speed limit'. I then considered flicking on my radar to determine the exact speed of the vehicle, which I quickly ascertained was fifty-five miles an hour,

three miles an hour within the established speed limit parameters.

I was about to make a left-hand-turn into the Maplewood IV Restaurant's parking lot when I observed the *Maxima* suddenly accelerate to a much greater speed. When my radar indicated that the car hit sixty-five miles-an-hour the sedan suddenly vanished into thin air right before my astonished eyes. Thinking that my pupils had experienced a visual aberration or some kind of amazing optical illusion I continued onward past Bartram Avenue and then drove past the busy intersection of Atco Avenue and the *White Horse Pike*.

A mile further down *Route 30,* I observed a red dump truck stopped in the middle of the busy highway. Then I noticed to the right the merlot *Maxima* upside down on its roof and its front hood wrapped around a sheered-off telephone pole.

The in-shock and bewildered dump truck driver identified himself as Harold Swift, who claimed that he never saw the *Maxima* and then heard a loud thud resulting from his vehicle's right-front-fender's collision with the merlot-colored automobile. Mr. Swift had difficulty fathoming how and why the tragic impact had occurred.

Credentials discovered both in the *Maxima's* driver's wallet and inside the glove compartment's registration indicated that the dead man's name was Mr. Jack Scanlon of 375 Valley Avenue, Hammonton, New Jersey, 08037. I recognized that particular name from a recent traffic speeding citation I had issued and the master computer at Waterford Township Police Headquarters showed and verified that Mr. Scanlon had indeed received a ticket on Thursday, August 4, 2005 for going sixty-five in a fifty mile-an-hour zone. Our records at headquarters also indicate that he was at the time driving a mint green *Nissan Altima*.

In conclusion, I must attest that this is perhaps the most mysterious and confounding motor vehicle accident I have ever investigated. Mr. Swift (the dump truck operator) and I never saw the speeding *Maxima* after it exceeded going a speed of sixty-five miles-an-hour. The accident remains an enigma in my mind and the disturbing impact (both in my imagination and in my recollection of events) seemed to result from the implementation of some super-advanced military technology like that currently employed on Air Force stealth bombers. At any rate this unfortunate traffic fatality is another in a series of similar bizarre automobile accidents that are presently baffling police departments from Atlantic City to Camden. In all those analogous cases, the speeding vehicles seemed to have disappeared prior to disaster resulting. Perhaps when all of the applicable information is accurately coordinated then a feasible explanation for the extraordinary number of audacious speeders losing their lives can be logically developed and explained.

"Mariner X"

St. Vincent's Hospital is a landmark New York City medical institution famous for its research, latest technology and outstanding service to lower Manhattan from Washington Square to Little Italy, from Greenwich Square to the Bowery. The hospital staff is comprised of some of the finest and most competent specialists in the United States and the nurses are reputed being compassionate, courteous and very professional.

On Wednesday morning, August 17, 2005, Intensive Care nurses Miriam Stevenson and Kristen Penn were briefing Dr. Edward Saunders and Dr. Joseph Walker of the status of an "unusual patient" that had just been taken to *St. Vincent's* Emergency Suite by ambulance for urgent admission. The strange new arrival had no identification or wallet on his possession, was badly beaten, battered and bruised and was unconscious and moaning. And to add to the general mystery the "close-to-death" man was dressed in a peculiar looking "sailor's uniform" that was made-up of an unknown synthetic material.

"The man talks from an unconscious state," Nurse Miriam Stevenson informed her two very interested male superiors, "but his words sound like random babbling. He was found lying on the pavement outside a Bowery bar and apparently was involved in an altercation, sustaining multiple facial and body wounds and apparent internal bleeding. It's amazing he's still alive!"

"How old would you say he is?" Dr. Saunders asked while staring down at the sailor's face. "Any imminent surgery might prove to be fatal if he's not strong enough!"

"It's hard to say," Nurse Kristen Penn hesitantly answered. "I have trouble judging age when a person is lying horizontal beneath me with his or her eyes closed," the veteran nurse honestly qualified. "But in my estimation, he looks too old to be in any navy, American or otherwise. I'd say by his facial wrinkles and gum recession he appears to be around eighty years old!"

"I have to concur with Nurse Penn's guesstimation!" Dr. Joseph Walker verified. "Nurse Stevenson, please cut off his uniform and get him on one of the *Emergency Room* operating tables as quickly as possible. Dr. Saunders and I will attempt to stop the internal bleeding and then do an in-progress evaluation. Has the patient spoken anything discernible from his subconscious state?"

"Well, yes he has," Nurse Stevenson remembered and mentioned. "Consistent with the weird sailor's uniform you see him wearing the old gentleman claims to be on the crew of a ship, actually he was mumbling the name of what sounds like a fictitious aircraft carrier, the….."

"The Richard M. Nixon!" Nurse Penn finished. "I'm never heard of such a ship since all major naval vessels dock at one time or another in New York and sailors are always getting injured and brought here for treatment. It's really a rather puzzling matter that defies explanation. The gentleman must be in great pain and currently being delusional in his subconscious mind!"

"This entire conversation is absolutely borderline ridiculous and counterproductive to the task at hand!" Dr. Saunders austerely maintained. "Whoever would dare name any naval ship, battleship or otherwise after Richard M. Nixon? He left his Presidency in total disgrace as a result of the *Watergate Scandal!* Nixon fully knew he'd be impeached if he didn't!"

"Let's get to work on this fascinating man right away!" Dr. Walker constructively recommended. "Nurse Stevenson, did our ancient-looking sailor happen to mumble in his unconscious state what date he thought it was? Does he know his name? Did he allude to any family members?"

"No Dr., he seems to be suffering from severe memory loss and his mind is evidently failing from amnesia," Miriam Stevenson related. "And to answer the first part of your question," the woman informatively continued, "strangely enough our Mariner X had the date correct but the year totally misconstrued. He claimed that it's August 17, 2083 AD!"

"This must be some sort of colossal hoax, a real conundrum, and I'll wager we're dealing with some kind of charlatan or impostor here!" Dr. Walker cynically presumed and declared. "If this man wasn't so seriously injured and traumatized, I'd say that he needs psychiatric assistance!"

"Hoax or charlatan, it really doesn't matter at this stage of the game, now does it Joe!" Dr. Saunders challenged his peer as he watched the nurses cutting scissors having difficulty slicing off the fabric of the futuristic-looking naval uniform that incidentally had the emblem *USS Richard M. Nixon* sewn onto the right shoulder section. "This case is already meandering somewhere between an enigma and a mystery. Let's first attempt saving this old man's life! If he ever regains his senses maybe then he can recollect the past and clue us in on what has happened in this chaotic and erratic world between now and 2083!"

"Are you being facetious?" the esteemed Dr. Walker skeptically asked his colleague. "I thought that *that* particular personality trait was exclusively my department!"

"Joe," Dr. Saunders replied in a somewhat chastising tone of voice, "if you have a more reliable theory about this unusual Old Salt then please advance it. Unlike you, I do believe in religion and have implicit faith in angels, demons and the like! Despite your pessimistic agnostic views of the world," the head *ER* surgeon mildly reprimanded his subordinate, "please respect the fact that *St. Vincent's* is still a functioning Catholic Hospital!"

"Sorry, Ed," the more dubious surgeon apologized, "but I'm not half as superstitious as you are. But we do share one commonality and that's the general welfare of humanity. In that ethical sense I suggest that we operate immediately!"

"Joe, let's not procrastinate and please finish scrubbing-up!" Dr. Edward Saunders advised. "We can't afford to hesitate another minute. This man's life is in jeopardy! I don't think any of his vital organs are damaged! And I do believe there's actually a remote chance of him surviving his ordeal!"

The expert surgeons made the necessary incision and soon found the major source of injury, a ruptured spleen that had been penetrated by an assailant's knife. After the small organ had been skillfully removed the wound was properly sutured. And then after the common but delicate procedure had been fully completed the four professionals congratulated each other on what they evaluated as "another Emergency Room success."

"The old man's again muttering something!" Head Nurse Miriam Stevenson recognized and reported. "His mind seems to still be mentally alert although his identity remains anonymous! I think we should try and find out who Mariner X really is!"

"What's he murmuring?" Dr. Walker curiously inquired. "It sounds like a lot of gibberish to me!"

"He's saying something about being a crewmember aboard the *USS Edgar Allan Poe*," Nurse Kristen Penn conveyed to her three medical companions. "That sort of odd language sounds almost as incredible as the *USS Richard M. Nixon!"*

"What year are you speaking from?" Dr. Saunders asked the unconscious but somewhat stabilized mariner. "Give me the exact date."

"August 17, 2045!" the *ER* patient remarkably uttered. "The destroyer's bein' attacked by enemy forces. Don't interrupt me! I gotta' fire these shells at approaching jet aircraft!"

"I've never heard of any destroyer named *Edgar Allan Poe*!" Dr. Walker criticized. "This entire scenario is nothing more than a preposterous charade! This man appears to be fighting a one-man war inside an American literature class!"

"Of course, you haven't heard of the Edgar Allan Poe!" Dr. Saunders volleyed back. "The ship probably hasn't been built or commissioned yet! I have a hunch that this pretentious old fellow is addressing us from forty years in the future Dr. Walker! Nurse Stevenson, see to it that this feeble patient is brought into the recovery room and given every attention. In four hours put him on intravenous. Maybe when he gets stronger we can induce him out of his deep trance and learn some pertinent information about his identity and about his past."

* * * * * * * * * * * * *

Three days passed, and the bed-ridden "ancient mariner" improved considerably in terms of health and vital signs yet he still remained in his ongoing "coma-vegetation state." The doctors on call were quite baffled and so were the nurses, who now showed a particular curiosity and intrigue about Mariner X's history and origin. On August 21st the Old Salt began uttering some new "jargon" to Nurse Stevenson, who was holding his hand trying to elicit additional bits and details from the fascinating occupant of Room 254. A conversation of sorts did ensue.

"I'm your friend and want to help you," Miriam Stevenson sympathetically comforted her newfound ward. "What date is it and what ship are you on?" the woman prompted and encouraged.

"It's the *USS Thresher* and the date's April 19, 1963," the elderly man answered in a voice sounding like it was coming from a hypnotic but rather disturbed state of mind. "The sub' is currently positioned underwater around two hundred miles off of Cape Cod. It's 9:18 in the morning and the submarine's breaking apart. Breaking apart! Do you hear me?"

Nurse Stevenson let go of the unconscious man's quivering hand, and then grabbed a ballpoint pen and notepad and began hastily and anxiously scribbling-down the hysterical man's exact words. Then the speaker provided some other relevant facts and the listener was almost mesmerized by his fantastic disclosure.

"The *Thresher's* supposed to be the finest new sub' in the U.S. inventory and now it's about ready to disintegrate!" the old man emphatically said and regretted as his forehead broke-out in a heavy sweat. "Damn the Portsmouth Naval Shipyard! Damn Kittery, Maine where she was built and launched! All 129 of us are doomed! The pressure's too much to bear! Sonar' be damned! The new weapons' system can't save us! Nothing can save us! We're all damned and doomed! Do you hear me?"

Nurse Stevenson panicked and ceased her documentation, when the old man suddenly stopped breathing. Then, responding to her professional training, she regained her composure and grabbed Mariner X's right hand. The remarkable patient's heart again began beating and the instruments to which he was attached began signaling life. 'Thank God he's still alive!' Miriam Stevenson thought. 'Could it be that this withered old sailor has led many lives in many centuries and that this is some sort of arcane transition in the making that I'm witnessing? I mustn't tell anyone about this bizarre development or else my reputation might be marred and my career placed in danger. I must zipper my mouth and remain mum about this *Thresher* incident!'

The following Monday morning, August 29, Nurse Kristen Penn was visiting the unconscious old sailor's room to check his charts and his physical condition when the remarkable patient started verbalizing some salient particulars about his past. The frightened woman asked the "ancient mariner" what day and year he was speaking from. She was astounded by his response.

"It's 9:10 a.m. December 7, 1941!" the inimitable man sputtered-out from his Room 254 hospital bed. "There's hundreds of Japanese planes attacking, wave after wave of them. The *Oklahoma's* been severely hit, the *West Virginia* too and so has the *Utah*. Don't you understand that I can't talk now because *Pearl Harbor's* being hit in a surprise attack'. Oh this is horrible, just plain horrible. New wave coming in from the Hickam Field side! Another enemy squadron's zeroing-in from the ocean! Head for cover! Don't ignore my warning! If you want to live take cover and trust that Almighty God will save us all!"

"What ship are you on?" Nurse Penn asked in amazement. "Tell me the name of your ship!" she repeated. "What ship are *we* on?"

"The *Arizona*!" the sailor loudly answered in a voice sounding like it was being transmitted from another dimension. "No time to talk! Duck down! Hurry! Here they come zooming in on us! Duck down! Heaven, save us all!"

'At least, he's gotten off the August 17th date!' Nurse Penn speculated and assessed. 'Maybe I'll ask him that question.' "Why isn't it August 17, 1941?"

"Because now it's August 17, 1944! I'm telling you about the devastating *Pearl Harbor* sneak attack, because I had survived the assault on the *Arizona* and have been re-assigned to the *Battleship New Jersey*. I can now have the time to talk more freely because right this moment, we're sailing the *Pacific* heading for the *Marianas* and presently not being assaulted by enemy fire! Ironically this juggernaut was launched on December 7, 1942, just one year after the *Arizona* was struck at *Pearl Harbor!"* God bless good old invincible *BB-62!"* The *New Jersey's* the best damned ship in the entire American Fleet!!"

Nurse Kristen Penn shuddered in horror as she gingerly stepped away from the bed. 'I mustn't tell anyone about this soul-wrenching experience! This old sailor seems to be eerily addressing me from another world! This phenomenon could only be described as being a paranormal experience! But the man's statements seem so honest and truthful! This has got to be the most extraordinary sensational testimony my ears have ever heard!'

On Tuesday, September 6, Dr. Edward Saunders stopped by Room 254 to check on the exceptional elderly sailor's condition. While the surgeon was studying the anonymous mariner's daily chart the patient began uttering discernible sentences in his bed. Dr. Saunders' ears immediately pricked up to interpret the nature of the old man's monologue.

"Captain says there's a three-hundred-foot gash torn in the hull!" the patient neurotically blabbered. "Orders are to evacuate the ship! All women and children climb into the lifeboats! All women and children into the lifeboats right now!"

"What is the date?" Dr. Saunders demanded in a firm tone of voice. "Where are you? What is your destination? Describe your situation!"

"It's the early morning of April 15, 1912 on the White Star Line *Titanic!"* the unconscious old fellow revealed in a ghastly almost spectral tone of voice. "It's the ship's maiden voyage from England to New York and this horrific tragedy had to happen! And everyone said that this ship's unsinkable! That iceberg has done us in! All women and children into the lifeboats if you want to live!"

"Are you sure it's not August 17, 1912?" the chief surgeon objectively queried. "August 17 seems to be a date you can't seem to ever escape!"

"Don't you understand man? I'm telling you about the end of my short tenure on the *Titanic* on April 15th, 1912 but I'm now speaking to you from August 17th, 1912. I miraculously was salvaged and was one of the last people to leave the *Titanic* before it submerged into the ice-cold *North Atlantic*! What a horrendous disaster! What a horrible catastrophe! It was a tragedy of epic proportions! Do you fathom my words?"

'This man's uncanny declarations defy both logic and sanity!' Dr. Saunders concluded. 'I must keep this *Titanic* incident a secret or else I might lose all credibility in the local medical community. My colleagues will call me 'a quack'! But I must admit that I'm staggered and fascinated at what odd comments the ancient mariner is reviewing and discussing. If my nautical history is correct,' Dr. Saunders recalled, 'another ship, the *Carpathia,* managed to rescue 705 survivors from the *Titanic* and according to *his* claim one of the passengers is lying before me. But that's got to be impossible! This admirable man would have to be at least a hundred-and-twenty-years-old, if his highly imaginative story has any validity or merit whatsoever! And around one thousand five hundred unfortunate victims had perished in the great calamity!' Dr. Saunders recollected. 'And isn't it a queer coincidence that many of the *Titanic* survivors were taken right here to *St. Vincent's Hospital* for recuperation from their traumatic tribulations! The Lord's sanity, have mercy on me!'

On Thursday, September 15th the always-doubtful Dr. Joseph Walker confidently entered Room 254 to examine the remarkable but still incoherent and comatose patient that had been given the appellation "Mariner X." While Dr. Walker was jotting-down some pertinent notes concerning the sailor's physical welfare, the ancient mariner recommenced narrating his unique recitation. The surgeon ceased his perfunctory activity and paid full attention to his subject's frantic oration.

"Help me! I'm drowning! Help! I'm drowning!" the mariner yelled from his hospital bed. Immediately Dr. Walker rushed over to close the room's door so that no one outside could hear the ancient mariner's emotional but amazing exclamations. "Captain Sigsbee should've anticipated such sabotage! It pays to be distrustful of everyone!"

"Where are you'? What is the date? What event are you' involved in?" the highly interested medical cynic' deliberately asked his' unknown patient in rapid-fire order. "Please answer me!" Dr. Walker pleaded.

"It's January 25, 1898 in Havana Harbor!" the Old Salt voluntarily disclosed as his mental state approached delirium. "I'm a U.S. sailor on the *Maine* and loud explosions have just rocked the ship. Water is gushing in through the walls! We're all gonna' drown like rats I tell ya'! And it happened right after the bugler finished playing 'Taps'! How ironic! Then the lights all went out and we're now all choking in the darkness from the intense smoke!" Mariner X divulged. "We'll all die from either asphyxiation or drowning, whichever menace happens first! The heat's intolerable! The heat's intolerable! We can't get out! We're all trapped in here like rats! We can't get out!"

'Over two-hundred and fifty seamen had died in that disaster!' Dr. Walker remembered from facts learned in an undergraduate college American History course. 'And then American 'Yellow Journalism' accused Spanish saboteurs of rigging underwater explosives or a mine to the *Maine* and next the villains cunningly detonated it from land. William Randolph Hearst was probably responsible for starting the *Spanish American War* that made Teddy Roosevelt and his intrepid *Rough Riders* famous!'

"You must've survived the *Maine* sinking or else you couldn't be telling me all about the adventure?" Dr. Walker plausibly pointed-out to his unconscious subject. "What date are you presently speaking from? Do you think it's August 17th, 2005?"

"No Sir, it's August 17th but the year is 1898. I'll most certainly and most undeniably be dead on August 17, 2005! You must surely know that!"

Dr. Joseph Walker inhaled a deep breath and meditated for a moment. 'This is enough to make me take up formal religion!' the modern-day Diogenes very solemnly considered. 'I must not discuss the nature of this encounter with anyone or else my impeccable medical standing will be sullied if not completely tarnished. I feel as if I'm communicating with some sort of primitive demon here!'

On Monday morning September 19th Dr. Saunders asked Dr. Walker and Nurses Stevenson and Penn to meet with him at 9 a.m. in Room 254 to discuss "the disposition of Mariner X's case." During the "impromptu conference" Chief Surgeon Edward Saunders explained to his dedicated associates that he had asked a chemist friend to analyze a swath of material from the futuristic sailor's uniform and the results indicated that the fantastic fabric used in manufacturing the anonymous unconscious mariner's "distinguished-looking costume" consisted of several amazingly durable but unknown synthetic compounds.

"I've kept the remains of his garb we had cut-away on the gurney here in this plastic bag," Dr. Saunders informed the others on his *ER* team. "But now our elderly sailor friend must be transferred to another *St. Vincent's* facility on Staten Island for continued monitoring observation. He has no identification and no health insurance and the administrative brass has made the decision to move him from our custody by noon."

Mariner X suddenly began wriggling-around in his bed and Nurse Stevenson held his hand to soothe the patient's obvious emotional distress. Soon the agitated sailor began compellingly expressing himself. Eight ears keenly perceived his every word. First the valiant Old Salt claimed to be a crewmember on the *USS Hatteras* representing the North during the *Civil War* but the Confederate raider *Alabama* had destroyed the Union vessel near Galveston, Texas on January 11th, 1863. Before any of the four witnesses could interrogate Mariner X about how he could be alive and making the noteworthy statement (since he had already died a hundred and forty-two years in the past) the whiskered man started mumbling about significant naval engagements involving ships commanded by Commodore Perry in the *War of 1812* and by Commodore John Paul Jones in the *American Revolutionary War*. All four objective medical professionals stood flabbergasted around the hospital bed with their mouths agape and incredulously staring at one another all throughout Mariner X's incredible revelation. But despite her great apprehension the totally bewildered Nurse Stevenson still firmly held the old sailor's right hand.

Before any of the four observers could verbally interact with their "favorite patient" the assumed beating victim took a final deep breath and then expired. Within ten seconds *his* standard hospital gown wondrously advanced through a progression of inexplicable changes, first transforming into the futuristic naval uniform in which he had been brought to *St. Vincent's Hospital*. But then in a chronologically backwards sequence the dead sailor was soon wearing various naval apparel characteristic of the years 2045, 1963, 1941, 1912, 1898, 1863, 1812 and finally 1778. The four hospital professionals peered at their patient in absolute astonishment as his body glowed in the bed and then totally disintegrated into ashes as if Mariner X had just been cremated. Finally only a lump of dust remained in dumbfounded Nurse Stevenson's trembling right hand.

"My word! He was telling us the honest-to-God truth all along!" Dr. Edward Saunders exclaimed. "Mariner X's soul has finally journeyed to the afterlife where it rightfully belongs!"

"All of our superiors and associates in modern medicine will consider us quacks if we dare report this spiritual incident in a medical journal article or dare share it with the police!" ever cynical Dr. Joseph

Walker warned his equally confounded comrades. "We mustn't communicate these spectacular details to anyone, especially the press or else we risk ridicule and condemnation!"

"It was amazing how his uniforms all regressed in a reverse chronological pattern in the exact sequence that he had so thoroughly described and uttered," the still-dismayed Dr. Saunders articulated. "But I only recognized the first original uniform with the futuristic-looking fabric, the uniform he had worn on the *Titanic* and the uniforms Mariner X had claimed to presumably wear on the *USS Hatteras* as well as the ones that were emblematic of the *War of 1812* and the prior sixteenth century *Revolutionary War!"* The second uniform we had glimpsed, I presume, was worn in 2045, on the yet-to-be-constructed *Edgar Allan Poe,* in the unconscious fellow's beyond-belief, reverse historical pattern. I caution you all that this Room 254 supernatural experience has indeed been an unbelievable occurrence of major magnitude."

And then, the radical uniform transformations made more sense when Nurse Miriam Stevenson broke her silence and mentioned Mariner X's claim to be on the *USS Thresher* in 1963 at the time of the submarine's demise. And next Nurse Kristen Penn confessed about the ancient sailor's presence aboard the *USS Arizona* and later as a crewmember serving his country on the *WWII USS Battleship New Jersey*. And finally, the normally skeptical and laconic Dr. Joseph Walker revealed about Mariner X serving his nation aboard the *Maine* peacefully anchored in 1898 in Havana Harbor.

"Mariner X finally died and disintegrated because in reality he had to be over two and a half centuries old!" Dr. Walker marveled and declared exhibiting a rare degree of emotion. "That's why he crumbled into dust right before our very eyes! I hate to admit it but the four of us have just shared a supernatural experience!"

"But Dr. Walker," the now grief-stricken Nurse Stevenson interrupted, "how could this incomparable man have died before our eyes when he had already most certainly died aboard the *Thresher* in 1963 and most probably on the *Maine* in 1898? Could it be that we've just witnessed the culmination of multiple reincarnations?"

"Well, the time spans between each nautical tour of duty or sea assignment does make sense. Mariner X could've lived and died over and over again," Dr. Walker hypothesized and stated, "but now contrary to my good judgment I'm totally wandering-off into the realm of conjecture. The entire matter most definitely transcends medical knowledge, that's for sure! I've never been so bewildered in my entire life."

"There's always the possibility of the medieval belief of the Transmigration of Souls!" Dr. Saunders suggested. "That idea was also a popular belief in the late sixteenth and early seventeenth centuries. It sounds like paranormal science fiction but perhaps Mariner X's soul had wandered into another prospective sailor each time he died," The Chief Surgeon hypothesized and commented. "A cat has nine lives and apparently so did our enigmatic Mariner X. It's conceivable that our anonymous Mariner X really had many names and many ranks throughout nautical history. May his troubled and tormented soul now rest in peace."

"What should we do with his mortal remains?" a very disconsolate Nurse Penn asked. "I would think that his ashes should be given the honor that they so justly deserve!"

"I'm going to buy a large cemetery burial plot out on Long Island and over Mariner X's grave we'll have an inscription on his headstone reading, 'Tomb of the Unknown Mariner.' I believe that the simple tribute would be a most appropriate and fitting one!" Dr. Saunders suggested.

"I'll generously contribute to the memorial fund!" Dr. Joseph Walker acceded. "Mariner X has definitely changed my life for the better!"

"Me too!" Nurse Kristen Penn agreed. "I want to contribute all I can to the worthy project!"

"Me too!" Nurse Miriam Stevenson concurred as she stared in shock at the very distinct ashes now glowing in her right palm.

“The Disfavored Son”

Stephen Boyd Showell disgustedly drove his dark blue *Mercedes S-Class* west on the *Atlantic City Expressway*. A pelting November rain was showering large drops on Showell’s expensive automobile as his windshield wipers swept back and forth during the heavy downpour. The exceptionally inhospitable rainfall was relentlessly drenching the entire Philadelphia metropolitan area. Such fierce storms are not uncommon in northern-latitude American cities as Mother Nature makes her annual predictable transition from late autumn into early winter. Cities situated along the U.S. eastern seaboard are often deluged by a late fall “northeastern.”

‘Pretty soon, I’ll be leaving the *Expressway* and be on the *Route 42 Freeway*!’ Showell thought. ‘Then it’ll be over the *Walt Whitman Bridge* into Philly’ and next *I-95* south to the airport to pick-up my older brother Jason. Those dark gray ominous clouds indicate gloomy weather and torrential rains for the next few days. This lousy storm is almost like a tempest or a typhoon!’

Stephen Showell had been delegated by his mercurial father to meet Jason at *Philadelphia International Airport* and then transport him to the family’s splendid mansion situated on the *Egg Harbor River* in Mays Landing, New Jersey. The disfavored brother was not only coming home from western Maryland to celebrate the *Thanksgiving* holidays. His father “Iron Mike” Showell had recently suffered a severe heart attack and then a stroke in September and had been taken home from the hospital to continue his rehabilitation. The elder Showell had become a wealthy entrepreneur by being South Jersey’s premier oil distributor selling his product to casinos, businesses and residences anywhere from Atlantic City to Hammonton and from Cape May to Berlin.

Undaunted by the nasty inclement weather, Stephen Boyd Showell steered his *Mercedes* across the wind-swept *Walt Whitman Bridge* on his way to United Airlines Gate 13, Terminal C inside *Philadelphia International Airport*. ‘Only five more miles and I’ll be reunited with my despised sibling rival, and childhood nemesis!’ the driver thought as he glimpsed-up at the smirk on his face in the rearview mirror. ‘I still loathe Jason after all these years of separation. Thank goodness he made himself an outcast in father’s eyes. But in all due respect I have to admire Jason’s proven stubbornness. My older brother had unwisely left the security of family wealth to become an idealistic middle-class college professor out *at Frostburg State* in western Maryland. His maverick decision has, by default, left me the prime beneficiary of father's will,' Stephen gratefully reminded himself. 'My future with Showell Oil has power and opulence written all over it. Jason on the other hand has by choice authored his own mediocre destiny. That's exactly what happens when one selects love over money and consequently must live with adversity! I'm sure glad that I'm divorced and that Jason's not! That's another reason why father has deliberately favored me over him!'

Old Iron Mike Showell desired for bliss and tranquility to exist in his family as long as *he* held supreme authority. But when Jason had eloped to Elkton, Maryland to marry a gorgeous Sicilian girl the family patriarch could not forgive his eldest son's indiscretion. Iron Mike had wanted Jason to wed a local hand-picked "English Episcopalian girl of decent descent" to not only propagate the oil dynasty but also the family's British-origin genes along with Iron Mike's inflexible *WASP* values. Obstinate Jason Showell had intentionally violated his domineering father's expressed edict and as a result became the disenfranchised black sheep of the all-too-sanctimonious clan.

'Father's death is imminent!' Stephen presumed as his *Mercedes* passed south over the *I-95 Bridge* overlooking *the Philadelphia Naval Yard*. 'And then the bulk of the family fortune will be mine! An ace of diamonds is better than an ace of hearts any day in my book!' the driver avariciously evaluated. 'I'm sure glad that Dad rejected Jason and that there's been little fraternity between my brother and me over the last twenty years. I'm safe because the foolish idiot has made himself into a pariah. When Jason first spotted Maria Marino in the halls of Oakcrest High School Cupid's arrow instantly pierced his vulnerable heart,' Stephen recollected. 'Maria had everything that father deeply despised: Catholic faith, middle-class upbringing, an immigrant tailor for a father and a dark complexion. Maria Marino embodied all that my father considered repugnant in a prospective daughter-in-law, especially her ethnic origin and her swarthy Mediterranean Palermo skin!'

After Jason and Maria had "surreptitiously eloped" Old Iron Mike had indeed become alienated from his older son and the oil czar's mood swings vacillated like a pendulum between despondency and hostility. The elder Showell's rigid Puritan mores had been defied and violated by his "disobedient son." Jason was automatically shunned because of *his* "on purpose deviation" from his father's inflexible will. The *Frostburg State* college professor had only been invited back to New Jersey "out of courtesy" to spend *Thanksgiving* (without his wife) at the Showell mansion, because of Iron Mike's failing health. The surprise invitation to the family estate (lording over the *Egg Harbor River*) was only a polite gesture that had been extended and nothing more. Despite Jason's visit to Mays Landing Stephen Showell believed *he* was still a shoe-in to inherit his father's vast commercial empire. 'Jason's no longer my rival or my principal obstacle,' Stephen Showell concluded. 'He's now been reduced to a mere minor irritation!'

Stephen parked his luxury car on the fourth level of Terminal C's high-rise garage and then briskly proceeded walking down the long concourse to Gate 13 where ten minutes later he met his older brother. Their handshake was cordial but lacked genuine warmth and animation. It had been performed solely out of societal necessity.

"How was your flight?" Stephen asked without showing emotion. "Were there any complications? The weather's been quite hostile around here the last several days."

"A little turbulent between Baltimore and Philly' because of the abominable storm pattern that's been harassing the eastern seaboard," Jason answered. "And I should tell you that Maria's pregnant again and we're expecting our third child in September. You' oughta' break away from Mays Landing for a few days Steve and come out to Frostburg and see Billy and Johnny, after all they are your nephews. How's dad doin'?"

"Not too well!" Stephen Showell confided feigning a degree of sadness. "He's become more miserable and sarcastic than ever! Pop's developin' Parkinson's in addition to sufferin' the heart attack and the nasty stroke. He's partially paralyzed on the left side and now his right hand trembles with the accompanying nervous system disease. And the worst part of the dilemma is that Iron Mike's now confined to a wheelchair. You know Jason how active our father used to be."

"Too bad!" the older brother replied with an element of empathy. "I'm looking forward to seeing him. Dad really had a volatile temperament that most of the time was directed towards me. It must really be very frustrating for him to be so handicapped and immobile. It sounds as if he's virtually an invalid."

The incompatible pair ambled the lengthy C Concourse to the luggage retrieval area where they impatiently waited a full half-hour to obtain Jason's black suitcase from the rotating oval carousel. While externally exhibiting outward sincerity Stephen Showell's scheming mind contemplated that his older brother's eighty-thousand-dollar professor's salary was only one-tenth *his* mammoth annual income (when including generous wage and stock dividends, provided by *their* father's prosperous oil corporation).

"I hear the Jersey oil business is really thriving," Jason related for the sake of conversation. "Dad's enterprise must be at least three times as big as it was when I left South Jersey twenty years ago. Pop always was a shrewd operator."

"Try seven times as huge!" Jason proudly boasted. "Once we acquire Bruno Oil in Hammonton and Senn Oil in Egg Harbor we'll have a virtual monopoly on all petroleum products from the shore to Camden County. Jason, I think you made a colossal blunder by secretly marrying Maria against Pop's will and then fleeing out to western Maryland. Dad has always believed that you had made an enormous error in judgment and had betrayed his confidence. And as you're well aware," Stephen emphasized, "our father has an abundance of obstinacy when it comes down to certain family matters like the continuation of his Victorian values."

"Even when we were rascally kids," Jason said while finally reaching down for his black suitcase gliding along on the moving luggage conveyor, "either you or I have been on the ins or the outs with Pop. He always played you against me and me against you and as it turned-out, you're now the prodigal son with the extravagant expense account, and I'm the Ishmaelite. Steve, what are you driving nowadays?"

"A navy-blue *Mercedes S-Class!*" the favored son haughtily returned. "It's one of my many fringe benefits. It sure beats a *Buick Century* or a *Ford Focus*."

"That's one of your special rewards for sacrificing your independence and your soul to Dad's almighty will," the all-too-honest Jason Showell asserted. "Pop was able to manipulate you and indirectly punish me by giving you promotions and rewards and simultaneously ignoring my twenty-year self-exile existence out in Frostburg. I guess pretty soon it'll be your turn to operate the Showell Oil Company merry-go-round. It'll soon be your time to be in the limelight and calling the important shots!"

"You blew your big opportunity by runnin' off with Maria to Elkton," the younger pretentious brother reminded his former chief contender for the family fortune. "But right now our major concern should be our father's health, or should I say his lack thereof. Old Iron Mike's spirits are low and he has trouble enunciating words and finishin' sentences," Stephen mechanically communicated with little empathy. "Besides his perpetual slurring, Pop's right-hand quivers incessantly and he boisterously yells out occasional fits of rage. I'm afraid that Dad doesn't have too much sand remainin' in his earthly hourglass."

"I suppose I really ruffled Pop's feathers by hitchin' up with Maria," Jason Showell acknowledged and elaborated, "but I'm happy and we're still in love despite the past twenty years of me being separated from the family mainstream. And ever since Mom died ten years ago, Dad's heart has known plenty of loneliness and loss. I might not be *that* successful in a capitalistic sense," Jason speculated and stated with conviction, "but I do believe Steve that I've achieved plenty outside my struggling financial situation. My only regret is that Dad has insisted on withholding his blessing on my marriage. That's what's really disturbed and bothered me over the last two decades, but I want you to know that I feel little guilt about what I had done twenty years ago."

Stephen Showell shook his head in disbelief' as his brother's words echoed and resounded throughout *his* greedy head. The 'fortunate son' viewed his older brother as a certain fool, an incredibly lost fool drowning in his own folly, which *he* was now attempting to rationalize and justify. Jason had earned for himself a dismal teaching position in a wicked and reprehensible dog-eat-dog world. 'My brother's basic stupidity has doomed him to a future abounding with economic mediocrity and Jason has no one to blame for his pathetic predicament except himself,' Stephen determined. 'My frivolous brother's romance with Maria has made Father altogether eliminate Jason's birthright. My older brother has by his own actions cancelled himself right out of Father's last will and testament and I suspect that Jason's now coming home to see what he can connive from Iron Mike.'

On the forty-mile drive from *Philadelphia International Airport* to Mays Landing, Stephen Showell again overtly demonstrated friendliness while his front-seat passenger discussed in-depth his professorship at *Frostburg State*. But then, the driver had to articulate some additional braggadocio in his older brother's direction. "When Iron Mike finally kicks-off, I'll sell my tiny million-dollar-home on Hammonton Lake and move right into the opulent mansion on the *Egg Harbor River*. Then, the family yacht will be all mine and I can't wait to navigate that sleek baby down to Ocean City, Maryland, the *White Marlin Capital of the World*."

"It's hard to believe that this family conflict all started with me marrying Maria," the passenger advanced, while trying to make the dialogue more objective.

'You're absolutely right, Jason," Stephen facetiously stated. "Maria was and probably still is a beautiful woman. But as far as Pop's concerned you and he always quarreled about how to run the business. You wanted to expand operations between Hammonton and Berlin but Dad...."

"Wanted to keep everything centrally located in Mays Landing," Jason accurately recollected and answered. "But then Pop winds-up doing precisely what I had recommended three years after I had called it quits; got married and pulled-up stakes to start a new life out in western Maryland."

"But you should've never lost your temper and punched Pop in the mouth during that wild argument the last day you were associated with the company!" the mean-spirited driver reminded his older brother. "That's when you fell out of favor and were banned from paradise just like Adam had been evicted from *Eden* in *Genesis*. And Maria never had the opportunity nor the privilege to be Eve, either!"

"Well, Steve," Jason adamantly challenged, "the oil business was not the only game I could play. I humbly started-out selling textbooks until I earned my Master's Degree and then began my teaching career from the same institution where I had done my graduate studies. I'm not a multimillionaire like you are but what little I have I've earned on my own initiative. And needless to say Steve I enjoy teaching American Literature to my academically oriented students, I'm happily married and I'm quite content to report that I'm virtually at peace with myself and with the apathetic cruel world we live in."

The dark blue *Mercedes* angled off *Route 322* onto *Route 50*, passed by the lengthy brick-structured County Seat Courthouse in downtown Mays Landing, whizzed by the landmark Sugar Hill Restaurant situated on the scenic *Egg Harbor River* and two miles further down *County Road 559* the driver turned right onto Clarktown Road just as the persistent rain stopped and a shaft of sunshine penetrated through the thick dark clouds. Jason Showell perceived the momentary sunshine as 'a good omen.' At the end of the winding road were high mounds decorated with fresh-seeded grass, stately evergreen shrubs and attractive floral arrangements, all the aforementioned landscaping effectively concealing the Showell mansion from public scrutiny. Stephen drove the dark blue *Mercedes* around the gray semi-circle, paver driveway, and stopped under the structure's impressive Greek columned front pavilion. The disfavored son felt exceptionally uneasy and distressed upon returning to his boyhood home.

"Grab your suitcase out of the backseat and go in and talk with Pop!" Stephen directed. "We just started-up a new heating and air conditioning division serving the Vineland, Bridgeton, Millville triangle and I'm scheduled to have a meeting with the managers in a half hour. If it's a bit chilly inside start-up the gas jets in the living room's fireplace. I'll return after the new distributors meeting and then we can reminisce old times."

"Any servants or relatives meandering around inside the castle?" Jason innocently asked.

"No, Iron Mike wants to speak with you in private without any busybodies around eavesdroppin' on your conversation! That's always been Pop's style and habit."

Jason latched onto his black suitcase, thanked his brother for the ride, closed the luxury automobile's back door and then entered the family palace through magnificent varnished solid cherry wood doors. As the visitor passed from the main entrance's pink marble floor foyer into the kitchen area the invited guest could see Old Iron Mike directly ahead sitting in a wheelchair while gazing out glass sliding-doors facing the picture postcard *Egg Harbor River*. On the ledge of the kitchen hutch the estranged Showell spotted a copy of Iron Mike's Will and upon initial examination was not-too-thrilled with its stipulations. The new arrival lifted the document from the ledge up to his eyes and the third paragraph read: "To my son Stephen Showell I leave the entire oil business, the Mays Landing mansion, my yacht and my *Merrill Lynch* and all other bank accounts, a total value of twenty-three million dollars." Paragraph four stated: "To my son Jason Showell I leave ten thousand dollars payable by check upon the probating of this will."

Jason then fully fathomed Iron Mike's animosity for *him,* marrying an Italian girl whose good-hearted father was a mere tailor. The disenfranchised son felt that he had been shunned, betrayed, overlooked and disinherited. The self-ostracized *Frostburg State* professor now fully realized that he was being punished for falling in love with what his stubborn father regarded as "the wrong woman." Jason Showell felt anger surging in his heart, an exasperation that was comparable to the intense rage he had experienced when he had punched Iron Mike in the face twenty years before. The perturbed professor angrily folded-up the will and roughly placed it inside a front pocket of his blue suit jacket. Trying to contain his jealousy at being "financially reprimanded," Jason turned the knob that opened the valve to the fireplace's gas-log insert. Then he intently peered at his notoriously cantankerous but ailing father, who had heard the gas jet flare-up, rotated his wheelchair and then slowly moved himself in the direction of his aberrant son.

"Welcome home, Jason!" Iron Mike said in a raspy gruff tone of voice. "I suppose you've come back to Mays Landing to see me one last time before I die! Now that's a rather discomforting statement to begin a strained conversation with, isn't it?"

"Let's quit all of the small-talk!" hollered back the normally placid and complaisant but now indignant son. "Mussolini and Hitler were saints compared to you! Just look at all the phony plaques gracing your paneled wall. Each one has a message that's contrary to your repulsive demeanor! I thought that we could reconcile now that Mom's dead, but evidently I was wrong! You're still a pathetic miserable ruthless dictator!"

"What on Earth are you ranting and carping about?" old man Showell defensively criticized. "You're making absolutely no sense whatsoever. What's your meaningless tirade all about? Can't you see that you're welcome here?"

"You know as well as I do!" Jason vehemently shouted back while still (out-of-anger) abandoning his usually benign disposition. "The New Jersey Chamber of Commerce Honors Michael Showell! The South Jersey Oil Distributors Recognize 'Iron Mike' Showell's Contributions! These awards are all fabrications," Jason uneloquently alleged. "You know as well as I do that your disgusting personality is the complete opposite of what these nice platitudes fraudulently say about you! Pop, you make Lucifer look like chopped liver!"

"Why are you' so angry at me?" Iron Mike nervously questioned. "If you had not married that Italian girl, you would still be living here in Mays Landing and enjoying all of the material comforts that Stephen's been appreciating! Son, you've brought your family dilemma on all by yourself!"

"Let's get down to the crux of the matter!" Jason vociferously yelled back. "I just accidentally saw a copy of your will on the kitchen hutch. It explicitly stated that...."

Iron Mike immediately interrupted his enraged son, claiming that Jason had always been "a rebel" and "a maverick" and that *he* constantly defied his father's intentions and discipline. "And now I was going to tell you son about a radical change of heart I've had, but as usual you've rashly ruined everything for yourself by being too damned obstinate and too damned impetuous! Once a fool, always a damned fool!"

"What insanity are you talking about?" Jason stammered. "Stop the damned riddles and speak plain and simple language. Don't forget that you're speaking with a highly educated English professor!"

"Jason, I'm going to tell you' some' things that not even Stephen knows," Iron Mike intimated with sadness in his voice. "From doctors' opinions Francine and I believed that we could never have any children so we went to an adoption agency and that's how you had entered the Showell family. You're not officially my biological son Jason Emerson Showell! But your mother made me promise not to ever reveal that essential secret to you, but now that she's deceased," the elder Showell explained, "I now feel that my pledge to her can be broken."

The appalled adopted son felt his knees buckle from the shock of hearing his father's unexpected announcement. "If you had married Virginia Littlefield as your mother and I had wished," Iron Mike slowly uttered, "then you would not have violated my intentions and would've remained in my good graces."

Jason could not control his temper any further. His wrath was about to powerfully explode like the crater inside *Mt. Etna*. "You rotten old snake, your will on the kitchen hutch stipulated that I would be given a token ten thousand dollars while your favored son Stephen will receive close to twenty-five million dollars in assets. That's just not fair under any circumstances!" Jason blustered. "You've always been biased towards Stephen and have meanly discriminated against me! That's totally unacceptable from my point of view! You're nothing more than a dictating pernicious old man! Your arbitrary twenty-year rejection of me has been an agonizing curse whether I'm your adopted son or your biological one!"

"You've been suspicious and presumptuous right up to the end!" Iron Mike sarcastically accused. "Here's the whole honest-to-God truth Jason. When I was young and foolish I had had an affair with an Italian waitress who worked at the Midway Diner over in Hammonton. She had gotten pregnant and I knew that having an Italian wife and a dark-skinned child would've been socially disastrous for my highly respected family name," Iron Mike informed his wayward black sheep. "Marrying a Sicilian woman would've been a gigantic scandal among the sophisticated local aristocrats of British descent. And so, after you were born, I arranged through several political bribes to get you back from the adoption agency that your biological mother, Carmella DeStefano, had agreed to place you in, for a mere five-thousand-dollar payoff!" Iron Mike divulged with his right arm trembling. "And that's precisely how you became a well-to-do Showell! And then you have the unmitigated audacity to go out and commit the same stupid mistake that I had done but instead of erasing the problem you obnoxiously proliferated it by getting married and then having mongrel children." "But the bottom line is that you still have basically disinherited me?" Jason protested with gesticulating arms. "Your will that was on the hutch attests that Stephen will receive all of your assets minus a measly ten-thousand-dollars allotted for me!"

"But don't you understand, you intentionally defied my will!" Iron Mike maintained. "That explains my absolute scorn for you!"

"I ought to report you to the *Civil Rights Commission* for an immediate investigation concerning ethnic discrimination!" Jason defiantly balked to his highly prejudiced father. "I'm now really glad that Maria and I had eloped to Elkton! You're nothing more than a petty WASP despot masquerading as a despicable father!"

Iron Mike could not tolerate any more of his adopted/biological son's insolence. The wealthy oil mogul nervously removed from his sweater a second will that he claimed overruled all items listed in the "obsolete will" that had been accidentally left (and discovered) on the kitchen hutch. "This document in my hand now is meaningless, because it's the only copy of the original will I have," Iron Mike bellowed as the invalid recklessly scooted his wheelchair over to the roaring fire, flaring-out from the gas log insert. And then, with an absence of ceremony the vindictive old man tossed the new revised will into the flames. "I had altered the will that you had indiscreetly examined in the kitchen and I decided to give you half of my estate, but as you can plainly comprehend I've now changed my mind. As far as I'm concerned Jason, the original will is still in effect."

"You dirty black-hearted inconsiderate evil man!" Jason Showell bellowed like a possessed maniac. "Now I know why you always looked at me with a jaundiced eye! I hope you burn and rot in hell for all eternity, you insensitive maniacal tyrant! You have the compassion of a dirty foul-smelling cockroach! I have more respect for Satan's armpit than I do for your lousy judgment!"

As Jason's diatribe reached its culmination, Iron Mike Showell gripped his heart, gave out an exclamation of pain and then slumped down in his wheelchair, dead as a doornail. His antagonist incredulously observed what had transpired and upon realizing exactly what had occurred Jason shuddered and began weeping. The front door of the prodigious mansion then opened, and seconds later, Stephen Showell stepped into the regally furnished living room.

"What happened to Pop?" the stunned newcomer on the scene asked. "Did he fall asleep? Why is his mouth wide open along with his eyes?"

"We had a mammoth argument and then Pop collapsed in his wheelchair Stephen! He's now on his way to the afterlife! His black soul has reluctantly departed his body!"

"What's that I see burning in the fireplace?" Stephen noticed and inquired. "I can only read the top. It says 'Last Will and Testament'."

"That's Dad's latest will! He tossed it into the fireplace while we were having our heated disagreement. Now that document is gone forever."

"What!" Stephen Showell lividly screamed before bolting to Iron Mike's mahogany desk and opening the top drawer. The incensed brother removed a pistol and pointed it at Jason. "If you want to live, you'd better level with me and lay all your cards on the table right this minute."

"Well, Steve," Jason responded in a confused and stuttering voice, "Dad told me that he had revised his will and that I was included and entitled to half the family assets!"

"That's the will burning in the fireplace, isn't it?" Stephen Showell demanded. "Tell me the truth! That's half my inheritance going up in smoke right this second. Is that the only copy?"

"Well yes," Jason hysterically answered without fully interpreting and comprehending his chief rival's statement. The older brother was completely rattled with the prospect of death staring him in the face. "But let me explain Steve! When I came into the mansion I noticed that...."

"You've said all I need to hear!" Stephen Showell antagonistically yelled. "Now it's time for you to join Pop in the afterlife! Hope you're on good terms with Jesus!" Bang, bang, bang.

'Now I'll just wipe my fingerprints off of the handgun with a handkerchief, and gently place it in Dad's good hand and press his fingertips around the trigger,' Stephen Showell cunningly imagined. 'If Jason couldn't have a profitable shotgun wedding then at least he can now have a decent handgun funeral! Ha, ha, ha!' the crazed man uttered to his two dead relatives. 'It's a good thing that I wield some influence around this town! All I have to do is phone the Mays Landing Police and alert them as to what I've shockingly discovered upon my return to the mansion. No way Jason was going to get half of Pop's fortune! Rest in peace, both you dirty bastards! What's this folded paper tucked inside Jason's blue suit jacket pocket?'

"Double Trouble"

Little honor exists between ignominious human beings and this story confirms that very valid social/ethical axiom. Charles Carlucci nervously fidgeted with his wristwatch during another boring Hammonton Lions Club meeting. The apathetic service club member hastily had eaten his delectable veal parmagiana meal, drank down two glasses of merlot wine, paid a dollar fine to the Tail-Twister (for forgetting to wear his membership badge) and was remotely listening to the litany of fundraising reports. The club's pie and muffin concession stand at the July 2nd blueberry festival had netted three-thousand-dollars profit, the gold raffle dinner had earned twelve-thousand-dollars, and the '50s dance committee chairman was now giving his glib presentation on the upcoming event.

After the lengthy civic club meeting, Charles Carlucci deliberately stayed another half hour conversing with the club's President and with the guest speaker for the evening, the distinguished Governor of New Jersey Lions Club District 16-C. 'By now Hank Cardone has murdered my wife!' Carlucci was thinking as the Governor was commenting on how inspiring and dynamic (and what a model organization) the Hammonton Club was when compared to less active and smaller clubs in District 16-C. 'Yes, by now Sandra is dead. All I have to do is pay that scoundrel Cardone $25,000.00 and then after the funeral collect on my wife's hefty $500,000.00 insurance policy. And I have a great alibi being here at the Lions Club dinner until 9:30 p.m. It sure pays to have out-of-state Mafia connections!' the conniving husband concluded. 'My wife has betrayed me a final time!'

Charles and Sandra Carlucci had been sweethearts at Hammonton High School, and both had graduated in 1960. After Charles attended *Rutgers University* in New Brunswick and Sandra graduated from *Glassboro State College*, the couple tied the marital knot. Then the ambitious husband became a local new car salesman at a Hammonton *GM* dealership and the wife an elementary school teacher in nearby Folsom. Everything went alright, with a son Daniel being born in 1965 and then twenty years quickly passed, but after the Carlucci's only child left the nest for higher education at *Boston University*, Sandra and Charles' relationship drastically changed. Each accused the other of "cheating" and at least three prolonged arguments developed every week with one spouse accusing the other of infidelity. The couple's happiness bubble had completely burst and hatred now dominated their rapidly eroding marriage, Things were getting ugly in a hurry, with the couple's relationship's accelerated deterioration.

'I'll hang around another ten minutes and pay the treasurer my back dues that I owe,' Charles decided. 'I don't want to barge in on a brutal murder-in-progress. I'll wait until Hank Cardone finishes the job without any complications or interruptions. Then I'll pay him the 25 Gs I have stashed in a suitcase in my car's trunk, wait a half hour for my hired gunman to get out of town and then phone the Hammonton cops about my gruesome discovery. By the time the police cordon off the house with their crime scene tape Hank will be going across the *Delaware Memorial Bridge* into Wilmington,' the lazy problem-solving Lion fantasized. 'I'm sure glad I had contacted the Delaware Mafia and not the Philly' mob'. The cops will never be able to trace Cardone because he told me his next contract obligation is out west in Palm Springs.'

Upon steering his aqua *Buick LeSabre* into his Oak Road asphalt driveway Charles Carlucci observed a late model black *Cadillac* parked beside his backyard garage. 'That's Cardone's vehicle,' Charles determined. Carlucci exited the *Buick*, removed the black suitcase from his trunk, and after slamming the auto's door shut the new car salesman rushed across the back lawn and excitedly climbed up the concrete steps leading to the kitchen. Hank Cardone was waiting for his "employer" with his .38 caliber handgun gripped in his right palm.

"I guess you've done the job!" Charles awkwardly began the conversation. "Yes, I can see my wife lying there in the living room. You do mighty good work Hank. You're efficient and professional, no doubt about it."

"Two slugs in the head finished her off!" Cardone bragged. "It's a good thing ya' live far away from any neighbors. No one was around at precisely 9:15 when the rubout took place, not even any random traffic passing by. Sorry I got some blood on your expensive Oriental rug Charlie."

"That's perfectly okay, Hank. But now you're goin' to have to get out of Hammonton fast, so that I can report the crime to the cops. Soon I'll be callin' the Hammonton dispatcher by dialin' *911*. And Hank, please don't peel out of the driveway and leave any skid marks. And I'm glad to see that you're still wearin' your plastic gloves! Ya' never know about evidence, fingerprints, *DNA* and the like."

"Ya' got the cash?" Cardone anxiously asked. "I hope ya' didn't withdraw it all at one time from a stock brokerage or bank account!

The more-savvy State Police investigators will look into that type of thing right away."

"No, Hank. I've been secretly savin' this money and keepin' it from my wife's scrutiny for three years now," Charles replied without showing any remorse for his spouse's horrible fate. "Here's all twenty-five-thousand clams in this black suitcase. Thanks for your very reliable services."

"Well now, Charles, thanks for the loot," Hank Cardone facetiously answered as he opened the suitcase and inspected and admired his remuneration. "Believe me Charlie I've earned every penny of it. But before I leave your stellar company, I have something important involvin' arithmetic to say to you. One-half only equals one-third."

"What kind of illogical math' is that?" Charles questioned. "Your arithmetic doesn't make any sense at all! One-half can't possibly equal one-third!"

"I guess that's a weird fraction puzzle you'll never understand!" Hank Cardone chuckled with an evil frown suddenly appearing upon his countenance. "Now it's time to officially join your wife in the afterlife. I'm not a cheap everyday run-of-the-mill thug, ya' know. You shouldn't be so frugal when dealin' with a professional murderer! You oughta' know better than that Charles!"

"But, but! What's the meaning of all this?" Charles pleaded almost crying as he frightfully and then hysterically stared down the barrel of the .38 caliber gun. "A deal's a deal! Why are you doin' this atrocious thing to me?"

"There ain't no guaranteed ethics when it comes-down to basic crime and money!" Hank Cardone countered, his frown gradually converting into a smirk. "Now it's your time Charlie to meet the legendary Grim Reaper! Just remember in your final thought that one half equals only one third! But I assure you ya' won't be able to figure the math' problem out before your butt hits the floor!"

The hired hit-man aimed his weapon at his most recent acquaintance's forehead and then without showing any pity or compassion pulled the trigger twice. Charles Carlucci's body fell to the tan square-tiled kitchen floor. Since no phone call to the local police would be forthcoming the ruthless murderer had more than sufficient time to escape the premises, drive back to Delaware and meet another client. Then two days later the very busy Hank Cardone planned to catch a jet from Baltimore out to sunny Southern California. The highly proficient criminal looked-down at his latest victim and smiled at his most recent conquest.

* * * * * * * * * * * * *

Before the cold-hearted hit-man departed the grisly-murder-scene, Hank Cardone made certain that he had pilfered Sandra Carlucci's pearl necklace, diamond earrings and other elegant jewelry from the woman's bedroom bureau. 'This way the local cops will think that robbery was the original motive and they'll be foolishly searching for clues locally while on the wrong trail. The fuzz will think the Carluccis' accidentally discovered a robber in their house and then had to face the consequences. That sort of confrontation happens all the time on *Action News*! Ha, ha, ha! This double homicide might someday be made into a *Hollywood* movie! I might even be called in as a consultant! Ha, ha, ha!'

The accomplished villain nonchalantly sneaked-out of the house with his cash bonanza, put the black suitcase into his *Cadillac's* trunk and after slamming it shut Cardone climbed into his classy getaway vehicle. Then the killer carefully removed his plastic gloves and stashed them under his seat. Fifteen minutes later Hank Cardone was motoring west on *Route 40* heading towards the *Delaware Memorial Bridge*. But his destination was not Wilmington. It was Smyrna, Delaware.

'There used to be a really neat place down a mile or so south of here in Penns Grove called Riverview Amusement Park,' Cardone remembered as his black *Cadillac* reached the summit of the landmark bridge connecting New Jersey and Delaware. 'I was thirteen years old when I won a subscription contest delivering newspapers for the *Philadelphia Bulletin* and my reward was a free boat trip down the *Delaware* to Riverview Park. How times have changed! The *Bulletin* went bankrupt thirty some years ago and Riverview Park is now defunct also. And I'm no longer a paperboy but I've advanced to doin' big-time criminal activity all over the *USA* from coast to coast!'

Then, the cunning murderer's mind exited its whimsical mood and seriously focused on the essential business at hand. 'When I finish crossing the bridge, I'll take *Route 40* south to *Route 13* just past the airport and then head east in the direction of Smyrna. There's a *McDonald's* I'll stop at and catch a bite to eat,' the syndicate's dangerous player decided. 'Then, I'll have just enough time to meet good old Danny Boy at midnight in the parking lot behind his Smyrna video store.'

Dan Carlucci was impatiently waiting in his dark blue *Honda Accord* for Hank Cardone to arrive at the designated rendezvous point behind his "Route 13 Movie Rental Store." When the black *Cadillac* halted the store's proprietor immediately exited *his* automobile with a satchel filled with hundred-dollar-bills, and next Dan Carlucci promptly entered Hank Cardone's vehicle.

"The Smyrna cops are on patrol tonight in this lazy hick town but at midnight they're usually at the diner getting coffee and doughnuts. So just to be safe Hank let's make the transaction fast and sweet," greedy Dan Carlucci suggested. "Did ya' pull the job off? Are they both dead? Did they both die instantly?"

"There sure are with two slugs into each of their heads," the heartless mercenary hit-man replied. "Your Mother was an easy target. She thought that I was your Pop returnin' home from his lousy Lions Club meeting. When she turned the corner from the hall into the living room I shot her twice at point-blank-range," the killer admitted without regret or conscience. "I gotta' confess it was a little messy and bloody. By the way Danny Boy, here's your old key I used to get in the back kitchen door. The baby still works like a charm so I didn't have to use Plan B and break into the house. Either way I'm glad that Oak Road is so desolate. I got a little tense when I heard myself breathin', before the back door lock clicked."

"Great!" Danny Carlucci jubilantly exclaimed. "My alibi is intact. Ironically, I had attended the Smyrna Lions Club's boring meeting and hung around the restaurant bar with several members until around 10 p.m. As you know Hank the video rental business is on a nation-wide decline with cable television havin' 'On Demand' movies so this cache of cash is really hard-earned money I'm offerin' you in this bag."

"I suppose tomorrow you'll get an urgent phone call from the minor league Hammonton cops about the Oak Road twin killings and then you'll have to leave Delaware and arrange two funerals after the coroner's office staff performs routine autopsies," the hired assassin speculated and stated. "Be sure Danny Boy to look shocked and melancholy when the cops get around to interviewin' you. Sorry that I'll be settin' up shop out west and I won't be able to make the dual viewings at…."

"Marinella's Funeral Home on North Third Street!" Dan Carlucci matter-of-factly finished his hired gun's sentence. "That's the best mortuary in Hammonton. But I fully understand that you'll be out in California workin' on your next important assignment. Here's the dough we had agreed on, fifty thousand cash-on-delivery and it's all in hundred and in fifty-dollar-bills. It's half my life's savings I've kept stashed away from the *IRS* in my cellar. I'll tell ya', Hank, if I didn't skim profits off the top, then Uncle Sam would definitely own my soul, considering all my detrimental gamblin' habits!"

"Thanks a lot, Danny Boy!" Hank Cardone callously remarked. "It' better all be stored in here or else I'll come back from my ritzy motel suite and hunt ya' down and shoot ya' in cold blood just like ya' see on TV. It's been a pleasure doin' business with ya'. I guess you'll have to wait a few months before receivin' your expected compensation."

"Correct, Hank!" Dan Carlucci concurred. "I figure my end will come to over a million bucks includin' the house that has no mortgage, their bank accounts, stocks, bonds and their hefty insurance policies plus the three building lots in Florida and the one in the *Poconos*. I've thoroughly read their wills and each one would inherit the other's assets, but if both of them die accidentally or otherwise...."

"Then, you bein' the only child are the chief beneficiary!" Cardone concluded and verified from past experience with other "clients." "Thanks for the fifty thousand Danny Boy'! And just to think that your old man introduced you to me at a family picnic when you were still a young buck attendin' Hammonton High. Just like I told your old man Danny Boy, right before I pulled the trigger, 'one third equals one half'!"

"What kind of strange math' riddle is that?" Dan Carlucci asked the wanton criminal. "How can one third equal one half? I'm no Einstein but that equation's absolutely irrational!"

"I'll make the explanation good and brief," the unscrupulous hit man indicated. "Your Pop had paid me $25,000.00 to eliminate your Mom, which I did. I had previously asked him for $50,000.00 to do the job but your father was obstinate and refused to agree to the higher amount. Let me tell ya', Danny Boy; it doesn't pay to be a frugal cheapskate in this business or you're askin' for trouble, but in your father's case double trouble!"

"It still doesn't make any sense with the two fractions you've mentioned," Dan Carlucci deducted and related. "One-third can't be the same as one-half, no way!"

"Ha, ha, ha!" the remorseless hit man indulgently laughed. "The way I figure it usin' my limited high school education your Old Man gave me twenty-five thousand for eradicatin' your mom and then you upped the ante and have paid me an additional fifty thousand to shoot and kill your Old Man. The sum of the payoffs comes to seventy-five thousand smackers. Your Pop had paid one-third of the seventy-five thousand, and you paid twice as much to have him rubbed-out."

"I get it!" Dan Carlucci exclaimed in amazement. "Pop's twenty-five thousand was one-third of your seventy-five thousand total fee and my fifty thousand was twice what my dead old man was willin' to pay so in effect Pop paid you half of what I did to have someone killed. But I don't think that your creative math' would work on any Algebra teacher's arithmetic test. Your final answer is just too bizarre and incorrect!"

The two men shook hands to consummate the settlement and then Daniel Matthew Carlucci departed the expensive black *Cadillac* and merrily re-entered his mediocre-looking dark blue *Honda Accord.* Daniel then realized that liars, thieves, connivers and murderers could only be trusted as cash recipients if the client happens to be the highest bidder in a deleterious Mafia-style auction. 'If Pop had raised his offer to seventy-five grand,' Dan Carlucci hypothesized, 'then he and Mom would be makin' arrangements to attend my funeral. Ya' just gotta' be both careful and lucky when sealing deals with unscrupulous and treacherous Mafia hit-men!'

"The Bed"

Arthur Kondrach drove his white *Chevy Malibu* south on New Jersey *Route 206* past Indian Mills heading towards Hammonton. 'I'm entering the *Wharton State Forest*. Pretty soon I'll be stopping at the Pic-A-Lilli Inn,' Arthur fondly considered. 'They have really terrific Buffalo hot wings and pork spare ribs. I can't wait to devour some of both those edibles along with a mug or two of cold beer. I'll just pretend I'm a regular patron and ignore all the pineys and deer hunters that hang out there.'

The wholesale goods traveling salesman parked his car in front of the famous Pine Barrens eatery and a pretty auburn-haired hostess escorted him to a small table. Arthur ordered his preferences without even looking at the menu. 'Selling merchandise to gift shops is really getting more difficult each year,' the on-the-road salesman thought. 'A lot of merchants are buying their wares and items online by computer nowadays. I guess I'm part of a dying breed and in ten years my species will probably be obsolete. I made reservations to stay five nights at the *Route 30* Hammonton Ramada Inn. Glad I brought along my trusty credit cards. Then I could easily commute back and forth to the motel and visit my Atlantic City, Ocean City, Egg Harbor, Absecon and Hammonton clients all in one trip!'

The jewelry and novelty salesman consumed his' very delicious meal, paid his modest tab and left a satisfactory four-dollar tip to the amiable accommodating waitress. Soon Arthur was inside his *Malibu* zipping by scenic Atsion Lake. 'Only seven more miles to downtown Hammonton,' Kondrach contemplated. 'I'll just relax in my motel room tonight and get to Atlantic City tomorrow. I've been doing this exact same routine for the past twenty-two years now and always in early April. I really think the monotony of it all is getting to me.'

The hundred-and-twenty-five-mile-ride from upstate Morristown to Hammonton usually took two and a half hours, including necessary time for Arthur Kondrach's traditional Pic-A-Lilli Inn annual pilgrimage. 'West Central New Jersey is more of a hilly *Piedmont* region compared to the South Jersey pinelands, but everything seems a little too flat around Hammonton and vicinity. I suppose that's the big difference between certain western parts of North Jersey and the *Atlantic Coastal Plain,'* Arthur assessed. 'Oh well, here's the *206* and *Route 30* intersection. Only a mile east, and I'll finally have arrived at the *Ramada*. I can't wait to get some much-needed shuteye. I hope I get a comfortable bed.'

Arthur checked into the motel at the main desk and then carried his large suitcase and two freshly dry-cleaned blue business suits to Room #13. 'I'm not generally too superstitious so this #13 foolishness doesn't bother me at all,' Arthur determined. 'Who knows? It might really be a lucky omen! It's only another number, that's all!'

The fatigued guest locked his room's door, unpacked his suitcase and then exited his quarters to obtain a bucket of ice from a vending machine. After returning from his self-appointed errand the traveling salesman unscrewed the cap to an extra-large bottle of *Southern Comfort*, poured himself' a double on the rocks and slowly imbibed his favorite whiskey. 'This should make me mellow enough to doze-off without feeling any stress or arthritis,' Kondrach convinced himself. 'Now it's time to lie-down and pay a much-needed visit to Mr. Sandman.'

That Monday evening, Arthur enjoyed a sumptuous steak dinner at Hammonton's popular Silver Coin Diner, returned to his motel room, took a hot shower, poured himself another potent whiskey double and watched television for two hours in his bathrobe. 'This room has a king-size bed with two side-by-side mattresses. That's a little peculiar!' Arthur evaluated. 'Ordinarily, I get a nice queen-size bed with one mattress. Oh well, what's the use of complaining? I'll just sleep on the left side mattress that's closer to the TV. When a man's as tired as I am right now all he wants is a decent bed, clean sheets, a nice bedspread and a soft pillow.'

Tuesday morning inside the *Ramada's* "Continental Breakfast Room", Arthur Kondrach recognized the desk manager filling a tray of bagels and asked him a salient question. "I'm in Room #13 and there's a very comfortable king-size bed in there with two separate box springs and matching mattresses. Is there any particular reason for *that* nice surprise?"

"That two-section bed used to be an automatic electric bed with the two sides going up and down independently," the mustached employee suavely answered. "That quality bed used to be in the Honeymoon Suite but then two of the electric motors went bad so we temporarily moved the item into Room 13 while waiting for the new motors to come in. If you'd like Sir, I can conveniently move you into another room with a queen-size bed for your' second evening here."

"No, thanks," Arthur bashfully replied with a smile. "I had an excellent night's sleep in that wonderful bed you just described and woke-up this morning with plenty of pep. I was just curious why that unique bed was in my room and now you've given me a satisfactory reason."

"Well, Sir, confidentially between you and me just two days ago we had replaced the original box spring and mattress on the right side along with the old motor," the manager confided. "And in a few days, the second motor should be arriving and then we'll replace the left side components as well. What side did you sleep on last night if I may ask?"

"The left side because it was closer to the television," Kondrach indicated, before biting into a delicious double chocolate doughnut. "And I gotta' tell you it was very comfortable and cozy. I had a great night's rest and feel quite robust this mornin'."

"Okay, Sir, but if you change your mind and request another room, I won't question your judgment."

"I'm perfectly content situated right where I am," Arthur articulated to the very amiable day manager. "But thanks for the information about the two-mattress bed. What seemed a puzzle now has a very plausible explanation."

The merchandise hawker had a most rewarding Tuesday in Atlantic City. Arthur received large orders from twelve of his boardwalk novelty shop stores and being conscientious had acquired three new accounts in *Bally's Casino*, in the *Trump Taj Mahal* and also in the opulent *Borgata*. 'I'll try my hand at blackjack here in the Marina District before I drive back to the *Hammonton Ramada*,' Arthur reasoned. 'I've already been to *Harrah's* and to the *Trump Marina* so I guess I'll stay right where I am and try the brand-new *Borgata*. This place is magnificent, and quite comparable to the *Mirage* out in Vegas! I might as well do some casual gambling right here and now just to see if my recent Atlantic City good luck skein is for real.'

Much to Arthur Kondrach's elation, that night he won three-hundred-and-fifty-dollars playing blackjack, two-hundred-and-fifty at the roulette table, and next hit a five-hundred-dollar jackpot on a very cooperative quarter slot machine. 'Wow! Eleven-hundred-bucks profit! I oughta' quit while I'm ahead!' the euphoric fellow decided. 'But I'll definitely return tomorrow night and see if I can duplicate my thrilling feat!'

Tuesday night, the lucky winner was tempted to sleep on the new right-hand-side mattress and box spring but because of his marvelous good fortune in Atlantic City Arthur was overwhelmed by superstition and feared he might jinx his 'winning pattern' by sleeping on and 'waking up on the wrong side of the bed.' So, the itinerant salesman

Nursed-down a *Southern Comfort* double and then gradually nodded off into Dreamland.

"Mr. Kondrach," the *Ramada Inn's* day-manager greeted the fortunate winner in the complimentary "Continental Breakfast Room" the following morning. "The second motor came in yesterday for the left-hand side of the bed. Should our maintenance crew change it today? It'll only take an hour or so, while you're away conducting your business."

"No," Arthur bluntly replied. "Today, I'm going back to Atlantic City where yesterday I was wearing-out my shoe leather hustlin' along the boardwalk. And I had a phenomenal day finding some new merchant accounts. I would prefer if you hold off on switching motors, box spring and mattress on the left hand side. Now confidentially I've become accustomed to the bed and quite frankly I'm rather attached to it just as it is."

"I understand perfectly, Sir!" the day manager pleasantly agreed. "You feel lucky and don't want to change anything right now. Have a good day in Atlantic City!"

On Wednesday morning, Arthur again experienced terrific luck on the world-famous boardwalk and managed to acquire six new accounts while selling over fifty-thousand-dollars-worth of jewelry and novelties to seven "loyal old accounts." Naturally the compulsion to gamble dominated the salesman's mind so instead of honoring his urge to try his luck at the *Atlantic City Showboat Casino* the anxious man drove again to the elegant regal-interior *Borgata.*

Consistent with his fabulous good luck winning' streak, Arthur accumulated earnings of twelve hundred dollars in almost an exact replication of his previous night's activities. The man was animated listening to the *Malibu's* radio and felt exceptionally exuberant driving his white automobile from the Atlantic City Marina District thirty miles east on *Route 30* to the *Hammonton Ramada*. 'Tonight I'm going to sleep on the left side again,' the merry reveler thought. 'I'll have to hit the *Southern Comfort* bottle again to celebrate my most recent fabulous success. Who needs Las Vegas or Reno when Atlantic City is within driving distance from Morristown?'

Wednesday night, Arthur again rejoiced in his good fortune and for good measure downed two doubles of *Southern Comfort* on the rocks from his large 1.75-liter bottle. 'Tonight, I'm going to try an experiment and sleep on the right-hand side of the bed,' Kondrach boldly decided. 'I just want to see what transpires or if there's going to be any different results in tomorrow's escapades. This business about right-handed people being normal and skilled and left-handed people being unlucky and distrustful is a lot of ridiculous medieval nonsense, nothing more than a foolish old-wives tale!' the half-inebriated man imagined.

Thursday morning, Arthur desired a standard bacon and eggs breakfast so he motored to the Silver Coin Diner and appeased his appetite and after three cups of hot coffee finally recovered from his mild hangover. After the rejuvenated salesman eventually arrived in Atlantic City an hour later he soon discovered that Lady Luck was already frowning on him. Three of his finest accounts were lost and so was six hundred dollars later that afternoon at the marble-floored plush-rugged *Borgata*. 'I gotta' go back to the old system and sleep on the left side of the bed,' Arthur concluded with superstitious regret. 'I'm trying to establish a cause-effect relationship here. I wonder if my eating breakfast at the Silver Coin Diner instead of having the redundant continental high-carb' diet at the *Ramada* had anything to do with my radical reversal of luck?'

Thursday night, the bewildered salesman slept on the left side of the giant bed and on Friday morning sacrificed his better judgment and ate the regular *Ramada Inn* continental breakfast. Arthur swiftly departed the premises and serviced his three Hammonton accounts and his six in Ocean City and was by noon in a very optimistic spirit upon driving north up the *Garden State Parkway* en route to the *Borgata*. 'I actually feel that I've regained my good fortune and my confidence,' the tenacious fellow audaciously thought. 'The moment of truth has arrived.'

Incredibly, the rejuvenated casino whiz hit a thousand dollar Triple-Diamond Jackpot on a dollar slot and he was equally as formidable playing at the blackjack and roulette tables, which together yielded total winnings of an additional eleven hundred dollars. 'I'm gonna' make gambling my profession rather than my hobby,' the traveling sales representative mused. 'I'll just live the rest of my life in Room 13 at the *Hammonton Ramada Inn* and suffer through their rather dull and mediocre continental breakfasts. Once in a while I'll just have to swallow down some heavy-duty antacid tablets for lunch.'

On Friday morning, Arthur woke-up, showered, put on his favorite blue suit and decided to eat the all-too-familiar complimentary continental breakfast and then attend to his remaining three prominent accounts on Pacific Avenue in Atlantic City. All went quite propitiously for Arthur, and after again visiting the palace-like *Borgata,* the visitor's luck was phenomenal. ' King Arthur' proudly

Motored west in the direction of Hammonton, with four-thousand-three-from the hall machine hundred-dollars in new-found, well-deserved earnings.

'I'm gonna' get loaded and down the rest of the *Southern Comfort,'* Arthur fantasized as the dreamer drove east on *Route 30* through Egg Harbor City. 'I might be so drunk tomorrow that I'll not be able to see my Absecon and Egg Harbor City accounts. Who really cares?' the ecstatic driver concluded as he whimsically challenged conventional wisdom. 'Maybe it's the giant bottle of terrific whiskey that's lucky and not the bed or the high-carb' continental breakfast. Who knows what's causing this remarkable series of fortuitous events? Who really cares as long as it continues? Looks like I'm gonna' need lots of ice from the hall machine to attempt finishing this daunting whiskey task!'

* * * * * * * * * * * * *

On Saturday, Arthur Kondrach failed to check out of the *Hammonton Ramada* by noon, so the day manager entered Room #13 with a house-key and was shocked to find the occupant lying dead on the left side of the king-size bed. The motel employee immediately contacted the Hammonton Police, who showed-up five minutes later to initiate an investigation into the cause of death.

"The coroner will be here in half an hour," Sergeant Aiello told the distraught day manager. "That whiskey bottle on the bureau is empty. Maybe alcohol contributed to *his* death. Maybe drugs. That's why the coroner is goin' to perform an autopsy to determine exactly what happened to him. I don't have to tell you that the main part of the word 'intoxicated' is 'toxic'! That's pretty obvious!"

"Well, Sergeant, the *Ramada* doesn't want to have too much bad publicity about someone dying here," the extremely upset day manager stated. "Especially since this has been the second death here in two weeks."

"Yes, you're right," the Officer recalled and verified. "And if I remember correctly the first one occurred in this same room, #13. What a terrible coincidence! Talk about ominous bad luck! But as far as the press is concerned," the Sergeant paused and qualified, "I really can't do anything about it. Once a police report is filed at the station the newspapers automatically have access to it. And quite frankly, it's my duty to file a complete report. Expect to be hounded by lots of media, I guarantee it."

"I really liked Mr. Kondrach!" the very upset day manager confided to the policeman. "He absolutely loved the king-size bed in this room. But unfortunately, yesterday was my day off, so I didn't have the opportunity to converse with him."

"Drugs might also be involved in this human tragedy!" Sergeant Aiello speculated and declared. "Just look at all the cash he has stuffed inside his suitcase. This untimely death is getting more and more interesting by the second."

Meanwhile, outside the dead customer's room, two *Ramada Inn* maids were having a private conversation. The topic of their verbal exchange was the sudden passing of Arthur Kondrach, hard-working and affable traveling salesman.

"He seemed like such a nice happy-go-lucky man who was always courteous and cheerful!" Juanita said with tears in her eyes. "And the one time I had extensively talked with him he said he was fascinated by the big bed in Room 13."

"That's the second man to die in that room in two weeks," Margarita replied, "and to tell you the truth it gives me the creeps just thinking about it."

"He kept saying that the left side of the bed was lucky for him," Juanita revealed. "He promised me that he would leave me a big tip at the end of the week too, but he died before he could ever get around to doin' it."

"You were off from work yesterday, weren't you?" Margarita asked Juanita.

"Why yes!" Juanita answered. "I had to attend a friend's retirement party in Vineland. Why do you ask?"

"Well, so was the regular day manager off from work, too," Margarita disclosed. "The substitute manager noticed that the second motor, mattress, and box spring had arrived so he and two workers tampered with the bed, not that I'm so superstitious that I believe that that fact is so important."

"What action could the substitute manager have done?" Juanita curiously queried.

"Well, not that it really means anything important, but he removed the old left side mattress and box spring and had the two workmen bring them to the storage area to be later disposed of. Then he and the men moved the right-side box spring, mattress and accompanying motor over to the left side, and finally," Margarita continued almost out of breath from sheer excitement, "the substitute manager had a brand new motor, mattress and box spring put into the right-hand side of the king size bed. Since the new motorized two-sided bed is too hard to move to another room, from now on, Room 13 is goin' to be the new Honeymoon Suite. But to tell you the truth Juanita, don't think that the information I had just mentioned is going to do much good for poor Mr. Kondrach!"

"You're right, Margarita," Juanita expressed with a solemn and genuine expression on her face. "Don't say too much when the police interrogate you. Less is sometimes best. But for poor unlucky Mr. Kondrach, the moment of truth has arrived! May God rest his troubled wandering soul!"

"The Alien Minority"

Growing-up, I had originally believed that my character had been formed by a combination of three powerful influences: the *Ten Commandments* along with the *Golden Rule;* Greek thinking, which translates roughly into "Be all that you can be; challenge the status quo; strive for perfection and excellence," and thirdly, Jeffersonian Democratic thinking, outlined and defined in the *Bill of Rights* of the *United States Constitution.* In my impressionable teen years, I was aware of my need to be respected as an individual and to always reciprocate courtesy, but I also realized that I was vastly different than most other people in my immediate environment.

When I became cognizant that there was a distinct difference between "my character" and my "personality". my mind recognized that my genetics compelled me to instinctively gravitate toward and gradually embrace the three already cited aspects (or concepts) that coincidentally developed my character. After analyzing my basic uniqueness, my heart and mind afforded me insights into identifying the traits of my personality that were reflected in my behavior, and around the age of 21, my psyche finally comprehended that I was a dye-in-the-wool alien, a human with humanoid thoughts and values, which incidentally incorporated Moses, Socrates. and Thomas Jefferson's contributions to civilization and to history.

Aliens on Earth tend to inadvertently gravitate towards the "helping professions". If we aren't teachers, scientists, or nurses ,then we're bound to be firefighters, policemen, or doctors. Earth Aliens are builders and not destroyers; our culture is pure-hearted and not diabolical, and we're also honest citizens without being criminals involved in illegal activities. Aliens believe that there's a "touch of the Divine" that acts as a moral compass, and helps govern *our* consciences. I suppose that this "out-of-this-world alien business" requires some fundamental, logical explanation, so here it is.

Aliens on Earth have been biologically programmed to appear during troublesome periods of world history. Our genes and chromosomes have been designed by *our* visiting space ancestors to be released at various timed-intervals that make our appearances on this planet inconspicuous to common ordinary earthlings. The whole genetically sophisticated process had been deliberately formulated to purify the Earth's population, along with the weak minds of its non-Alien dwellers. Now, I'll provide the characteristics that are emblematic of genetically engineered "Earth Aliens".

Earth Aliens have narrowly escaped death on more than one occasion, and these "close encounters" are necessary "Wake-up calls" that allow *us* to fathom the "Urgency of *our* mission". These near-death-events validate *us* to ourselves, and allow *us* to eventually identify others of our species. When I was fiv- months old in February of 1943, I required a tonsillectomy, which at the time happened to be an extremely dangerous and life-threatening surgical procedure during the *WWII* era. My chance of surviving the operation was only thirty percent, but if I hadn't undergone the surgery in Baltimore, then I most certainly would have died in infancy. Remarkably, I pulled through and came out of it against very formidable odds. Later in life, I understood that I was quite different than the seventy-percent of the United States population that would have died from infection, or perhaps from the risky operation.

The Catholic Church has sacraments that are practiced so that the congregation members could unify and ultimately strengthen parishioners' faith. Around the age of puberty, *Confirmation* is given to teenage boys and girls to "awaken them" to the importance of leading exemplary lives, so that they could earn eternal happiness as a just reward. Biologically programmed Earth Aliens (as teenagers) usually "awaken", confront death, and manage to escape their ordeals, thus making them aware that *they* are different than "the congregational flock adolescents" that the Bishop and the Pastor (remember, the designation "Pastor" means "shepherd") must initiate into either manhood or womanhood. Yes, regular earthlings need to be constantly preached to, disciplined, and reminded of their religious duties and civic responsibilities (both to themselves and to their fellow man). Conversely, Earth Aliens soon realize (after their traumatic near-death experiences) that *they* don't need Popes, Cardinals, Archbishops, Bishops, Monsignors, Ministers, and Priests to show *them* the path of moral wisdom. *We* automatically are knowledgeable of the righteous path of wisdom and of honor, not only in thought, but also in deed. And *we* instinctively practice the preacher's important precepts without having to be constantly reminded of our temporal existence on this sometimes-diabolical planet.

When I was fourteen, I narrowly escaped drowning. It was January of '56 in Levittown, Pennsylvania. A friend and I were ice skating on the *Delaware Canal,* with him pretending to be the goalie and with me hitting a hockey puck (with an improvised stick) at a makeshift goal we had constructed out of lumber scraps and a very old fishing net. Suddenly, I fell through the ice into eight-foot-deep-water. Before I perceived exactly what had happened, I was under the surface, and all that I could recall at the time was seeing everything peaceful and tranquil, with me seemingly suspended in emerald green water. I must have been suffering hypothermia and shock, because the underwater canal reeds and algae all seemed enchanting when my ice skates finally had made contact with the canal's bottom. Fortunately, I surfaced directly into the hole into which I had plunged. My goalie friend was lying flat on the cracking ice, and he vigorously tugged my half-frozen body out of my "near-death" dilemma. That near-tragedy represented my young teen supplement to the *Sacrament of Confirmation*. It was *my* personal "wake-up call" that I had to explore my "assigned mission in life".

Fate and coincidence ordinarily and amazingly schedule other reminders of his or her "role obligation" in an Earth Alien's direct participation in history-in-the-making. These significant events reinforce the esoteric principle of "Who *we* really are!" In 1970, I was parked at a gas station pump getting my tank filled when an inattentive driver rapidly backed his car out of a garage bay without ever looking into his rear-view mirror. A terrible collision resulted, and it was a miracle that neither his nor my automobile had caught fire. Another time in 1990, I had fallen asleep late one night while driving east on the *Atlantic City Expressway*. A fly landed on my nose, and I instantly awoke just in time to turn my steering wheel and swerve back into the right-hand-lane and out of the path of a car I had nearly sideswiped. To this day, I believe that the fly that saved my life was "no accident".

I've had three other "near-death" experiences that I consider signals from "the Universe", instructing me not to deviate from the "building of character" teachings of Moses, Socrates, and Thomas Jefferson. One such incident had me rolling off my parents' house's roof (while installing a TV aerial), and then having my back safely landing in a soft evergreen bush, rather than smashing into the hard ground. That "destined situation" was a radical wake-up call for me to get my life together, and to get my mind on task and focused, in order to accomplish certain constructive goals before I die. If I had horizontally plunged from the roof to the ground, I might right-this-minute be either dead or paralyzed.

Earth Aliens have active protectors that many Catholic priests and Protestant ministers believe and preach are "guardian angels". These anonymous protectors assist *us* Earth Aliens through arduous times; through family members' deaths; through devastating natural catastrophes, and the moral benefactors insulate *us* from horrors like drowning and auto' accidents. By salvaging us from almost certain

Doom, these guardian angels are reviewing for *our* benefit that *our* general purpose for inhabiting the Earth is to advance the human condition by advocating peace, harmony, justice, truth, beauty, and good spirit. Earth Aliens are not particularly religious, but we are indeed specifically beings who possess abundant "Alien inspired spirituality".

I estimate that Earth Aliens constitute a mere three percent of the world's population. Certainly, and arguably, all of our great scientists, philosophers, teachers, authors, leaders, and inventors have been inspired by the need *they* had felt to "stay the course", regardless of opposition generated by less cerebral non-Alien Earthlings. We special Earth Aliens tend to have high *IQs,* and our breed features such notable people as Albert Einstein, Thomas Edison, Marie Curie, George Washington, Abraham Lincoln, Plato, Aristotle, Miguel Cervantes, and William Shakespeare. Earth Aliens show-up (and make their presence known on this planet) usually during times of crisis where action, leadership, moral clarity, and sage discretion must be exercised to neutralize public indecision and/or confusion.

It is good that only a three-percent minority of the Earth's population happen to be Earth Aliens. If all of this planet's inhabitants were of superior intelligence and of a creative nature, everyone would be attempting to out-create and out-invent the other, and such reckless competition would surely lead to inevitable conflict among tenacious rivals. Oftentimes, when a great Earth Alien emerges, his or her ideas are rejected by the mediocre masses. Some *EAs* like Galileo might have to face adversity in the form of an *Inquisition,* and others like Socrates might be put to death for "corrupting the minds of others". It usually takes the more belligerent and barbaric Earthlings a hundred-years to decipher and learn that threatening, persecuting, and executing *EAs* represents the ultimate in human ignorance.

Most *EAs* don't like the limelight, and actually shun and despise it. Only out of necessity will one become a President, or a great General, to verify and implement the axiom, "Crisis determines the great man!" And for the most part, Earth Aliens indubitably are unselfish helpers, thoroughly dedicated to constructively expanding and exploring the perimeters and parameters of culture. *EAs* practice a brand of "Reverse Transcendentalism" where (as opposed to false Emersonian philosophy) reason triumphantly supersedes and trumps emotion. Non-Aliens tend to be biologically oriented, nondescript, hedonistic humans that are principally governed and driven by primitive, selfish feelings.

Generally speaking, Earth Aliens are not affectionate. *We* don't like perpetually hugging and kissing one another, or our spouses or relatives. *We* instinctively know that *we like* most people, and *we* have a sixth sense that can detect a potential evil person's sinister motives. *EAs* don't equate love with affection; we believe that love is a transcendent, abstract quality represented in honor, respect, courtesy, kindness, caring, helping, courage, justice, beauty, and fairness. For example, Earth Aliens believe that the *Commandment* "Honor Thy Father and Thy Mother" literally means just that, without perpetual phony hugging and sloppy kissing dominating family relationships.

Earth Aliens are very sensitive. We believe that a person's feet and toes are the ugliest parts of the human anatomy. Nothing is more disgusting to an Earth Alien than to go to the grocery store and see people casually shopping-around wearing hideous clogs and sandals.

EAs would make terrible political candidates going from town to town insincerely kissing and hugging crying babies, just to selfishly accumulate votes. The erudite members of *my species* fully understand that any citizen/individual has tremendous difficulty governing himself' or herself, without pretending to be capable of governing thousands of people by holding a public office. *We* diligently attempt to execute *our* illustrious, aforementioned abstract virtues every day of the year, so *we* don't really place a greater value on anniversaries, birthdays, *Father's Day, Mother's Day,* wedding-dates, *Christmas, Thanksgiving, Fourth of July, and Easter*. To *EAs,* every day is equally as important as any other twenty-four-hour period, and *our* vital missions are essentially needed all twelve-months on the calendar.

Here's precisely what showing affection between non-Alien humans does and fosters. It stifles children's growth and spiritual maturity. Affectionate children tend to be raised thinking that they are the center of the Universe, and they often evolve into arrogant, selfish, egotistical brats. Children exposed to too much affection tend to fear competition, and are intimidated by free enterprise, the essential tools that (in America and the rest of the Free World) can contribute to amassing wealth and developing moral strength and an ethical character. Affectionate children are too dependent on their doting and compromising parents. You don't teach a child a good example when the parents themselves act like four-year-old children, and constantly hug and kiss their over-protected offspring. This is why spoiled children often lack self-discipline and long-term-commitment to complete difficult goals and achieve full independence. And "the pursuit of happiness", as prescribed by Thomas Jefferson, is the ultimate goal of every Earth Alien. Affection between parents and children basically stifles the child's initiative to experiment and discover, and the continuous bonding makes the child helplessly *dependent* on its parents. Affectionate children are quite used to instant gratification, and the doltish brats don't possess the wherewithal to study, grow, sacrifice, struggle, and demonstrate the capacity and the perseverance necessary to elevate themselves above mediocrity through continuous industry, application, persistence, and self-discipline. Affectionate children don't have the propensity to understand and distinguish that they are part of a "Universal Soul", and that *EAs* are very unique and rather extraordinary global inhabitants, willing to take their helping roles.

Indeed, in a biological sense, kissing promotes the sharing of billions of germs from one person to another, and it astounds hybrid *EAs* that most non-Alien beings prefer doing *it,* when science has discovered that there are five times as many germs and bacteria in a person's mouth than in that same person's rectum. And since monkeys always feel that they need to groom, touch, hug, and embrace one another for security, then *that* bad habit is genuine proof that ninety-seven percent of the Earth's inhabitants require continual bonding to feel safe, while the three-percent *EAs* find other more creative things to do with their limited tenure in this imperfect world. The general non-Alien population is a product of *Darwin's Theory of Evolution,* while the mentally superior three-percent *EAs* are the requisite *Missing Links,* responsible for most of the creativity and progress evident throughout the ages.

EAs are essentially *intellectually affectionate* and not physically demonstrative about expressing their feelings. *We* don't have to kiss someone for that person to know that *we* strongly like and admire him or her. Over the eons, *EAs* have evolved from other self-motivated space traveling ancestors and benefactors residing on distant planets, and conversely, the Earth's ninety-seven percent general public can trace *their* origin back to prehistoric chimpanzees and apes. This simple explanatory principle of the minority "Intellectual Earth Aliens" and the corresponding majority "Simian-origin Earth Non-Aliens" has confounded Earth scientists for over a century. Cerebral *EAs* think more objectively and demonstrate more creativity than feel-oriented, subjective non-Aliens do.

A popular Seals and Croft '70s song has the lyrics: "We are stardust, we are golden!" I honestly believe that those wonderful words express both the essence and the function of being a complex Earth Alien. *We* love challenges and adventure, even if our endeavors pertain to us making imminent enemies or opponents. *EAs* are "genetically blessed" with enough fortitude, perseverance, tenacity, ingenuity and spiritual strength to crusade for virtue in order to ultimately triumph over wickedness during any prospective formidable adversity, ranging from violent nuclear war to disruptive economic depression.

EAs' don't savor loud raucous parties, and we absolutely loathe *Mardi Gras* and *New Year's Day* celebrations, when obnoxious Non-Alien Earthlings pursue their absurd folly, which in truth is reminiscent of Moses climbing *Mt. Sinai* with all of the Israelites deviating from the *Ten Commandments'* wise teachings and acting like inebriated, out-of-control juvenile delinquents on the desert plain below. Rap music, boisterous parades, large crowds at football games, and big audiences at rock concerts are all repugnant to *our* value systems and those kinds of disturbing occurrences invariably bring-out the baser emotions of regular non-Alien Earthlings.

EAs generally abhor tattoos and body piercing, and assess those "grotesque externalizations" as being examples of primitive and anachronistic body desecration and mutilation. *Our* more judicious "three-percent sage species" realizes that a person's mind and achievements are what distinguishes *him* or *her* from the remainder of society, and not gaudy tattoos, and earrings through the tongue or cheek, being indicative of "individuality." And oh yes; most *EAs* prefer to be altruistic, left-handed, creative folks to deliberately separate *us* from our Darwinian, Earth-generated, right-handed counterparts. Regrettably, throughout history, left-handed *EAs* have been unjustly persecuted by envious and jealous right-handers that fear *our'* potential, and envy *our* unselfish pursuit of excellence. Motivated by fear, the traditional non-Alien Earthling wants to reject the truths that *we* mercifully offer, and the dolts perpetually keep attempting to discredit, punish, control, and manipulate *us* less-greedy and happy *EAs*.

Our breed wholeheartedly supports the institution of marriage as a privilege enjoyed between a husband and a wife, whose indispensable mission is to "guide" *our* children through the myriad dangers and pitfalls associated with everyday life. *EAs* feel a natural compulsion to be monogamous, and we will devotedly live with that one chosen mate and make every effort to avoid marital arguments, while continuously pursuing mutual compatibility. And if *our* husband or wife (usually a regular Earthling) dies, *we* seldom remarry out of respect to the person *we* had (nurtured and) shared *our* wedding vows with.

EAs are sometimes criticized as being "domineering" and "tyrannical", but this is only because *we* candidly believe that the human body should be maintained naturally. An *EA* male's wife might insist on wearing red, black, green, or purple fingernail polish, but since the husband admires "natural beauty", just plain, glossy, clear nail polish is tolerable as an alternative. Light red lipstick on a woman is alright, because it enhances the *natural* color of a woman's lips, and therefore, does not project any outward artificiality, which obviously connotes phoniness.

In conclusion, although *EAs* are not formal religious churchgoers (in the orthodox sense), *we* have much more faith than those "sheep" that must listen to a Pastor once a week to fortify *their* vulnerable hearts and consciences. *EAs,* on the other hand, have sufficient faith in *our* very pertinent Earth mission, which is to morally purify ever-developing non-Alien human intelligence, and to directly influence those aberrant individuals to walk the "Avenue of Righteousness". *We* have little apprehension of death or about dying, and *EAs* don't preoccupy *our* inquisitive minds with perpetually contemplating such triviality. If and when *we* die, *our* superior species lucidly discerns that *we're* just involved in another inconvenient transit on the way to a new assignment, somewhere else within the enormous *Milky Way Galaxy,* or perhaps somewhere else inside the infinite *Universe.*

Yes, *EAs* are worthy candidates for reincarnation, and non-Aliens are earmarked for and doomed to death. In the final analysis, Earth Aliens have souls of fire, and non-Aliens have souls of clay. And I firmly believe that when I die, I'll be spiritually reincarnated into another humanoid body (and this phenomenon will happen redundantly) until my soul is finally pure-enough to reach Nirvana (Heaven).

But to the ninety-seven percent primate-to-man non-Alien Earth dwellers, *death* will mean either Hell or Purgatory, the latter being enforced with the clay-souled recipient reappearing as another lackluster ninety-seven percent personage on this humdrum planet, or as a miraculous transformation into an *EA* on another world, with a bona fide opportunity choice) to legitimately attain Heaven (Nirvana).

"City Councilmen"

The thriving New Jersey coast has a number of excellent boardwalks famous for amusement arcades, piers, rides, gift shops, pizza parlors and various games of chance. With the legalization of gambling Atlantic City's boardwalk now features multi-million-dollar casino hotels, which have significantly revitalized the city's economy. Other popular boardwalks exist along the Jersey shore in Seaside Heights, Asbury Park, Ocean City, Cape May and Wildwood, with all of those terrific beach towns being annually commercially promoted as "traditional family resorts."

The Wildwood Boardwalk is best known for its marvelous amusement piers and for its numerous games of chance and myriad gift shops. A typical boardwalk block facing the white sandy beach would feature a hot dog/hamburger stand, a pizza place, several video game amusement arcades, a candy shop selling homemade chocolates and salt water taffy, a glassblower's shop, a gift shop and several games of chance featuring stuffed animals for prizes. "Old Money" landlords charge exorbitant rents of up to two thousand five hundred dollars per frontage foot with the average store occupying twenty-two feet along the wooden promenade. Many of the hard-working store renters diligently labor from *Memorial Day* to *Labor Day* just to pay their' enormous expenses and in reality, the hard-working merchants earn their annual profits when staying open before May 31st and after September 1st.

Thomas and Warren Wallace have owned and operated the Atlantis Coastal Hotel, which had burned down twice since 1900 when the landmark structure had first opened its doors for business. Brick-façade storefronts had been built in 1965 with ambitious tenets signing long-term leases to launch their prospective enterprises. In the year 2002 "agreed upon rents" were paid sixty percent by check (reportable to the *IRS*) to the greedy Wallace brothers and the remaining forty percent "hush money" was involuntarily contributed by means of "cash under the table."

Clint Vaughn was a wily Wildwood entrepreneur that owned a novelty shop and a shuffleboard bowling game since 1994 on the Wallace Brothers' lucrative boardwalk block. But Clint Vaughn had aspirations of becoming "a serious boardwalk operator" and eventually acquired other establishments on other well-trafficked blocks, a bold practice which Thomas and Warren Wallace did not entirely savor.

In the winter of 2002, Clint purchased from an elderly gentleman the Surf Bar two blocks north of the Atlantis Coastal Hotel, and then two years later, he acquired a busy lemonade and pretzel concession located next door to his "drinking hole." And then a haunted house was added to Vaughn's holdings in the fall of 2004 and a water gun game at the boardwalk's south end in 2005 was next obtained to further expand the ambitious fellow's burgeoning Wildwood property portfolio. The all-too-wary Wallace Brothers thought that Clint Vaughn (and his ever-growing retail empire) was getting "too big for his britches."

"Something's got to be done with Clint Vaughn," Warren Wallace said to his older brother in late July of 2005 in the Atlantis Coastal's Victorian-style lobby. "That guy came here in 1994 and didn't have two nickels to rub together, and now he's takin' over half the damned boardwalk," the older brother hyperbolized. "I say let's boot him out of his novelty shop and out of his shuffle bowling game arcade, and get two new tenets in those properties. And Tom, I think we oughta' consider changing the rental formula to one havin' us ownin' a percentage of the new businesses comin' in. That oughta' generate more revenue for our corporation than the present basic rental system does."

"Clint Vaughn's a good proprietor, who always gets his rent in on time," Thomas Wallace corrected his younger and more callow brother. "He always pays his under-the-table debts on schedule, but you're right Warren. He's getting too big for his own sake and his bar is a general nuisance with all the derelicts it attracts. It caters to too many town drunks and to underage drinkers havin' false *IDs* too! Mr. Vaughn's walkin' a thin tightrope and he's bound to tumble from grace by stumblin' over his own clumsy feet. Let's just bide our time with good old Clint and see what happens," Thomas Wallace prudently suggested. "I hear he's now negotiatin' to get the Telescope Picture business up on Boardwalk and Pine. Clint's definitely walkin' on quicksand Warren, and pretty soon he's about to sink down over his head."

"Old Money" that had been transferred from generation to generation (like the big bucks belonging to the Wallace brothers) was at odds with the "New Money" being made and invested by upstart wheeler-dealers like Clint Vaughn. The Wallace brothers deeply resented their risk-taking tenet because the shrewd operator was acting independently in the free enterprise marketplace without *their* expressed permission, input or consent. The all-too-perceptive brothers wanted Clint Vaughn to be answerable to them and subordinate to *their* whims and fancies. Conflict between the avaricious landlords and their adventurous shopkeeper seemed quite inevitable.

Meanwhile, Clint Vaughn was dissatisfied with the Wildwood Police "relentlessly harassin' and arrestin' my Surf Bar patrons" outside his drinking establishment after midnight. The boardwalk bar owner decided to rally some political support among his local customers and well-networked contacts and run for city council with the intention of controlling and/or influencing the shore police department. But a major obstacle stood in Clint's political path: his Atlantis Coastal Hotel landlord Thomas Theodore Wallace was already a prominent member of the city council, and *his* seat was scheduled to be contested on the upcoming November ballot. Clint Vaughn's risky maneuver would certainly cause imminent friction between the aggressive tenet and his grudge-holding senior landlord.

Clint was the Wildwood citizens' favorite candidate, and he boldly predicted he would win the "up for grabs" council seat, much to his envious opponent's chagrin. Thomas Wallace's animosity for *his* industrious tenet now rivaled that of his more argumentative younger brother. Just before August 10th of 2005 Clint Vaughn received his termination of leases (eviction notices) for his novelty shop and for his shuffle-bowling arcade. But the "hungry newcomer" continued to aggravate his former landlords by announcing in the local papers that he was relocating the two businesses four blocks south with Henry Thompson, a fourth generation Wildwood tycoon, who absolutely despised the snobbish Wallace Brothers. And when it became public knowledge that Henry Thompson and Clint Vaughn had agreed in principle to form a partnership to construct "fifty top-shelf bayside condominiums", the Wallace Brothers' blood pressures climbed to very high danger levels.

"Warren, Clint's goin' big time with our rival Henry Thompson," Thomas Wallace informed his more outspoken brother. "Ya' know Warren, pretty soon those two chummy clowns are goin' to take over Wildwood if we allow them. We gotta' do something about it, and something drastic mighty soon too!"

"Don't worry, Tom," Warren cavalierly answered. "I got some Mafia friends over in South Philly' that'll help us out. They're just itchin' for a little out-of-the-city job money. It pays to have the right alliances both in warfare and in local money battles. Those two connivin' boardwalk rip-off artists will get their just punishments, but right now, Tom, I loathe Clint Vaughn a lot worse than I despise Henry Thompson, whose father and grandfather our pappy and granddaddy hated with a passion. Let me give you the details of what I have in mind."

In late August of 2005, Thomas and Warren Wallace put their strategy (to "once and for all reprimand Clint Vaughn") into action. Like other boardwalk merchants Clint skimmed cash from his businesses and kept his "off-the-top" cache of hundred-dollar-bills stashed in a large safe in his apartment that was conveniently situated above *his* Surf Bar. The unscrupulous Wallace brothers had a South Philadelphia Mafia hit squad conduct a secret operation by breaking into the small upstairs residence, cracking Vaughn's unsophisticated safe and easily heisting a hefty hundred-twenty thousand dollars from the enclosure. The "found loot" was then split fifty-fifty between the appreciative mob members and the always-scheming Wallace brothers, who had been awarded the handsome "finders' fee."

Thomas and Warren Wallace were ecstatic upon reviewing their half of the recently confiscated booty. The pair merrily sat and chatted about their fantastic good fortune in their tiffany-lamp-lit Atlantis Coastal Hotel office.

"Yes Sir, Warren. This is the easiest sixty-thousand we've ever made," Thomas proudly bragged. "Clint's probably havin' severe conniptions and naggin' hemorrhoid flare-ups as I speak. And Councilman Vaughn will never go to the police, because his money that had been expertly pilfered would not have been reported to the *IRS* because..."

"Because the hidden loot wasn't designated for reporting to the *IRS* in the first place!" Warren Wallace confirmed with a healthy laugh. "That's the benefit of ownin' cash businesses Tom. The downside is that it's hard to keep a secret from your enemies and when Clint least expected it, whammo! He gets robbed but can't call the authorities into the fray because he's been skimmin' cash from *Uncle Sam* for over a decade now. Tom, ya' can count this most recent wonderful treasure as found money! Vaughn's already blown his main gasket, I betcha'!"

"Clint's loss is our gain, our capital gain, ha, ha, ha!" Thomas Wallace verified and chortled. "Now if that rotten skunk Vaughn had played his cards right by not runnin' against me for city council, then he'd be a hundred-and-twenty-thousand-dollars richer now, and would still have his two stores conductin' legitimate trade on *our* boardwalk block! Renters oughta' know their place in Wildwood society and stay humble and subordinate! Mr. Vaughn bit-off more than he could chew, and the fool found-out the hard way!"

"Say, Tom," Warren said after some lengthy rumination. "I got this here idea in my head and I wanna' know what you think of it! Here's some logistics I have in mind."

"Sure thing!" the older Wallace swiftly acknowledged. "If your concoction is half as decent as this Mafia grand larceny job has been then my sensitive ears will prick-up and listen. I always enjoy kickin' an enemy when he's down! Makes me feel mighty glad it's not me bein' stomped on!"

A week later in early September, the Wallace brothers made a surprise afternoon visit to the Surf Bar, specifically to fake commiserating with Clint Vaughn and to offer their condolences at his "rumored loss." Clint invited the two unexpected guests into his establishment's rear office to provide an appropriate setting for the impromptu conference.

"What are you guys here for?" the bar owner began. "Can I get ya' a couple of beers from the tap? How about some whiskey on the rocks?"

"No, thanks!" Thomas Wallace promptly and politely answered. "There's scuttlebutt along the boardwalk that you've recently been robbed. Estimates range anywhere from a hundred fifty-thousand to a half million."

"People tend to exaggerate after hearin' some random juicy gossip like that," Clint Vaughn readily admitted. "By the end of the day it'll probably reach a staggerin' million dollars! But I don't know how the theft news leaked-out since I haven't told anyone except my mother after I swore her to secrecy."

"Well, Clint," Warren Wallace said with a grim face. "If your mother ever goes to a beauty shop or to a charity function, the gossip is bound to slip-out. Women can't control their need to prattle all day long, especially when in the dignified company of other females. It's their form of oral tabloid journalism."

"You might be accurate this time," Clint returned. "Now, why are you gentleman really gracin' me with your presence? Do ya' want me to relinquish my council seat? If that's your goal, forget it. I can't be bribed."

"No, not exactly," Thomas Wallace snickered in an effort to conceal his ongoing contempt for his principal adversary. "We just want you to know that we sympathize with your plight because we had a terrible robbery occur to us too."

"What happened?" Clint asked, showing a degree of sincerity. "Who do ya' think pulled the caper? How much was stolen? Where did the theft take place?"

"Four days ago, our hotel office safe was broken into and three hundred thousand was removed," Thomas dramatically lied to his despised adversary. "We couldn't go to the cops or else big problems might result after the newspapers and the Feds got a-hold of the personal information. Can't trust anybody nowadays, Clint. But as soon as Warren and I heard that you had experienced something similar, we figured we'd pay you a little visit and let you know that we're sufferin' a gigantic monetary loss too."

"Thanks for stoppin' by," Vaughn said. "Is there anything else you'd like to discuss?"

"My brother and I were thinkin' things over," Thomas Wallace mentioned, "particularly recent negative events. I think that you and us oughta' be friends again in light of our similar unfortunate circumstances. Next Monday is *Labor Day* and things slow-down on the boardwalk to almost a standstill until the following weekend. What do ya' say Clint that you' come out on our yacht for a private fishin' party?" the older Wallace brother rhetorically asked. "We'll reminisce old times, drink a few beers, catch a few white marlins and then get your opinion on a possible business deal we're gonna' cut you in on. How about accompanyin' us on our scheduled fishin' expedition next Tuesday morning? I guarantee you'll be excited at the nifty offer we got in mind?"

"What time next Tuesday?" Clint asked with avaricious-looking sparkling brown eyes.

"Nine a.m. at Thomas's house on the other side of the bay," Warren indicated. "And whatever ya' do, don't disclose anything to anyone, including your aging mother. If we find out that you've spilled the beans about our dynamic proposition," Warren Wallace threatened, "then the deal's off and we're all back to negative square one again. Are our cordial and genuine terms of consultation acceptable to you?"

"Sure thing!" Clint replied ineffectively holding back his mounting enthusiasm. "I'll meet you at your dock at quarter to nine on Tuesday. I gotta' confess I'm really speculatin' about what you fellas' have cookin' on the drawin' board. Maybe we can find middle ground and agree on something substantial and call a permanent truce. Cooperation is always better than hostility, that's my family credo even though I gotta' admit that my father was a notorious loan shark!"

Clint Vaughn shook hands with both clever brothers to seal the general terms of their "financial arrangement." "I've always wanted to take a ride on your terrific cabin cruiser," the Surf Bar owner confided to his prominent visitors. "I hear that baby is worth over a half million. We're we goin'? I'm not the best fisherman when it comes to big game."

"That's perfectly alright," Warren Wallace diplomatically stated with a false grin upon his countenance. "We're goin' out to the Baltimore Canyon just southeast of Cape May. And don't worry about a thing Clint. The *Atlantic* in early September is as calm as Lake Placid. Our very interesting mission will be accomplished and everything's gonna' be peaceful and friendly."

At 8:45 a.m. on the Tuesday after *Labor Day,* Clint Vaughn showed-up at Tom Wallace's dock for his ocean fishing excursion out to the renowned Baltimore Canyon. The conniving Wallace Brothers greeted their guest and extended to Vaughn full courtesy and hospitality. Soon the three men boarded the impressive *Point of No Return* and after the mooring ropes had been unraveled the awesome fishing yacht gently left the dock and headed south toward the Cape May inlet directly where *Delaware Bay* meets the majestic *Atlantic.*

"Never had the pleasure of riding in something so fabulous!" Clint praised Warren Wallace as the craft opened-up its dual inboards east of Cape May heading towards its Cape Henlopen, Delaware destination. "When are you' fellas' gonna' tell me your big investment plan? Not that I don't relish white marlin fishin' but sooner or later I know my curiosity is gonna' be getting the better of me."

"Here's a cold beer!" Thomas Wallace offered his inquisitive passenger in an ice-chilled brown bottle. "After each of us reels in a white marlin, then we'll stop our activity and my brother and I will sit down and confidentially disclose our intentions. And my brother and I are sure you won't be disappointed."

"Show some patience and self-discipline!" the equally devious *Point of No Return* co-navigator chided his anxious passenger. "The summer boardwalk season's just about over and it's now time to relax and reflect on the great business trade we all enjoyed. There's plenty of time to settle down and converse about our grand opportunity," Warren Wallace advised his invited guest. "But let's collect those three white marlins and I assure you Mr. Vaughn that by noon you'll fully learn about *our* special project," the younger brother insisted. "The purpose of this little trip is to solidify *our* trust so that we can be three respecting partners in an ironclad joint development that'll make you glad you've accompanied us today on this terrific white marlin exploit. We'll cross *Delaware Bay* and when we're finally parallel to

Rehoboth Beach," the pilot elaborated, "then we'll swing east to the Baltimore Canyon."

"Okay," Clint amiably acceded. "But you guys oughta' write mystery novels, because you really know how to keep an already intrigued passenger in suspense."

A mere forty-five minutes later, the magnificent pleasure yacht/fishing boat finally arrived at its twenty-five-mile offshore objective. The handsome craft was now stopped with its engines off so that the three "sailors" aboard could conduct their friendly fishing contest. By eleven-thirty Clint had reeled-in a forty-five-pound white marlin, which eliminated him from continued participation in the competition because Warren was able to bring in and gaff a forty-nine-pound fish, and Thomas Wallace later skillfully landed an enviable fifty-three pounder that was laid writhing and wriggling on the *Point of No Return's* deck.

"Looks like you lost our little contest!" Warren snidely said to the now-fatigued Clint Vaughn. "But I gotta' tell ya' that you're gonna' badly lose in an even bigger way with your precious life!"

"What are ya' talkin' about?" Vaughn vehemently objected. "I think you've had one beer too many, or maybe the hot sun has melted your brain cells."

Just then, three formidable Mafia hit men rapidly climbed the steps from the cabin cruiser's galley and menacingly confronted Clint with their raised revolvers. Spiteful Warren and Thomas Wallace laughed exceedingly as the surrounded boardwalk mogul finally realized the gravity of *his* predicament.

"What's this ugly-lookin' scam all about?" Vaughn adamantly protested. "This is a lousy setup! I've been duped!"

"Exactly," Warren Wallace replied with a huge smirk apparent on his face. "My brother and I have been thinkin' about disposin' of you ever since you foolishly decided to challenge Thomas and run and obtain your coveted city council seat. Now distinguished Sir, it's time for you to leave this evil dog-eat-dog diabolical world and visit the afterlife so that you'll never be around to annoy and aggravate us again."

"That's what the hell you think!" Clint audaciously answered. "Tony, Lucky, Frankie, let these two turkeys have it!" Clint commanded the three hired Sicilians. "These two aristocrat punks have been a thorn in my side for all-too-long now!"

The three dedicated Mafia hit men turned their bodies and their revolvers and pointed their weapons at the two suddenly flabbergasted Wallace Brothers. Before either Thomas or Warren could ever utter a plea (or even a defiant shout) three triggers were pulled six times each and the two boardwalk tycoons fell like heavy sacks of potatoes to the *Point of No Return's* now-bloodied deck.

"Thanks for agreein' to get involved in the neat double-cross!" Clint commended his three hired henchmen. "It was well worth three-hundred-thousand-bucks to exterminate those two pathetic, miserable creeps."

"It pays not to be too frugal when dealin' with professional hit men!" Tony Brigandi concluded and articulated. "You were lucky enough Mr. Vaughn to be the highest bidder to do an assassination, actually two assassinations!"

"First, we'll tie these two deceased creeps up and chain them to portable anchors," Lucky Battaglia chimed-in. "Then, we'll toss the scumbag evidence overboard."

"Hey, guys," Frankie Errera pointed-out "Here comes our boat that's right on schedule for our rendezvous at sea. Say, we can tie each corpse to a white marlin that could serve as chum for other big fish to nibble on! After that, we'll tow the *Point of No Return* five miles from here and dynamite it. That ought to confuse anybody investigatin' the two missing persons lost at sea theory. I never did like those two pompous WASPS!"

"Okay, men," Clint Vaughn finished with a smile. "Let's do those things before anybody accidentally spots us out here. And as a generous reward you three guys can keep the sixty thousand portion ya' stole from me and then gave back to me. And thanks for getting out the word to the Wallace Brothers and givin' those dead knuckleheads the dual theft idea, too! I almost laughed my rear end off after they came and visited me at my bar. And gentlemen, as an added bonus, I'm goin' to give Frankie "the Fish" Errera the third remaining white marlin as a special souvenir for his stellar loyalty and his superb cooperation!"

“Fixtures”

Connor Murphy, a forty-three-year-old Hammonton, New Jersey bachelor had a fascination for collecting unique wall ornaments, particularly tapestries, paintings, murals and unusual fixtures. In response to a small advertisement in the classified ads section of a local gazette the accountant decided to visit an antique shop in nearby Sweetwater to browse-around for an item to hang on an empty wall in his computer room. After enjoying his early Saturday morning April ride into the South Jersey pine barrens the credit and debit guru arrived at the desired Pleasant Mills Road shop situated near the historic but now defunct Old Mill Play House. Connor noticed a certain circular bronze shield mounted upon a sword and an accompanying battleaxe, and the uniquely interesting item immediately captured the collector’s attention.

“How much is that beautiful shield with the sword and battleaxe background?” Connor asked Mr. Gene Domenico, the quaint curio shop proprietor. “If the price is reasonable, I might be interested in purchasing it.”

“Eight-hundred-dollars!” the establishment’s owner answered. “It’s certainly a novelty item and I’ve never carried anything quite like it. The article I believe is of European origin, British I presume. It’s a rare specimen indeed.”

“What if I offered you six-hundred-and-fifty for it?” the frugal Murphy haggled. “It’s just what I’ve been searching for, and I have a special place in my home to hang it! And I suppose the thing even comes with a mounting hook on the back.”

“Well, sir, if you’d like to own the fixture, it’s slated to be up for auction bid tonight at eight p.m. I think I’ll get at least a thousand for it during the bidding,” the wily proprietor insisted. “So, I’m really being very generous permitting it to be sold for eight hundred dollars in a private sale.”

“You drive a hard bargain,” Connor conceded. “Okay, I’ll give you eight-hundred for it. My guess is that its composition is solid iron gilded with brass,” Murphy speculated and related as he respectfully touched the object. “And it genuinely looks medieval, although I must confess, I’m no authority on artifacts and the like. If the sword and battleaxe weren’t attached to the shield,” Connor stated to Mr. Gene Domenico, “from a distance, the arrangement appears to have three separate components.”

"I'm sure you'll be thoroughly delighted with it," Mr. Domenico agreeably replied. "It's a unique conversation piece, no doubt about it. It's what we in-the-business call 'a collectors' item'."

Connor Murphy readily purchased his "authentic-looking shield from antiquity," drove his black *Mercury* sedan five miles south from Sweetwater past blueberry fields to Hammonton and after arriving at his Packard Street rancher proudly hung the object on his computer room's formerly blank wall. 'On second impression, this splendid shield looks like it was recently manufactured,' Connor thought as he admired his latest acquisition. 'It doesn't even require brass polishing. But I'm tickled pink that I bought it. The thing looks like it once belonged to Richard-the-Lion-Heart, or to the villainous Sheriff of Nottingham. I'm no historian, but maybe,, if I ever have the time, I'll research shields, swords and battleaxes on the *Internet.*'

The following week in April of 2005, Connor Murphy parked his *Mercury* sedan at the expansive *Philadelphia International Airport* ground level lot, caught a shuttle bus to Terminal C and after clearing security boarded a *United Airlines* flight to Las Vegas to attend the annual *CPA* Convention. 'I'll be staying at *Harrah's* across the street from the *Mirage* and *Caesar's Palace*,' the passenger contemplated as the sleek jet ascended to cruising altitude. 'I love Vegas and all its glitter. I'll be combining business with pleasure and getting a little gambling in, too, besides some quality pool time. I can't wait to check into my room and then hit the tables.'

The five-and-a-half-hour direct flight went smoothly, and the jumbo jet landed on schedule at Las Vegas's busy *McCarran International Airport*. After successfully retrieving his two pieces of luggage from the *United Airlines'* baggage carousel, Connor Murphy stepped outside the terminal and caught a mini-bus to *Harrah's Casino/Hotel* situated on the famous Vegas strip.

'They've really modernized this place,' the accountant thought upon finally arriving at his much-anticipated destination. 'Harrah's used to look like a sparkling, all-lit-up Mississippi riverboat at night. But now, its main tower look like it blends in perfectly with its neighboring high-rise structures along the strip. I suppose that's what casino architects call 'progress'.'

After checking into the hotel at the main registration desk, the somewhat weary traveler was escorted by a bellboy to an elevator just off the main lobby that then conveyed them up to the ninth floor. The hotel employee opened the door with Murphy's electronic key, and

Immediately, the visitor's keen sense of smell detected a certain recognizable odor.

"I can smell fresh paint," Murphy complained to the attentive bellboy. "The odor isn't exactly aromatic if ya' know what I mean. I'll give you a twenty-dollar tip if you can have my room changed to something more favorable. I think the smell is comin' from the bathroom where painters must've just done a bit of touch-up work."

"I can smell it, too!" the amiable bellboy concurred and verified. "I'll call the main desk right now and report the abnormality. You have a perfect right to request switchin' your accommodations. I'm sure we'll get you a new room in a jiffy."

While the conscientious bellboy was calling the main desk, Connor observed what his mind evaluated as a 'weird coincidence.' 'That gold framed mirror hanging on the wall is a facsimile of the one I used to have in my Park Avenue condominium before I moved into my Packard Street ranch home. I then sold the piece to my cousin Robert who had always admired the mirror and insisted on owning it. I really didn't mind,' Connor rationalized, 'because I got tired of the cumbersome square object and bought a new smaller rectangular foyer mirror instead.'

"Sir, the desk manager apologizes for the inconvenience and the hotel's oversight!" the bellboy cooperatively announced. "You've been transferred to Room 666 on the sixth-floor. Let's go down three floors and check it out."

"Don't we have to take the elevator down to the main desk to obtain a new key?" Connor asked.

"No, Sir," the bellboy promptly answered. "The lock combination on Room 666 has been changed to accept your Room 928 key. Isn't modern technology amazing? The central computer at the registration desk can work magic."

"Sure can," Connor admitted with a wide grin. "I'm definitely impressed. Whoever owns the patent to that technology must be a rich man living in luxury by now. I wish I had the imagination and the ability to think of something as useful as that. I guess the cliché 'Necessity is the mother of invention' is truth after all."

"It's just a modern marvel that makes life easier for everybody working in the hotel," the bellboy intelligently acknowledged. "Computer science is changin' our lives every day. I'm just glad that we could help you out and make your stay here as comfortable and as memorable as possible."

"I really appreciate your help," Connor honestly returned. "I'm a little fatigued from my flight from Philly' and I need to take a nap to fully recover. As I grow older, m stamina level is gradually decreasing."

The visitor was quite pleased with Room 666's appearance, and its clean fresh air and gladly gave the pleasant hotel employee the twenty-dollar tip *he* had promised. After the elated bellboy left the quarters, Murphy then unpacked his bags and stored his clothes and suits in the master bureau and in the room's closet. 'That's odd!' the new arrival thought as he hung his favorite blue business suit inside the closet. 'I was born on June 6, 1966, so Room 666 and the numbers 6666 seem to coincide, when I include June as the sixth month. Maybe I'll find and buy an authoritative book on numerology in the hotel's gift shop, and see if that strange number relationship has any relevance or significance that might pertain to me.'

Connor took his traditional late afternoon nap, and upon waking-up, his eyes perceived a familiar-looking object hanging on the wall opposite his bed that previously had gone unnoticed. 'That's really bizarre!' Murphy contemplated with mild apprehension. 'I had dreamt that I was vacationing in Venice and there's a tapestry of *St. Mark's Square* that I had failed to notice, tacked to and suspended on the wall. And the *Venetian Hotel* is next door to *Harrah's* and it has a replica of the *Campanile* bell-tower on its premises. Perhaps I dreamed of Venice because I had viewed the *Venetian Hotel* when the mini-bus had dropped me off at the main entrance to *Harrah's*,' Connor conjectured. But then the now-nervous visitor realized something that seemed totally implausible. 'That tapestry is identical to the one I have hanging in my home's guest room. Now that astounding coincidence is absolutely inexplicable! Perhaps I should be staying at the *Mirage* across the street!' the room's occupant imagined and reckoned. 'Then this uncanny phenomenon would make more sense. First, it was the gaudy gold gilded mirror in the ninth-floor room, and now this identical tapestry being on the wall when I woke-up here in my sixth-floor suite. This is all becoming too weird and baffling for my brain to comprehend.'

That Monday evening, Connor enjoyed an excellent meal at the *Harrah's* buffet and then spent the remainder of the evening merrily gambling at the blackjack tables. Satisfied that he had achieved winnings of two hundred dollars the accountant decided to return to Room 666 and get some necessary rest to compensate for his 'three-hour jet lag time differential.' The man eagerly showered and then entered his clean and tidy bed. Murphy stared at the *St. Mark's Square* tapestry one final time, shook his head in astonishment, turned-off the light and then gradually fell asleep. Soon, Connor was dreaming that he was an intrepid sailor on a sixteenth-century Spanish galleon, having characteristic square sails fluttering on its masts. In a matter of minutes, the wooden vessel was engaged in a fierce naval battle with a ruthless crew aboard a sinister-looking pirate ship. Connor Murphy awoke in a cold sweat resulting from his seemingly surreal nightmare ordeal. After swallowing a prescribed sleeping pill the anxious *Harrah's* guest finally achieved a well-deserved slumber.

When Connor woke up on Tuesday morning, he recollected his dream of being a shipmate on a Spanish galleon engaged in a brutal sea battle with barbarous swashbucklers. 'The Spanish ship was shaped just like the expensive metallic wall fixture hanging in my dining room back in Hammonton,' the occupant of Room 666 soberly realized. 'That's really peculiar. Must be some kind of oddball aberration. The Spanish galleon is hanging right up there on the damned wall! Oh well, I'll have a big breakfast, and then attend the slated morning seminar over at the *Mandalay Bay*. That lecture ought to clear the cobwebs out, and get my mind thinking objectively again with basic numbers, statistics and facts.'

On Tuesday night, the rejuvenated accountant spent three-hours playing the slots at the *MGM Grand*, not far from the magnificent *Mandalay Bay*. 'I'll walk the mile up the strip back to *Harrah's*. The exercise will do me good. Then I'll order a nice steak dinner from room service, take a hot bath, watch the late-night news and then sleep like a log.'

At 3 a.m. Wednesday, Connor was tossing and turning in his sleep and then the restless dozer woke-up from his distress. 'I was dreaming I was duck hunting near a country pond, but then I fathomed that I was shooting at ducks inside the mural that is glued to my den's wall. What is happening here?' the bewildered man thought. 'First, the wall-mirror up on the ninth-floor; next the Room 666 St. Mark's Square tapestry; then, the Spanish galleon that was a duplicate of the one in my dining room, and now, I'm dreaming about my home's den duck mural.' The perplexed vacationer awkwardly turned on the bed table lamp, and was dumbfounded to see that the duck mural he had envisioned in his dream was now situated on the wall above the bureau, and it had remarkably replaced the metallic Spanish galleon. The incredulous hotel guest wiped his eyes to express his total disbelief. 'I better not discuss this delusion with anyone, or else I'll be directly referred for psychological examination,' Connor assessed and determined. 'I've never had any paranormal experiences before, and I now believe that I don't relish them one iota.'

After washing and shaving at 7 a.m., Connor dressed, took the elevator to the ground floor, and out of anxiety, devoured a big buffet breakfast at *Harrah's,* and then an hour later attended an informative *CPA* conference across the strip at *Caesar's Palace*. The man's afternoon was spent casually touring the marble-façade casino/hotel's extensive Roman Forum-style shopping mall, featuring rounded and illuminated blue cloud-laden skies that majestically curved across the ceilings from horizon to horizon. 'This beautiful sight ought to clear all of the cobwebs from my head,' the still-befuddled man pondered. 'I wonder if the stylish duck mural is still on Room 666's bureau wall. It's gotta' be more than an anomaly. I mustn't drink any alcoholic beverages tonight at the gambling tables, because I think that's what's causing me to be having these terribly inexplicable dreams, and hallucinating about objects appearing and then magically changing into other wall ornaments inside my room,' Connor admonished himself'. 'Those abnormal mystifying room fixtures are pushing my self-control and my self-discipline to their limits. Am I becoming certifiably insane, or what?'

Finally, just before midnight in the city that never sleeps Connor Murphy gulped-down a sleeping tablet and a glass of water and managed to slowly drift-off into dreamland, mentally attributing his 'fixture encounters' as 'imagination caused by extreme mental exhaustion.' Connor's active subconscious mind conjured-up a scenario of him standing in a Roman-style villa next to an ancient atrium witnessing a darkened sky raining down hot ash, pumice, and lapilli upon the entire city. In the distance, *Mt. Vesuvius* was exploding its summit, and the violent eruption was causing the citizens and slaves of Pompeii to frantically scurry in all directions, seeking shelter from the unexpected violent eruption.

Connor awoke in a panic state-of-mind and quickly sat-up in his bed, sweating profusely. 'This is impossible!' the harried fellow ascertained and concluded. 'Pompeii was destroyed in 79 A.D. Now wait a minute!' the paranoid man thought. 'There's a mural of Pompeii in my living room on the wall above my sofa. And in it an inactive *Mt. Vesuvius* appears in the background. But that horrific nightmare seemed so real, so visceral, and so life-threatening!'

The extremely paranoid man reluctantly flicked-on the bedside table lamp, and was astonished to observe that the Spanish galleon decoration' had been replaced by a colorful Pompeii mural, which was a duplicate of the scene adorning Murphy's living room wall, back in

Hammonton. 'It's a good thing I woke-up, or I might've been suffocated by carbon monoxide poisonous gas or killed by having a roof collapse upon my head,' Murphy considered as his challenged mind had difficulty distinguishing fantasy from reality. 'I dare not reveal this fantastic sequence of events to anyone. They're so extraordinary that the weird events defy all standard logic and all conventional reason.'

The confused occupant of Room 666 was so unnerved and so upset from his nightmare experiences that he dressed, washed his face in the bathroom, ventured out of his room and onto the elevator and spent three frustrating hours losing four hundred dollars at various casino games of chance. Weary and defeated, the exhausted man returned to Room 666 to retrieve some of the sleep he had voluntarily missed.

'Well, at least it's now daybreak and soon light will be filtering into the room,' Connor rationally determined. 'I'll open the heavy drapes and allow radiant sunshine to penetrate through the interior sheer curtains. I'll feel safer knowing that daylight surrounds me, instead of darkness.' Then, Murphy's eyes stared in amazement at the Pompeii mural that still ornamented Room 666's wall above the main bureau.

After counting three-hundred sheep jumping over a white picket fence, Connor Murphy finally achieved a deep sleep. In his slowly developing dream the traveling accountant imagined that he was a participant in the September 27, 1066 A.D. *Battle of Hastings*. The soldier was dressed in armor disembarking (along with thirty comrades) from one of Duke William the Conqueror's ships with the rest of the invading armada anchored just offshore in the English Channel.

'Oh my God!' Connor thought in his hellish dream. 'It's the *Norman Invasion* of England! I'm carrying a carbon-copy of a very familiar shield, sword, and battleaxe, but all three are separate objects, and not welded together like the fixture that's hanging on my computer room wall!'

Desperately, Connor attempted to shake himself' out of his wicked dream and regain consciousness in his more comfortable 2005 reality, but his efforts were to no avail as the two opposing eleventh century armies converged on the battlefield. The invaders from Normandy under Duke William and his loyal barons (supported by eleven thousand obedient and subordinate soldiers) were about to engage the army of Harold II, the last Anglo-Saxon King of England. Ironically, Connor Murphy was presently involved (as an anachronism) in a huge battle that represented a major turning-point in British and in World History, which resulted in the three-hundred-year occupation and rule of England by Normans, who had clandestinely organized their English invasion from the Normandy Peninsula of western France.

Connor Murphy never awoke from his savage nightmare because an accurately shot enemy arrow had pierced his heart. The following morning, the sixth-floor housemaid discovered the accountant's bloody-chest and body partially lying under the bed covers, and the hysterical woman immediately notified House Security, who then summoned the Las Vegas Police. A thorough investigation ensued, but the inspectors, the detectives, and the forensic squad experts assigned to the case were all baffled by what their pupils detected.

"This is one for the books!" Inspector Henderson said to Detective Brubaker. "This unfortunate guy has been killed with a primitive-looking arrow, and there's no apparent explanation to account for the murder. And I must emphasize that the arrow seems ancient, like those used in medieval battles."

"And Inspector," Detective Brubaker interrupted. "How do we account for the blood dripping down from that shield ornament on the wall? And look, there's blood on the sword and on the battleaxe backgrounds, too!"

"This one is too crazy to even try and figure-out," added William Bevins, head of the investigating forensic team. "Fact One: The man's dead because he had been shot through the heart with a medieval arrow. And Fact Two: that gory-looking wall fixture that looks like it belongs in an antique auction or in a museum is thoroughly smeared with blood. We'll have to take several vials and compare the blood on the shield, sword and battleaxe with the victim's *DNA* samples. We're hopeful that the appropriate tests will confirm our findings!"

"This is the third incredible homicide that's happened in this Room 666 in the past year," Inspector Henderson contributed to the general discussion. "Perhaps we should consult with the hotel management and advise *Harrah's* to change the ominous room number to something more satisfactory. Not that I'm superstitious," the investigator continued articulating to his colleagues, "but I'm mighty suspicious of the astounding sequence of inexplicable murders that have ominously been occurring in this very jinxed hotel room!"

"The Jewelry Box"

James Donovan was feeling despondent when he left his 108th Street Stone Harbor, New Jersey two-story modular home. He checked his wristwatch and it was five p.m. September 2, 2005. The particular date haunted the man's already depressed mind. September 2nd marked the one-year anniversary of his wife Jackie's death, a victim of breast cancer. The retired *Camden Community College* professor reviewed his circumstance as he trudged down the full block to Bradley's Sub Shop on Third Avenue and 108th to order for supper a cheese steak sub' with ketchup and fried onions.

'The kids are all grown-up and on their own with their own families and concerns to worry about,' the lonely man sadly contemplated. 'Billy's living in Princeton and Heather has her condo' up in Long Branch. And Jackie was really excited about us knocking down our old little Stone Harbor bungalow and building our pre-fabricated house. The place is on valuable seashore property and it's now worth 1.2 million, but what good is it? I would give the residence away in a second to have Jackie back,' Donovan lamented and sobbed. 'The house is an empty shell without my wife's love and companionship to share it with. Sometimes life is cruel and unfair!'

Jim entered the popular Stone Harbor eatery, plopped himself down on a Bradley's counter stool and patiently waited for his order to be given and completed. Ten minutes later Donovan sipped a large *Pepsi Cola* through his straw and the melancholy man pondered other fond recollections. 'Jackie always wanted a nice home in a pleasant community at the Jersey shore. Now I would trade the home and my entire Merrill Lynch Cash Management Account just to have her back again,' the widower nostalgically regretted. 'If only I could turn the clock back to our wedding day, April 24th, 1966. Those thirty-eight years of marriage were the happiest days of my life. I feel guilty that I wasn't kinder to her, and now she's gone.'

After engaging in some small talk with the cute blonde college-age waitress, Jim began consuming his delicious steak sub'. All the while the Bradley's patron wished that some new woman with Jackie's grace, charm and good looks would enter his life. 'Jackie and I very seriously discussed the matter before her succumbing to cancer,' Donovan justified, 'and I know that I have her approval to date and remarry. If only the right refined lady would step into my life and bring me bliss. I do miss Jackie's companionship greatly, but as is often said, 'Life must go on'!'

After paying his five-dollar tab, James Donovan left the attractive tanned waitress a generous five-dollar tip. The depressed customer then lethargically exited the establishment with a full belly and an empty heart. Upon arriving at his 108th Street front doorstep the disconsolate citizen saw that the *UPS* deliveryman had left a package on his porch. The driver's brown truck was now observable two blocks east making a delivery somewhere between Donovan's expensive prefab' home and the dark blue *Atlantic Ocean*.

'This item is rather heavy,' Donovan evaluated as he lifted the carton up from his front porch. 'And the package's return name is really a strange coincidence,' the recipient acknowledged as he read the sender's identity on the shipping label. 'From: James Donovan, 437 Cactus Drive, Palm Desert, California 92210. Ship To: James Donovan, 232 108th Street, Stone Harbor, New Jersey 08247. 'What's this all about?' the confused man wondered.

James Donovan eagerly entered his two-story home and carried his newest possession through the living room into the kitchen. With his curiosity peaking, the retired political science/history professor cut the hemp that bound the package and then anxiously ripped away the exterior cardboard that enveloped the interior carton. Soon, the object of interest was fully perceived and Donovan stared at the item with heightened curiosity.

'It's an ebony jewelry box with silver hinges and a single silver-plated lock,' James marveled, 'and it's shaped like a miniature pirate's chest. Who is this other James Donovan of Palm Desert California?' the receiver asked himself. 'Is this some sort of prank or practical joke, or am I a mistaken relative of this anonymous man that bears my name?'

Being very motivated and curious, Jim Donovan slowly unlocked the silver fastening and raised the box's lid. His eyes were amazed at the container's sparkling contents. The ordinary-looking jewelry box possessed no upper tray, but instead the entire interior was a receptacle filled with dazzling diamonds, emeralds, rubies, pearls and sapphires. 'Oh my God! These precious gems must be worth millions!' Donovan greedily assessed. 'I'll rent a large safety deposit box at the bank and secretly keep this magnificent treasure there, until I need to redeem a few of these exotic beauties for cash.' The thrilled man picked-up and admired a glittering diamond and then performed a rudimentary experiment to test the mineral's authenticity. The recipient scraped the gem against a glass surface, and instantly, his little test verified that the invaluable lustrous stone was indeed genuine.

After relocating his bonanza in a newly acquired bank safety deposit box, James Donovan thought about his fantastic gift for the next several days. Then, while watching *Action News* the following Thursday evening, the anchorman announced that the New Jersey Pick-6 Winning Number worth seven million dollars is: 6,10,18, 27,35,42. 'Oh no! I forgot to play this week's lottery, and those are my six favorite numbers!' Donovan remembered five hours too late. 'Oh well! I still have my precious stones that are probably valued at more than the seven-million-dollar lottery jackpot. Who needs the lottery when I can sell the fabulous jewels individually for cash whenever I want at any reputable New York jewelry dealer's place of trade?' the man rationalized. 'If I had won the Pick-6 Lottery, I would've had to pay forty-percent of the winnings up front in taxes, just to satisfy state and federal governments! I'm much better off owning the jewels.'

When James stepped upstairs to take his nightly shower (before retiring for the evening), he felt compelled to look inside his exquisite ebony jewelry chest that was positioned atop his bedroom bureau. Donovan carefully lifted the lid and to his utter astonishment a lottery ticket dated "Thursday, September 8th" was inside with the numerical combination: "6,10,18,27,35,42!"

"Eureka!" Donovan exclaimed in total delight, almost loud enough for his nosy neighbors to hear. "I can't believe that the winning lottery ticket is situated safe and sound inside this incredible jewelry box! It must indeed be magical!" James incredulously whispered to himself. 'Maybe it'll find me a new wife to share my good fortune with. I'll just think of pleasant things and settings involving romance, and possibly, my fondest wish for female companionship might just come true!'

The following morning, the ecstatic James Donovan contacted *New Jersey Pick-6 Lottery* officials in Trenton and that evening on New York and Philadelphia news channels the winner was shown receiving his check for the colossal amount of four-million-two-hundred-thousand-dollars (with the appropriate taxes already deducted). Within the next month, the enthralled rejuvenated fellow received in the mail twenty-three marriage proposals from various aggressive women (mostly widows), the majority of whom had also sent glossy photographs. But the shrewd Stone Harbor resident was aware that those tantalizing marriage offers had only resulted because of *his* recent wealth proliferation, and not because of him or his bashful personality. 'My checking and savings accounts have never been so fat. I'll find the right lady on my own,' Donovan said to his inanimate bureau jewelry chest the following Sunday night. 'And I know that you'll adequately assist me in my endeavor. Now, Dear Chest, how can I invest a hundred-thousand-dollars of my new-found money wisely, and eventually achieve tremendous capital gains?'

On Monday morning, the retired professor woke-up in a cheerful spirit and quickly ambled-over to his most munificent ebony jewelry chest. 'Please treat me favorably today!' Donovan prayed as he gingerly lifted the very commonplace lid. Inside the wondrous ebony treasure chest was a type-printed list of ten fledgling companies' penny stocks, with the very interesting heading: "Guaranteed Big Gainers". 'This is a dream come true!' James impetuously evaluated. 'I'll invest ten-thousand-dollars in each of these recommendations, and follow the small cap companies' progress over the *Internet.* My broker will think I'm insane buying equity in upstart corporations, but he doesn't know about the mystical powers operating my special magical charm.'

Within three months, the market value of the ten small-cap corporations in Donovan's portfolio rose from the initial hundred-thousand-dollar investment to over five-million. Jim's astounded account executive phoned the widower and asked if *he* had any other "penny stock tips", but the euphoric owner of the equities stated that he had exhausted his hunches (while Donovan thought that the percentage commissions his now-inquisitive broker would earn upon selling the selections would warrant handsome compensation without the dangerous risk associated with speculative investing).

On the second Wednesday in February of 2006, "Lucky Jim" rose from bed, approached the bureau's supernatural pirate's chest, and lifted the cover. Much to the inspector's bewilderment, a sequence of ten numbers was represented on a small sheet of white paper: '1. 8, 17, 36, 47, 51, 63, 72, 76, 79,' the mystery progression read. 'What is the relevance of these ten numbers?' Donovan thought. 'They must involve some sort of gambling. Could they pertain to two consecutive Pick 5 Lotteries? There's no heading above the numbers to identify their significance. What could they pertain to?' the puzzled man pondered as his brain analyzed and attempted to interpret the challenging riddle. 'I'll memorize the ten numbers in their exact order, and later apply them to the right situation, once I finally establish a definite relationship.'

The third Friday of March, the cold, harsh winter weather finally broke along the Jersey shore, and with the coming vernal equinox, the first signs of spring were in the air. James motored his tan auto' out of Stone Harbor and took the *Garden State Parkway* fifteen-miles north to Ocean City to have a pleasant stroll on the scenic boardwalk. 'Stone Harbor doesn't have a boardwalk, and I can buy some fudge and salt water taffy at Shrivers, and have a few slices of pizza at Mack and Manco's. It's really great that Old Man Winter is finally losing his tug of war with Mother Spring. Life is full of wondrous miracles,' the invigorated man realized, but then, James Donovan recollected Jackie's 'premature death. 'Life also has its sorrowful aspects as well as its moments of triumph,' the beach-town visitor very rationally concluded.

After buying his confections and downing his delectable two slices of pepperoni pizza, James Donovan had an inspiration. 'I'll drive eight miles north to Atlantic City and try my luck at the *Tropicana Casino*. I'll make it a decent day by visiting two famous boardwalks.'

Donovan hopped into his brand-new tan *Lincoln* sedan, and soon was heading north again on the *Parkway* to *Route 322,* also known to locals as the Black Horse Pike. In another fifteen-minutes, the spur-of-the-moment visitor was turning his luxury automobile off of Pacific Avenue and soon steering the luxury car into the *Tropicana's* high-rise parking garage. 'I should've done valet parking,' the man reconsidered during his impulsive rush in judgment. 'I certainly can afford it!'

After trying several quarter and dollar slot machines, the indecisive and itinerant fellow passed by an alluring Keno lounge. Donovan watched a game in progress, and noticed that ten balls representing ten numbers had been randomly selected out of a field of eighty distinct possibilities. 'That's it; the ten numbers,' the retired political science/history instructor instantly realized with controlled enthusiasm. 'The ten numbers I've memorized from the jewelry chest list must relate to the ten balls that comprise a winning Keno jackpot. I'm no expert in mathematics, but the odds of getting all ten numbers correct are astronomical! It's probably almost as rare as hitting two Pick-Six Lotteries back-to-back!'

The prospective-but-confident player accepted a card from a pleasant hostess, and she carefully punched the dictated numbers 1, 8, 17, 36, 47, 51, 63, 72, 76 and 79. Next, the player feigned nonchalance as James impatiently waited for *his* ten accurate numbers to pop out of the bin, and then light-up on the overhead screen. Donovan was tense as the suspense he felt gradually ascended to a culmination. Finally, the game bin was activated and spontaneously filled with eighty bouncing and ricocheting plastic balls. But despite his general haughtiness, the Keno player was astounded and flabbergasted when his eyes and mind confirmed that his card undeniably contained all ten of the "lucky numbers".

"The chances of what you've just accomplished happens once in a leap year purple moon!" the astonished casino employee standing behind the cage window exclaimed. "I'll notify the manager and get a photographer over here right away. Mr., I believe you've just won yourself a staggering twenty-three-million-dollars! And that's just a conservative estimate!"

"Pay me fifteen-thousand in cash and the rest by check!" the fortunate, newly recognized number wizard commanded the still-in-shock casino manager. "Five-thousand will be for you, kind Sir; five-thousand for the cage cashier, and the remaining five-thousand cash will be for the hostess over there, who had punched-in the lucky digits. If I'm Mr. Lucky, then by George, she's gotta' be Lady Luck!"

A similar phenomenon occurred to James Donovan in late June, when a list of numbers provided by the remarkable jewelry chest represented a winning Trifecta at Monmouth Park racetrack, and the owner's sagacious ability to connect the three given numbers with three long-shot race winners afforded the gambling guru the courage to confidently bet the sum of five-thousand-dollars on three separate winning Trifectas. 'I'll donate the proceeds to charity, because a couple of hundred grand is mere chicken feed, compared to my priceless jewels and to my massive lottery and casino earnings. I could've easily bet a hundred-thousand on a hundred different Trifecta tickets, but I didn't want to bankrupt the racetrack. I'll give some of the dough to the Stone Harbor Lions Club; some to Catholic charities, and the remainder I'll donate to the *Red Cross* and the *Salvation Army*. After all, I'll need all of the deductions I can muster, when my accountant finally figures-out my income tax obligations! I'm not that greedy!' Jim sanctimoniously concluded. 'I still have a heart, a conscience, and some compassion too.'

Although James Donovan had masterfully accumulated great wealth in his various gambling enterprises, the man still lacked female companionship and essential love in his rather drab life. The wealthy 'calculated risk taker' whimsically flirted with the idea of discovering the 'second ideal woman' in an *Internet* chat room, but then, he judiciously nixed the temptation, since James didn't desire to pursue a female acquaintance when the stranger might, in reality, be 'an avaricious economic parasite'. Instead, Donovan wished for the fantastic jewelry chest to provide him with the name and email address of the perfect mate, designated to become 'Jackie's worthy substitute.'

In early July, Jim Donovan sauntered-over to his bedroom bureau's all-too-enticing jewelry chest, and deliberately and methodically opened the lid. His blue eyes detected certain information neatly typed on a sheet of computer printer paper: Gretchen Vanderhoff, *gvanderhoff@yahoo.com*. The lonely man wasted no time in authoring a letter of introduction to his ideal mate, and after several casual exchanges of emails and electronic photos'- the back-and-forth correspondences soon took on a romantic quality. Donovan agreed in his latest dispatch to travel by plane down to Oranjestad, Aruba, where his Dutch sweetheart resided and worked as a skilled legal secretary.

'I'm going to board a jet and take a flight out of Philly' to Aruba in August,' Donovan decided and planned. 'But first, I can't seem to locate my birth certificate with the raised seal, so that I can obtain a passport and photo' I.D. I wish that I could find it. I've searched all through my legal papers and documents, and can't seem to stumble across it.'

On the morning of August 10th, the retired professor opened his magical jewelry chest, and miraculously, inside was a bona fide passport accompanied by a valid-looking birth certificate with a raised seal, along with a new and updated New Jersey Division of Motor Vehicles' photo' I.D. driver's license. 'I'm surprised that the jet plane ticket to Aruba wasn't also included!' Donovan mildly mentally criticized. 'Oh well, I suppose nothing's perfect, not even magic!'

On August 27th 2006, James Donovan boarded his American Airlines jet, his destination the Dutch Antilles island of Aruba just off the Venezuela mainland. After fastening his seatbelt prior to takeoff from Philadelphia, the passenger recalled the exceptional box, which he had carefully packaged and superstitiously taken along onto the plane as a carry-on. 'Seven is a lucky number,' the now-neurotic and excited fellow thought, as the plane passenger reviewed the chronological order of bizarre events over and over in his sharp mind. 'And the outstanding ebony chest has worked like a wizard's wand seven wonderful times. First, there were the excellent jewels now secure in my Stone Harbor safety deposit box; second, the *Pick-6 Lottery* winner; third, the ten penny stock' big gainers; fourth, the once-in-a-lifetime Keno kill at the *Tropicana;* fifth, the *Monmouth Park Racetrack* success and subsequent charity donations; sixth the discovery of vivacious Gretchen Vanderhoff, and finally seventh, the acquisition of a passport and accompanying photo' *I.D.* Now, I've gotten everything including all the materialistic riches a man could ever covet! And thank God I've become happy again! I hope I haven't exhausted all of my good fortune! That's the paramount question!'

The flight from *Philadelphia International Airport* to Aruba was both smooth and enjoyable, and the plane finally touched-down on the *Caribbean* island paradise. After removing his favorite object from his seat's overhead compartment, the jubilant tourist disembarked the *737* and proceeded to "Customs." Suddenly a police dog began ferociously barking at the package containing the incomparable magic jewelry box.

"Sorry, Sir, but we'll have to inspect that item!" an Aruban customs agent demanded. "I have to determine exactly what's inside! Airport security is on high alert these days, you know!"

"It's only a cherished jewelry box! I'm taking it to my girlfriend who lives in Oranjestad," the new arrival stammered and explained. "She's going to meet me on the main concourse!"

"This precautionary search procedure will only take several minutes!" the customs official advised. "Sometimes, our dogs do detect a false positive in their sniffing, so we just have to fully check this matter out to be sure. Again, Sir. Sorry for the unexpected inconvenience!"

The two customs' agents cut the hemp and adroitly removed the outer brown paper wrapping. Gently, the customs officials extricated the ebony jewelry box from its brown paper enclosure. Then, the searchers meticulously opened the lid, and to James Donovan's utter surprise and alarm, concealed inside were four packs of an illicit white substance that the authorities immediately identified as "high quality cocaine". Instantly, the island visitor was taken into custody, and then swiftly conducted to an airport interrogation room.

Later that day, James Donovan was incarcerated in the Oranjestad jail, waiting conviction and sentencing, which would then have him transferred to the Aruban prison, a structure standing like a citadel on the north side of the island. Learning of her adventurous beau's terrible plight, Gretchen Vanderhoff, an ambitious and dedicated legal secretary, immediately abandoned her amorous affair with James Donovan and decided to pursue her lifelong aspiration of becoming a certified, practicing attorney on the island.

The imprisoned man was allowed to have his Stone Harbor mail forwarded to his Oranjestad cellblock for him to keep up-to-date on his monthly bills and other relevant financial responsibilities. The last Friday in September, the disgraced American received an unusual letter from *his* West Coast counterpart, James Donovan of Palm Desert, California. The beleaguered Aruban prisoner nervously held the missive close to his eyes. The surprise correspondence read as follows:

437 Cactus Drive
Palm Desert, California 92210
September 22, 2006

Mr. James Donovan
232 108th Street
Stone Harbor, NJ 08247

Dear James Donovan,

By now, you' have figured-out that the ebony jewelry chest I had sent you possesses magical powers that can be accessed and used only seven times. After the seventh successful employment, the jewelry chest begins generating evil events that could prove especially detrimental to your career, to your love interests, to your bank accounts, and to your entire life.

To erase the heinous Devil's curse that you have obtained, it is necessary for you to forward the box to another James Donovan, other than myself, the individual residing somewhere else inside the United States. That namesake person' you will have selected will enjoy seven terrific wishes, but then, his good luck will consequently turn sour, expire, and finally act against him.

Furthermore, Sir, do not leave the USA or else the negative realities following fortuitous event number seven will become doubly egregious. In conclusion, Mr. James Donovan, one remaining serious instruction must be communicated. You must intelligently dispose of the jewelry chest to another James Donovan within the next year. If you fail to comply with that particular mandate, then by the Will of Satan, you, James, will surely die and the diabolical Prince of Darkness, Lucifer himself, will triumphantly, and most assuredly claim your accursed, immortal soul.

Sincerely,

James Donovan
Prisoner: San Diego Jail

"The Victim"

I opened my eyes and everything I discerned appeared nebulous and hazy. My mind was dizzily vacillating-around in suspended animation and my perception of my immediate environment was definitely distorted and quite convoluted. My only recollections were fluorescent lights behind translucent ceiling panels and what my addled brain vaguely recognized as an I.V. bag hanging from a portable stand. A gentle female voice assured me that I was safe and resting. My thoughts were still in a quandary, my encumbered brain attempting to interpret my surroundings more lucidly. "Where am I?" I asked the figure dressed in white standing above my horizontal position.

"You're in a private room at Kessler Memorial Hospital, Hammonton, New Jersey," the attending nurse informed. My eyes then scanned the room to further validate the woman's statement. "You've just come out of unconsciousness. You've been in that condition for six hours now. Besides having a nasty bump on your head," the benign nurse proceeded, "you've sustained a number of minor injuries ranging from skin lacerations to a dislocated shoulder. But the Emergency Room doctor said you would pull through and so you have. But you must be in pain."

I repeatedly blinked my eyelids endeavoring to clear some of the mental images that were cluttering my inquisitive mind. "Well then nurse, who am I?" I desperately wanted to know. "I can't seem to remember who I am."

"We're still trying to determine that!" the sympathetic caregiver informed me. "That's why two gentlemen are here to ask you some questions. Dr. Kalani has given approval for them to discuss certain matters with you."

The sympathetic nurse stepped out of the room and two men, one in plainclothes and the other wearing a police uniform entered from the hallway. Immediately the tall detective introduced himself along with his austere-looking colleague. My erratic thought processes were still laboring to distinguish the true nature of my situation. My disheveled mind required more data to evaluate.

"Hello," the man in the business suit began. "I'm Detective Pete Reynolds from the Winslow Township Police Department and this is Sergeant Tony Dunsmore from the Williamstown Police. We're here to ask you' a few questions. Dr. Kalini told us that your physical condition is strong enough to endure a brief interrogation. If you cooperate," the grim-faced detective elaborated, "we'll be able to piece missing parts of the puzzle together and then have some solid answers about the circumstances relative to your injuries and also about your identity Everything' is a bit sketchy at the moment."

"Our departments are also working closely with the Hammonton Police, and all information we obtain will be shared with them," Sergeant Dunsmore added. "In your sleep, you kept mysteriously mumbling the words 'weed spray!' Sir, does 'weed spray' have any particular importance to you? We couldn't directly establish its significance!"

"No," I emphatically replied with excruciating pain being felt in my right shoulder. "I can't seem to associate that reference to anything right now. And I can't see how weed spray could land me in a hospital bed, other than the fact that it's poisonous. Have I been poisoned, too, besides having my right shoulder in a harness?"

"No, Sir," Detective Reynolds assured me. "But I believe we have to go back to square one to ascertain certain facts. Tell Sergeant Dunsmore and me what you recall about getting that massive lump on top of your skull. Were you in a fight? Did more than one person assault you?"

My brain was still a little fuzzy with general ideas expanding and contracting like the colorful elements viewed inside a kaleidoscope. Then finally, one thought settled and materialized in my head, like eddying dust collapsing onto a wet pavement. I was finally capable of communicating something I deemed relevant to the investigators. "I remember waking-up lying on the side of a road," I related. "My head hurt really bad, just above my right eye. An old bicycle was right there on the ground next to me, and it had a flat tire with a broken front rim. My first impression was that I had been riding the bike, and then got clipped by a passing vehicle in a hit and run accident," I candidly expressed as my right shoulder throbbed. "But after feeling my aching head I then realized that I was not wearing a safety helmet. And then everything went blank again."

"I see," Detective Pete Reynolds said as he hastily scribbled down some pertinent words onto his notepad. "Do you remember checking for your wallet before you passed out? You didn't have any credentials on your possession so that's why we have no *I.D.* for you."

"No, Sir," I respectfully returned, slowly shaking my head in disappointment. "My sole concerns were the severe ache in my head and getting someone to help me. Everything else was a big senseless blur. Maybe some relative or friend will show-up here to identify me."

"Can you describe the road where you were dropped-off?" Sergeant Dunsmore asked. "For example, was it a dual highway, a farm road, an avenue?"

"There were woods on both sides, that I'm pretty sure of," I recalled and shared. "And the telephone poles appeared different than usual, with larger wires, and I remember that there was a road-level wooden bridge to my left. And oh yes," I recalled and verbalized. "Incidentally, it was a two-lane country road with plenty of garbage strewn in the woods. The trees were mostly evergreens. Yes, that's correct, mostly evergreens," I reiterated with a degree of certainty.

"You've just described the Winslow-Williamstown Road," Detective Pete Reynolds of the Winslow Township Police Force verified. "It has two lanes, woods on either side, a wooden bridge, and a brook that separates Winslow Township from Williamstown Borough. The tall thick telephone poles on that road are of the high-tension variety. And litter is often tossed into the woods and the debris can be seen strewn along the highway. But we don't yet know whether or not you were riding a bicycle before suffering your trauma! Are you familiar with Winslow-Williamstown Road?"

"No, Sir," I reluctantly answered. "Never heard of it. Is it near Hanf Avenue?"

"Where's Hanf Avenue?" Sergeant Dunsmore chimed in. "I'm familiar with Winslow Township, Williamstown and the Hammonton area and there's no Hanf Avenue anywhere in those three South Jersey municipalities. We'll have to run a thorough computer check and locate Hanf Avenue. That search might help us figure out exactly who you are since you had no wallet or *I.D.* on you when you were admitted into Kessler Hospital. How do you spell Hanf?"

"H-a-n-f!" I articulated from what was left of my somewhat disintegrated memory. "Yes, H-a-n-f! And how did I get here in New Jersey?"

"What state do you live in?" the detective inquired. "If we can learn that detail it would make our job a lot easier and also assist you in putting together your *I.D.*"

"I can't seem to remember," I honestly acknowledged. "But my street address is 8507 Hanf Avenue. Maybe I'm sufferin' from temporary….."

"Amnesia," the Williamstown Sergeant competently completed my thought. "That often happens after receiving a wicked blow on the head. Did you snap out of your stupor after going unconscious along the wayside? I mean to say, what happened next?"

"Well, Officer, I staggered to my feet and my head was really throbbing like crazy as if it was goin' to explode. I was very groggy, to say the least," I declared in a frustrated tone of voice from my hospital bed. "I think I walked about a hundred feet or so and passed the wooden bridge I have already told you about. Suddenly, a dark red car stopped and offered me a ride. Naturally I got inside."

"How many people were in the red car?" Detective Reynolds asked.

"Three," I promptly replied. "The driver and a passenger in the front and another man seated in the rear."

"What nationality were these men or was it a mixed group?" Sergeant Dunsmore queried.

"They all spoke Spanish and looked like Mexicans," I visualized and uttered. "Yes, Sergeant, I'm almost sure they were Mexican farm workers by their dress, their complexions and their language."

"What kind of dark red automobile was it that picked you up?" the Winslow Township Detective asked. "A *Toyota Camry*, a *Dodge Intrepid?* A *Pontiac Grand AM?"*

"I didn't get a good look at the car so I can't really say," I sincerely replied still a trifle addled. "It had good air-conditioning, that I can tell you! And the car was definitely red."

"Where were you taken?" the Winslow Township investigator questioned. "I mean, our report indicates that you were dropped-off here in front of the Emergency Ward at Kessler Hospital! You' were discovered lying on the pavement by an outpatient and the woman immediately summoned a security guard. After you were taken inside the building, the security guard immediately contacted the Hammonton Police," the capable detective further contributed. "Captain Martinez is waiting downstairs and the three of us are going to coordinate all of our information and develop a few possible scenarios to explain your injuries. Captain Martinez has already interviewed Dr. Kalani and Mrs. Hutchins, your nurse, and they've provided us with everything you've been mumbling while you were unconscious. After our conference, we'll get back to you. I must admit that this is indeed a very fascinating case."

"Thank you," I solemnly said with an element of gratitude. "I'm very weak now and need to shut my eyes. Please get back to me with an update when I'm more rested! Maybe my dilemma will make more sense during your next visit."

* * * * * * * * * * * * *

The following afternoon, I was visited by Detective Pete Reynolds of the Winslow Police Department, Sergeant Tony Dunsmore of the Williamstown Police and Captain Jerry Martinez of the Hammonton Police Force'. It seemed logical to me that since my disappearance and travels had occurred in three separate political jurisdictions that naturally three simultaneous investigations were being jointly conducted.

"Good morning, Mr. Robert Berkheimer of 8507 Hanf Avenue, Baltimore Maryland, Zip Code 21236," Detective Reynolds greeted. "May I have the pleasure of introducing you to Captain Jerry Martinez of the Hammonton Police."

"Hello," I automatically responded. "Glad to make your acquaintance. Now Officers, I do remember that my name is Robert Berkheimer and my wife's name is Mary. If my memory serves me correctly, I had come to New Jersey to visit my cousin John Wiessner who lives on...."

"The White Horse Pike, *Route 30,"* Captain Martinez capably finished my sentence. "699 North White Horse Pike to be exact. Your cousin is a retired English teacher that lives in a light gray two-story colonial house with dark blue shutters and matching garage doors. There's a wide u-shaped driveway in the front."

"Yes, now I recall," I stammered as my fragile mind gradually exited its prolonged stupor. "Cousin John and I were going to attend a *Phillies-Baltimore Orioles* game, which I guess I missed because I'm here recuperating in the hospital. He's an avid *Phillies* fan and I'm an ardent *Orioles'* rooter. Cousin John had two box seat tickets at *Citizens Bank Park.* His wife Joanne and their children were spending the week in Ocean City, New Jersey at a rented beach house. I arrived early," I continued my narrative, "and Cousin John was busy mowing his lawn and asked me a favor. He asked if I could drive to the local Hammonton *Wal-Mart* and buy him a quart of...."

"Concentrated weed spray," an animated Sergeant Dunsmore injected into the discussion. "*Round-Up* was the particular product's name, I do believe. But anyway Robert, after your cousin gave you directions to the local *Wal-Mart* store you made the purchase and when you left the place...."

"You were accosted by six Mexican farm workers that were planning to kidnap you and steal your car," Captain Martinez deductively informed me. "During the scuffle that ensued, you were hit over the head with a blackjack and were knocked unconscious.

The Mexicans were hanging out there at the *Wal-Mart* because they had just gotten-off work early from a blueberry farm. They clobbered you over the head, and then recklessly tossed your limp body into the back of the white van. And then others in their party stole your dark red…"

"*Nissan Maxima!"* I realized and exclaimed with apparent disgust. "Actually, the car's official color is merlot. Hey, I just comprehended something awesome. After I was dropped-off by the white van into the woods, the other Mexicans that had taken my keys, and had stolen my treasured vehicle in the *Wal-Mart* parking lot, stopped and picked me up in my merlot *Maxima.* And that business about the bicycle lying beside the road…."

"Was just a crazy coincidence Mr. Berkheimer that made you think that you might've been riding the object prior to going unconscious along the roadway," Sergeant Dunsmore intelligently communicated. "The bike was just a discarded piece of litter. And when your cousin got done mowing his acre property three hours later he waited another two hours and then got nervous and finally reported you as missing to the Hammonton Police."

"Unfortunately, your pilfered *Maxima* has not been found," Detective Reynolds piped in. "But the Mexicans in the white van feared that you were not regaining consciousness so they then abandoned their kidnapping plan. It's amazing that most of these summer migrant laborers have their own cell phones, so what we' think happened next was that the Hispanics in the white van called their amigos in your merlot-colored *Maxima.* Your six abductors were probably afraid that you might die, and they decided to drive you to the nearest hospital and inconspicuously drop you off. They were smart enough to know that auto' theft is a much lesser crime than murder, and that their chances of getting caught and convicted were much greater for committing a homicide than for engaging in grand theft and selling your highly coveted *Maxima* to a Philly' chop shop. Unfortunately," Detective Pete Reynolds persuasively concluded, 'these transient farm workers have a knack for finding nefarious American citizens willing to collaborate in illicit business deals with them. That's at the moment what we think has happened in regard to your missing *Maxima*."

"I really loved that car with a passion!" I attested with a saddened heart. "But the honest-to-God truth is that most people value life over property. The 2002 *Maxima'* is fully insured and can be replaced. But my life can't be! Thank the Lord that my captors got cold feet and had the decency to deposit me in front of the Emergency Room!"

"The funny part about this entire episode is that you never realized that you had been beaten again and then dropped-off by the side of the Winslow-Williamstown Road by the Mexicans in the white van, which immediately took off," Sergeant Dunsmore emphasized with a wry smile accentuating his facial features. "Several minutes later, when you revived, you were apprehended and captured by the second wave of alleged criminals riding in *your* fancy merlot *Nissan Maxima*. And if you didn't pass-out and go unconscious for the third time after you were forced into your vehicle to be kidnapped for ransom…."

Just then, cousin John Wiessner stepped into my hospital room to pay me a visit. "Heard you had quite a spine-tingling adventure this morning Bob," my blood relative on my mother's side sarcastically announced and laughed. "That's the last time I'm ever going to ask you to do a favor or run an easy errand. I had no idea that I was putting your fragile life in jeopardy. From all of this, I've learned that even performing a casual chore at the neighborhood *Wal-Mart* could result in a life-threatening situation!"

"You said it, Cousin John!" I concurred while feeling a degree of embarrassment. "Nowadays, a person isn't even safe livin' inside the main gold vault at *Fort Knox*."

"You' said a mouthful!" Captain Martinez chuckled and supplemented. "The next time' Mr. Berkheimer you have to perform an errand around town, kindly hire the Hammonton Unit of the *New* Jersey *National Guard* to protect you. And for added security, you might want to take along two dozen well-trained *Secret Service* agents too!" the amused cop exaggerated as if he was doing stand-up comedy. All four thoroughly entertained visitors laughed indulgently at my expense. But then Cousin John had something else pertinent to relate that added more accumulative mortification to my humiliation.

"Cousin Bob," he seriously addressed me with a stern expression on his countenance, "the *Phillies* won the baseball game against your beloved *Orioles*, 5-3. But more importantly, Bob, I want to know where's my weed spray? How could you be so unreliable as to have misplaced it?"

Cousin John was literally and effectively adding insult to my aggravating and agonizing injuries. "It's either in the back of the Mexicans' white van or concealed somewhere inside my precious missing-in-action *Nissan Maxima,*" I sorrowfully lamented and reported. "That regrettable occasion happens to be the last time I'm ever goin' to voluntarily do *you* a personal favor! I feel much more comfortable and less flustered ridin' around metropolitan Baltimore than I do drivin' around rural South Jersey!"

"The three police authorities, hearing *our* harmless, quarrelsome exchange, broke-out into a boisterous roar, as if Cousin John and I were two famous veteran comedians, engaging in and debating humorous on-stage banter.

"Justification"

A front-page article recently appeared in the *Hammonton Gazette* with similar reports filed and documented in both the *Hammonton News* and the *Atlantic City Press.* The three newspaper dispatches chronicled a devastating luxury boat explosion on the historic *Mullica River,* a shallow body of water that lazily meanders through the legendary Jersey Devil pinelands of Burlington and Atlantic counties. Here is a duplication of the aforementioned journalistic account that had appeared in the *Atlantic City Press*.

Two Killed in Yacht Explosion

Two prominent Hammonton residents were killed on the *Mullica River* when (according to eyewitnesses) their luxury yacht spectacularly exploded at approximately 1:30 p.m. fifteen minutes after leaving the Sweetwater Casino/Marina dock. The victims of the unexplained blast were Mark Ranger, a successful multimillionaire/banker and real estate investor and his wife Marjorie Ranger, formerly married to a Hammonton peach and vegetable farmer Thomas Richard Crescenzo, now deceased.

The fatal incident occurred about a mile north of the recently renovated Lower Bank Bridge that crosses the scenic river. Area residents as far away as Green Bank to the west and Port Republic to the east heard the tremendous explosion, which then sent debris flying and scattering onto opposite banks of the *Mullica.*

"We're intensively investigating the matter but there's very little physical evidence to go on at the moment," State Police Captain Gordon Philbin stated. "To my knowledge nothing like this has ever happened on the river before. Our experts suspect that the accident must have been caused by mechanical failure but as of this interview, we aren't exactly ruling out the possibility of foul play, either."

"The couple had just enjoyed lunch at the Sweetwater Casino Restaurant," according to a waiter who wishes to remain anonymous. "The Rangers seemed to be having some sort of argument or loud discussion, but I don't know if that disagreement had anything to do with the terrible tragedy occurring."

The luxury yacht "Bound to Happen" was sailing downstream and heading for Chestnut Neck Marina at the river's origin on the bay where the craft is usually moored when not docked at Sweetwater. The *Press* hopes to have a more definitive follow-up article providing additional detailed information in tomorrow's early edition as soon as more facts are gleaned from the ongoing investigation.

* * * * * * * * * * * * *

Hammonton, NJ farmer Anthony Domenic Crescenzo was a hard-nosed, brawny parsimonious, second-generation Sicilian who (like most other offspring of Italian immigrants) understood the Old-World language when it was spoken but did not openly converse in it. Anthony and his many old *WWII* vintage cronies traced their roots back to Messina, Sicily and vicinity. The fraternal order of Sicilian Americans spent many evenings socializing at the Hammonton Garibaldi Lodge 1684 of the Sons of Italy on North Third Street, and often engaged in throwing "fingers" while shouting numbers in Italian, and sharing their ethnic camaraderie while imbibing plenty of beer and "homemade dago wine". But despite *his* proclivity for nighttime frivolity with old Sons of Italy chums at the lodge (and also on his farm during the daytime), Anthony Domenic Crescenzo maintained an inflexible Old World work ethic, characterized by thick calluses on his hands and heavy sweat accumulating on his brow. The uncompromising old man's hardcore personality and language always projected the philosophy: "My way or the highway!"

When not boisterously interacting with his loyal paesans Anthony Crescenzo was obsessed with strictly managing his five-hundred-acre peach, tomato, pepper, and sweet potato farm, that bordered the *Wharton State Forest* on two-lane *Route 206*. According to family tradition (during the planting and harvesting seasons), Crescenzo assiduously labored from sunrise to sunset, and the temperamental fellow was the austere overseer of every facet of his much-envied agricultural operation. Local admirers often affectionately called Anthony Domenic Crescenzo "the Mussolini of Hammonton area fruit and vegetable farming".

Anthony and wife Annie had one spoiled and doted-on child, Thomas Richard Crescenzo, named after *his* fraternal grandfather. Thomas was generally a cooperative and obedient son, but after graduating from *Temple University,* the industrious-but-hardheaded Catholic broke away from family expectation by dating a suburban Philadelphia girl, Marjorie Westbrook, whom Thomas had met at a friend's wedding, celebrated at a prestigious Malvern *Main Line* country club. But besides being a born-again Baptist, Marjorie Westbrook was of middle-class means, and immediately, old Anthony Crescenzo resented and despised the attractive young woman as if her name was "Sin."

"She's nothing but an avaricious social climber, a dedicated gold digger," the elder Crescenzo admonished *his* enchanted son. "I only wish that you would think more practically and marry the daughter of a rich Hammonton or Vineland Italian farmer. That's how things like weddings are done between influential South Jersey families, usually by arrangement and accommodation to the families' approval."

"But I love Marjorie, and would like to spend the rest of my life with her," Thomas futilely argued to deaf ears in defense of his favorite woman. "We're getting engaged in the fall and married next spring."

"You'll be sorry!" the father hostilely predicted as if his son' were destined to become involved in an abomination. "That woman's trouble with a capital T! She wants what we have, without working for a share of it. I know her kind, and women of that damned ilk will worm their way into your life, try and steal most of your assets, and then leave you high and dry without ten-cents to buy a piece of licorice. Tom," the distraught father recommended, "I'm advising you by strongly suggesting that you drop that greedy witch, and then find a nice rich Catholic Italian farm girl, instead."

Much to Anthony's chagrin, Thomas did violate his father's wishes and married Marjorie Westbrook the following April. At age seventy-five, the senior Crescenzo had to honor reality and surrender his majority interest in his fruit and produce empire to his only "obstinate child". The elder's wife Annie was dying of breast cancer, so the plantation owner's options to ensure the continuation of the prosperous estate had been drastically limited. The physically failing patriarch revised his will and generously turned over most of his assets to his perfectly disobedient but content son.

Annie Crescenzo finally succumbed to cancer and died three years later, and thereafter Anthony was heartbroken at his spouse's passing. But other annoying factors began to excessively aggravate the "semi-retired lame duck President of Sunsweet Farms, Incorporated." Anthony had heard rumors abounding around Hammonton that Marjorie was having a love affair with a certain "too big for his britches" town bank manager, Mr. Mark Ranger. Using his influence in the rustic, rural community, the vengeful patriarch surreptitiously had the amorous Ranger moved to another branch of the regional bank, located twelve miles away from Hammonton in Mays Landing.

"You'd better be careful!" Anthony cautioned his aberrant but idealistic son in the packinghouse's main office. "That money-hungry woman will steal the eyes off a blind man! And I hear around the gossip mill she's havin' an affair with a flirtatious bank manager named Mark Ranger."

"Don't listen to that cheap scuttlebutt circulatin' around town, Dad!" Thomas answered in loving defense of his wife. "She, Mark and me are good friends, and that's all there is to it! But Mark's just been transferred to the bank's Mays Landing branch, so I suppose Marjorie and I won't be seeing as much of him now. Mark's really a pretty decent guy, and you shouldn't prejudge him on the basis of some wild town hearsay."

"You' naïve fool!" the now-livid father reprimanded. "I turned over most of my assets to you, so that hopefully, you'd see the truth as clearly as I see it. But unfortunately, son, I had made a terrible mistake in judgment."

"Dad, I wish you'd stop being so distrustful and cynical and learn to accept Marjorie into the family," Thomas honestly and genuinely stated. "You've been discriminating against her right from the start. And you've treated her cruelly these last four years, and it's severely damaged *our* relationship. I mean, I appreciate you giving me control of the farm, and all that, but I can't tolerate any longer how flagrantly mean you've treated my wife."

Without old Anthony Crescenzo's knowledge or approval, Marjorie convinced her gullible husband to finance Mark Ranger's acquisition of a local shopping mall for a twenty-five percent interest in the property, after the ambitious banker's three-hundred-thousand-dollar loan would be eventually paid-off with the terms of the

Promissory Note being "satisfied in full". Thomas Crescenzo never realized that he was subsidizing his wife's trysts with Mark Ranger, along with her secret infidelity. Each lovers' rendezvous would occur when Thomas was away attending County Board of Agriculture meetings in May Landing, and State Board of Agriculture meetings in Trenton. In fact, whispers were rampant throughout the State that the next Republican Governor might appoint Thomas Richard Crescenzo as the next New Jersey Secretary of Agriculture.

The animosity between Marjorie and her stubborn, rigid father-in-law was ever mounting, especially after the power and control of Sunsweet Farms Incorporated had been officially transferred from the patriarch to his only son. But as Mark Ranger's investment enterprises flourished, Anthony Domenic Crescenzo's huge farm saw "lean years" when California peaches began taking market share away from Jersey fruit growers, particularly in the New York, Philadelphia, Baltimore, Albany, and Boston food distribution centers. And when Thomas Richard Crescenzo finally determined that Marjorie was betraying his trust and involved in a two-male one-woman love triangle, the normally tranquil farmer violently erupted into a rage, suffered a massive coronary, and died in his kitchen before rescue squad paramedics ever arrived at the farmhouse.

Thomas's viewing and funeral were well attended by most of the Hammonton high society aristocrats, but a week after the burial big trouble between Anthony and straying daughter-in-law Marjorie Crescenzo was imminent. It all started when the elder arrived at his deceased son's mansion to make amends, but then the feuding pair became embroiled in a heated argument at the kitchen's back doorstep.

"Here's a copy of my husband's will," Marjorie indicated to her longtime enemy, without mincing any of her words. "A,nd it clearly states in paragraph one that I've inherited *his* farm. I never want to see you step foot onto the packinghouse, into the office, into the cold storage, or into any of the fields and orchards again, or else I'll go to a judge and get a restraining order, and have you arrested on the spot for trespassing!"

"What?" the elder Crescenzo incredulously exclaimed. "I toiled all my blessed life here in New Jersey building-up this successful business, and now you're kicking me off my own premises! I built this plantation up from seventy-five acres to a five-hundred-acre empire, and now you're trying to push me out, and evilly capitalize on my life's labor. This is a wrongful deed you're blatantly committing, young lady, and I'll not stand for it! I was right when I told my son that you were trouble with a Capital T!"

"You have no legal grounds to stand on, regardless of what your opinion is," Marjorie insisted. "You voluntarily gave your farm away to my husband, who died and then generously transferred the property to me in his will. That's what you get for being a mean old coot all these years. The chickens have finally come home to roost. You foolish, old, demented man! You outsmarted yourself royally and you've no one to blame but yourself!"

"But all of the improvements I've made, all the money I've invested in buildings, machinery, and equipment, and to think that those investments are no longer mine! I knew I should've listened to Annie and not have signed over my estate to my all-too-innocent and gullible son," the woebegone aged Sicilian lamented and answered. "I hope to live to see you die, just like you and Mark Ranger have lived to see my dear Thomas pass on!"

"Not a snowball's chance in Hades!" Marjorie scornfully yelled. "And from now on, I never want to see your ugly wrinkled face again on *my* property, as long as I live! And furthermore," the incensed widow continued her antagonistic tirade, "you ought to stay confined to your small house that was the original homestead. If you recall, Mr. Crescenzo, you poor excuse for a human being. You also signed over the manor house to Tom, and now my husband has fortuitously willed it to me. There's no retroactive clause in Thomas's last will and testament, and you never for a moment ever suspected that you would outlive your son, you miserable old goat! Live like a pauper on your meager monthly Social Security check, my dearly beloved father-in-law," the angry woman sarcastically ranted. "And may your pathetic soul burn and rot in hell a hundred times over for every instance when you had mercilessly berated me in front of the hired help!"

The shocked old man left his former house with his head crestfallen at learning the specific terms of his deceased son's 'surprise will'. 'I developed and expanded the farm, and now that witch owns the result of sixty-years of blood, sweat, and tears,' Anthony bitterly sobbed. 'But I'm not defeated yet, by any legal documents, and I'll not be a victim of my own stupid indiscretion. My greedy daughter-in-law and her playboy banker/lover will pay for their arrogance! One thing we Sicilians know well is how to be vindictive when our due respect is not given!'

The wily old farmer made several relevant phone calls to begin consummating his black-hearted revenge scheme. First, Anthony contacted several South Philly' Mafia acquaintances he had known from their frequent visitations to the local Sons of Italy Lodge and to the Hammonton Mt. Carmel Society Meeting Hall. Next, the irate elder Crescenzo converted into cash several bank accounts he had shrewdly "squirreled away" as "necessary compensation money" to initiate his retribution scheme. The highly motivated miser had ample incentive to retaliate and old Anthony was inclined by spite to use every ounce of energy in his body and every penny in his bank accounts to seek his personal reprisal. 'My daughter-in-law and her gigolo lover have tangled with the wrong Sicilian!' the embittered widower flattered himself and thought. 'I'll live to see my avowed enemies destroyed and eliminated! This promise I pledge to my deceased wife and son!'

The Mafia "rub-out" would cost Anthony Domenic Crescenzo a hundred-thousand-dollars, the bank account withdrawals virtually wiping-out his dwindling cash assets. But in the final analysis, the domineering, rancorous old codger (with the convoluted value system) believed that the tidy round-numbered sum of $100,000.00 was "morally justified to squander".

Humans generally are creatures of habit, and Mark Ranger and Marjorie "Crescenzo" Ranger were no exceptions to that simple rule. Every Friday during autumn, the happily eloped couple would have an early lunch at the nautical-themed Sweetwater Casino Restaurant, and then leave the popular back-river establishment just after noontime. According to their weekly schedule, the unsuspecting pair would board Mark Ranger's yacht at the restaurant's marina, and then travel from Sweetwater seventeen-miles down the *Mullica* to the Chestnut Neck Marina.

Anthony Domenic Crescenzo's ruthless Mafia associates imported and delegated several of their "hired help" from Miami "to erase a few undesirable characters." The assigned henchmen happened to be accomplished scuba divers, who on Thursday night, stealthily swam underwater to the designated pleasure craft, and then skillfully attached several powerful explosive devices onto the exterior hull of Mark Ranger's streamlined, ocean-worthy yacht, the "Bound to Happen". The timers were very meticulously set to detonate at 1:30 p.m. the following day, just minutes after the expensive yacht would predictably leave its Sweetwater mooring.

'He who laughs last laughs best!' Anthony Domenic Crescenzo thought and chuckled as the revenge-seeker carefully read the front-page story of the Saturday early-bird edition of the *Atlantic City Press.* 'I had told my son on many occasions that there are millions of beautiful Catholic-Italian girls he could have fallen in love with. The lesson here is to never cross paths with a vengeful, old Sicilian! Even though I've lost my life's sacrifice, I can now thankfully die in peace! But first, I'll see if I can successfully challenge my dead daughter-in-law's will at the County Courthouse over in Mays Landing, and hopefully, with a degree of political influence, I'll get my rightful assets back in my name! Tom never learned that there's no sweeter justice than vindictive Sicilian justice!'

"Cemetery Walk"

Brian Riley was a retired Edgewood Regional High School English teacher who resided on French Street in Hammonton, New Jersey. The manic-depressant widower had three grown sons, Frank, David and Stephen, all living in various parts of the *Garden State*. Brian's wife Lisa had died from *ALS* on 10/06/2000. The last ten months of Lisa's life were most difficult for Brian to endure, watching his spouse's health deteriorate, her knuckles becoming gnarled and her windpipe narrowing to the point where breathing eventually became an impossible task.

Whenever the weather and temperature were favorable during the spring, summer, and fall, several times each week the former educator would walk a mile in Hammonton's Greenmount Cemetery on First Road south of town, but for the most part Brian Riley preferred getting his daily exercise in the smaller but more aesthetic and serene Oak Grove Cemetery situated across from the newly constructed Hammonton High School on the corner of Old Forks Road and busy *Route 30*, the White Horse Pike.

On an early October Thursday morning, Brian left his French Street bi-level home and motored to Oak Grove hoping to be inspired by the many autumnal hues of the resplendent deciduous trees. Brian's intention was to meditate in private and to reminisce the glorious past by recalling people the introverted retired pedagogue had once known. The driver parked his automobile in his favorite corner spot under a canopy of stately oaks. Each 'good-weather-day ramble' through Oak Grove Cemetery brought back many nostalgic memories to the very sensitive stroller's usually melancholy frame of mind.

'If I walk all of the asphalt cemetery lanes the distance is exactly one mile,' Brian reminded himself as he admired the many tall magnificent oak, elm, sycamore and tulip trees that abounded in the old graveyard. 'I know this fact to be true because I once recorded the distance on my car's odometer.' But then a rather disturbing realization entered the man's presently unsettled mind. 'I actually know more dead people than living ones. I suppose that's what happens when one reaches Social Security age. Next to May, I think that October has to be my' most appreciated month of the year. This year's fall leaves are really spectacular in appearance.'

Along his daily jaunt, Brian would occasionally stop to read the names of deceased loved ones, friends, and acquaintances now permanently resting in peace, their short epitaphs carved on various-shaped tombstones verifying each individual's identity and earthly tenure. 'Most of my immediate family and my long-gone ancestors are buried here in Oak Grove,' Brian sadly contemplated. 'And their granite monuments are testaments to their lives and also to man's mortality. If only I could magically bring them all back to life and let each one of them know how much I had truly valued their company and their friendship. You don't know how much you care for people until they're gone forever.'

Just adjacent to where Brian had parked his black *Honda Accord* under the beautiful oak tree canopy were the graves of *his* maternal grandparents with his father and mother's headstones located directly behind the large front stone. 'Grandpop Tony used to take me in his black stake body truck each morning to Olivo's Grocery Store on Central Avenue and buy me a package of three *TastyKake* chocolate cupcakes,' Brian fondly recollected. 'And when I was a kid Grandma Annie would always give me ten dollars of hard-earned money to spend at each of the two summer carnivals that annually came to town. It's all of the little things in life that when added-up really matter, each one accumulating onto the pile to contribute to a young person's wholesome maturation and development,' Brian fondly evaluated. 'And how could I ever forget Dad having baseball catches with me in our backyard and Mom's delicious apple pies and homemade spaghetti. But these remembrances only make me wish that my folks were alive again, animated, giving me guidance and contributing to my welfare and general happiness,' Riley assessed. 'God! How I genuinely do miss all of you! Perhaps someday we'll all be happily reunited in a bigger and better place!'

Directly behind his mother's grave Brian's Aunt Frances had been buried and right behind his father's final resting place Uncle Ben had been interred and laid to rest. 'Every late December in the years 1957-61 Aunt Frances would drive Grandpop Tony, Grandma Annie and me down to Florida on *Route 301* before *Interstate I-95* had been completed. My grandparents owned a ranch-style home in North Miami Beach and the three adults would always give me spending money to buy candy, play pinball and to enjoy hot fudge sundaes and banana splits at corner pharmacy and department store ice cream counters,' Brian sadly recollected. 'And Uncle Ben taught me how to correctly hit a punching bag if I ever needed boxing skill to defend myself and he taught me how to drive a truck through peach orchards and tomato and pepper fields. Gee,' Brian reflected, 'I really miss all of you. If only I could bring each and every one of you back to life for just one day. But alas, how futile and foolish it is to engage in wishful thinking! I've always been a dreamer and a romantic!'

Not situated too far away from his immediate family were the gray stone memorials of Uncle Tim and Aunt Katherine Falcone. 'Aunt Katherine was a kind-hearted but domineering woman that always treated me nice and poor Uncle Tim was a shy and bashful Walter Mitty-type fellow who always honored commands sternly issued by his bossy wife,' Brian recalled. 'And their oldest son Johnny and I are best friends to this day and often go out on the *Mullica River* in his small boat or we'll scoot over to the Hammonton *Applebee's* or to the Mill Street Pub in Mays Landing for hamburgers and fries. And I know that Cousin Johnny thinks about his deceased parents just as often as I mediate about my relatives now, ghosting around in the hereafter.'

The next stretch of asphalt road in Oak Grove Cemetery led to the graveyard's maintenance building, which was in need of a new roof along with a new paint job. And then the cheerless trekker's feet walked around a lengthy oval-shaped lane that was shaded by majestic tall oaks, several of them having exposed insides, their barks being hit and torn away by lightning.

'There's Larry Bertino's grave,' Brian recognized. 'Larry was a friend who was also born in October of 1942 just like me nine months after *Pearl Harbor*, and that's no strange coincidence. He had two hundred acres of peaches but then unfortunately got involved in several unsavory business deals, lost his savings and had to dissolve all of his assets to pay off his debts. But still Larry and I took several business trips together to Washington DC, where we had invested in small companies that exhibited their innovative products at trade shows,' Brian recalled. 'Sorry to say to you' Larry that the two upstart corporations went bankrupt shortly after your departure from this Earth. But as you had always told me, 'Nothing ventured, nothing' gained or lost'. Oh well Larry,' the trekker lamented and mused while wiping a tear away from his right eye, 'you went from millionaire to liquidation while I'm still working on becoming a millionaire. And just to think that you had inherited, bought and once owned four houses while I'm still paying off the mortgage on my first one. But what good did all of that materialism do you? What good is being the richest or the poorest man in the cemetery?'

Fifty-feet from Larry Bertino's weed-infested grave rested Tony DiCicco, a happy-go-lucky builder that had lived every moment as if it was his last. 'I once worked sixteen summers back in the late '60s through the early '80s, owning and managing an Ocean City, Maryland boardwalk amusement arcade,' Brian remembered, 'and one gloomy rainy night, I took Lisa out to dinner at the Ship's Café Marina Restaurant on 15th Street and the bay. I was surprised to see Tony partying there a long' one hundred and seventy-five miles away from Hammonton. Tony, you had explained to Lisa and me that you were down in Ocean City doing cement work on a high-rise condominium project and then you joined us for supper and generously picked-up the dinner and drinks' tab,' Brian's mind resurrected from memory as he peered down at the nicely maintained sod gravesite. 'Little things sure mean a lot Tony, especially unexpected acts of courtesy. As Bob Hope often sang, thanks for the memories. And when I think of *you* there are many pleasant ones.'

On the opposite side of the well-shaded oval lane was the gravesite of Dave Anderson, who back in 1985 was a strong-looking New Jersey State Trooper that shockingly had suffered a fatal heart attack in the prime of his life. 'The Lord took you away Dave four decades too soon,' Brian thought. 'We were in the Hammonton Lions Club together and of all the guys I knew, you were in the best physical condition, the ideal human specimen. You' religiously ran ten miles each day rain or shine, diligently lifted weights and had a thin, trim muscular physique. Every man in the club was envious of your svelte well-built appearance. But then Dave you collapsed coming out of a hot shower and an autopsy revealed that you had died from an enlarged overdeveloped heart. I miss you, Dave. You never realized that the heart is a muscle that shouldn't be overdeveloped by being overworked. I must admit that the Lions Club meetings aren't quite the same with your illustrious humor being absent.'

At the end of the impressive, picturesque oval lay Buddy Zarro and Frank Cramer, two local peach growers that ironically had farms that paralleled one another just as *their* Oak Grove graves presently do. 'Buddy, you were extremely funny. And you always stuttered when you were anxious or nervous and your self-deprecating good humor represented in your telling of silly jokes and puns always cracked me up when I was a kid looking for adults to model my behavior after. And Frank,' Brian gratefully remembered the second peach farmer, 'you would take me on bumpy dirt road rides in your flat-body truck and you would drive me into your dad's orchards and we would stop and load your vehicle up with baskets of soft peaches. Then we would deliver the delicious fruit to area farm markets, go back to your dad's farm and repeat the process all over again,' Brian rehashed. 'You and Buddy were good neighbors and *we* spent many good times together when I was growing-up back in the fabulous '50s. And both of you would often drive me out to Royale Crown Custard Stand as a reward for helping you pick-up and deliver baskets of peaches. And Buddy, how could I forget that your favorite ice cream flavor was vanilla fudge and Frank, you had a weakness for butter pecan. Some things, some special wonderful little marvelous things, I'll never forget in my old age even if I ever suffer from dementia!'

A left turn onto a circular asphalt lane brought Brian to a mausoleum where his father-in-law, Domenic Russo, a legendary area peach farmer was resting in peace. 'You and I never saw eye to eye and always argued on every subject from religion to politics,' Brian considered as he slowly approached the granite structure. 'But I suppose you now know the truth about Christianity and all of its promises of eternal reward or of infinite punishment. Nevertheless I'm sorry for offending and upsetting you on many occasions where our views and opinions about running *your* huge farm clashed,' the trekker candidly weighed and regretted, 'but I want you to know that I harbor no hard feelings or antipathy towards you. Domenic, let's allow bygones to be bygones!'

After the walker had completed the impressive circular path Brian Riley had to hike a long straight quarter mile length, which marked one side of the outer perimeter of Oak Grove Cemetery that presently faces the new Hammonton High School, which had been erected behind well designed sod-mounded landscaping on Old Forks Road. The new school's contemporary-architecture structure appears palace-like, situated behind the series of irregular high manmade banks.

Midway down the asphalt lane rests Mikey Harkins, a former close friend of Brian's son Stephen. Mikey's parents had been killed in an automobile accident when *he* was a youngster and so Mikey was raised and provided for by his grandfather. 'I had always felt sorry for you Mikey,' Brian thought in an informal prayer, 'especially when I would drive you home after you and Steve had middle school baseball games or basketball practices. And to think that you too coincidentally died in an auto' accident shortly after you had turned seventeen and had obtained your driver's license. Steve has never quite gotten over your sudden violent death. May perpetual light shine upon you'. I hope Mikey, that you're happy now wherever you might be. The Lord had taken you way too soon!'

A little further down the lengthy lane lay Heather Cataldi, a former Accelerated English student whom Brian Riley had taught at Edgewood High. Heather had died at age twenty-two when she had been a passenger in a speeding car that veered off a local back road and severed a telephone pole in half. 'You were a good student and you deserved a much better fate,' Brain meditated as he respectfully stood before the young woman's tombstone. 'You never had a chance to realize your potential! The last time I saw you' Heather you were a waitress serving dinner at a local caterer's place of business. I wish we had talked more that day but you were in such a rush. If anyone deserves a second chance at life,' Brian Riley critically analyzed, 'it's either you Heather Cataldi, or you Mikey Harkins! I hope that you two auto' accident victims have become close friends in the afterlife.'

Making a right angle turn at the end of the lengthy, straight Oak Grove Lane (that rises on an incline alongside Old Forks Road), Brian arrived at the gravesite of Harry Olive, who stipulated in his will that he preferred to be cremated rather than be embalmed. Even in his old age Harry was a handsome man who liked gambling, playing cards, flirting with gorgeous women, and even late into his Golden Years Harry Olive also demonstrated a definite enjoyment of rye whiskey. When sober and focused Harry Olive' was a highly skilled carpenter that made "from scratch" many benches while working on "handyman projects" for Brian's father and for his maternal grandparents' farm markets. 'Well Harry,' Brian thought, 'you now know whether or not St. Peter guards Heaven's pearly gates. I hope the legend isn't just some fanciful glorified religious mythology. If the fabled gates to a blissful Heaven really exist,' Brian speculated, 'then kindly meet me there whenever my number comes-up with my corresponding name being selected in the eternal lottery.'

Further down the asphalt lane Brian passed the inimitable tombstone of Daniel Domenico, a dedicated and competent attorney who for several decades served as the Edgewood Regional High School Board solicitor. Brian considered and reviewed in his mind all of the heated debates that Dan and he had had when Riley was serving as the President of the high school teachers' association and Domenico was on the opposing side of the negotiating table faithfully safeguarding the taxpayers' dollars. 'The important thing is that you and I respected one another despite our widespread differences in educational philosophy and in school management matters,' Brian thought as he stopped to keenly peer at Dan Domenico's headstone. 'And you, Dan, like my father had been a *World War II* veteran and I have to hold your name in high regard for your admirable and honorable service to your country. You risked your life so that others could live in freedom.'

And on the opposite side of the tranquil lane rested Robert Rodio, who was an opinionated garrulous Sicilian that frequently wrote controversial 'Letters to the Editor' to local newspapers, successfully stirring up public debate. Brian and Robert Rodio had their differences and they usually advocated conflicting points of view. Their intense 'opinion battles' had often been fought on the *Hammonton News* and the *Hammonton Gazette's* Op/Ed pages. But then Robert developed a malignant brain tumor that eventually took his life, and now Brian felt guilty about having his fierce journalistic war of words (ranging in subjects such as "How to Cure the Pollution Problem in Hammonton Lake" to "How to Make Public School Education More Economically Efficient") with the now-deceased medical supply salesman.

At the cemetery's next corner there is a looping lane that forms a peculiar-shaped bow and next the asphalt road arrives back at its original corner origin. Near the loop's middle rests Jeff Corma, an outspoken and tough dwarf that had earned a satisfactory living (and a fine reputation) growing and selling cucumbers, peppers, corn and zucchini squash. As Riley ambled by the former diminutive farmer's grave Brian recollected how *he* had worked the full summer of 1986 for the hard-to-please vegetable grower and how the two were always at loggerheads as to how certain mechanical problems should be solved and the two often disagreed on how certain selling strategies should be employed. But despite their many disputes and verbal wrangles Jeff Corma and Brian Riley always managed to compromise in the end and find a mutually compatible answer to the two egomaniacs' crisis-in-progress. 'One never knows his or her longevity on this Earth,' Brian solemnly concluded.

And three-quarters around the unique cemetery loop rested the remains of Vince Campione, a crackerjack Hammonton attorney who in 1971 had helped Brian Riley obtain a copyright for a board game drawing that never quite materialized into a bona fide manufactured product. But the legal experience opened the door for Riley to later in life pursue and acquire copyrights for his twenty-eight self-published fiction books, many of the titles now top sellers at Amazon, at Barnes and Noble, at Booksamillion, at AllDirect, and at Buy.com.

And after rounding the loop's bottom corner and entering the lane leading to his parked black *Honda Accord* Brian passed by the grave of *World War II* veteran and I have to hold your name in high regard for your admirable and honorable service to your country. You risked your life so that others could live in freedom.'

And on the opposite side of the tranquil lane rested Robert Rodio, who was an opinionated garrulous Sicilian that frequently wrote controversial 'Letters to the Editor' to local newspapers, successfully stirring up public debate. Brian and Robert Rodio had their differences and they usually advocated conflicting points of view. Their intense 'opinion battles' had often been fought on the *Hammonton News* and the *Hammonton Gazette's* Op/Ed pages. But then Robert developed a malignant brain tumor that eventually took his life, and now Brian felt guilty about having his fierce journalistic war of words (ranging in subjects such as "How to Cure the Pollution Problem in Hammonton Lake" to "How to Make Public School Education More Economically Efficient") with the now-deceased medical supply salesman.

At the cemetery's next corner, there is a looping lane that forms a peculiar-shaped bow and next the asphalt road arrives back at its original corner origin. Near the loop's middle rests Jeff Corma, an outspoken and tough dwarf that had earned a satisfactory living (and a fine reputation) growing and selling cucumbers, peppers, corn and zucchini squash. As Riley ambled by the former diminutive farmer's grave Brian recollected how *he* had worked the full summer of 1986 for the hard-to-please vegetable grower and how the two were always at loggerheads as to how certain mechanical problems should be solved and the two often disagreed on how certain selling strategies should be employed. But despite their many disputes and verbal wrangles Jeff Corma and Brian Riley always managed to compromise in the end and find a mutually compatible answer to the two egomaniacs' crisis-in-progress. 'One never knows his or her longevity on this Earth,' Brian solemnly concluded.

And three-quarters around the unique cemetery loop rested the remains of Vince Campione, a crackerjack Hammonton attorney who in 1971 had helped Brian Riley obtain a copyright for a board game drawing that never quite materialized into a bona fide manufactured product. But the legal experience opened the door for Riley to later in life pursue and acquire copyrights for his twenty-eight self-published fiction books, many of the titles now top sellers at Amazon, at Barnes and Noble, at Booksamillion, at AllDirect, and at Buy.com.

And after rounding the loop's bottom corner and entering the lane leading to his parked black *Honda Accord* Brian passed by the grave of Tony "the Fox" Cirillo, a local gangster having Philadelphia Mafia connections. Decadence and crime meant little to Tony the Fox, who Brian had suspected of sending in a team of hit men to rob his father-in-law's house in the summer of '69 and stealing the peach farmer's weekly payroll. Domenic Russo and his wife Charlotte were then tied-up with wires from their telephones and next bound and gagged. 'The slickly executed cash heist had all of the markings of a mob raid. But now you Tony the Fox and my father-in-law are neighbors residing on different blocks in Oak Grove Cemetery and somehow your troublesome pasts must be erased and an atmosphere of harmony between you two created,' the penitent pedestrian hypothesized in what constituted an erudite mental conjecture. 'I know at least fifty other people that are buried in this cemetery,' Riley sadly estimated, 'but the ones I've thought about today are the folks I remember most.'

Finally, Brian was coming to the end of his standard early morning Oak Grove Cemetery itinerary. Just beyond his parked black *Honda* was Lisa's peaceful gravesite with her name and month of death 'October 2000' engraved on the polished brown headstone. The distinct memory of his wife and the years of joy they had shared made the cemetery trekker suddenly feel very sentimental. 'I wish I could be with her right this moment,' Brian sincerely desired with all his heart. 'I was born on October 6, 1942, Lisa died on October 6th, 2000, and today October 6th 2005 marks the fifth anniversary of my wife's death,' the disconsolate man reminded himself. 'What a terribly cruel diabolical coincidence! My sixty-third birthday is also the five-year-anniversary of Lisa's death!' Then the perplexed reader became very jittery and paranoid.

The customary blank space on the right-hand-side of the granite headstone represented Brian Riley's future interment along with the month of his demise. But then the unsuspecting trekker stopped in his tracks and was astounded at what his eyes perceived. Riley's fantastic discovery was not serendipitous.

'This is impossible!' the stunned observer thought. On the right-hand side of the polished brown tombstone the viewer's name "Brian Riley" and the etching "October 2005" had been mysteriously and freshly inscribed. The shocked observer momentarily held his chest and his heart was pounding incessantly in a rather frightening rhythm. Then the afflicted man's knees buckled and he collapsed to the ground, an apparent victim of supernatural intervention disguised as coronary thrombosis. Twenty minutes later Brian's lifeless body was discovered without any pulse or corresponding vital signs by the Oak Grove Cemetery caretaker', who panicked and frantically dialed *911* on his cell phone.

After Hammonton paramedics and police finally arrived at the venerable cemetery the rescue squad personnel desperately attempted performing a resuscitation using a defibrillator, but it soon became quite evident that Brian Riley's restless spirit had already departed planet Earth.

"This man is dead! He's expired! He can't be revived!" the Hammonton Rescue Squad Captain yelled.

"He's Brian Riley!" the chief paramedic's assistant exclaimed. "He's in the Lions Club with me! Let's try again! This man's too young to die!"

The only cause/effect clue for the befuddled body discoverers to interpret and decipher was the copy of the morning edition of the *Atlantic City Press* left on the front seat of the black *Honda Accord,* the innocuous date reading: “October 6, 2005.” No one present on the cemetery scene had the wherewithal or the imagination to comprehend and articulate that date’s esoteric significance. The coincidences associated with October 6th had only been fathomable to the now-deceased Brian Riley.

"The Fountain of Youth"

For centuries, the *Fountain of Youth* legend has captured the imagination of adventurous men. The mythological spring was thought to be able to guarantee eternal life and to heal the maladies of any human that drank its reputed precious water. Early Spanish explorers believed that the magical fountain was located somewhere in the vicinity of what is now St. Augustine, Florida, but local Indians embellished the tale by suspecting that the much-sought-after rejuvenating wonder existed somewhere in the Bahamas. But a quiet shy man named Ricardo Cortez had the advantage of knowing exactly where the mythical *Fountain* was to be found.

In July of 1930 Ricardo Cortez retired at age seventy from his employment as a locomotive engineer practicing his trade on the *Pennsylvania Railroad.* Three months later the widower packed his bags, sold his South Philadelphia row house and moved to Ft. Myers, Florida. Ricardo stayed in a downtown hotel until he purchased a dilapidated house on Flamingo Lane just off *Route 41* in Bonita Springs, ten miles south of Ft. Myers.

The property (including the in-need-of-repair bungalow) had been purchased from the heirs of the estate of one Gonzalo Pizarro, who according to *his* two surviving sons had accidentally died at age 97 when a speeding automobile hit him while the elder was crossing a busy downtown Ft. Myers intersection. Being a handyman with a good knowledge of machines, carpentry, electricity, and masonry, Ricardo Cortez was content during the next five years making much-needed renovations to the ramshackle one-story wooden frame home. Much to his satisfaction Ricardo remained living for seventy-five additional years while still maintaining the decent physique of a seventy-five-year-old man (without showing any apparent aging), and the remarkable Bonita Springs resident finally died in the fall of 2005. Here's how it all happened.

One morning in late September of 1935 Ricardo Cortez was preoccupied cutting down dense underbrush and tangled vines in his Bonita Springs, Florida backyard when the retired railroad engineer discovered water gurgling out from an underground spring'. A closer examination of the liquid's source (that had been found under a jangle of tall weeds) fascinated the conscientious homeowner. Ricardo astutely observed that fresh water was bubbling-up from a coral rock basin. Every day the man sipped cold refreshing water from "the fountain", and several years later Cortez reached the pertinent conclusion that his arthritis had been cured, his rheumatism no longer pained him, the wrinkles had vanished from his face, ugly brown age marks had disappeared from his skin and his stamina reverted back to how it had been in the 'Gay 1890s.'

"I think I've actually found the *Fountain of Youth*," Ricardo said to his rippling reflection in the coral rock basin. 'And now I know why Gonzalo Pizarro lived to be spry right up to age 97,' the newly revitalized man realized and considered. 'Old Pizarro must have regularly drunk water from this splendid fountain, which naturally preserved his health and cured all his diseases. And Pizarro probably kept the fantastic spring a secret all to himself. I suspect that Gonzalo's sons probably never learned of the wonderful water's existence otherwise they would've never sold me this fabulous Florida property at such a bargain price.'

Being inspired by his 'outstanding new-found possession, Ricardo Cortez did extensive research on the life of Juan Ponce de Leon and soon became an expert on the early Spanish explorer's biography. In fact,'s Cortez became the foremost authority on Juan Ponce de Leon in all of Bonita Springs, Florida.

'Ponce de Leon was born in San Servos, Spain and participated in the final Spanish war against the Moors,' Ricardo recorded in his spiral notebook. 'He sailed with Columbus in 1493 on the sea rover's second voyage to America. De Leon later conquered Puerto Rico in 1508 and the city of Ponce on the south side of the island is named in his honor since de Leon was Puerto Rico's first governor,' the self-appointed biographical authority recollected from his recent studies and then enthusiastically jotted-down the commonplace academic information in his personal journal.

Ricardo's ballpoint pen ran out of black ink and so Cortez opened his desk drawer and obtained another similar writing utensil. 'In 1513 Ponce de Leon finally reached the American mainland. The ambitious Conquistador then explored much of the newfound peninsula and boldly claimed the territory for the Spanish Crown,' Ricardo scribbled onto paper, 'naming the land Florida because of its many varieties of beautiful and exotic flowers. Soon the famous explorer became familiar with an old Indian myth that told of a magical fountain that afforded its drinkers' excellent prolonged health and eternal life,' Ricardo recalled from his astute investigation and then entered into his historical record.

The writer's second ballpoint ran out of black ink and so Ricardo Cortez again opened his desk drawer and found a third pen with which to continue his scholarly enterprise. 'Ponce de Leon never quite fathomed that the incomparable *Fountain of Youth* superstitious tale told to him by Florida and neighboring islands' Indians was really a retelling of a fabled spring in the *Garden of Eden,* that incidentally and ironically had been related to native Indians by Spanish soldiers and priests that had recently traveled to the Bahamas and to Florida. Those imaginative narrations led to later speculation among the triumphant Spanish Conquistadors that Bimini Island in the Bahamas was the home of the mythical *Fountain of Youth,*' Ricardo mentally summarized and chronicled in his spiral notebook. 'Ponce de Leon attempted to colonize Florida but his efforts eventually ended in defeat. The Conquistador suffered a severe wound in a conflict with local Indians and the brave man's last expedition resulted in his demise. The legendary hero died in Cuba of injuries that had been inflicted during his final battle with the Florida peninsula's native Indians.'

By the summer of 2005 at the ripe old age of 145 Ricardo Cortez had outlived his two sons and his seven grandchildren in addition to all of his brothers and sisters, friends, acquaintances and elderly Bonita Springs neighbors. 'I've been faithfully collecting *Social Security* checks since 1945,' Ricardo acknowledged and mused. 'I'm surprised that the federal government hasn't investigated me as a fraud or as some kind of hoax. Oh well,' Cortez reflected. 'I suppose that bureaucracy has its benefits. Those computers in Washington D.C. can't think on their own and they can't realize I've been merrily milking and bilking the government for over seventy years now. I'll just keep on cashing my checks as long as good old mentally lame *Uncle Sam* keeps sending them. I can honestly say that I've thoroughly beaten the Feds' at their own silly bottom line game.'

On Thursday September 1st, 2005 Ricardo Cortez's ever-growing entrepreneurial spirit had wholly captivated the man's heart and mind. The Bonita Springs recluse had an inspiration where he believed he could immensely capitalize on his illustrious *Fountain of Youth.* 'I possess what Juan Ponce de Leon only dreamed of owning!' Ricardo selfishly concluded. 'I can make millions bottling my sparkling spring water and marketing it to rich senior citizens that don't want to die.'

Then Ricardo fantasized some more. 'If I could convince a water company that it would be profitable to market and distribute my miraculous product,' the excited man hypothesized and fancied, 'I could easily become richer than Bill Gates. Just think of all the income I could generate and amass getting handsome royalties. A twelve-ounce bottle of my terrific magical water could go for at least a thousand-dollars. I have no problem about exploiting my *Fountain of Youth,* and I must have millions of gallons running under my land.'

Much to his gratification, Ricardo successfully arranged a meeting with important decision makers at a large Miami spring water bottler and the appointment was scheduled for Friday, September 9th, 2005. Cortez had agreed to be interviewed about the prospect of his wondrous "miracle water" by the nationally known company's *CEO* Francisco de Soto and its President, Sergio Balboa. At first, both executives cynically thought that Ricardo Cortez was something between a novelty and a quack. A courteous receptionist showed the aged solicitor into the corporation's main office.

"Mr. Cortez, what proof do you have that your marvelous water can prevent disease and can increase a person's longevity as your letter of introduction indicates?" Francisco de Soto skeptically asked the aspiring capitalist. "I must confess with all candor that I've never heard anything quite so extraordinary!"

"Well, Sir, I'm now a hundred-and-forty-five-years of age, and I have the body and the dexterity of a fifty-year-old man although my general appearance is around twenty years older than that," Ricardo answered the gregarious *CEO* with admirable confidence. "The way I feel right now I could easily live another century and a half, no doubt about it."

Sergio Balboa was not immediately persuaded by Ricardo's exceptional boasts and claims. "What specific proof do you have to confirm your extremely outrageous statements?" the dubious company President soberly queried. "You must certainly understand our concern that your proposal does seem quite preposterous! Do you have any affirmative documentation?"

The fidgety visitor reached into the interior pocket of his only blue business suit and produced two very important legitimate-looking papers. "Gentlemen, here's my original birth certificate. Notice the official raised seal, the date and the place, July 21st, 1860, Camden, New Jersey. Mr. Balboa, I was a *Civil War* era baby, yes, I was. But I don't want to be listed in the *Guiness Book of World Records* until I start collecting lucrative profits from my sensational *Fountain of Youth* drinking water. In fact," the overzealous aged man continued and editorialized, "I think Gentlemen that's what the product, or should I say elixir, ought to be called, *Fountain of Youth!"*

Both *CEO* Francisco de Soto and company President Sergio Balboa carefully examined the faded certificate with their mouths agape and quickly looks of incredulity appeared on their countenances, expressing both their dual interest and their mutual consternation. Finally, the dumbfounded *CEO* garnered the mental and emotional wherewithal to ask an obvious question.

"What is the other validating paper in your possession?" the pallid-faced Mr. de Soto nervously asked. "Show it to us!" he emphatically implored. "Show it to us!"

"Here is my discharge paper showing my honorable release from the *United States Army* dated May 22nd, 1890," Ricardo explained to the two thoroughly astounded corporate administrators. "That official document was issued two years before I began working for the *Pennsylvania Railroad.* Now, I have additional papers at home that can also verify my tenure of employment there, too! I'm sure that you can have these credentials expertly tested in laboratories to determine their authenticity. In my time I've seen Presidents like Cleveland, Garfield, McKinley, Taft and Teddy Roosevelt come and go along with the *Spanish American War* and *World War I* too!" Ricardo Cortez matter-of-factly insisted in not exactly chronological order.

"Mr. Cortez," the temporarily flabbergasted *CEO* of Eternal Springs Water Company said before clearing his throat, "Mr. Balboa and I find your business proposal to be most enticing. We'll send several of our laboratory scientists out to Bonita Springs immediately to obtain samples of your excellent water for analysis. What a terrific and delightful coincidence!" Francisco de Soto enthusiastically marveled and exclaimed, his hands showing uncharacteristic animation. "Your magical *Fountain of Youth* spring-water is located in a place called Bonita Springs!"

Mr. Sergio Balboa had an idea to challenge the veracity of Ricardo Cortez's medicinal therapeutic water. "Tell us kind Sir," the company President queried, "how can Mr. de Soto and I be certain that all of the water lying beneath Bonita Springs doesn't possess the divine properties of your so-called *Fountain of Youth* formula? That's my principal concern at the moment because the water all must come from the same aquifer."

"Well, Sir, most of my neighbors have well water, and all of them have either gotten diseases or have died except me," Ricardo haughtily replied. "Now if I'm the only human in the place who is over a hundred years of age," Cortez argued and maintained, "then there's no way on Earth that I could be an impostor fabricating crazy stories ad making exorbitant claims, now is there?"

The two befuddled executives apologized for their demonstrative pessimism and proceeded listening to Ricardo's astonishing rhetoric. Neither corporate executive could refute the old fellow's undeniably meritorious but seemingly ludicrous statements. Finally, Mr. Balboa collected sufficient emotional fortitude and gathered enough of his cerebral wits to make the budding capitalist a feasible offer.

"Mr. Cortez, Mr. de Soto and I are prepared to have our attorney draw-up a letter of intent that we believe will meet your wholehearted approval," Sergio Balboa very politely asserted. "The appropriate language should be ready for our signatures in about a week. Naturally background research has to be done in this matter before a final contract is eventually negotiated. Do we have your consent to perform preliminary scientific tests on your wonderful *Fountain* and the feeding stream that runs beneath it?"

"No problem whatsoever!" the jubilant Ricardo Cortez responded. "In fact I'll be there on the spot to supervise the entire testing. I know that my water is pure and bona fide so I have no qualms about your scientists doin' the testing!"

"Well, all right then!" Mr. Francisco de Soto concurred. 'Let's shake hands on our present understanding as a sign of our mutual good faith. By next Wednesday Mr. Cortez we'll send a team of specialists out to Bonita Springs to conduct their appropriate experimentations! I trust that the results will be beneficial both to you and to our corporation."

The euphoric prospective multimillionaire left the offices of Eternal Springs Water Company without a suspicion that his suddenly greedy heart might be engendering certain dangerous egregious consequences. Ricardo Cortez blithely sauntered to a public parking lot across the street from the headquarters of Eternal Springs Water Company.

'I never felt so buoyant and so happy,' the old man thought. 'A year from now I'll be wealthy and famous. Tabloid magazines and television talk shows will be clamoring for my interviews,' the *Fountain of Youth* owner considered with great anticipation. 'No more mediocre existence for me because I plan to change the world by being one of its most influential people, perhaps the world's most influential person,' the dreamer clarified for his own self-indulgent appreciation. 'My photo' is destined to appear on the cover of *Time Magazine* as its distinguished 'Man of the Year'.

The elderly man paid the parking lot attendant and then gave the surprised fellow a generous five-dollar tip. Ricardo clambered into the cab of his dull red 1952 Ford pickup truck, fired-up the engine and swiftly drove out of the lot pretending that his vehicle was a brand-new Ford *SUV*.

But a mile outside of Miami Ricardo Cortez's vicarious fantasy came to an abrupt end. His ancient red Ford pick-up stalled while crossing a railroad track. Seconds later the railroad warning lights flashed on and off and the accompanying gates descended. The occupant desperately tried opening the left side door but his panicky efforts were in vain. Seconds later the oncoming locomotive crashed into the stalled vehicle in its path and then dragged the red truck a quarter of a mile down the tracks until the engineer finally was able to bring the locomotive to a stop.

Ricardo Cortez lay dead behind his crumbled red pickup's steering wheel. The *Fountain of Youth* spring-water only allowed for immortality and the preservation of optimal health but it provided no viable defense against accidental injury or incidental death. A coroner was summoned and the county official immediately pronounced the victim dead on the scene with a white sheet then ironically covering the former train engineer's limp crushed body, which was slumped over inside the dull red '52 truck's cab.

A small but dignified funeral was held in Bonita Springs attended by Ricardo Cortez's elderly great-grandchildren and the deceased man's five great-great-grand-sons and three great-great-grand-daughters. The deceased man's estate was valued at a shameful $75,000.00, but Ricardo's heirs were thrilled upon learning that the Eternal Springs Water Company of Miami, Florida was offering the colossal sum of $500,000.00 to purchase the dead man's ruinous Bonita Springs' property. The sale of the shabby bungalow and its attendant one-acre of land was finally legally consummated on Thursday December 22nd, 2005.

"Modern Mythology"

Dr. Bertram Novac was finishing-up his end-of-semester lecture to a self-motivated graduate class in his second-floor *University of Pennsylvania* Logan Hall classroom. The eminent world-renowned Anthropology Professor was reaching the culmination of his presentation on the subject of how the ancient Greeks had misconstrued the nature of dinosaur fossil remains and ascribed *their* origin to the existence of mythological creatures and monsters. The lecturer's dissertation held his captivated audience both alert and spellbound.

"Certainly, the ancient Greeks that were glorified in Homer's *Iliad* and *Odyssey* and also in many classic myths were believed to have battled bigger-than-life monsters such as the Nine-headed Hydra giving Hercules a difficult time, Scylla and Charybdis going-up against Odysseus, the Sphinx threatening to eliminate Oedipus with its puzzling riddle, Medusa the Gorgon challenging the dauntless Perseus, the Minotaur confronting Theseus and the Chimera waging combat against the hero Bellerophon," Professor Novac eloquently stated, "and I hereby claim that those imaginative myths depicting man challenging and defeating wretched creatures all have a very plausible explanation. The embellished tales all attest to ancient man's inability to draw the correct conclusions from physical evidence and from direct observations. Their hypotheses were completely erroneous because the people of ancient cultures lacked advanced science to fully comprehend their surroundings."

A perceptive student sitting in the small auditorium's second row raised his hand to clarify something that remained nebulous in *his* understanding of the distinguished professor's profound statements. "Dr. Novac," *U of P* senior Demetri Callas respectfully addressed his anthropology mentor, "I'm a little confused and I don't exactly fathom what you mean but you certainly have my attention. Could you give the class several concrete examples to illustrate your thesis?"

"Why certainly!" the accommodating instructor answered. "The fossils of prehistoric animals like dinosaurs for instance were around in ancient Greece and very visible to anyone coming across them, especially on the island of Seriphos, but quite evident most anywhere else from Athens in Thessaly down to Sparta in the Peloponnesian Peninsula. Upon finding these colossal-sized dinosaur bones embedded in mountain ridges and marble quarry pits," Dr. Novac elucidated, "the ancient Greeks had no workable frame of reference and little scientific basis to accurately classify them. Consequently, since dinosaurs, mastodons and the like were not animals living alongside ancient man in the prehistoric humans' natural environment," the professor proceeded, "the Achaeans and the Minoans conjured-up exotic myths explaining what they thought the dinosaur and mastodon bones represented. Hence my dear students, you have Minotaurs, Gorgons and Cyclopes evolving out of dinosaur and mastodon skeletons and fossils scattered all over. And this practice probably held true for the Mesopotamians and the Egyptian cultures as well. The horrible creatures found in popular myths were probably based on false assumptions and deductions the Greeks had made about the prehistoric fossils that were quite prevalent in their physical environment."

"I see!" Demetri realized and exclaimed to the amusement of his fellow graduate students. "Those crazy elaborate myths and wicked monsters you had mentioned were created by the Greeks to explain the existence of what seemed to be to them very confusing bones of unknown origin. They never knew about the Brontosaurus, the Trachodon, the Allosaurus or the Tyrannosaurus and the like so the Greeks invented creatures and incorporated them into their folklore. That's quite academically interesting Professor Novac, and now the scenario you've described all makes absolute logical sense."

"And furthermore," Dr. Novac suavely elaborated, "when the stories were passed on as oral tradition from one generation to the next, and considering that all of this creative fabricating was happening before men knew how to write and accurately record events as actual history, let's say before 1,000 B.C., individuals added and subtracted details and the stories gradually became grossly amplified and exaggerated. The monsters and creatures became even larger and more formidable and ostensibly more evil with the retelling of the myths by each subsequent generation of storytellers and bards. And even though mythology significantly contributed to the birth of literature," the erudite speaker emphasized, "its totality unfortunately was being interpreted as fact and truth and ultimately incorporated into the Greek religion, into the Greek value system and also into the Greek morality."

The 9 p.m. bell rang indicating the end of the fascinating lecture session. The twenty-nine students in the second floor *U of P* Logan Hall classroom stood and left the temple of learning all abuzz and quite impressed with the sophisticated knowledge their ears had just heard. Demetri Callas, a third generation Greco/American, had been particularly influenced by erudite Professor Bertram Novac's very enlightening presentation.

* * * * * * * * * * * * * *

In early June of 2005, young Demetri Callas was touring Sicily with his mother's brother, Nikos Mitropoulos, an acclaimed educator in his own right. The *U of P* graduate student's uncle was a prestigious literature professor at *Princeton* and Dr. Mitropoulos was also recognized as the foremost authority on ancient Greek civilization, proficiently speaking several dialects of the language of Demosthenes and Homer besides sporting an international reputation for being an avid big game hunter. Dr. Mitropoulos was sitting behind the steering wheel of a rented car driving his favorite nephew along the rugged eastern coast of Sicily from Messina through Catania, their destination being the ruins of Syracuse.

"I suppose to Archimedes and to his contemporaries Syracuse was known as Siracusa," Dr. Nikos Mitropoulos explained to his passenger as he steered the rented red *Volvo* around a series of mountainous bends overlooking the dark blue *Mediterranean Sea*. "I love this rough terrain between *Mt. Etna* and Syracuse. And it's very scenic, starting south from the *Strait of Messina*. No wonder why the ancient Greeks were attracted to and colonized this area of the island, around 700 B.C."

"I guess the Romans conquered and took control of Sicily later on," Demetri added, trying to impress his uncle with his knowledge of history. "Just what my college history professor often said, 'Greek culture and Roman rule of law'."

"Generally correct Nephew!" the driver replied with a broad smile. "Sicily was a popular crossroads in ancient times and in addition to Roman occupation the island was also ruled by Carthage and by the Saracens, whom you may more readily know as Muslims from Northern Africa. That's why the Sicilian natives even to this day are distrustful to government rule of any kind," Nikos communicated. "People here have a code of ethics called 'omerta,' which means that they'll refuse to report any sort of irregular activity including crime to the government. That's why Demetri the Mafia has thrived on Sicily for over a century. The people here have traditionally resented foreign rule, and even today they're leery about the Italian government on the mainland. Their antipathy to foreign rule dates back over two millennia to Rome's domination."

“Weren’t the Cyclopes described in Homer’s *Odyssey* supposed to be residents of this island?” the all-too-inquisitive Demetri asked. “I recall my Anthropology Professor stating that.”

“Yes, very good again Nephew!” Nikos Mitropoulos amiably complimented. “The individual Cyclops that Odysseus and his men had encountered was very independent-minded and acted hostilely to the visiting Achaeans just like the natives of this island had treated the Romans. As you can plainly determine Demetri this particular business of the Sicilian natives despising foreigners goes back a very long time.”

As Nikos steered his rented red vehicle through Catania Proper he answered Demetri’s curious inquiries about ancient Syracuse’s most popular resident. Nikos was very happy to educate his precocious nephew about Archimedes, one of the acclaimed scholar’s most revered and respected personages of ancient *Western Civilization.*

“Archimedes lived from 287 to 212 BC,” the prestigious self-appointed expert began as he adroitly negotiated a difficult curve, “and the inimitable fellow was perhaps the most accomplished inventor and mathematician of his era. The genius was the founder of what we now know as experimental science and perhaps his most important invention was the Archimedean Screw’, which as you know functioned by raising water from one spiral of a large screw to the next groove. The Egyptians used that same basic principle to drain and irrigate land along the *Nile.* The great inventor also refined the use of the lever and the pulley, which as you know are employed in the operation of simple machines.”

“Sounds like he was a pretty amazing guy,” Demetri readily admitted. “But didn’t Archimedes conduct some sort of nifty experiment involving a crown. I recall reading that he put it in water and.....”

“Well Nephew, here’s what I think you’re attempting to explain,” Nikos interrupted his verbose eager-to-learn young companion. “A fellow named Hiero was King of Syracuse who had his doubts about a crown that he suspected was not made of solid pure gold. Archimedes thought that if the crown had some silver being intentionally substituted for gold, then since gold has a different volume per pound than silver does, the resourceful experimenter figured he could therefore establish the existence of silver by quantifying water displacement.”

“Exactly what do you mean?” Demetri queried. “I don’t quite get the water part!”

"Well, Nephew," Nikos answered as he nonchalantly negotiated another precarious curve, "when Archimedes was taking a bath one morning he had an inspiration. He recognized that some of the water spilled over the sides of the tub. This process is called displacement. Archimedes reasoned that the volume of spilled water would be the same as the volume of *his* body if the tub was absolutely filled to the brim."

"I believe I get it now!" Demetri excitedly exclaimed. "It's really quite remarkable and rather simple at the same time! Archimedes put the king's crown in water and found that the goldsmith that had manufactured it had used some silver because of the difference in volume between a pound of silver and a pound of gold. The King was right thinking he had been cheated. That's when Archimedes shouted out...."

"Archimedes shouted 'Eureka'!" Nikos yelled as he pounded the steering wheel with his left fist. "It's meaning is 'I have found it'! And that's when Archimedes got the idea to explore and define the laws of buoyancy in water that submarines honor even to this day. And besides that," the renowned literature professor continued, "Archimedes discovered the functionality of Pi, being the first one to figure out that 3.17 diameters of any circle always equals the circumference of the circle being studied. Hence," Professor Mitropoulos continued, "the equations for the area and for the circumference of any given circle can easily be mathematically determined. Now you know why Archimedes is one of my favorite ancient Greeks along with Homer, Aristophanes, Socrates, Plato and Aristotle."

"Didn't Socrates teach Plato and wasn't Aristotle a student of Plato?" Demetri inquired as he stared at an oil tanker in the dark blue *Mediterranean*. "I think I remember those historical facts from one of my high school teachers."

"Well, that's true Nephew, but the three philosophers did have their fundamental differences," the driver pointed-out to his callow protégé. "Socrates was a moral philosopher mostly concerned about ethics and about what is right and what is wrong. Plato was more concerned about determining what form of government was most advantageous for the people and he concluded that it was the idea of a *Republic*," the sagacious speaker clarified. "And then Aristotle diligently classified science into the different categories that we study today: biology, anatomy, chemistry, astronomy and physics. That's the major distinctions among and between Socrates, Plato, and Aristotle."

"Not to change the subject," Demetri injected into the dialogue, "but why are you smuggling those two rifles you've concealed in the trunk? Do you think we're going to encounter some ferocious tigers or some wild panthers up here in this secluded mountainous terrain?"

"You never know!" the amused uncle heartily laughed. "Actually the rifles are for a little off-the-beaten-path target practice. I brought along a dozen tin cans in a brown paper bag for us to shoot at when we get bored of being bounced around on remote bumpy country dirt roads. In fact my dear Nephew I think I'll take a detour off of this coastal highway and get in a little target practice en route. I gotta' keep my marksmanship up to world class levels. You never know when the skill will come in handy!"

* * * * * * * * * * * * *

As Nikos Mitropoulos drove his rented automobile up a steep incline, he attentively listened to Demetri telling him about Professor Bertram Novac's theory accounting for the origin of mythological monsters being imagined by means of ancient Greeks viewing and subsequently misunderstanding the exact nature of dinosaur and mastodon fossils. The driver was fascinated by Demetri's revelation. "That sounds quite logical!" Nikos praised as his red *Volvo* ascended along the bumpy dirt road higher into the mountains. "Oh no! The car's being enveloped in fog. I'm going to stop right here Demetri. We'll get out our rifles and do a little target shooting as soon as this wayward low cumulus cloud drifts across the mountaintops. I can't back-up because visibility is too bad and I don't want to risk damaging our vehicle with us in it tumbling off a cliff. We'll just have to wait this one out," Nikos decided and urged his young companion. "I was so busy speaking and then listening to your rendition of Professor Novac's theory that I completely lost track of the gradual change in atmospheric conditions."

The occupants exited the car and Nikos removed the rifles and a box of shells from the trunk and then handed one of the weapons to Demetri. "Take along the tin can bag, the two flashlights and please shut the trunk," the uncle directed. "We'll hang-out nearby and do some basic target practice until this low-drifting cloud passes. That's one very distinct disadvantage of being temporarily stranded in the mountains. You have to contend with the whims of Mother Nature."

"Look!" young Callas hollered. "There's an opening in the side of that hill big enough for a person to squeeze into. How's your spirit of adventure Uncle?" the youth rhetorically asked. "How about if we take along our flashlights as well as the guns and conduct a little amateur exploring."

"That's fine with me!" the elder answered in sheer admiration of his nephew's initiative. "Maybe we can catch a glimpse of some beautiful stalactites and stalagmites. I'm especially intrigued by unusual rock formations almost as much as I savor Archimedes, Socrates, Plato, Aristophanes, Aristotle and Homer."

The two momentarily inconvenienced men soon escaped the fog that had enveloped them by leaning down and carefully stepping into what turned-out to be a limestone hollow. The duo very cautiously meandered through a long narrow winding tunnel that soon led to a huge chamber having a vast arched cathedral-shaped rock ceiling. Much to their utter amazement and bewilderment a blazing fire was flickering off the distant walls. Nikos then whispered an intelligent suggestion to his now-almost-mesmerized nephew.

"Let's turn off our flashlights," the uncle strongly recommended. "There's sufficient illumination ahead for us to further investigate. And I also detect light being admitted into the cavern through that giant circular-shaped opening in the front of the cave. Quiet Demetri! I think I hear movement. Someone's approaching the entrance right now!"

"Uncle, look at the giant primitive-looking chair and the goats, sheep and rams kept in the enclosed pens. And over there is a colossal bucket brimming with milk. Do your eyes see what mine' do? Is this a grotesque illusion or are we hallucinating?"

Before Dr. Nikos Mitropoulos could render a reply a vast shape ducked-down and awkwardly entered the enormous cave. The two-legged creature had a form as large as a mountain crag and the hideous brute was as ferocious-looking as any twenty-foot-tall one-eyed primate monster imaginable. The awesome creature then rolled an immense circular stone to fully cover the cave's entrance, thus preventing any of *his* non-penned animals from escaping. However the awesome one-eyed giant dressed in animal skins appeared to be injured, bleeding profusely from his singular foot-long eye situated directly above his dirty nose. But apparently (from studying the awesome creature's behavior) the powerful ogre's sense of smell had become keenly accentuated with his loss of vision.

"Who are you that have come uninvited into my cave?" a tremendously loud dreadful voice thundered in an ancient Greek dialect that Nikos Mitropoulos immediately recognized. "Identify yourself! Are you more scurrilous plunderers arriving from Troy?"

“We’re your guests who have come in peace?” the literature professor unconvincingly answered the barbaric-looking giant. “Are you the Cyclops known as Polyphemus, son of Poseidon the sea god?”

“Yes,” the enraged creature responded in a highly perturbed tone of voice. “I was just blinded by a hostile Greek named Odysseus and now I suspect that you’re one of his men that failed to leave my cave,” the grotesque-looking creature accused as he began feeling around the back of the cavern for whom he believed to be his newfound tormentor. “Ah hah!” Polyphemus shouted. “I now smell that there are two of you!”

“Don’t come any closer!” Nikos shouted-up as Demetri trembled expressing his genuine fear. “We have weapons that can kill you!” the elder intruder intrepidly yelled as he handed his frightened nephew two shells and motioned for him to load *his* gun.

“Do you think that I’m stupid?” the deformed giant bellowed. “Your puny swords and spears could scarcely cut a scar into my thick skin. I seek revenge for your sly Captain Odysseus blinding me! I shall dash your brains out upon the ground and then promptly devour each of you intruders for supper!”

“Cannibalism goes against the laws of man and God!” Nikos boldly hollered up to his formidable very imposing adversary. “If you dare attempt grabbing me I swear that you’ll die!”

Not heeding the trespasser’s threat the wounded Cyclops reached down with his right hand and barely missed making contact with his tormentor’s head. Demetri and his uncle simultaneously raised their rifles and fired two shells into the creature’s forehead, making the already encumbered clumsy giant moan from pain. But soon Polyphemus’s knees wobbled and in another moment the savage freak-of-nature collapsed to the ground screaming in agony from his recently inflicted head injuries.

The two daring encroachers flicked-on their flashlights and hightailed it through the winding tunnel-labyrinth back to the rear entrance to the cave (that was only big and wide enough to accommodate human-sized wanderers). And upon exiting the limestone mountainside Nikos hastily opened the *Volvo’s* trunk, recklessly threw the two rifles and ammunition inside and then quickly slammed the hatch shut. Next the fearful fleeing interlopers hurriedly opened the sedan’s front doors and quickly leaped inside. Nikos turned on the ignition and quickly put the auto’ in reverse.

“The fog’s lifting just in time!” the driver noted to his petrified passenger. “If Homer’s description is correct Polyphemus lives in a colony of Cyclopes and his friends obediently come to his rescue. That's why we have to hightail it out of here. A single one-eyed monster was more than enough for us to wound and escape!"

Demetri finally regained his sensibilities and now had the capacity to mentally focus and to speak. "I might watch too much science fiction on TV but I think that the fog cloud was some sort of mysterious time portal that for thirty tense minutes had dramatically transported us over three thousand years back into history. Say Uncle!" the youth exclaimed as Nikos frenetically maneuvered the *Volvo* into an improvised K-turn and then instantly headed back down the bumpy dirt road leading to the coastal highway. "Dr. Novac's hypothesis about the monsters of mythology was totally incorrect. Our bad Cyclops experience back there in that dank dreary cave certainly disproves it."

"I now seriously believe Demetri that there exists some phenomenon called 'modern mythology', which you and I both have witnessed and survived! I only wish that I had brought along a camera to catch the entire Cyclops confrontation on film! Then you could've taken it to Dr. Novac and have him try and explain it all rationally!"

"We now know that mythology is just as valid as history is," the restive rider intelligently realized and articulated, "but we'll never be able to duplicate or verify that truth and no one will ever believe our bizarre testimonies. We would be the laughing stock of the academic world if we dared share our exploit with Polyphemus in any university lecture hall."

"Sometimes, reality seems like fantasy, and sometimes the pattern operates in reverse," the still nervous driver noted as the red *Volvo* finally approached the paved coastal highway. "Demetri, what did you ever do with the bag of tin cans we were going to use for target practice once the fog lifted?"

"I accidentally left then in the Cyclops cave during our hasty departure," the nephew remembered and related. "I guess that old Polyphemus's one-eyed comrades will be puzzled when the blind fellow finds and shows the tin cans to his belligerent neighbors. Those inbred imbeciles won't be able to identify the purpose of the metallic material composing the strange anachronisms from the future!"

"You're assuming Demetri that Polyphemus will be able to survive his devastating gunshot wounds to the forehead," Nikos logically declared. "The Cyclops was no match for our superior, modern weaponry. But from our recent thrilling exploit, I've learned two very salient facts."

"What are they?" the vernal passenger curiously asked his esteemed vacation guardian.

"That the hero Odysseus described in Homer's *Odyssey* was a real person, Demetri, and that contrary to what your knowledgeable Professor Bertram Novac maintains," Dr. Mitropoulos declared, "the mythological Cyclops was also really an honest-to-goodness, true-to-life historical character."

“Higher Stakes”

Eddie Kern had honestly owned and operated his modest but quite profitable blackjack/poker Ocean City, MD boardwalk amusement arcade under the Pier Ballroom opposite Wicomico Street for ten wonderful years without a problem. Despite paying a high summer rental fee, the wholesale cost of prizes (including stuffed animals and assorted merchandise) along with the cost of labor and other high operating expenses, Eddie’s arcade always managed to turn a decent profit. The coin-operated games’ setup was an ideal situation for the hard-working Hammonton, New Jersey English teacher, providing Kern with a cash-oriented summer business that more-than-equaled his diminutive public school teaching salary.

Eddie maintained three apartments above an amusement/kiddie rides pavilion near South Division Street on the “bay/inlet end of the boardwalk.” The furnished upstairs accommodations all had air-conditioning with the first apartment housing his wife, his three small children and himself and the other two living spaces being utilized by college and high school students that constituted Kern’s loyal arcade management team and floor workers, all imported to the popular resort from *his* New Jersey hometown.

The Ocean City, Maryland arcade was what boardwalk people called “a grind joint.” Customers would put dimes in the blackjack and pokerino machine slots and then reels with cards glued on them would spin around. Blackjack or poker hands would be developed with the players (customers) pushing buttons on the machines. Blackjack or poker combinations (“Jacks or Better”) would earn the players coupon tickets redeemable in money values ranging from ten cents to twenty-five dollars in merchandise. And a poker machine player was awarded a top prize for achieving a rare Royal Flush. And on the two-reel card machines, a blackjack combination would earn the player a five-dollar coupon that was exchangeable for a prize or was accumulative with other money value poker machine tickets added together to obtain a larger more expensive gift.

The floor workers would hustle around the boardwalk arcade awarding the players *their* appropriate payoffs in coupon values before the patrons’ inserted additional dimes in the slots for new cards to be selected. A ten-cent ticket would yield the player a comb or a plastic spider ring (“plunder”) or the dime ticket could be added with others in money value towards “plush” (stuffed animals) or towards “high line gifts” (toasters, blenders or other kitchen appliances)

A Royal Flush on the poker machines would yield the lucky customer "Choice of the House," an item worth twenty-five dollars.

Eddie had purchased his "amusement devices" in 1990 from Ken Hoffman, who planned to manufacture more of the "patent-pending" blackjack and pokerino machines and then franchise the operations on New York, New Jersey, Virginia and Ocean City, Maryland boardwalks. But then contrary to a verbal agreement Eddie Kern had reached with Ken Hoffman the latter businessman soon installed a similar competing arcade at the "South End" of the boardwalk, thus cutting into the Wicomico Street Pier operator's "bottom line." When Ken Hoffman put in a similar operation distributing "red and white coupons" going up against Eddie's "black and white" ones, the pair ceased being friends and ignored each other when sharing a common space in a restaurant or occasionally passing one another in opposite directions on the crowded boardwalk.

A year later the conniving Ken Hoffman sold an arcade's worth of thirty pokerino machines and twenty blackjack "amusement devices" to a tough Sicilian named Carmen Francona, who opened an amusement arcade on North Division Street and the Boardwalk, five blocks above Eddie's Kern's "Wheels and Deals" Wicomico Street place of business. Francona's arcade gave out blue and white coupons to its customers that were only redeemable at his place, so Eddie was "surrounded" on two sides by similar arcades and many of Hoffman's and Francona's customers tried redeeming their tickets at Kern's centrally located establishment ideally situated in front of the "Amusement Pier." Hoffman and Francona were often seen talking with each other but Eddie Kern felt that both "devious men" had violated the verbal pact he had originally made with the all-too-shrewd South Division Street boardwalk merchant/machine manufacturer.

On July 6th 2000 something exceptional happened that affected the relationships among the three aforementioned boardwalk operators. Two well-dressed suit and tie *IRS* agents stepped off the boardwalk and entered Eddie Kern's humble Wheels and Deals Arcade. Eddie reluctantly answered exploratory questions advanced by agents Ralph Parsons and Allen Cohen out of the Salisbury, Maryland *IRS* office.

"Mr. Kern," Agent Parsons began, "Agent Cohen and I have good reason to believe that these poker devices you have here in your arcade are actually *gaming devices*. They run like slots, and the outcome of each game is determined by chance and not by player skill."

"They definitely are not gaming devices," Eddie nervously returned. "They're *amusement devices*. Just take a look at my city and county licenses posted here on this back wall. My fifty machines are registered in the State of Maryland as *amusement devices* and I pay city and county taxes on each one of them. If they were *gaming devices* as you fellas' insist they are," Eddie anxiously qualified and stipulated, "then I couldn't get city and county licenses to own and to operate them."

"That's your personal opinion on the matter," Agent Cohen (playing the classic role of "bad cop") interrupted. "The federal government's rules, laws and policies always trump those of state and local jurisdictions. I'm afraid that you're operatin' sophisticated gaming machines similar to illegal slot machines and not utilizin' simple amusement devices as you claim."

"How long have you had these machines Mr. Kern?" Agent Parsons (playing the role of "good cop") asked. "That to me is a very important issue."

"Why I've had this summer business for ten years now!" Eddie reluctantly acknowledged. "And I pay plenty of federal income taxes for this arcade, too. You can check your records to confirm that I'm tellin' you the honest-to-God truth. Ever since 1990 I've operated a clean and ethical business gentlemen and my customers are happy and satisfied and they come back year after year."

"We aren't here to check your federal income tax returns or your employment wage withholdings," Agent Parsons explained. "We're here for another reason."

"Well, don't keep me in suspense!" Kern answered as politely as he could. "Why are you here takin' up my valuable time? My wife has a doctor's appointment in an hour and she wants me to drive her over to *his* office."

"Since we contend that you're using gaming devices instead of amusement devices where chance and not skill determines the outcome of each game," Agent Cohen sternly prefaced, "therefore Mr. Kern you must pay the federal gaming tax on each assessed machine you own and operate."

"How much is this gaming tax you've just alluded to?" Eddie queried before nervously gulping down a mouthful of *Pepsi Cola* from the can he was holding. "I've never heard of such a tax!"

"A hundred-and-fifty-dollars a year per machine," Agent Parsons replied as Eddie almost choked on his beverage. "Times that figure by fifty machines in your establishment and we figure you owe us $7,500.00 for this summer alone."

"What do you mean for this summer alone?" Eddie challenged as calmly as he could utter the words.

"Well Mr. Kern, since you've been in business for ten summers, retroactively you owe the *IRS* seventy-five thousand dollars not counting accrued interest and penalties, which haven't been assessed yet. Count on over a hundred thousand dollars in back and present revenue including the ten years accumulative interest and penalties that you owe."

"You're legal crooks!" Eddie vehemently accused his newfound tormentors. "You're holding me up for a hundred thousand dollars that I don't have and can't afford to pay. This is unmitigated blackmail! It's government extortion run amuck! I oversee a legitimate business here!" Kern testily ranted. "If I pay you the money you're demanding then I'm admitting that I have gaming devices and not amusement devices and I'm then risking losing my city and county licenses because the documents specifically state that I maintain amusement devices."

"That's the chance you gotta' take!" Agent Cohen argued. "Life is a gamble, now isn't it Mr. Kern! Don't trifle us with your county and city responsibilities and license commitments. We represent the federal government!"

"That's nor funny one iota!" the intimidated arcade owner volleyed back. "You're knocking me out of business! And besides, I can easily demonstrate that these poker and blackjack machines are not slot machines. First of all, a slot machine shuts itself off and determines the winning or losing combination for the player. None of my machines have timers on them that limit the duration of a game or the development of a winning card hand," the proprietor yelled at his unconvinced antagonists. "The player determines the outcome by pushing either two buttons on a blackjack machine or five buttons corresponding to each of five card windows on a poker console."

"These devices still look and work like slot machines," Agent Cohen stubbornly insisted. "They're reel games that have the look and feel of slot machines."

Eddie was more aggravated and flustered than he had ever been in his entire respectable life. He then told the adamant *IRS* agents to observe a demonstration that would conclusively prove that the blackjack machines and the poker machines were games of skill and not of chance. Kern summoned three of his workers to verify to the 'obstinate intruders' his assertion.

The first employee predicted to Agents Parsons and Cohen that he would get a blackjack combination on a machine and after inserting a dime into the slot wound-up with an Ace of Spades and a Jack of Diamonds. The second "manager" indicated he would obtain "four Aces" on a poker machine and with admirable eye-hand dexterity accomplished his stated objective within a minute. The third floor worker boldly promised his amazed *IRS* audience that he would expertly achieve a "Royal Flush in Hearts" and incredibly attained his haughty prediction much to the federal agents' astonishment.

"And a Royal Flush is Choice of the House!" Eddie reminded the *IRS* men. "A customer could earn a twenty-five-dollar prize for the mere investment of one thin dime!"

"The essential problem is that your patrons play these machines like they're slot devices and assume that they're games of chance and that they can't be beaten," Agent Cohen declared. "True Mr. Kern, your employees can beat the machines because they've played them thousands of times. But the wheels spin around so fast that the average boardwalk customer can't pick-up the cards' rotations and their random locations on the wheels. It's still our educated opinion that these machines of yours are gaming devices."

"And what if I refuse to pay the gaming device tax either for this summer or for the ten years retroactive?" Eddie lividly asked his dual aggravators. "If I pay the tax once then I'm admitting guilt. By paying the exorbitant tax I'm indirectly confessing that I own and operate gaming devices, which coincidentally is your position Mr. Cohen and Mr. Parsons!"

"Well then, if you neglect to cooperate, we'll show-up in your store with the County Sheriff and the local Chief-of-Police accompanied by a slue of patrolmen and proceed to confiscate all of your machines in what is known in *IRS* parlance as a 'jeopardy seizure.' Then we'll padlock your doors, your landlord will be angry and you'll risk losing your lease."

"And what if I hire an attorney to represent me?" Kern incredulously wanted to know. "Don't I have any rights in a court of law or have I unknowingly already sacrificed my *Constitutional* rights to the *IRS*?"

"Well Mr. Kern," Agent Parsons (who had suddenly turned "bad cop") returned, "then we won't do a jeopardy seizure and padlock your doors right away, if you elect to go that route. But please remember one pertinent thing!" Parsons cunningly continued. "You can't take the *IRS* to a regular court until you've thoroughly exhausted going through the federal administrative code system, which is a series of tax courts and their attendant appeals. In other words Mr. Kern," Agent Parsons qualified, "the tax courts always rule in favor of the *IRS* and you can't appeal to a regular civil court until after the tax court system has been completed and the fines and financial obligations paid. You're talking about over a hundred thousand in lawyer's fees tacked onto the hundred thousand you already owe us. You'll only be entitled to *your* concept of justice after you've gone through the complicated and expensive tax court system. Now what's your pleasure Mr. Kern?"

"The lawyers are legal crooks just like you two gumshoe extortioners are!" Eddie yelled and rankled. "I'm not surrenderin' any hundred-thousand-dollars to you fellas' without a fight! I'm getting a lawyer first thing tomorrow morning!"

"I resent your insinuations!" Agent Parsons protested.

"Have it your way!" Agent Cohen emphatically exclaimed. "You'll be getting an official letter citing your violations by certified mail. Our Salisbury Office will be in touch with you and your hired attorney shortly! All you've done is bought yourself some additional wiggle time at a very hefty price. Have a pleasant day Mr. Kern!"

Eddie Kern nearly cried as he watched the two uncompromising agents leave his suddenly dismal-looking boardwalk arcade. 'So this is what it means to practice free enterprise economics in a democratic system of government!' Kern thought and lamented with his head crestfallen. 'I should've listened to my parents and become a priest!'

* * * * * * * * * * * * *

One of Eddie Kern's managers was friendly with one of Ken Hoffman's managers and the two subordinates arranged a "meeting of necessity" between Kern and Hoffman inside the friendly-atmosphere Regal Restaurant on Baltimore Avenue. "Hoffman's manager had stated to me that he was also hit by the *IRS* guys and owes them almost as much as you do," Kern's trusty employee revealed to him. "But word is out on the street that Carmen Francona up on North Division hasn't been hit yet. Could it be that he's miraculously escaped the rap?"

"I'll give Francona a call, even though I hate his lousy guts!" Eddie confided to his loyal lieutenant. "Thanks Jimmy, for settin'-up the conference between Hoffman and me. I guess now that we have something in common the greedy parasite and I gotta' ally together and lick this stinkin' *IRS* scam. I always thought Jimmy that the government was supposed to help its citizens and not bankrupt them and put them out of business so that they can't pay federal income taxes!"

The following afternoon, Edward Kern and Kenneth Hoffman did meet at the Regal Restaurant on Baltimore Avenue for supper and agreed to split the cost of attorney fees to fight the impending *IRS* allegations. The pair shook hands on their pact only because they shared a joint need for economic survival on the highly competitive Ocean City, Maryland boardwalk. And Hoffman had several salient points to add to the over-dinner conversation.

"I've been in touch with Carmen Francona up on North Division, and he says he'll pitch-in for some of our legal expenses," Ken Hoffman informed his business rival. "He says he'll contribute up to ten thousand in financial aid. I know the finest lawyer in town who will represent us."

"Did the *IRS* nail Francona, too?" Eddie curiously asked Hoffman. "I heard that he wasn't approached or accosted. Is that guy Houdini, or what?"

"That's the word around town!" Hoffman said shaking his head in disgust. "The two federal punks never walked up the boardwalk that far. I guess the agents reached their quota between you and me and stopped hittin' the pavement before they ever got to North Division to bust Carmen."

"But that's discrimination!" Eddie loudly yelled getting the attention of other less distraught Regal Restaurant clientele. "We're bein' singled-out Ken and Francona's escaped the dilemma smellin' like a rose."

"He's gonna' say he's good enough to help us out with ten grand legal money and that we shouldn't get him in trouble boilin' in the same pot as we're in," Hoffman vociferated. "Francona's gonna' say it's unethical for us to report him to the *IRS* since he's contributin' to *our* legal fund. What could we do? He could ruin our reputations around town!"

"It all stinks worse than four-day-old rotten fish!" Eddie angrily opined. "That lousy creep's still in business after magically avoiding the *IRS* firing squad, and we're critically wounded and hemorrhaging to death. Explain one thing to me, Ken. Where's the justice in this world?"

"There ain't none'!" Hoffman lividly returned with a grim expression on his facial features. "That's why we gotta' patiently wait for the next world to finally get it!"

* * * * * * * * * * * * *

Three years elapsed and still after forty thousand dollars in legal fees the *IRS* case against Edward Kern and Kenneth Hoffman had not been resolved. Both men adapted to their monetary crises and added money pushing games into their arcades and the new Splash-Down, Pot of Gold and Flip-A-Winna' machines provided the businessmen with much need additional boardwalk revenue to cover their heightened operating expenses.

But Carmen Francona was still operating his North Division Street arcade with apparent impunity from *IRS* interference. Several times Carmen Francona had conspicuously entered Eddie's busy Wicomico Street amusement center and promised to donate additional money for legal expenses on the condition that Kern not report him to the *Salisbury IRS Office* and Eddie acceded to the slick operator's entreaties.

"Nice money pushin' games you've strategically added over there in the center of the floor," Carmen Francona complimented his principal competitor. "That octagon-shaped Spash-Down looks like a real winner! Eight people can play it at the same time. How much can it do in a day?"

"Well, confidentially, Carmen," Eddie whispered to his sly business adversary, "*Memorial Day* it took in thirteen hundred dollars in dimes all on its own. It's salvaged my arcade and has financed my portion of the legal fees to defend myself against *our* intrusive federal government."

"I'm gonna' get me one of them Splash-Downs!" Francona enthusiastically informed Eddie. "It has the players fascinated watchin' their dimes drop-down, bein' pushed against a big pile of dimes, and when some of them drop-down to the second level, the fallen coins are then pushed against another pile and if dimes fall down into the player's chute, tokens come out the bottom worth ten cents apiece."

"That's right!" Kern acknowledged. "And the customers then exchange their tokens for coupons of equivalent money value. The players can go from the Splash-Down, the Flip-A-Winna' and the Pot of Gold money-pushin' machines', exchange their winning tokens for regular coupons, and then play the blackjack and poker games' matching coupons that can be added up together. It's like all of the machines in the arcade are networked and coordinated with each other in terms of the payoffs. The customers really love it! Everything's now connected and easy to understand!"

* * * * * * * * * * * * *

In mid-August in the summer of 2004, two on-a-mission agents from the county licensing division entered Eddie Kern's thriving Wicomico Street boardwalk amusement arcade. The proprietor as usual showed the inspectors his county arcade licenses just like he had done for the past ten summers.

"Sorry to tell you something you might not savor, Mr. Kern," Inspector Fortis abruptly stated. "But those money-pushing games in the center of your arcade have been judged illegal by a county prosecutor out in western Maryland. You're goin' to have to remove them before next summer season or else we'll have to take decisive appropriate legal action against you."

"What's wrong with them?" Eddie futilely countered. "They're fun to play and give a handsome return to the customer. I'm involved with a similar dispute with the *IRS* over whether the pokerino and blackjack machines are games of chance or games of skill. They're licensed as games of skill by the county and can be demonstrated as such."

"We have no objections to your card machines bein' games of skill," Inspector Franklin assured the now-frustrated Eddie Kern. "They're perfectly legal as games of skill as far as we're concerned. But the money-pushing machines warrant no skill whatsoever and in our estimation the outcome is completely governed by chance. That county prosecutor in western Maryland already has proven that contention in an indictment against a travelin' carnival operator," Inspector Franklin clarified. "Now I'm afraid Mr. Kern that similar allegations and action as had occurred out in Frederick County will have to be directed against you here in Worcester County unless you comply with our steadfast recommendation to remove the money-pushers."

"I can't afford another expensive lawsuit!" Eddie pleaded and complained to the apathetic county inspectors. "I suppose I'll have to attend a few amusement trade-shows next winter,` and come across other arcade devices that can generate decent revenues and put them in as substitutes for the money-pushers in the center of my arcade. Are the money-pushers outlawed in any other states? Or is this only a Maryland thing!"

"At the moment, not to our knowledge," Inspector Fortis divulged. "But you never know about these things. They're always subject to change and open to legal interpretations."

"Then, I'll sell them back with a clear conscience to the Pennsylvania amusement game distributor from whom I had purchased them," Eddie promised the inflexible county licensing officials. "At least I'll salvage some of my original equipment investment."

That winter, during one of his weaker moments, Edward Kern received a surprise telephone call from Carmen Francona, who had an enticing business proposition to offer the generally meek Hammonton, New Jersey English teacher. "How ya' doin' with the *IRS* case?" Carmen aggressively inquired. "Been any federal settlement yet?"

"I'm thinkin' about borrowing a hundred grand and then mortgagin' my house to make a two hundred thousand settlement," Eddie disclosed a little-too-frankly. "I've already paid over forty-thousand in legal defense expenses and the cost is gonna' soar even higher pretty soon. My wife's threatenin' to divorce me!"

"Tell ya' what I'm gonna' do!" Carmen cunningly suggested sounding a lot like a used car salesman. "I'm gonna' make you an offer ya' can't refuse. I'll give ya' a hundred-thousand to take over your arcade. That includes your machines, your lease with your landlord, your' red restaurant stools in the floor, your good will and everything else. What do ya' say?"

"Sold!" Kern gleefully answered without giving the matter a second thought. "What are ya' gonna' do without bein' able to have money-pushers in the place?"

"I got another type of business in mind. I've already talked to your landlord and he says I can rent the space for sixty thousand a summer, same as you're payin'," the slick wheeler-dealer reported. "He said everything's kosher as long as I get your stamp of approval. I figured I'd help ya' out and get ya' off the hook."

"Well, what are ya' goin' to do with my thirty pokerino and my twenty blackjack devices if you're puttin' another kind of business in under the Pier Ballroom?" Eddie asked.

"I'll use 'em for spare parts for my North Division Street arcade," Carmen related while feigning sincerity. "Ya' never know when these things break down and gotta' be fixed quick. So basically, Eddie, I'm offerin' ya' a hundred-thousand up front just to get the key to your location and to acquire your spare parts. This deal should get you off the hook with the IRS!"

"Alright!" Kern instinctively agreed. "I'm sick and tired of forking-over all this money to bureaucratic lawyers and to the even more bureaucratic Federal Government. It's a deal Carmen, or better yet, it's a 'Wheel and a Deal'."

"I'll drive-up to Jersey next Friday night and cut ya' a check for the hundred thou'!" Carmen Francona promised. "You got a good career goin' for ya' as a school teacher and a decent pension awaitin' you when ya' retire. Me, I gotta' struggle with crummy nickels, dimes and quarters for the rest of my damned life. Have a good one Eddie." Click.

Eddie gladly received the hundred thousand dollars from Carmen Francona the following Friday night inside Hammonton's Rocco's Town House Restaurant on North Third Street. The troubled man next mortgaged his house and from the proceeds he managed to pay his remaining attorney fees and finally "get off the chopping block" with the relentless *Internal Revenue Service*.

'When I went to Washington to pay off my alleged debt assessment the *IRS* couldn't even locate my folder and luckily I had *Xeroxed* all of my records and at the conference eventually wound-up indicting myself before I paid my massive settlement, interest and penalty charges. How incompetent can you get?' Eddie pondered. 'And when I entered *their* sterile-looking headquarters and sat down at one end of the long table, the three clowns representing the government's case for Parsons and Cohen actually thought I was someone else and had the other unfortunate sucker's folder on the table. How incoherent and unprofessional can the *IRS* be?'

In July of 2005 Edward Kern decided to take a casual hundred-and-seventy-five-mile drive from Hammonton, New Jersey to Ocean City, Maryland to check-out his former arcade location now under the management of one slippery Carmen Francona. Much to the naïve traveler's bewilderment the boardwalk pier arcade was still in operation with the familiar poker machines and the blackjack devices lined-up against the side and back walls with their accompanying luncheonette-style red stools (along with certain illegal money-pushing games functioning like clockwork in the center of the store).

'What's going on?' Eddie wondered. 'I'll have to check-out Carmen Francona's arcade up on North Division and Ken Hoffman's place down on South Division to see if those dumps are still in operation too!'

Kern paced the Ocean City boardwalk and soon discovered that the two competing arcades were still accepting customers' money and that the reel games and the Splash-Down, Pot of Gold and Flip-A-Winna' money-pushing apparatus were still viably in business. The perplexed man ambled with a strident step to the popular Cork Bar on Wicomico (a block off the crowded boardwalk) to chug-down several frosted mugs of beer and to contemplate possible explanations to account for the present confusing scenario. Soon Harold Melendez, a legitimate boardwalk tee-shirt store merchant entered the well-trafficked watering hole and after swallowing-down three cold drafts gave Eddie "the scoop" on what had actually transpired.

"Don't tell anyone a word about this private conversation," Harold said to his old-time boardwalk acquaintance, "but here's what went-down according to scuttlebutt I've heard. Hoffman and Francona were in cahoots all the time right from the get-go. They wanted to get rid of you Eddie because you had the most successful and honestly run arcade on the boardwalk," Melendez confidentially related. "They couldn't compete with your fairly run business so they sat down and contrived a pretty clever scheme."

"Which was what?" Kern asked with his mouth agape expressing his astonishment.

"Well," Harold Melendez continued before scanning the crowded bar for some snoops that might be eavesdropping, "Hoffman and Francona swindled you by bribing the two *IRS* guys to just prosecute *you* while Hoffman pretended that he too was on the hook while Francona had supposedly escaped government scrutiny. And the two jerks also paid off your fancy Baltimore Avenue lawyer too and he held *your* joint conferences knowin' full well that only *you* were bein' officially charged by Parsons and Cohen."

"I was naïve and set-up as the fall guy!" Eddie gasped almost choking on his last gulp of cold beer. "I had always thought I was bein' discriminated against but now I know exactly how and why! So Hoffman never paid a penny while he insisted he too was bein' targeted and Francona talked me out of rattin' on *him* to the *IRS* because Parsons and Cohen had inadvertently overlooked his arcade. And now I'll bet…"

"That Francona and Hoffman both own your old arcade fifty-fifty because they each forked over fifty grand to bait you into selling," Melendez filled-in the missing pieces to the complicated but now very comprehensible jigsaw puzzle. "And the nefarious swindlers got you out of their hair cheap, and begrudgingly, now share what each one had always coveted, your very prosperous and reputable Wheel and Deal arcade."

"But what about the county inspectors?" Eddie asked Harold. "Where do they fit into the mix?"

"Those two bureaucratic Bozos were paid-off too to put the pinch on you Eddie!" the tee-shirt retailer shared. "Now I figure ya' got the entire picture and it ain't too pretty. Extortion committed by corrupt government agents is really ugly stuff!"

"I'm incensed!" Eddie protested to his sympathetic listener. "I've been had and I've been used! Those monkeys treated me like I was chopped liver! I'm glad I've always trusted you, Harold!"

Harold Melendez hastily scribbled a phone number on the back of one of his business cards and then handed the confidential intelligence to the still-seething Eddie Kern. "Now good buddy here's an indispensable item for ya' to consider so use your own wise discretion in pursuing it," the compassionate boardwalk merchant advised his exploited friend. "You've always impressed me as bein' an honest guy Eddie and I like ya' a lot," Harold almost apologetically claimed. "And I don't appreciate one-bit what Francona and Hoffman did to you and I want ya' to know that I was also cheated by that sniveling craven Baltimore Avenue lawyer that cost you a small fortune, too! So if ya' feel inclined Good Buddy, give this guy 'the Sheik' a call. You'll find him very sympathetic to your situation!"

Harold Melendez quaffed down the remainder of his cold draught', rose from his wooden bar stool, shook hands with the beleaguered Eddie Kern and stepped out of the busy Cork Bar premises. Eddie stared at the Sheik's phone number and decided to give the anonymous man a call the following evening from his Hammonton, New Jersey residence.

* * * * * * * * * * * * *

A full week later, sensational headlines appeared on the early morning front-page editions of the *Philadelphia Inquirer*, the *Baltimore Sun* and the *Atlantic City Press*: "Three Ocean City, MD Men Savagely Beheaded." Eddie then removed all three competing newspapers from the rack at Tapper's Stationery Store and eagerly bought them.

Eddie Kern sat in his silver *Toyota* on Bellevue Avenue and earnestly read with keen interest the three very graphic newspaper columns situated below the three separate mastheads. Kenneth

Hoffman, Carmen Francona and prominent attorney Winston Howell had all been "barbarically decapitated" in Arab execution-style in their separate Ocean City, Maryland offices. Police and veteran *FBI* agents were currently intensively investigating the "gruesome horrendous incidents" and have promised that the mendacious criminal or criminals responsible for the heinous murders would be apprehended and prosecuted to the fullest extent of the law.

'I'm really glad I hired the Sheik and his competent henchmen to perform their invaluable services!' Eddie concluded. 'The Arab syndicate is much more ruthless and much more efficient than the Mafia! And it only cost me a hundred and fifty thousand to get even with those three double-crossing miserable creeps,' Eddie recollected. 'I don't know if the Sheik is associated with any Arab terror organizations,' Kern evaluated, 'but in my opinion I don't really care! Immoral and unethical goons like those three swindlers don't deserve to be alive!' the avenged English teacher justified in his mind. 'I feel much better about my massive debts now that those three evil parasites have been eliminated! It's a good thing I had five years' worth of skimmed arcade dough stashed away (from *IRS* scrutiny) to subsidize 'the three vermin eradications!' I think I'll take a casual drive over to the West End Bar and Grille and enjoy a few ice-cold *Coor's Light* frosted mugs!' Eddie reflected. 'Thank you Harold Melendez! Only ten more years until I can collect

"The Traffic Ticket War"

Several years ago, a little publicized traffic ticket war had occurred in New Jersey, until state officials finally intervened and stopped the proliferating conflict. The friction developed between two New Jersey units authorized to issue traffic citations throughout the state, the New Jersey Motor Vehicle Department highway patrols, and the standard and more prevalent New Jersey State Police. Eventually, numerous participants on both sides of the rivalry became involved in the ongoing controversy.

The escalating difficulty began when a maverick Motor Vehicle officer routinely stopped a speeding off-duty State Trooper on *Route 130,* just south of New Brunswick. The aggravated trooper was not in uniform and was driving his own private vehicle. As standard procedure, the trooper showed the Motor Vehicle patrolman his driver's license, his automobile registration, and then obtrusively flashed his badge and identified himself as a certified officer of the law. Contrary to common practice, the Division of Motor Vehicles' patrolman did not honor professional courtesy and allow the off-duty trooper to be merrily on his way, free of penalty. Instead, the "by-the-book" officer issued the State cop a speeding ticket. That particular Central Jersey incident initiated the "Traffic Ticket War" between the two state law enforcement agencies.

Word of the embarrassing incident circulated around New Jersey State Trooper barracks from hectic Bergen County down to somnolent Cape May. Soon, State Troopers were issuing violations to off-duty Motor Vehicle cops that had been routinely stopped, and the instigated MV highway patrollers quickly reciprocated. The "assumed ethics" of law enforcement was running amok as more stubborn individuals became involved in the rapidly expanding dispute.

Judges all over the State were complaining to Freeholders, to Legislators, and to the Governor's Office of wasting their valuable bench time addressing "frivolous charges" being aggressively waged between warring members of the two, rival, ticket-issuing, highway enforcement departments. The imbroglio reached the point where vindictive cops from both camps were traversing the State's highways, specifically hunting for and ferreting-out each other, and ignoring common "civilian abuses of traffic laws," particularly on the *New Jersey Turnpike*, the *Garden State Parkway,* and the *Atlantic City Expressway*.

Bob McCormack was an off-duty Hammonton, New Jersey

policeman driving his wife Helen in the family car to the *Home Depot* in the neighboring South Jersey community of Berlin, Bob was grieving to his apathetic spouse that he had received a speeding ticket from "an overzealous State Trooper" in Vineland the week before, when suddenly, red-flashing lights appeared in his rear-view mirror, just as the driver was entering the congested Berlin *Route 73 Traffic Circle*. The frustrated fellow negotiated the circle and then entered *Route 561,* where McCormack angrily stopped his black 2003 *Chevy Malibu* and threw his hands up in the air to emphasize his total disgust.

"Here we go again, Helen!" Bob strenuously beefed. "This traffic ticket war is spilling-over into the local police departments, where town law enforcers are being given frivolous citations. Neither the State cops nor the Motor Vehicle guys are honoring professional courtesy. If I stop a trooper or an MV guy tomorrow, I'll give him a ticket without even blinkin' an eye!"

"Stop being so presumptuous! Just be polite and tell the officer who you are and where we're going!" Helen prudently advised her husband as the Motor Vehicle Highway Inspector approached the *Malibu's* driver's side, and then gruffly requested Bob's license and registration.

"You were goin' sixty-five in a fifty-mile-an-hour-zone!" the Motor Vehicle official imperatively claimed. "I got it all on my radar. No sense even appearin' in court to challenge this one. It's a slam dunk! An easy home run!"

"Here's my badge," Bob interrupted at an appropriate moment during the verbal ,exchange. "I'm a Hammonton cop just takin' my wife over to *Home Depot* to buy a new brass handle for our home's front door. I got a ticket from a Trooper last week on Landis Avenue down in Vineland," McCormack protested, "so how about goin' easy on me. I'm not a Statie! I'm just an ordinary town cop tryin' to make a buck and get a family goin'."

"Sorry, Mr.," the Motor Vehicle patrolman answered with a grim expression on his countenance. "Last week a couple of guys from my department got citations from wise-guy town cops in Stratford and in Waterford Township. It seems like local police are getting in on the free-for-all fun, too. You're goin' to become my next victim, so just take a deep breath, cross your legs, stop complaining, obey the process, and grin and bear it!"

"Whatever happened to professional courtesy?" Bob bitterly objected. "I mean, I could understand sockin' it to some southern hillbilly cop from Alabama or Mississippi, flyin' through Jersey, because those wise-guys have reputations for givin' multiple citations to out-of-state badges. This craziness of cops giving tickets to cops has got to stop! It's both unethical and unprofessional! And besides that, it's not good for morale!"

"Not until the gutless Governor steps-in to quell the wild altercation!" the veteran Motor Vehicle agent countered. "And you know how bureaucratic, how slow, and how utterly wimpy politicians are! The next time I stop one, I'm goin' to lay the wood to him or her big time, just outa' general contempt. Now, Mr. McCormack. Here's your ticket. Please take it easy on *Route 73* the next time ya' wanna' leave Hammonton and go to *I-HOP* or to *Pizza Hut!* Maybe when Hammonton gets a little bigger and more urbanized, you'll have your own *Home Depot,* your own national pancake house, and your own franchised pizza joint! Then, you won't have to travel all the way to Berlin for those special services!"

A half-hour later, Robert Patrick McCormack remained reticent during the *Home Depot* experience, permitting Helen to dominant their communication and take command of selecting the store's "most attractive" replacement brass-plated door handle and accompanying key lock. During the shopping excursion, the Hammonton cop was weighing how he would get even with off-duty State Troopers and Motor Vehicle Inspectors that dared traverse through the Hammonton Corporate Limits at an excessive rate of speed, going to and from their myriad South Jersey destinations. The couple finally left the huge hardware/lumber supplies' mart, and upon Helen's request, had lunch at a nearby *Boston Market,* where the wife liked the chicken platter special with two sides, mashed potatoes, and brown sugared apples, and Bob preferred consuming the sliced ham entrée with rice and corn, washed-down with a medium-sized *Diet Coke.*

"Are you goin' grocery shopping this afternoon?" the husband mechanically asked as McCormack finally snapped-out of his Hammonton policeman role-playing trance.

"Yes, I'm commandeering the car and going over to the Hammonton *ShopRite,"* Helen replied between *Diet Coke* sips. "A woman's day has no end!"

"There's a bigger and better *ShopRite* right here in Berlin, right next to the *Home Depot,"* the normally laconic and laid-back husband challenged. "Why don't you just do your food purchases there? Doesn't that make better sense?"

"Because in Hammonton, I buy some items at *ShopRite,* and others across the highway at *SuperFresh,"* the wife lectured and explained. "And if we stop and grocery shop at the Berlin *ShopRite,* I don't know the aisles where the goods are located, so, I'll wind-up having to push three shopping carts inside three separate supermarkets in two different towns, instead of the normal two grocery carts in

Hammonton. Does that female logic satisfy your inquiry?"

"Women! Who could ever figure them out?" Bob exclaimed with an exaggerated frown upon his face. "Who could ever decode what nuances go through their enigmatic minds? And let me tell you, Helen," the disgruntled and irritated husband persisted. "If a lady State Trooper or female Motor Vehicle person tries stopping me on the road, I'll simply smile at them and not stop until I reach the Hammonton Police Station. That's my new battle strategy."

"Now that you know my lady's plans for this afternoon," Helen diplomatically replied while adroitly changing the subject, "what's on your agenda? Are you going to the video store and renting *Smokey and the Bandit* again?" the wife sarcastically bantered.

Even a subtle comment was sufficient to provoke the now-emotionally unstable Robert Patrick McCormack. "Very funny!" Bob reflexively answered back. "I'll be supervising replacing the analog cable box for our den's television, and replacing it with a digital one. After the cable guy comes at 3 p.m., and if the spirit then moves me, I'll ambitiously attempt changing the front door handle and lock."

"Just be around the kitchen to help me carry-in the heavy grocery bags," the wife insisted with a frown. "I want to visit the hairdresser later this afternoon, so that I look presentable at your cousin Mark's wedding reception tomorrow night. Didn't he just become a State Trooper?"

"I don't want to discuss it right now!" Bob McCormack flippantly replied. "Some sensitive topics are now off-limit,s and that's definitely one of them!"

When the quarrelling couple finally arrived back at their *Route 30* Hammonton home, Helen then climbed behind the wheel to obediently perform her shopping chores, and Bob carried the newly acquired brass-plated door handle into the living room to be installed, after the cable employee would arrive with the highly-anticipated digital reception box.

'I can't wait to get the digital box,' Bob thought while getting his mind off of his dissatisfaction with "letter-of-the-law" State Troopers and Motor Vehicle officers. 'For only four dollars more a month, I can have the 'On-Demand' feature and watch free movies and concerts whenever I want. And also, for a reasonable monthly fee, I could have my computer hooked-up with high speed, broadband access. And there's a variety of terrific music channels I can listen to whenever I so desire!"

At precisely 3 p.m., a courteous *Comcast* cable-man rapped on the front door, and Bob eagerly opened the portal, which was indeed in need of a new brass-plated handle. It required only thirty-minutes to have the digital replacement box installed, and then the amiable cable repairman calmly explained to the homeowner how to use the remote control.

"Be very careful because there are more selections than you've been accustomed to that you have to consider," the cable employee suggested. "If you press the wrong button, you might find yourself floating in TV cyber-space somewhere, if you aren't absolutely careful. Now pay close attention. here's how to use the very functional On-Demand feature."

Bob paid mild attention to the mini-course, and then thanked the friendly cable rep for his time and for the brief remote control introductory lesson. "Where ya' heading now?" the curious *Route 30* resident asked. "Another house call?"

"Over to the *WaWa,* down the street," the cable representative answered McCormack. "I'm hungry for some *TastyKake* cream-filled chocolate cupcakes with vanilla icing, and a sixteen-ounce cup of hot coffee to wash the treats down. My wife says I'm a candidate for cardiac city, but I don't really care. You only live once, that's my' philosophy, Mr. McCormack. Now please; just apply your signature to this mandatory company work order, and I'll be on my way to WaWa Snacksville."

"I know where you're comin' from when you mentioned your wife's carpin' about your natural eatin' habits," Bob replied as the disgruntled town cop scribbled his chicken-scratch John Hancock onto the *Comcast* work order. "Women! Ya' can't live with 'em, and ya' can't live without them! It's a real paradox!"

"Hope ya' enjoy your new digital box!" the hungry snack food junkie stated. "I know you'll appreciate it, especially the 'On-Demand' choices and the many 'Pay-Per-View' channels. Sometimes, a man's gotta' watch *Wrestlemania,* or a good R-rated movie to escape his wife's inexplicable idiosyncrasies. Divorce is always an unrealistic and an impractical alternative, because it's too expensive of an option that could bankrupt an ordinary citizen. Have a good day!"

"As they say, 'It takes two to tango! But to tell you the truth," the homeowner facetiously said to the affable installer/repairman, "I've always preferred basic '50s jitterbugging to complicated South

American dancing! See ya', and thanks for bein' punctual and puttin' in my digital box before my opinionated wife comes home from grocery shopping and instinctively finds fault with it."

When the *Comcast* white van eventually exited the driveway, Bob McCormack nonchalantly picked-up his remote control to begin experimenting with the fascinating device. 'This is one time I don't want to procrastinate!' the proud owner of the versatile digital box thought. 'I want to have this thing up and running before Helen returns from the Peach Tree Plaza *ShopRite* and proceeds to criticize my inability to operate the system smoothly. I only wish I had paid better attention to the *Comcast* guy's instructions. Oh well, here we go, trial and error!'

The "Power" button was pressed, and then the "On-Demand" feature was quickly activated. A complex menu appeared with an overwhelming number of possible selections. 'Oops! Wrong channel!' Bob's mind synthesized, trying to keep pace with his new-found dilemma. 'I'd better stick to basic cable channels until I thoroughly master this 'On-Demand' feature. For starters, let's try Channel 3 out of Philly'.'

Bob inadvertently neglected to press the "Exit" button to escape the "On-Demand" domain on the menu, but instead, pushed "03" for basic Channel 3 reception. 'Maybe I'll think better and be less impulsive if I drank a few cold *Budweisers* out of the 'fridge!' McCormack mused. 'That reminds me. I gotta' get to the liquor store and stock-up. My beer supply is runnin' low. I think I'm down to my last six pack.'

Channel 3 appeared on the TV screen, and Bob was befuddled by what the picture depicted. 'This isn't Philadelphia being shown!' the viewer dubiously reflected. 'It's that same Motor Vehicle cop that just ticketed me. He's stopping a car at the Ancora Railroad Bridge, just five-miles west of here. Hey! Now this is totally impossible! I know that guy in the stopped vehicle! That's Frank Longo, a New Jersey State Trooper that lives over on Eagle Drive on the other side of town!'

McCormack's eyes carefully scrutinized the bright TV screen, and his pupils perceived that off-duty State Trooper Frank Longo stepped on his accelerator, and then his dark-green *Buick Century* had shot-out from the *Route 30* right-side shoulder onto the highway, and quickly ascended the newly re-constructed Ancora Railroad Bridge. Bob rubbed his eyes and imagined that he was having a massive 'video hallucination'.

'This weird fiasco is absolutely arcane and surreal!' McCormack believed and thought. 'How could this video scene ever be taken!

There aren't any TV cameras or cameramen anywhere around the traffic incident. Cameramen don't hang-out at the Ancora Bridge, that's for sure! This new remote control and cable box must be some sort of diabolical satanic device, possibly possessed by pernicious demons or evil spirits! What's causing this abnormal paranormal experience? I'm getting spooked out of my mind, and *Halloween* is still a couple of months away!'

McCormack nervously switched the TV setting to #4, which ordinarily was Public Television NJN (New Jersey Network). A high-speed automobile chase was in progress, with off-duty Trooper Frank Longo in his *Buick Century* being pursued by the determined Motor Vehicle Officer, as the fleeting cars passed a familiar White Horse Pike landmark, the twenty-foot-tall three-dimensional Renault Winery Champagne Bottle, appearing in the background. 'They're now only four-miles from my home!' Bob marveled. 'This strange happening is becoming too eerie for words to describe!'

Bob changed the digital cable box to #5, the Philadelphia Fox News station. The white Motor Vehicle patrol car was now chasing the dark green *Buick* under the seventy-year-old Railroad Bridge that crosses *Route 30,* just before Pastore Orchards Farm Market. Flashing red lights appeared upon the TV screen, and were accompanied by a loud shrill wailing siren blasting-out from Bob McCormack's television speakers. 'This whole scenario seems too real to be imagined! That farm market is only three-miles from Fairview Avenue. The chase is heading my way, but I'm too captivated to turn the damned television off! I'll see what's happening on Channel 6, WPVI, the Philadelphia *ABC* network channel.'

On Channel 6, the white Motor Vehicle auto (with its flashing lights and screaming siren) was closing-in on the dark green *Buick Century,* the vehicles speeding in front of the Heart-of-Elm Restaurant. Then, Bob McCormack realized something very contradictory and seemingly illogical. 'The Heart-of-Elm went out-of-business twenty-years ago, and it was demolished by a crane's wrecking ball and by bulldozers a few years later. Say, who's taking these crazy pictures anyway? Is this some sort of practical joke?' the observer worried. 'How could it be? The Heart-of-Elm was only two-miles from Fairview Avenue. But the place is now just a mere memory. Now *that* non-existent restaurant can't possibly be photographed! No way! I gotta' try Channel 7, WPHL, an independent Philly' station. I need to have a feasible answer to this fantastic phenomenon that's wickedly plaguing my mind!'

The exciting high-speed chase on Channel 7 zipped right past the Silver Fox Tavern, a longtime business located just one-mile west of Bob McCormack's *Route 30* home. Soon, they'll be speeding past Oak Grove Cemetery, Ideal Clothes Manufacturing Company, and the new Hammonton High School. How could this be happening and me seeing it all on cable television?' the perplexed homeowner wondered. 'This new digital cable box must be haunted! I should've pressed 'Exit' to escape the 'On-Demand' menu, and then switched to standard cable programming! I swear this new setup is eerily haunted! It's beyond haunted! It's the work of the Devil!' McCormack theorized. 'Hey, what's those noises I hear approaching the house? Maybe I ought to shut-off the TV before it's too late! But I can't! My curiosity is too high! I gotta' find-out what's goin' to happen next in the spectacular police chase!'

Helen McCormack was dutifully returning from her grocery shopping and passing the *WaWa* in the family's 2003 *Chevy Malibu,* as her automobile slowly passed by the Fairview Avenue traffic light. The wife put on her left turn signal to cross four-lane *Route 30,* wanting to proceed into her driveway, when the harrowing high-speed pursuit approached coming from the opposite direction. A *Honda Odyssey* van was rapidly closing in behind Helen, and so Bob's wife hit the gas pedal to prevent being rear-ended. In the meantime, off-duty State Trooper Frank Longo realized that a collision with the *Malibu* was imminent, so the neurotic cop veered his *Century* to the right and smashed into Helen's right rear fender.

The *Odyssey* van tried avoiding involvement in the accident, and it swerved to the left, clipping the *Century's* back left wheel, and then careening-off of the speeding, out-of-control white Motor Vehicle Department auto'. The white *MV* Ford flew into the air without the aid of a ramp, and crashed right into Bob McCormack's living room, immediately killing the off-duty Hammonton policeman.

The tragic *Route 30* traffic-accident had the largest number of fatalities in Hammonton's entire recorded history. Bob McCormack, his wife Helen, Trooper Frank Longo, Ralph Sinclair (the obsessed Motor Vehicle Officer), and finally the driver and three occupants of the *Odyssey* van were all declared dead by the county coroner's staff, that had been immediately dispatched to the gruesome highway accident tragedy. The devastating motor vehicle disaster prompted a thorough investigation by the Governor's Highway Advisory Committee, whose recommendations ultimately contributed to the cessation of the great "New Jersey Traffic Ticket War".

"Family Resentment"

Established in 1935, the Bronson Family Vegetable Farm remotely situated on rural rustic Third Road in Hammonton, New Jersey was a brand name famous for quality produce in food distribution centers along the East Coast from Baltimore to Boston. The business started-out during the *Great Depression* as a modest truck farm hauling its freshly picked and packed vegetables to Dock Street commission houses in Philadelphia and to Hunts Point food centers in New York City's Bronx.

In 1960, old Joseph Bronson faced reality and handed-over the reins of the reputable operation to his two sons, Dennis and Ben, who specialized in raising asparagus, corn, green peppers, zucchini squash, cucumbers, eggplants and tomatoes. Over the past several decades the farm gradually expanded from the original hundred and fifty acres to a huge plantation of six hundred.

The industrious Bronson brothers missed-out on the post-*World War II* peach boom when the luscious fuzzy fruit was the top producer in the Hammonton area where over three thousand acres of the "Queen of Fruit" were annually grown and harvested. But then in the 1960s blueberries began rivaling peaches as Hammonton's chief crop and the eight-week short-season "blue fruit" eventually dominated the town's agriculture when the chain-store-popular California O. Henry variety knocked New Jersey peaches out of popularity and virtually out of production.

But through the evolutionary transformation from peaches to blueberries (in the local Hammonton farming economy) the Bronson brothers still stuck to what they knew best, growing and harvesting vegetables even though the Town of Hammonton to this day prides and promotes itself as "The Blueberry Capital of the World." Two shopping centers on *Route 30* attest to and verify the municipality's past and present agricultural glory, Peach Tree Plaza and Blueberry Crossing.

Like many working partnerships on various South Jersey farms, conflict between hard-headed owners often arise when one sibling desires to either be the dominant corporate authority in the daily operations or wants to create and develop a reputation as a successful independent grower on his own. The harmony that prevailed between Dennis and Ben Bronson in the early 1960s gradually disintegrated into distrust, discord and animosity by the year 2000. The formerly compatible owners decided to divide-up all their equipment, assets, irrigation lines, buildings, and families into two separate entities on either side of Third Road: Dennis Bronson agreed to own and farm three hundred acres on the north-side of the two-lane county highway and Ben Bronson consented to owning and operating the three hundred acres that existed on the south-side of Third Road.

Over the ensuing five years, the two brothers became resentful and envious of one other and their families didn't openly quarrel or feud but instead virtually ignored each other, even at relatives' weddings, funerals, *Communions*, *Confirmations* and also at graduation parties. Cousins living on opposite sides of Third Road never acknowledged each other's passing on tractors or in pickup trucks and the two families pretended that "the other entity" wasn't of the same blood, sweat, tears and genetics.

In mid-January of 2005, Dennis Bronson really splurged and took his wife and family on an expensive two-month South Pacific vacation including stops and stays in exotic paradises Honolulu, Tahiti, New Zealand, Bali and Australia. The Dennis Bronson family returned from their' sixty-day hiatus refreshed, renewed and ready to engage in the redundant annual activities know as planting, cultivating, irrigating, fertilizing, growing, harvesting, packing and selling their high-quality fancy vegetables. But unfortunately- memorable South Pacific leisure and pleasure soon turned into heartbreaking tragedy. On April 7, 2005, Dennis Bronson unexpectedly died of a massive heart attack after all desperate attempts at reviving him (by first his frantic delirious sons and then by Hammonton Rescue Squad paramedics) had failed.

On Monday evening, April 10th, a viewing was held for sixty-seven-year-old Dennis Bronson at the spacious Marinella Funeral Home on North Third Street and over five hundred local socialites including prominent Hammonton farmers, politicians, school board members and doctors and lawyers filed-past the casket and expressed their condolences to the grieving family. Everyone expected to attend was observed in the long line but the family of Ben Bronson had been conspicuously absent. In fact the south side Third Road Bronsons weren't even mentioned in Dennis Bronson's extensive obituary appearing in the *Hammonton News,* the *Hammonton Gazette,* and the *Atlantic City Press*. And then, on Tuesday morning, jealous Ben Bronson, his wife, and his sons and daughters did not have the basic decency or the expected courtesy to be present at Dennis Bronson's well-attended High Mass at St. Joseph Church and his subsequent burial inside a magnificent marble mausoleum in the First Road Greenmount Cemetery.

* * * * * * * * * * * * *

Dennis Bronson was indeed the more gregarious of the two feuding brothers. While sixty-two-year-old Ben was introverted and introspective his older "sibling rival" Dennis was outgoing and more "public friendly". Dennis had belonged to service clubs like the Hammonton Lions and the Knights of Columbus and Ben Bronson contemptuously resented his older brother's cordial nature, especially when the elder Bronson ran for Town Council on the Republican ticket and easily won a seat by campaigning vigorously and beating his Democratic opponent in a landslide election.

Indeed, Dennis had been the more community-oriented and citizen-popular of the two. The likeable elder brother enjoyed public speaking, club leadership responsibilities and working the grills and promoting good will at political banquets and at church barbecues. But the local politician further incurred *his* brother's jealousy when Dennis Bronson used *his* political influence for what Ben and his envious family believed to be "excessive and decadent personal gain."

In 1995, the local Town Council had declared a building moratorium on all new house construction to abide by recently legislated strict New Jersey forest conservation laws. In the early 1980s the New Jersey lawmakers in Trenton had established the creation of the Pinelands Commission, which had the expressed authority to regulate population growth in and around the environmentally sensitive Wharton State Forest.

According to careful definitions enforced by the new bureaucratic Commission, the "New Jersey Pinelands" extended from Absecon just west of Atlantic City to Atco seven miles west of Hammonton and from Vincentown seventeen miles north of the agricultural community to Vineland seventeen miles south. The "Pinelands" had Hammonton and its proud farmers located directly in the middle of the "core area" where building and population growth was both restricted and limited and new houses in the town's jurisdiction that weren't connected to water and sewer lines required the approval of the "Almighty Pinelands Commission".

Hammonton farmers were deeply affected by the Pinelands and its governing Commission. Since *their* land value was now exclusively restricted to farm use, property (that would ordinarily be worth a hundred-thousand-dollars an acre to an entrepreneurial real estate developer) was devalued to a meager five- thousand dollars an acre because presently only other farmers would want to purchase the land for agricultural purposes.

Consequently, because of the stringent Pinelands regulations,

Hammonton fruit and vegetable growers had trouble borrowing money from banks and from farm credit bureaus to conduct their businesses since *their* credit lines were determined by using their now devalued land assessments as "collateral." It cost most area vegetable growers like Dennis and Ben Bronson three hundred thousand dollars of "seed money" to get started each spring because big bucks had to be placed on the table to purchase the upcoming summer's fertilizers, sprays and special customized packages and cartons (with the farm's brand names printed on them), payrolls before crops were picked, packed and shipped along with myriad other miscellaneous accumulative spring expenses.

Farmers doing business in the Hammonton "highly governed and restricted Pinelands core area" were also limited in deciding *who* could build houses on their property. Their children were allowed to build new homes on three-acre tracts and desperate farmers had to otherwise have their land divided into ten-acre zones if they wanted to sell those sub-divisions to non-family strangers (with a lot of money) desiring to erect dwellings on such sizeable tracts.

Since the autocratic New Jersey State Pinelands Commission required "core area residents" to hook-up to Hammonton city water lines and to town sewer lines, new growth was hampered by the State in the name of "natural environment preservation." And when the old outdated Hammonton sewer plant began operating at full capacity a restrictive building moratorium was adopted and enforced and the Town Council (including staunch Republican Dennis Bronson) had to abide by the State's inflexible land-use mandates.

The Hammonton area farmers, along with peeved real estate developers, boldly challenged the Pinelands Commission's authority in State courts claiming that the new environmental laws were "Unconstitutional" and violated the farmers' rights to own and sell land at face value. The disgusted real estate moguls maintained that their "civil rights" to build and make profits were being abused. The costly litigations were aggressively pursued but in the end the challenges to State Authority were to no avail. The Pinelands Commission prevailed and won every legal wrangle intensively argued before sympathetic judges and the court decisions maintained that the "State's general good" was being upheld by the intelligent planned regional conserving and by the prudent preserving of South Jersey forests, lakes and wildlife.

But the wily Hammonton farmers suspected that the real reason for the "stranglehold" Pinelands legislation (and its accompanying land restrictions) was more than mere discrimination against fruit and vegetable growers. Joseph Wharton of Philadelphia, founder of the prestigious *University of Pennsylvania* Wharton School of Business once owned the South Jersey land today known as the Wharton State Forest. Wharton was a venture capitalist at heart whose ownership of the pineland forests (on either side of *Route 206* surrounding Atsion Lake and vicinity) had by coincidence seven trillion gallons of excellent pristine water reserves directly under the virgin forestland, and the attendant Pinelands were fed by the close-to-the-surface Cohansey Aquifer. Capitalist Joseph Wharton's grandiose scheme was to pump clean fresh water from the Wharton Forest Tract to the Philadelphia and New York metropolitan areas and economically profit from his diligent endeavor, but near the end of his life the nineteenth century investor changed his mind and heart and benevolently donated the beautiful acreage to the State of New Jersey. The shrewd Hammonton farmers had suspected all along that the austere Pinelands building restrictions were not so much about protecting the pine trees as the State had asserted but about preserving the seven trillion gallons of pristine water lying beneath the forest trees as a reserve emergency water source for Philadelphia and New York.

In the late 1990's, the rift between the Bronson brothers became more intensified when the Town Council (of which Dennis Bronson was an influential member) passed a resolution to have a new sewage plant constructed (with Pinelands Commission approval) at local taxpayers' expense. When the Town's petition was studied and finally endorsed by the State, plans for new Hammonton sewage and water lines were quickly drawn-up. With the acceptance of the new high-capacity sewer system some lucky farmers in the correct "building zones" could sell one acre parcels to real estate developers at a hundred thousand dollars an acre because those properties could now link-up with city water and sewer usage and not require sophisticated septic systems and water wells that were strictly regulated by the supreme New Jersey Pinelands Commission.

Dennis Bronson was well-networked in the community and through his strong contacts with the City Zoning Board and with his noteworthy "political clout" on Town Council convinced other people in city government that (with the State approval of the new higher capacity sewage facility) it would be wise and judicious for the Town to have new water and sewer lines installed along the north side of Third Road that was more conveniently situated "closer to town". The local politicos supported Bronson's proposal and in 2002 the new water and sewer lines were installed to Dennis's benefit.

Ben Bronson and his jealous family despised what had transpired in what they labeled "Dennis's selfish and arrogant actions." The older brother's three hundred acres on the north side of Third Road was much more valuable than Ben's three hundred acres on the south side of the Atlantic County highway. By political savvy and by shrewd manipulation Dennis's land was worth approximately 60 million dollars while Ben's property (under the jurisdiction of strict Pinelands' regulation) was valued at only 1.5 million at five thousand dollars an acre (when exclusively sold to another farmer interested in acquiring additional land). Needless to say Ben Bronson and his family felt that they had become victims of Dennis Bronson's greed and cunning political maneuvering.

In March of 2003, Ben Bronson requested through his lawyer that the original six hundred acres be "re-divided equitably" but then the older brother acting through *his* attorney's advice bluntly refused the "retroactive suggestion." Then six months later Ben had requested through his accountant that his older brother purchase *his* land for five million dollars but the older brother answered through a letter from *his* accountant that the price was "three million dollars too much."

Finally, Ben ate humble pie and requested through his lawyer that Dennis lend him five hundred thousand dollars so that the younger sibling could avoid declaring bankruptcy and thus continue the operation of *his'* faltering vegetable farm, but the older brother declined to cooperate citing that Ben's three-hundred acres were no longer considered part of the "family legacy." The mounting antipathy between the two Bronson families was reaching a crescendo. The Bronson brothers were no longer sibling adversaries; they were now bona fide bitter sibling enemies.

* * * * * * * * * * * * *

Police Chief Anthony Presti summoned Detective Mark Cirillo into his office (located in the police department in the basement of Town Hall on Central Avenue) for a private conference. The topic of discussion was the sudden unexpected death of prominent Hammontonian Dennis Bronson. that was more conveniently situated "closer to town". The town politicos supported Bronson's proposal and in 2002, the new water and sewer lines were installed to Dennis's benefit.

"You know, Mark," the Chief prefaced, "Dennis Bronson and I were really close friends. In fact, confidentially, I own ten acres of ground on Chew Road between several large sections of the Bronson brothers' farms. I acquired the ground dirt-cheap after Denny clued me in about the probable lifting of the building moratorium and about the sewer and water lines goin' in on Third Road," the Chief elaborated. "I saw my pal's advice as an excellent opportunity to make a good quick capital gain on my recently acquired real estate property that incidentally Mark has been changed from farm zoning to residential. That's one advantage of bein' a public official in this town," the Chief expressed to his loyal subordinate before lighting up his long fat *El Producto* cigar. "You kinda' know what's goin' to happen before it actually does happen and a savvy inside person like myself can capitalize on the special knowledge before it becomes public."

"Well, Chief, why did you call me in?" the sharp young detective asked his superior. "Are ya' thinkin' about getting a real estate license or what?"

"Mark, I'm warnin' ya' to stop bein' so sarcastic and please kindly show me more respect. I'm a little suspicious about the circumstances surrounding Dennis Bronson's death," the Chief confided as he heavily puffed on his immense cigar. "I want to see if you can dig-up any information about possible foul play bein' involved. Your off-the-record investigation might be able to pin something tangible on that rotten skunk Ben, who didn't even have the common decency to pay his last respects to his brother. That's gratitude for ya'!"

The conscientious detective reflected deeply for a moment and then had several inspirations to share. "Well Chief," Detective Mark Cirillo said, "a couple years ago I understand that Ben had asked Dennis to re-divide their original six hundred acres so that each brother would have the same valued land assessments, but your good buddy Dennis nixed the idea when it was certain that the new Third Road sewer and water lines were to be laid town. Those combined factors would certainly give Ben a definite motive for wantin' to eliminate his brother."

"A motive does not constitute a crime," Chief Presti impressively articulated while remembering something salient from Law Enforcement 101. "And the exact cause of death was officially determined to be a heart attack. Now Mark, I believe that something sinister might've triggered the coronary but I can't prove it; it's just a suspicion, a hunch without any substantial evidence. And the Hammonton area farmers, along with peeved real estate developers, boldly challenged the Pinelands Commission's authority in State courts, claiming that the New Jersey environmental laws were "Unconstitutional" and violated the farmers' rights to own and sell land at face value. The disgusted real estate moguls maintained that their "civil rights" to build and make profits were being abused. The costly litigations were aggressively pursued, but in the end, the challenges to State Authority were to no avail. The Pinelands Commission prevailed and won every legal wrangle intensively argued before sympathetic judges and the court decisions maintained that the "State's general good" was being upheld by the intelligent planned regional conserving and by the prudent preserving of South Jersey forests, lakes and wildlife.

But the wily Hammonton farmers suspected that the real reason for the "stranglehold" Pinelands legislation (and its accompanying land restrictions) was more than mere discrimination against fruit and vegetable growers. Joseph Wharton of Philadelphia, founder of the prestigious *University of Pennsylvania* Wharton School of Business once owned the South Jersey land today known as the Wharton State Forest. Wharton was a venture capitalist at heart whose ownership of the pineland forests (on either side of *Route 206* surrounding Atsion Lake and vicinity) had by coincidence seven trillion gallons of excellent pristine water reserves directly under the virgin forestland, and the attendant Pinelands were fed by the close-to-the-surface Cohansey Aquifer. Capitalist Joseph Wharton's grandiose scheme was to pump clean fresh water from the Wharton Forest Tract to the Philadelphia and New York metropolitan areas and economically profit from his diligent endeavor, but near the end of his life the nineteenth century investor changed his mind and heart and benevolently donated the beautiful acreage to the State of New Jersey. The shrewd Hammonton farmers had suspected all along that the austere Pinelands building restrictions were not so much about protecting the pine trees as the State had asserted but about preserving the seven trillion gallons of pristine water lying beneath the forest trees as a reserve emergency water source for Philadelphia and New York.

In the late 1990's, the rift between the Bronson brothers became more intensified when the Town Council (of which Dennis Bronson was an influential member) passed a resolution to have a new sewage plant constructed (with Pinelands Commission approval) at local taxpayers' expense. When the Town's petition was studied and finally endorsed by the State, plans for new Hammonton sewage and water lines were quickly drawn-up. With the acceptance of the new high-capacity sewer system some lucky farmers in the correct "building zones" could sell one acre parcels to real estate developers at a hundred thousand dollars an acre because those properties could now link-up with city water and sewer usage and not require sophisticated septic systems and water wells that were strictly regulated by the supreme New Jersey Pinelands Commission.

Dennis Bronson was well-networked in the community and

through his strong contacts with the City Zoning Board and with his noteworthy "political clout" on Town Council convinced other people in city government that (with the State approval of the new higher capacity sewage facility) it would be wise and judicious for the Town to have new water and sewer lines installed along the north side of Third Road that was more conveniently situated "closer to town". The local politicos supported Bronson's proposal and in 2002 the new water and sewer lines were installed to Dennis's benefit.

Ben Bronson and his jealous family despised what had transpired in what they labeled "Dennis's selfish and arrogant actions." The older brother's three hundred acres on the north side of Third Road was much more valuable than Ben's three hundred acres on the south side of the Atlantic County highway. By political savvy and by shrewd manipulation Dennis's land was worth approximately 60 million dollars while Ben's property (under the jurisdiction of strict Pinelands' regulation) was valued at only 1.5 million at five thousand dollars an acre (when exclusively sold to another farmer interested in acquiring additional land). Needless to say Ben Bronson and his family felt that they had become victims of Dennis Bronson's greed and cunning political maneuvering.

In March of 2003, Ben Bronson requested through his lawyer that the original six hundred acres be "re-divided equitably" but then the older brother acting through *his* attorney's advice bluntly refused the "retroactive suggestion." Then six months later Ben had requested through his accountant that his older brother purchase *his* land for five million dollars but the older brother answered through a letter from *his* accountant that the price was "three million dollars too much."

Finally, Ben ate humble pie and requested through his lawyer that Dennis lend him five hundred thousand dollars so that the younger sibling could avoid declaring bankruptcy and thus continue the operation of *his'* faltering vegetable farm, but the older brother declined to cooperate citing that Ben's three-hundred acres were no longer considered part of the "family legacy." The mounting antipathy between the two Bronson families was reaching a crescendo. The Bronson brothers were no longer sibling adversaries; they were now bona fide bitter sibling enemies.

* * * * * * * * * * * * *

Police Chief Anthony Presti summoned Detective Mark Cirillo into his office (located in the police department in the basement of Town Hall on Central Avenue) for a private conference. The topic of discussion was the sudden unexpected death of prominent

Hammontonian Dennis Bronson. that was more conveniently situated "closer to town". The town politicos supported Bronson's proposal and in 2002, the new water and sewer lines were installed to Dennis's benefit.

"You know Mark," the Chief prefaced, "Dennis Bronson and I were really close friends. In fact, confidentially, I own ten acres of ground on Chew Road between several large sections of the Bronson brothers' farms. I acquired the ground dirt-cheap after Denny clued me in about the probable lifting of the building moratorium and about the sewer and water lines goin' in on Third Road," the Chief elaborated. "I saw my pal's advice as an excellent opportunity to make a good quick capital gain on my recently acquired real estate property that incidentally Mark has been changed from farm zoning to residential. That's one advantage of bein' a public official in this town," the Chief expressed to his loyal subordinate before lighting up his long fat *El Producto* cigar. "You kinda' know what's goin' to happen before it actually does happen and a savvy inside person like myself can capitalize on the special knowledge before it becomes public."

"Well, Chief, why did you call me in?" the sharp young detective asked his superior. "Are ya' thinkin' about getting a real estate license or what?"

"Mark, I'm warnin' ya' to stop bein' so sarcastic and please kindly show me more respect. I'm a little suspicious about the circumstances surrounding Dennis Bronson's death," the Chief confided as he heavily puffed on his immense cigar. "I want to see if you can dig-up any information about possible foul play bein' involved. Your off-the-record investigation might be able to pin something tangible on that rotten skunk Ben, who didn't even have the common decency to pay his last respects to his brother. That's gratitude for ya'!"

The conscientious detective reflected deeply for a moment and then had several inspirations to share. "Well Chief," Detective Mark Cirillo said, "a couple years ago I understand that Ben had asked Dennis to re-divide their original six hundred acres so that each brother would have the same valued land assessments, but your good buddy Dennis nixed the idea when it was certain that the new Third Road sewer and water lines were to be laid town. Those combined factors would certainly give Ben a definite motive for wantin' to eliminate his brother."

"A motive does not constitute a crime," Chief Presti impressively articulated while remembering something salient from Law Enforcement 101. "And the exact cause of death was officially determined to be a heart attack. Now Mark, I believe that something sinister might've triggered the coronary but I can't prove it; it's just a suspicion, a hunch without any substantial evidence. And the Atlantic County coroner's office's autopsy found no signs of poison or drugs present in Dennis's body. But I still have an inkling that there's more to his sudden death than meets the eye."

"Well then, Chief, it's rumored all over town in every barber shop and beauty salon that Dennis refused to buy his financially strapped brother out for five million smackers, but your friend declined and rejected Ben's humble solicitation. And then Dennis again denied Ben's request for a $500,000.00 loan according to coffee shop conversations. All of these facts could easily provide Ben with a good motive to eliminate Dennis, but like you said Chief, motives don't constitute crimes."

"Look, Mark," the Chief expounded on his hypothesis. "We know that Dennis's property is valued at over sixty million with the re-zoning of Third Road and with the heavy-duty north-side sewer and water lines bein' operational. We also know that Ben feels dejected and cheated because his three hundred acres is only worth 1.5 million if sold to another farmer because of the lousy Pinelands' regulations. There's still another viable motive, but like we already know, motives...."

"Do not constitute crimes!" Detective Cirillo robotically answered. "So, what do you want me to do Chief? Watch some old Peter Falk *Columbo* stories on cable TV and develop some brilliant idea?"

"Stop actin' so juvenile and bein' so damned cynical!" the Chief admonished his favorite detective on the force. "I want you to figure out some new angle that somehow implicates Ben Bronson in his brother's untimely death. I hate the no-good scoundrel with a passion and would like to see him put behind bars, maybe not for murder but for some less egregious offense. It could even be trespassin' or spittin' on the sidewalk or loiterin' as far as I'm concerned. Now get on that secret detail and find me something relevant!"

Detective Mark Cirillo left Chief Anthony Presti's downstairs office with a resolute mind to excavate some heretofore unknown significant facts within the community, that were relative to Dennis Bronson's much-grieved departure from this Earth. The investigator did not employ the conventional direct approach using interviews and interrogations. Instead, the alert plainclothes cop kept his eyes and ears open and closely listened to community gossip. 'If some skull-duggery were involved in Dennis Bronson's death that had not been indicated in the coroner's bland report,' Mark Cirillo conjectured, 'then surely someone in Ben Bronson's family would eventually slip-up and then make a boastful comment to a close friend or to a casual acquaintance at a bar or at a *Confirmation* party.'

Two weeks later, a very exuberant Detective Cirillo entered Chief Presti's downstairs office all out of breath. The Chief cavalierly glanced-up from reading the front-page headlines of the *Atlantic City Press* to precisely discern what *his* principal informant had to divulge.

"Well Mark, what is it?" the Chief rhetorically asked. "Did your ridiculous girlfriend propose to you again or what?"

"No Chief, it's something more vital and important than that!" Detective Cirillo replied without realizing exactly what his mentor had said. "There's something pretty essential in the wind concerning Dennis Bronson's death that wasn't chronicled in his obituary and wasn't identified and cited in the coroner's autopsy report."

"Well Sherlock Holmes, gather your breath and collect your senses and please tell me!" the usually skeptical Chief-of-Police characteristically chided. "Get to the point, even though I believe that points are for pinheads!"

"Well, I just contacted the *EPA* and the New Jersey Pinelands Commission on the phone and discovered that a week before Dennis Bronson's unexpected death his three hundred acres of choice real estate had failed the State's harsh standards for property development," the Detective revealed to his highly focused boss. "It seems that the farm ground north of Third Road was saturated with *DDT*, a banned toxic chemical pesticide that had been popular among local farmers in the 1950s. His entire farm is contaminated. The ground has been condemned!"

"Were soil tests performed in the past?" the now-concerned Chief wanted to know.

"Yes, four years ago while the building moratorium was in effect Dennis Bronson's farm had passed the environmental tests with flying colors," Detective Cirillo stated. "It's my theory that while Dennis and his family were vacationing in Hawaii and Tahiti for two solid months that Ben and his sons conspired and poisoned the north side Third Road three hundred acres with an abundance of *DDT*. But I believe we need additional evidence to substantiate my findings and build a case against that dastardly hermit Ben and his ornery sons."

"Well Mark, *DDT* shouldn't be hard to trace because the chemical is both obsolete and forbidden to be used," Chief Presti related. "We might not be able to prove murder but we might be capable of sending Ben Bronson to the county clinker for a couple years on charges of polluting the environment, trespassing, vandalism and crop devastation. Now, I got a stellar idea that might help us in arrestin' and convictin' that slippery weasel Ben Bronson. I truly now believe Mark that Dennis suffered his lethal heart attack wonderin' how his ground had gotten poisoned with an obsolete chemical and theorizing who would have the unmitigated audacity to commit such a cruel deed."

"What is your instruction?" the young detective demanded. "Give me your corroborative evidence so that we can conduct a collaborative investigation," Cirillo reflexively laughed as he thoroughly appreciated his slightly clever play-on-words.

"Well Mark, while you were yappin' away, I've just made a brilliant deduction," the egocentric Chief commended himself as was his bad habit. "As you know I own a fairly large parcel of ground on Chew Road situated directly between sections of the Bronson brothers' farms. Now if Ben and his sons drove their tractors and sprayers across my land to get to Dennis's back acres while the older brother and his entire family were celebratin' their prospective sixty million dollar bonanza in the South Pacific," the Chief objectively pontificated, "then some of the poisonous chemical would've leaked-out of their sprayers' tanks and left an invisible toxic trail clear across my ten acres. That'll be all the corroborative evidence necessary to launch charges against that yellow-bellied rogue Ben Bronson. I order you to get in touch with some soil testing experts right away and have sand, dirt and gravel samples taken from the main roads runnin' through my property and then have the evidence fully analyzed. Like they say Mark," Chief Presti elucidated, "there's more than one way to skin a cat, whatever the hell that means!"

"Yes Sir, even though Ben probably caused his brother's death, if we can't get the culprit for murder," the quick-learning detective insisted to his vindictive superior, "then we'll throw him in the Mays Landing' county slammer, for other less horrendous violations."

"The Pondarosa"

In 1990, Stanley Adler sold his very successful garden mart, greenhouses and fifty acres of Colts Neck, New Jersey land to a real estate consortium and (with his wife Sylvia) moved a hundred and thirty miles south to rural Vineland. The couple had a son Jason who was struggling as an aspiring stage actor and who loathed his father's good fortune and his mother's domineering nature. Despite many attempts by Stanley and Sylvia to make amends with their stubborn impractical gay son, Jason eschewed his parents' truce-overtures and lived with his male-companion-boyfriend in Glendale, California.

Stanley Adler loved to tinker around in greenhouses and so he used some of his excessive profits he had received from the multi-million-dollar Colts Neck deal to purchase a thousand acres of prime virgin real estate on *Route 47*, Delsea Drive near Wheat Road several miles west of downtown Vineland. Stanley and Sylvia had good instincts in regard to intelligent land investments and had thoroughly researched their Vineland area acquisition since the property was situated just outside the New Jersey Pinelands environmental restrictive area, which limited housing development and building construction in order to preserve the natural pine barrens environment and the accompanying seven trillion gallons of pristine water lying beneath the bountiful coniferous trees.

"That's why we used our brains and chose land outside the Vineland city limits and not that similar property we were considering twenty miles north in Hammonton," Stanley orally reviewed with Sylvia. "That's why it always pays to do your homework and use your imagination where New Jersey real estate is concerned."

"Bravo!" his supportive wife commended over Saturday morning breakfast. "The Vineland, Bridgeton and Millville areas are growing like gangbusters but Hammonton is fiscally stagnant because of the severe Pinelands' restrictions. And we now have three interested syndicates bidding on our valuable thousand acres. And you're right Stanley about your bright idea that it pays doing our homework, especially the math'."

"That's pretty humorous!" Stanley concurred. "Our five-hundred-thousand-dollar investment has proliferated into a top bid of eighteen million for a hundred and fifty store shopping mall. Life can't get any better than that! Say Sylvia, do ya' have any major appointments for this afternoon?"

"I'll be gone most of the day," the wife informed. "This morning I'll be at the hairdresser's getting beautified and then I'm going over to my girlfriend Sarah's place to have lunch and play cards with our bridge club. And finally later this afternoon I'll be hitting the *Wal-mart* and *ShopRite* scenes so as you can see I have a full plate on my hands. I'll probably be checking back home around 5 p.m.," the wife rambled-on without taking a breath. "What happens to be on your' agenda today?"

"I just have to mow the front lawn since I got the back and sides done yesterday before it started to rain," Stanley related. "It's not that easy taking care of a one-acre property, but after we sell our land to the highest bidder, we'll be on Easy Street spending the winters in Florida, the springs in California and the summers and falls right here in good old New Jersey after we buy a four-million-dollar house near the ocean in either Stone Harbor or Avalon. Ya' know Sylvia, I don't really like Sea Isle City, Ocean City or Cape May because they get too many tourists there. And Atlantic City is definitely out of the question."

"Okay Stanley, I'll see you later this afternoon," Sylvia promised as she gave her spouse the customary little peck on his right cheek. "Have fun mowing the front lawn."

Sylvia Adler merrily departed the handsome ranch home and Stanley then lethargically ambled out to the backyard utility shed to fire-up his ten-year-old sit-down lawnmower. Just before noon a white Cadillac with a twenty-foot-long fishing boat attached to the rear pulled into the concrete driveway of the well-secluded Vineland Main Road home. Three casually-dressed gentlemen exited the luxury automobile and approached Stanley, who was just finishing-up mowing his front lawn. The curious rider shut-off his sit-down's Briggs and Stratton engine to hear what his unexpected visitors had to say.

"Mr. Adler, do you recognize who we are?" the first tall burly gentleman asked without waiting for an answer. "I'm Victor Conrad but you can call me Vic. And this here is George Griffith and the third fella' is Alex McMillan. We're the three...."

"The three gentlemen interested in buyin' my thousand acres to erect a fancy shopping mall on Delsea Drive just below Wheat Road," Stanley alertly responded after formally shaking the men's hands from his position sitting atop the old red mower. "I remember you three gentlemen from a meeting four months ago we had over at the *Trump Plaza* on the Atlantic City boardwalk. Welcome to my humble home."

"I have a *Toro* sit down mower," Victor Conrad voluntarily explained, "George here has a *John Deere* and old Alex has a *Kobota* because he prefers those Japanese products to American ingenuity. How do you like that baby you're riding for reliability and maintenance?"

"Well, Mr. Conrad, it's always served me fine. Now, let's cut to the chase and find out what really brought you here besides our common interest in lawnmowers."

"Now, Mr. Adler," Vic Conrad said very deliberately. "The boys and I figured we'd come out here and up the ante for your thousand acres from fourteen million to fifteen. What do ya' think of our new offer?"

"To be honest with you, Mr. Conrad," Stanley replied while gathering his thoughts, "there are three consortiums including yours that's bidding on the property, and wantin' to build an ultra-modern shopping center to compete with the newly renovated *Cumberland Mall* on the other side of town. And quite frankly," Stanley expressly qualified, "yesterday I received an offer of eighteen-million plus several performance incentives and the ownership of two of the proposed hundred and fifty stores if I go along with the sweetened deal. Sorry to say that your alternate bid isn't anywhere near the highest at this moment."

The three disappointed men debated with the property negotiator for five full minutes, and then Victor Conrad noticed that Stanley Adler had a small fishing boat resting on a trailer, parked behind his backyard utility shed. The tall muscular astute businessman brought the remarkable coincidence to Adler's attention.

"Mr. Adler, I see you have a fishin' boat too," the visitor commented. "Do ya' enjoy fishin' as much as ya' like mowin' your lawn?"

"More so," Stanley promptly returned. "I don't like to fish. I *love* to fish, particularly in large well-stocked fresh water lakes like they have over near Glassboro and around Hammonton."

"Well now, we really do share common hobbies!" the slick Vic Conrad noted and stated while his companions grinned like contented Cheshire cats. "The boys here and I have a terrific log cabin over near Winslow west of Hammonton that we affectionately call the Pondarosa."

"After the Ben Cartwright homestead outside Virginia City, Nevada that was made famous on the TV show *Bonanza*?" Stanley asked his visitor.

"That's correct!" Vic Conrad confirmed as George Griffith and Alex McMillan nodded their heads and smiled. "But that ranch was spelled 'P-o-n-d-e-r-o-s-a' and ours is spelled 'P-o-n-d-a-r-o-s-a.' Anyway Mr. Adler, your idea of association was generally right! Now our secluded Pondarosa getaway is situated near Turtle Lake in an area that the local Winslow Village residents call Inskips. The lake's very isolated as I've already said and it's stocked with fantastic pike and huge catfish. And since we have access to the Pondarosa Lodge, we also have the privilege of fishin' at Inskips all the time."

"Well, what are you suggesting?" Stanley bluntly asked. "Are you in the process of invitin' me to accompany you on a fishin' expedition?"

"Now that you've mentioned it'," Vic Conrad affirmed with his two pugnacious-looking escorts very obviously nodding their heads in approval, "as sure as God made little green apples, you're definitely invited to accompany us."

"Well then, Mr. Conrad, I'll go along with you on two conditions. That I can bring my boat along and that you and I ride in my car that I'll hitch my boat trailer to," Stanley stipulated. "And when we're on the lake, you and I will fish from my boat, and your two buddies can fish out of yours. Maybe if you fellas' sweeten your cash offer a little bit, and sprinkle it with a few incentives, let's say a total package to the tune of a nice round twenty-million, then I'll be inclined to ink my signature to an official contract first thing Monday morning."

"Okay, Mr. Adler, your terms seem satisfactory and quite amenable too," Victor Conrad attested as he appointed himself official spokesman for his more laconic muscular partners. "Now get that old rusty red lawnmower into your utility shed, and we'll help ya' connect your boat trailer to your vehicle. Is that your brown *Lincoln* parked over there?"

"Yes, it is!" the dedicated fresh water fisherman verified. "I can't wait to start castin' my line into that lake ya' mentioned!"

"And after we do some serious fishin', we'll have a few cold beers out of the 'fridge over at the Pondarosa," Victor persuasively added. "And you'll just love Turtle Lake. It has a very convenient concrete ramp, where we can easily launch our boats. Mr. Adler, you've really made my day by sayin' ya' relish fishin'!"

The red rusty lawnmower was quickly returned to the backyard utility shed; the boat and trailer were connected to the rear mount of the brown *Lincoln,* and Stanley Adler (with Victor Conrad as his front seat passenger) followed the white Cadillac driven by George Griffith and the accompanying trailer onto busy Delsea Drive, their final destination being Inskips, near Winslow Village, five-miles southwest of Hammonton.

The conversation between Stanley Adler and Victor Conrad during the pleasant twenty-mile-long excursion encompassed a variety of subjects ranging from fishing to baseball and from bowling to stock market investing, but not once did the two businessmen discuss the sale of the thousand acres of ideally located Vineland land for the specific purpose of shopping center development. At last, the two vehicles and their attached trailers pulled off of Winslow Village's Hall Street onto a desolate, bumpy side dirt road that led to Inskips.

In another fifteen-minutes, the two boats had been successfully launched down the concrete ramp, and Mr. Conrad proposed that he and Stanley engage in a friendly two-hour fishing contest with the occupants of the second boat, George Griffith and Alex McMillan. "The winners get to drink as many beers as they want but the losers are limited to imbibing just two bottles!" Victor Conrad mandated and laughed in a jovial tone of voice. "And then, Stanley, the disgruntled losers will have to watch the victors, including me *Victor,* ha, ha, ha, and you, ha, ha, ha, drink as many brews as we so desire."

"This lake is quite immense and so clean!" Stanley admiringly observed and vocalized. "How come I've never seen it on any South Jersey map?"

"It's our little secret rendezvous that we keep hidden from the rest of the world!" Victor Conrad chuckled. "And when you join our select fraternity, Stanley, you'll have complete access to the lake and to the Pondarosa Lodge, whenever your greedy heart desires doin' some serious fishin'."

George Griffith and Alex McMillan were having better luck at the contest's outset reeling-in several foot-long pikes. But then Stanley felt a fierce tug on his line, and a gleeful expression instantaneously appeared upon his visage. Soon, the veteran angler was wildly and enthusiastically reeling-in an enormous pike, that certainly dwarfed the two that had been caught on the competing boat.

The thrilled fisherman lifted his line out of the water, proudly exposing a really healthy eighteen-inch-long fresh water fish. The jubilant fellow hoisted the wriggling prized catch up to waist-high level, and was about to triumphantly show his trophy to Victor

Conrad and the two men seated in the adjacent boat. Suddenly, Victor leaned forward and violently pushed his fishing companion into a six-foot-deep section of Turtle Lake.

"What did you do that for?" Stanley complained to Victor Conrad as the surprised speaker bobbed up and down in the six-foot-deep-water. "Get me out of here this instant! Now I'm not gonna' sell you my thousand acres just for spite!"

"We don't really think you have much of a choice in the matter!" Mr. Conrad arrogantly exclaimed. "Pretty soon you'll be feelin' a few tugs at your pants and legs."

"What do ya' mean?" Stanley Adler yelled back in a frightened tone of voice just as several tugs confirmed Victor Conrad's stark prediction.

"Why do ya' think they call this here remote body of water Turtle Lake?" Victor Conrad joyfully hollered back like a possessed madman, as his two brawny colleagues in the other boat let out a boisterous roar. "Besides a few random pike and catfish, this here scenic lake is stocked with an abundance of hungry snapper turtles that could bite flesh off of a man as if they' were a school of hungry piranhas, yes sir. Nice knowin' ya', Mr. Adler!" the heartless tormentor yelled to the duped victim, as a crimson pool of blood surfaced and surrounded the petrified, hysterical victim, hopping around in the shallow lake.

"George Griffith skillfully maneuvered the second boat to be parallel to Stanley Adler's "Love to Fish", and then Victor Conrad gingerly clambered into the other craft "Catch of the Day," climbing aboard just in front of the *Mercury* outboard motor. The three villains laughed indulgently at the completion of their nefarious scheme, while poor Stanley Adler's head submerged beneath the crimson-colored water's surface.

"Don't forget to re-install the 'Danger: No Swimming: Snapper Turtles' sign next to the boat ramp," Mafia chieftain Victor Conradi reminded his associates-in-crime, Georgio Griffani and Alexandre Milano. It goes to the right of the concrete boat ramp."

"Boss, I gotta' confess that the Pondarosa story was a terrific setup," Georgio 'the Snake" Griffani commended with a wide grin. "We ain't got no damned log cabin out here in the Pinelands' wilderness, but it's not such a bad idea after all. That imaginary log cabin next to Turtle Lake was just thrown into the mix to enhance and embellish our foolproof murder setup," Georgio noted with very evident admiration for the ruse's success. "But on second thought Boss, it ain't such a bad notion to make fiction into reality!"

"If Mr. Adler wasn't so damned greedy, he'd still be alive and nearly sixteen-million bucks richer," Alexandre "the Brute" Milano (alias Alex McMillan) effectively reminded his villainous "syndicate comrades." "The papers are gonna' erroneously report that Mr. Adler went alone on a fishin' trip, clumsily fell off his boat, and was viciously attacked and eaten by snapper turtles, which he never suspected were prowlin' around in the water. What a shame!"

"And that snoopin' around Vineland that you guys did the past month has paid off handsome dividends," Mafia Don Victor "the Moose" Conradi praised his henchmen. "You guys figured-out through workin' the grapevine that Stanley's wife was gonna' be away from the house doin' her weekly beautification appointment she had made at the hairdressers; playin' bridge with her card club, and goin' to *Wal-Mart* and the Vineland *ShopRite,* so the stupid dame never got the privilege of meetin' us in person. Only her deceased husband ever got the wonderful opportunity to greet us face to face." "And Adler's gay kid Jason that we contacted out in California has agreed to sell us the thousand-acres for a paltry te- million. He's gonna' inherit the land in good old Stanley's Last Will and Testament," Georgio Griffani reminded his avaricious confederates. "It's a good thing that the kid hated his old man, and that we were smart enough to capitalize on the tense situation. And Adler and his gullible wife never imagined in a million years that Stanley would accidentally die before the sale of their thousand- acres was ever consummated," Georgio verbally reviewed. "The greedy, idiotic fool didn't even trust havin' his wife's name on the deed, or listed in his Will as the surviving heir. What a pathetic dolt that egotistical jerk was! Only his raunchy kid's name is listed!"

"That only proves that a dead guy ain't worth a plug nickel in the eyes of the law," Alexandre "the Brute" Milano philosophized. "Even if the dumb punk was a multimillionaire before he kicked the bucket! And thanks to our good team work, we knew that Stanley loved fishing, and that the elderly codger had an old tub of a boat sittin' in his backyard on that rusty trailer. Those facts were bits of information that we could easily exploit. And the imbecile even promptly drove his own car and boat attached, twenty-miles to the death scene!"

"Hey fellas'!" Victor "the Moose" Conradi bellowed with a lusty laugh. "Guess what kind of red riding lawnmower Mr. Stanley Adler was sittin' on this morning?"

"A *Snapper!"* Griffani and Milano simultaneously boomed in amazed voices. "He was ridin' on a damned *Snapper!"* the amused hit-men simultaneously declared and then indulgently laughed.

About the Author

Jay Dubya is author John Wiessner's initials (J.W.) and also his pen name. John is a retired New Jersey public school English teacher and he had taught the subject for thirty-four years. John lives in southern New Jersey with wife Joanne and the couple has three grown sons.

Jay Dubya has written other adult literature besides *Two Baker's Dozen. Black Leather and Blue Denim, A '50s Novel* and its sequel, *The Great Teen Fruit War, A 1960' Novel* are humorous literary endeavors. *Frat' Brats, A '60s Novel* completes the action/adventure trilogy that had been begun by *BL&BD* and *Fruit War*. *Pieces of Eight*, *Pieces of Eight, Part II, Pieces of Eight Part III and Pieces of Eight, Part IV'* are short story/novella collections featuring science fiction, paranormal and humorous plots and themes. *Nine New Novellas, Nine New Novellas, Part II Nine New Novellas Part III and Nine New Novellas, Part IV are sci-fi paranormal short fiction stories written in the spirit of the four Pieces of Eight novellas' collections.* And *So Ya' Wanna' Be A Teacher* is a satirical autobiography describing the author's thirty-four-year educational career in American public schools.

Ron Coyote, Man of La Mangia is adult humor and the work is an imaginative satire/parody on Miguel Cervantes' *Don Quixote*, published in 1605. *The Wholly Book of Genesis* and *The Wholly Book of Exodus* are also adult satirical humorous works. *Thirteen Sick Tasteless Classics*, *Thirteen Sick Tasteless Classics, Part II*, *Thirteen Sick Tasteless Classics, Part III and Thirteen Sick Tasteless Classics, Part IV* are adult satirical rewrites of famous short fiction. *Mauled Maimed Mangled Mutilated Mythology* satirizes twenty-one popular ancient tales into humorous adult versions. *Fractured Frazzled Folk Fables and Fairy Farces* (Parts I and II) are adult-oriented parodies of classic children's stories.

John has also authored a trilogy of young adult fantasy novels, *Enchanta*, *Pot of Gold* and *Space Bugs, Earth Invasion. The Eighteen' Story Gingerbread House* is a new collection of eighteen diverse and creative children's stories.

Jay Dubya likes '50s rock and roll music, and he also enjoys pop' songs by the Beach Boys, Beatles, Fleetwood Mac, the Eagles, the Rolling Stones, *ELO,* John Mellencamp and by John Fogerty.

Author Biography

Born in Hammonton, NJ in 1942, John Wiessner had attended St. Joseph School up to and including Grade 5. After his family moved from Hammonton to Levittown, PA in 1954, John attended St. Mark School in Bristol, PA for Grade 6, St. Michael the Archangel School in Levittown for Grades 7 and 8, and then Immaculate Conception School, Levittown, PA for Grade 9. Bishop Egan High School, Levittown PA was John's educational base for Grades 10 and 11, and later in 1960, the aspiring author graduated from Edgewood Regional High, Tansboro, NJ. John then next attended Glassboro State College, where he was an announcer for the school's baseball games and also read the nightly news and sports over WGLS, GSC's radio station.

John Wiessner had been primarily an English teacher in the Hammonton Public School System for 34 years, specializing in the instruction of middle school language arts. Mr. Wiessner was quite active in the Hammonton Education Association, loyally serving in the capacities of Vice-President, then building representative, and finally, teachers' head negotiator for a period of 7 years. During his lengthy teaching career, John had been nominated into "Who's Who among American Teachers" three times. He also was quite active giving professional workshops at schools around South Jersey on the subjects of creative writing and the use of movie videos to motivate students to organize their classroom theme compositions.

In addition, John Wiessner was very active in community service, being a past President of the Hammonton Lions Club, where he also functioned for many years as the club's Tail-Twister, Vice-President and Liontamer. John had been named Hammonton Lion of the Year in 1979 and in 2009 received the prestigious Melvin Jones Fellow Award, the highest honor a Lion can receive.

John also was a successful businessman, starting with being a Philadelphia Bulletin newspaper delivery boy for two-years in the late 1950s in Levittown, Pennsylvania. After his family moved back to New Jersey in 1959, John worked at his grandparents and his parents' farm markets, Square Deal Farm (now Ron's Gardens in Hammonton) and Pete's Farm Market in Elm, respectively. He later managed his wife's parents' farm market, White Horse Farms in Elm for three summers.

Also in a business capacity, for 16 summers starting in 1967 John Wiessner had co-owned Dealers Choice Amusement Arcade on the Ocean City, Maryland boardwalk and also co-owned the New Horizon Tee-Shirt Store for eight summers (1973-'81) on the Rehoboth Beach, Delaware boardwalk. In addition, "Jay Dubya" was a co-owner of Wheel and Deal Amusement Arcade, Missouri Avenue and Boardwalk, Atlantic City. And then, for 18 summers beginning in 1986, John had been the Field Manager in charge of crew-leaders for Atlantic Blueberry Company (the world's largest cultivated blueberry farm), both the Weymouth and Mays Landing Divisions.

After retiring from teaching in 1999, writing under the pen name Jay Dubya (his initials), John Wiessner became the author of 75 books in the genre Action/Adventure Novels, Sci-Fi/Paranormal Story Collections, Adult Satire, Young Adult Fantasy Novels and also Non-Fiction Books. His books exist in hardcover, in paperback and in popular Kindle and Nook e-book formats.

In January of 2022, John Wiessner (Jay Dubya) was nominated into Marquis Who's Who in America, and in April of that same year, was one of nine distinguished Who's Who in America members honored with receiving Lifetime Achievement Awards, all nine sharing a news article of recognition appearing in the Wall Street Journal.

Google: Jay Dubya, books
Google: Walmart, Jay Dubya